FLATMATES

Never, ever, ever live with your friends. You may well ask 'who better to live with?' But, rest assured, there are millions of better people whom you don't yet even know. Take Fiona, Linzi and Kerry; friends since their first day at senior school when Linzi borrowed Kerry's compass to stick Fiona in the thigh. Twelve years down the line, they felt ready to make it something more. To make the commitment of sharing a house. They thought they knew and liked each other well enough. Little did they know that all those hours spent fighting over who had the best selection of Bros posters had done nothing to prepare them for the agony of the itemised phone bill.

Also by Chris Manby

Running Away from Richard
Lizzie Jordan's Secret Life
Deep Heat
Second Prize

About the author

Chris Manby grew up in Gloucester and published her first short story in *Just Seventeen* at the age of fourteen. Now in her late twenties, she lives in London and writes full-time.

Flatmates

Chris Manby

CORONET BOOKS

Hodder & Stoughton

First published in Great Britain in 1997
by Hodder and Stoughton
First published in Coronet paperback in 1997
by Hodder and Stoughton
A division of Hodder Headline

This Coronet paperback edition 2001

10 9

A CIP catalogue record for this title
is available from the British Library.

ISBN 0 340 68960 9

Printed and bound in Great Britain by
Mackays of Chatham PLC, Chatham, Kent

Hodder and Stoughton
A division of Hodder Headline
338 Euston Road
London NW1 3BH

To Mum and Dad

ACKNOWLEDGEMENTS

Special thanks are due to David Garnett, Peter Hamilton and Helen Pisano for their professional guidance and support. Thanks also to my agent Antony Harwood, my editor Kate Lyall Grant and to Kate and Lee Arnold for the bridesmaid experience. Love and gratitude to Ryan, Vicky, Ed, the two Janes, Jools, Bill, Anna, Tom C., Nick, Laura, Kim, Gerry(!), Rico, No. 17 and Collin for their support, their printers and numerous free dinners. Finally, extra big thanks to Guy 'Biscuit-boy' Hazel for believing I could do it without reading a word and to Mum and Dad for not making me get a proper job.

CHAPTER ONE

How to make fatal pesto:
1. Prepare as ordinary pesto.
2. Leave dirty plate in the sink for up to a week.

The screaming started shortly after seven o'clock one ordinary Saturday night. Kerry, who was upstairs in the bathroom, froze in the act of brushing her hair and strained to catch the words stirred into the cacophony of terror. It was hard, for as usual the screaming was accompanied by the fervent whirring of a fast rotating wheel . . .

Fiona was on the exercise bike again. She usually started an argument then, as if speaking over the sound of the spinning gave her an excuse to raise her voice.

'I'm not saying it's you,' she was screaming. 'But it only takes a couple of seconds, for heaven's sake . . .' There was a sudden bleep and the whirring stopped. The bike stopwatch had measured twelve minutes exactly. 'No, I don't think I'm being pedantic, Linzi. You know dried pesto sets like glue and it's always me who has to come in after a hard day at work . . .'

Yes, thought Kerry, stress that.

'. . . to face an archaeological dig before I can find a single plate clean enough to put my toast on. It's not even as though I can scrape the remains of your lunch easily into the bin because that is always overflowing. Why do you always have to cram the pedal-bin to the point that when I try to get the bag out it splits and goes all over the floor? I got sodding spaghetti rings all over my new Pied-à-terre sandals last week. I certainly never eat spaghetti rings and I know that Kerry . . .'

Oh no, thought Kerry, putting down her brush. Don't bring me into this.

'I know that Kerry feels the same way about . . .'

Kerry bounced down the stairs and into the open-plan living room, stopping Fiona mid-flow before she could implicate her more.

'I've had my hair done,' Kerry said quickly to change the subject.

Fiona and Linzi broke off from arguing just long enough to say 'that's nice'.

'I only went in for a trim but then I decided "what the hell", I'll have the lot off. If I don't like it it'll always grow back, won't it? What do you think?'

Linzi looked up from her little nest she had made with her duvet on the sofa and smiled her approval. There was a tuft sticking up from behind Kerry's ear that made her look like a mandarin duck.

'*Très* Suzi Quatro.'

'Yes. Lovely,' added Fiona, grudgingly. Kerry had broken her stride. Fiona jumped off the exercise bike with an exaggerated sigh and went to slam a lasagne into the microwave. The volume on the television was turned back down again. The pesto incident was over, and this time there were no fatalities. Just.

Never ever ever live with your friends. You may well ask 'Who better to live with?' but, rest assured, there are millions of better people who you don't yet even know. Take Fiona, Linzi and Kerry; friends since their first day at senior school when Linzi borrowed Kerry's compass to stick Fiona in the thigh. Twelve years down the line, they felt ready to make it something more. To make the commitment of sharing a house. They thought they knew and liked each other well enough. Little did they know that all those hours spent fighting over who had the best collection of Bros posters had done nothing to prepare them for the agony of the itemised phone bill.

They had been at number 67, Artesia Road for almost a month. It was their first Greater London address. In fact, it was the first house they had seen in London, chosen in a blind panic because the letting agent had assured them that hundreds of people were queuing up to spend 75 per cent of their take-home pay on a place so compact and bijou that even the carpet lice had claustrophobia. And only seventeen minutes from the nearest tube station, the nice young man had stressed . . . If you were Linford Christie. Not that you could actually guarantee transport when you got that far since the nearest tube was on the Northern Line, which is the only part of the London Underground system that still runs on batteries. Not Duracell, of course.

The letting agent gave the girls just twelve minutes to make a life-changing decision.

But the house itself was OK. It was a thirties mid-terrace affair that had been refurbished by its owner in the late eighties and looked it. The two front rooms had been knocked through to create one marvellous cavernous living space that had plenty of potential for parties but would soon prove impossible to heat. A three-piece suite in bachelor-grey Draylon dominated the room and the walls had been stripped down to the bare brick for a rather chi-chi rustic effect. The kitchen was nice, though, and there was even a washing machine (with an overflow straight on to the terracotta tiled floor for convenience, which Fiona discovered to her horror on the day the pipes froze and the resulting flood ruined her brand-new suede boots).

Upstairs, number 67 was a rather peculiar mixture of bachelor-pad black and Laura Ashley. Linzi fell in love with the bathroom, which had two sinks, stripy wallpaper and a bulb-surrounded mirror. It put her in mind of post-sex soap opera scenes. Of cleaning your teeth while your hero is having a shave. The three bedrooms, however, were more accurately described as two bedrooms and a box room – no, make that a shoe-box room – the two bedrooms having double beds and space to put your pot-pourri; the box room being just too small to accommodate a single bed and still allow you to swing your hamster.

Bedrooms provided the focus for the first shared-house debate. Fiona and Linzi felt that the distribution of spoils was obvious. They were both dating. Kerry was not. So Fiona took the front room with the pink curtains and newish carpet. Linzi had the one at the back with the flowered wallpaper and the rocking chair and Kerry moved into the box room, with its dirty white walls and the crusted remains of the previous tenant's Blu-Tack. The fact that Linzi chucked her Latin lover, a visiting Italian language student, a week later, did not seem to offer an opportunity to re-examine the status quo. Kerry had to send most of her belongings back to her parents' house in Bristol and Fiona very kindly suggested that she should perhaps pay a whole pound less rent per week. And they would think about changing rooms at a later stage. Honest.

Anyway, where she slept at night was the least of Kerry's worries when she moved into Artesia Road. She wasn't just starting out in a new house; the Monday after moving in she started a new job as a trainee booker for a voice-over company called Verbal Tix. It wasn't exactly what her biology degree had prepared her for but the tiny Soho office looked nice enough and the money they were offering was OK for a beginner. Kerry thought it might be a route into television and dreamed of being discovered when having to step in and record a radio ad because one of her clients had gone sick.

Fiona had strolled into her rather more high-powered job straight after graduation. No one was surprised when she took up her position at the Japanese First Orient Bank and declined their generous offer of a year's deferred start to 'find herself' beforehand. She had never been the type to dream of six months' slumming it in India and the starting salary they offered her was the stuff of a politician's arms deal dreams. Linzi, on the other hand, had yet to join the rat-race proper. She had just finished another course in alternative therapy (was it shiatsu this time?) and was waiting for 'something to grab her, careerwise'. Her television producer parents were divorced and guilty and it seemed that she would be getting a double allowance for the rest of her golden life anyway. However, a month into the Artesia Road period there were rumblings that her father thought that, at the age of twenty-four and three-quarters, it was time Linzi got herself a 'proper job'. She signed up with a temping agency that specialised in supplying secretarial support to the advertising industry and tried to be out when they called.

So, things went happily enough for a while. The complicated telephone pad system where you had to write down who you called and for how long quickly went by the by, as did the rota for doing the cleaning and the washing-up.

Sometimes there might be a war of attrition over the pesto problem but Kerry would usually step in and wash up before the crockery, piled high in the sink, went crashing to the floor; and, when their periods weren't synchronising in a huge hormonal scream of a week, the girls would sometimes even sit around and think that they were lucky to be living with their pals. It saved bothering to go out and meet them after all . . .

Blind Date came on and Linzi turned the volume of the television back up to get the full force of the 'jokes'. Unable to get comfortable on either of the remaining armchairs, which were comfy in name only, Kerry wandered aimlessly into the kitchen where Fiona was scientifically prodding her lasagne with the tip of a sharp knife. She put the kettle on to make herself a cup of tea but the tea-bag jar was empty, again. The curly-edged rota on the fridge door suggested that it was Linzi's turn to refill it. Kerry would have to have coffee instead.

'Do you want a coffee?' she asked Fiona, who had decided that the lasagne was still half-cooked.

'No,' said Fiona. 'I've given coffee up.'

'Oh. Even decaff? Why?' Kerry asked disinterestedly.

'It aggravates your cellulite.'

'But you haven't got any cellulite.'

'I assure you I have.'

'Please don't start that again,' sighed Linzi. She had appeared at the kitchen door with an empty mug found beneath the sofa which was only slightly green at the bottom with mould. She rinsed it out beneath the cold tap until it looked almost hygienic. 'I'll have a coffee please,' she told Kerry. 'I don't give a toss about my bum.'

Fiona shot her a dangerous look. The kind of look that only the painfully thin can give the painfully thinner. As it was, neither of them needed to worry about their bums, thought Kerry sadly as she ladled coffee and sugar into two mugs. At school they had been known as the 'Twiglet Sisters'. Kerry herself had been 'Podge'. Now she had long given up preventative measures with regard to her own posterior and was relying largely on the magic of Lycra to get by.

'No, look at this!' Fiona was grabbing a thimbleful of thigh and roughly pulling it out to demonstrate her 'obesity'. 'I'm all wobbly!!!'

'For heaven's sake, Fiona, you couldn't make a fairy's pin-cushion out of that. You're not fat. You've got thighs like a pair of nutcrackers.'

'Nutcrackers? What do you mean, nutcrackers? Are you trying to say that I've got bandy legs?'

This was fairly typical of Fiona. If you told her she looked nice, she would only ask you why you hadn't said that yesterday. Now she was staring at the gap between her denim-clad thighs, trying to decide whether early ballet lessons had really turned her into some kind of physical freak. Linzi threw her a musty Christmas walnut that lived alone on the spice shelf and shouted, 'Crack that'. She was hardly renowned for her tact.

'So, what are you two doing tonight?' Kerry asked hurriedly to avert the brewing row.

'Nothing much,' shrugged Linzi.

'I'm going out with Tim,' said Fiona.

'Now there's a surprise.'

Tim was Fiona's boyfriend, a merchant banker with a regime of work hard, play hard and fall over after twelve pints on an average Friday night. Kerry and Linzi didn't really like him. Linzi even claimed to have seen him snogging a fair-haired gatecrasher at the Artesia Road house-warming party they'd had, but Fiona had countered that Linzi needed glasses and the incident had never been mentioned again. At least, not to Fiona's face.

'I've got a party to go to,' Kerry added casually, as she poured boiling water into the mugs. 'But I don't know whether I want to go or not.'

'Where is it?' asked Linzi.

'Battersea.'

Kerry stirred the coffee clockwise until all the nasty floating brown bits were dissolved.

'That's not far,' said Linzi.

'Well, distance isn't actually the issue. It's just that I won't really know anyone there.'

'Whose party is it?' Linzi asked. She had just fetched a tomato out of the fridge and was eating it like an apple. As she bit into it, pips spilled out and dribbled down the front of her shirt. 'Oh no.'

Linzi reached over the sink to grab a piece of kitchen roll. Fiona turned from the chopping board, where she was dicing a carrot into calorie-counted chunks, to see what was going on and her eyes suddenly widened with rage.

'For goodness' sake, Linzi!! You're wearing my shirt again. My bloody Nicole Farhi shirt. When did I say you could borrow it? No, don't do that!'

Linzi was already damping the kitchen roll beneath the warm tap and moving to apply her now wet-wipe to the stain. Fiona snatched the damp ball of paper from her hand.

'It's pure silk. It's got to be dry-cleaned . . .'

Here we go again. Kerry tactfully sneaked away from the kitchen and stole Linzi's place on the sofa. She needed more sugar in her coffee but she wasn't prepared to risk going back into the fray.

'Take it off!!' Fiona was shrieking.

'You never wear it!!' came Linzi's reply.

'Take it off!!'

'It doesn't even suit you!'

'What do you mean? It looks perfect with my hair!!!'

God, thought Kerry, was it always going to be like this? She had hoped that such kitchen-sink nightmares would end when she moved away from Bristol and her sisters. But, no. This was worse. And her mother wasn't even around to intervene. Kerry flicked through the television channels with the remote control. There was a buzz at the door. It was Tim. He'd come early. Hearing the sound of his baritone voice, Fiona switched suddenly from screaming harridan to sweetness and light and whisked him straight upstairs to her lair. Talk about saved by the bell. Linzi slunk back into the sitting room when she was sure that the worst of the danger had passed.

'Lend me a shirt for tonight will you, Kerry? I'm meeting Eddy in the pub at ten and everything I own is in the wash.'

'You can wear my black one from Oasis,' Kerry said graciously. 'But only if you promise to come to this party with me first.'

Linzi looked down at the pink stain on Fiona's pale blue silk. The Nicole Farhi was unwearable and she didn't have a thing in the world of her own that didn't smell of fag ash or armpit.

'And I'll let you off that tenner you owe me from last week-end.'

What choice did Linzi have?

'Battersea, wasn't it?' she replied. 'Shall I call a cab?'

CHAPTER TWO

You've heard of the Bermuda Triangle of course. But I bet you didn't know that there's an area of Clapham Common that has exactly the same effect on passing cars. The taxi company that Linzi called to get a ride from Balham to Battersea promised a quick service, friendly drivers and nice clean vehicles. It didn't, however, promise that it would actually get you anywhere near your chosen destination in that double-quick time.

Clapham Common seemed to be a stumbling block for most of the minicab drivers of Balham. Inevitably speaking barely a word of English, they would turn up on time, claim to know where they were taking you, perhaps even point out the road you were looking for in their battered *A to Z*, and three-quarters of an hour later you would be on the wrong side of Clapham Common, getting out of the car to walk the rest of your journey, to the tune of approximately fifteen pounds.

'He's going the wrong way, isn't he?' Linzi hissed nervously. Indeed, he was. The cab driver had bypassed Battersea and was heading straight for Wandsworth instead.

'Queenstown Road?' Kerry reiterated hopefully.

'Yes, I know, Quinston Road,' said the driver with a sigh. He drove on towards Wandsworth Common and turned the stereo up pointedly.

'Kerry, he is still going the wrong way,' Linzi persisted. 'Why don't you tell him?'

'Why don't you tell him?' Kerry rejoined.

'Because I don't know the address of the party.'

Kerry cleared her throat, but that didn't stop her next sentence coming out as a strangled gasp. 'I said Queenstown Road,' she gurgled.

'Yays, I know it,' said the cab driver again, fixing her with a fierce glare in the rearview mirror. 'Quinston Road, I know. I know.'

'I don't think so, actually,' Linzi interrupted. 'It's over on the other side of the Common, mate. You're going the wrong way.'

Linzi leaned over into the front passenger seat and snatched up the grubby *A to Z*. She flicked through the tattered pages angrily. Most of central London was missing or had been Sellotaped back in upside-down. She eventually found what she was looking for, with no help from the largely absent index, and jabbed at it with a vicious finger. 'Look, Queenstown Road, mate. There. It's in Battersea. You're taking us the wrong bloody way.'

'I not know this area,' the cab driver protested. 'I only come to England for to do my cartography degree.'

'Oh, Christ on a bike,' sighed Linzi. 'You obviously haven't had time to go to many of your lectures, have you? Look, turn right here. At this next corner.' She tried to get him back on course. 'And when you get to those traffic lights, turn left, then take a left again.'

The driver threw a right at the lights.

'Left, I said.' Linzi pointed wildly. 'Left at the lights . . . Oh, bloody hell. This is ridiculous. Stop the car,' she shouted. The driver pulled up abruptly without bothering to turn into the kerb. Linzi opened her door and pulled Kerry out on to the pavement after her. The taxi was now blocking the traffic, a queue of irate drivers already forming behind.

'Three pounds fifty. Three pounds fifty!!!' the driver protested with an open hand. He wasn't going to move until he got paid.

'You can sing for it, mate,' Linzi told him, flicking the V-sign as she stalked off down the road. Kerry froze at the taxi's door and fumbled for the right money. She had a solitary fiver in her faded Body Shop 'Save the Endangered Species' purse.

'I got no change,' said the cab driver rudely when she handed the crumpled note over.

'Have it,' Kerry whispered in a fluster. The man in the huge car behind the taxi was sounding his horn and making her too nervous to wait for any change. The cab driver slowly folded the note into his wallet and tutted. Kerry had to run to catch Linzi up.

'We should have walked in the first place,' Linzi muttered.

'Three pounds fifty indeed!! He's got a nerve asking for that. How much did you give him?'

'I gave him a pound,' Kerry lied.

'That's a pound too much. You're soft in the head, you are, Kerry Keble. The whole point of taking a cab is that it gets you to where you want to go with no hassle. You're not supposed to have to navigate as well. He should have given us a pound for teaching him a new route.'

'He's not from the area,' Kerry whined. 'And the one-way system can be really confusing if you don't know it.'

'Its not his job to be confused,' Linzi sighed. 'Honestly, Kerry, if you don't stop being such a soft touch I'm going to go straight home right now, shirt or no borrowed shirt.'

'I just didn't see the point in getting angry with him, that's all,' Kerry squeaked. But her voice was lost in the din of the Saturday-night traffic heading down Queenstown Road and into town.

The girls finished their journey to the party on foot in almost half the time it had taken them to circumnavigate Clapham Common in the cab driver's old blue Astra. They recognised the venue because one happy reveller was already hanging out of a downstairs window, puking his guts out, and the creamy yellow splashback of his vomit very nearly got Linzi on her suede knee-high boots. Fiona's suede knee-high boots to be more precise. The ones that had already barely survived the washing-machine disaster.

'Kerry, this had better be a good one,' Linzi hissed as she skipped out of the way of the chunder fountain.

She couldn't guarantee it. Kerry suddenly wished she had come alone. At least then she knew that she wouldn't have moaned to herself all the way home. Linzi was so difficult to please. She and her trendy aromatherapy friends were an entertainment Gestapo, unimpressed by anything falling short of Elvis Presley coming back from the dead to hold a reunion party for the great and the good at the Grosvenor House Hotel. A house-party in Queenstown Road was hardly likely to cut the mustard. Blinking back the urge to run back to Artesia Road and bury herself under her duvet, Kerry quickly pressed the doorbell, which was hanging loose from a single wire.

* * *

The party was being thrown by one of Kerry's clients at 'Verbal Tix – your one-stop voice-shop'. Lance Sylvester had been a big name in the early eighties. He had played the teenage tearaway son in a television sit-com that had run for almost three years. During that time his roguish face had graced the gossip pages of the tabloids daily and he'd been voted a 'top-ten hunk' by the readers of *Just Seventeen*. On her first day at Verbal Tix, as she leafed idly through the details of the artistes who she was going to be representing, Kerry had been thrilled to find the career résumé of Lance Sylvester among them. And she had been ecstatic when he called in that morning to say that he would drop by the office to meet her later that very day. When Lance turned up, however, Kerry barely recognised the man who had played such an important part in her third-form fantasies. He was shorter than she had imagined and his hair, dyed bright blue for his role in *Family Affair*, had all but fallen out. As had half of one of his front teeth which he couldn't afford to get capped. Lance had barely worked at all since a couple of criminal cameos for *The Bill* in 1989. It was obvious that he drank like a fish these days and his hand felt just like one when he tried to rub it across Kerry's backside.

'Ignore him and he'll go away,' was her boss Leon's advice.

But he didn't. Lance Sylvester popped up at the office every day, as early as his hangover would allow, in the vain hope that someone wanted him to do his American accent for a cornflakes commercial or something paying even half as well. And Kerry knew that if she didn't go to his birthday party, Lance would make her life a misery by harping on about how good it had been for at least the next five weeks, if not for the rest of her days on this earth. Her head ached with the nuisance of it all. There's nothing like having to enjoy yourself under duress.

As he opened the front door to Kerry and Linzi, Lance was already in a state of advanced inebriation. 'Where have you been, Kelly-man?' he slurred as he slumped against the door-frame with a bourbon bottle clenched in his hand. 'The party's been going on since three o'clock this afternoon . . . Hey,' he perked up, suddenly noticing Linzi, 'you didn't tell me you were bringing your sister.'

'Linzi, this is Lance Sylvester. Lance, this is Linzi, my house-mate.'

Lance took Linzi by the hand and kissed it theatrically.

'I've been on the telly, love,' he told her as his mouth twisted into a leer. 'Fancy a shag?'

Linzi graciously forced out a laugh.

He ushered them into the purple-painted hallway. Kerry with a wave. Linzi by the old hand-on-bum control. She removed his fingers from her bottom casually, as if she were dealing with someone below the age of three who didn't really know any better. But she made sure she cracked them as she did so, and when Lance hopped in front of the girls to guide them into the fray, he was blowing on his digits as if they might be broken.

'He is disgusting,' Linzi hissed to Kerry. 'And he's wearing a Level 42 T-shirt, for God's sake.'

'I think he knows the drummer.'

'Yeah, right. Look, let's find a phone, call a proper cab, and go to meet Eddy now. What do you say, Kez?'

'I say I've just got to say "hi" to my boss before we can go.'

'Say "hi" to your boss?' Linzi mimicked. 'You absolute bum-licker. Make it quick, eh?'

'I'll see what I can do.'

Lance led them into the sitting room, where the party had already fragmented into little cliques which hung around the walls as though the centre of the floor might be carpet over quicksand. Almost blind in the ineffective ambient lighting, Kerry nearly tripped over Lance's girlfriend, who looked at the arm belonging to Lance which had wound its way around Kerry's waist as though she might have been able to help it. Tactfully, Kerry wriggled free of Lance's octopus grip and he made a dangerous sideways lurch, until his empty hand hit a table which put a rather abrupt stop to his listing.

'Drink?' he asked. At least, that was what it sounded like.

They nodded politely.

They weren't going to survive this party without it.

Lance stumbled off in the direction of the kitchen, taking the bottle of Chardonnay they had bought for personal consumption with him. They wouldn't see that again.

'Can you believe that people still have this stuff on their walls?' Linzi was off on a rant already, this time picking literally

at the woodchip wallpaper. It had been painted over with a
very dark red emulsion that made the room look like the
lair of Count Dracula after a night of projectile vomiting and
each picked-off chip revealed a nasty, bright white wound
beneath. Kerry tried to slap Linzi's hand away as Lance re-
emerged from the kitchen with a different bottle and two very
smeary glasses. Linzi casually leaned her hand over the bald
spot she had so recently made and even managed a wink of
thanks.

'Nice place you have here, Lance,' she told him.

'Fanks,' he slurred. 'I interior-designed it myself.'

'Yes, it's very interesting. Very . . . um, vibrant. I can see that
your personality is stamped all over the place . . .'

Kerry rewarded Linzi's flattery with a sharp dig in the ribs.
But she needn't have worried because Lance had missed out
on Linzi's lack of sincerity altogether. 'I'm gonna do the dining
room next,' he told her excitedly. 'In maroon with a gold trim.
It's gonna look quite baroque, don't you think.'

'Oh yes. *Très* baroque,' said Linzi sweetly.

Lance poured each of the girls a glass of the very best
Lambrusco Frizzante. Linzi held hers stiffly, without taking so
much as a sip. She claimed she was waiting for the bubbles to go
down but when Lance had to leave them to answer the door, she
poured her drink straight back whence it had come. A cigarette
end was already floating in the bit that remained at the bottom
of the bottle. 'I'm not drinking that piss,' she told Kerry in no
uncertain terms. 'And this is the kind of party where it probably
is piss. Lance looks just the type who would urinate in a bottle
for a laugh.'

'Oh, he's all right really.'

'All right really? That man is one down from a rat. What did
he do with our Chardonnay?'

'You didn't have to come with me,' Kerry protested.

'You said that if I did, I wouldn't have to pay you back that
tenner I owe you from last Friday. I had to come, Kerry, because
I don't get paid until the end of next week. Besides, I quite like
this shirt.' She smoothed the clingy black material down over
the waistband of her jeans.

'Yeah, it suits you,' Kerry said grudgingly. She hadn't worn it
at all since bringing it back from the shop. It had been bought

in a bit of a hurry and when Kerry got it home, she discovered that she couldn't do the middle button up.

Kerry took a sip of her Lambrusco and decided to her horror that Linzi was probably right about the piss. She put her glass down discreetly on a table covered with the detritus of a buffet. Two cans of Special Brew in a Threshers bag nestled behind a washing-up bowl full of potato salad. At least Kerry hoped it was potato salad. She fought shy of picking up a fork and finding out. Linzi snatched up the abandoned cans with glee. 'I hope Lance wasn't saving these for later,' she laughed. She handed one over to Kerry. 'At least they're still sterile and sealed.'

It didn't taste that much better than the piss but, at eleven per cent or whatever the alcohol content of the damn stuff was, Kerry figured that by the time she had finished the first half of the can, she wouldn't be able to taste the second half anyway. Linzi leaned back against the woodchip and continued to survey the party with a jaundiced eye from her sartorial highground. She tutted in despair at a forty-something gothic in lacy leggings who was picking over the remains of the cheeseboard. Nothing and nobody had met with Linzi's approval so far that night.

'Have you spotted your boss yet?' she moaned. 'Because I am more than ready to go.'

Lance staggered past again. This time, his eyes were barely open. He was wiping his nose and sniffing hard.

'Having a good time, girls?' he asked.

'Yeah, yeah. Great time.' Though obviously not as great as the time he was having, thought Kerry. 'Where's Leon?'

'Leon's over there,' Lance told her, waving an arm in the vague direction of the other side of the room. Kerry strained through the smoke to catch a glimpse of her boss. He had indeed appeared and was standing by the window, flanked by two smaller guys. One of them was wearing a beanie cap on his largely bald head. That must be Sam, Leon's boyfriend. Leon had mentioned him a few times, and though he hadn't really described his paramour's physical attributes at great length, his anecdotes about him were usually preceded by 'that bald bastard'. Leon himself looked incredible, as usual, in a dark blue velvet jacket over straight cut jet-black jeans. He had said that he was going to get his hair cut that weekend and the shorter look made the most of his textbook handsome face. Leon was the best thing about

Kerry's job. He was unlike any boss she had met before. You could actually have a laugh with Leon . . . not to mention the fact that she fancied him like mad.

'There he is,' Kerry whispered. 'That's my boss.' Linzi made a face that suggested she approved.

'Whooah! He's a bit gorgeous, isn't he?'

'I'm afraid so. And utterly unavailable.'

'Never say never, Kez.'

Catching Kerry's eye, Leon motioned them over, looking almost relieved to see another familiar face. When they reached him, he kissed Kerry on both cheeks. She stepped backwards with a blush. The sweet smell of his expensive aftershave clung briefly to her skin.

'This is Sam,' Leon said, introducing the bald one of his companions. Suspicions confirmed. 'And this is Andrew.' Sam and Andrew acknowledged the girls briefly but were quickly back in conversation between themselves.

'Great party, eh?' Leon asked.

'I think the answer to that question has to be "eh",' said Linzi.

'Oh, yeah. Leon,' Kerry interrupted, 'this is my housemate, Linzi. I bribed her to come with me.'

'I didn't think we paid you that much,' Leon laughed. 'How long have you been here?'

'Ten minutes.'

'We've been here since eight,' Leon said, rolling his eyes. 'I didn't think that Sam would want to stay for one second but then he bumped into Andrew and now I can't persuade him to leave. Andrew works for Sony. I think Sam's angling for a three album deal.'

'Any chance?' asked Kerry.

Sam was a singer. He had actually been the voice of a small frog on the soundtrack of the latest Disney cartoon and now he was trying to break into the dance scene.

'I think not,' Leon smiled dryly. 'Little does he realise that Andrew is low down in accounts.'

'Perhaps he just fancies him,' said Linzi, not realising her *faux-pas*. Kerry stared at her meaningfully but Linzi wasn't even looking in her direction anymore. The front-door bell had just rung again and, ever hopeful, Linzi wanted to see who was coming in. 'Wow,' she murmured suddenly. 'Things are looking up.'

Linzi drew Kerry's attention to the back view of a tall, dark-haired man, wearing jeans clinging tighter than a skin graft, who was leaning over an unsteady three-legged coffee table while attempting to roll a spliff. He was more than a little drunk, and the paper kept slipping from his fingers and unfurling again to lie flat. He tucked his long curly hair behind his ear to stop it from breaking his concentration and began the operation once more. Linzi affected a mock swoon. Kerry tipped her head to one side in appraisal and had to agree, 'Not bad from the back.'

'Not bad? He's incredible, Kez!'

Leon was looking in the same direction now, to find out who or what had attracted their attention.

'Oh, no,' he groaned. 'Please tell me it's not Gaetano.'

'Gaetano?' the girls echoed at once.

'His parents are Italian,' Leon explained.

'How exotic,' said Linzi.

'He's up his own arse,' said Leon.

'Wish he was up mine,' Sam quipped as he passed them by with an anaemic-looking sausage on a stick.

'So, you know him?' Linzi asked excitedly, clutching the lapels of Leon's velvet jacket. 'He's completely gorgeous. You've got to tell me everything you know.'

'I don't really know him, Linzi. We've only been introduced a couple of times,' Leon said warily. 'Sam knows him far better than I do.'

'What does he do?' Linzi asked Sam.

'He's a drummer,' said Sam.

'A musician?' asked Linzi.

'Well,' Leon murmured for the benefit of Kerry, 'he's certainly someone who bangs things. But he's only a drummer in the evenings. By day he works in some trendy clothes shop on the Kings Road.'

'He's the most amazing man I've ever seen. You've got to introduce me to him,' Linzi begged.

'Well, I don't really . . .'

'Introduce me or I'll die . . .'

As it was, Gaetano's attention had already been attracted by the bizarre sight of a girl sinking to her knees at the feet of

Leon Landesman. He raised a beautiful eyebrow quizzically as Leon beckoned him across. Gaetano walked towards them with the feline grace of someone who had been brought up on the catwalk. In fact, the proudest moment of his life had been almost getting a casting for a Dolce & Gabbana shoot.

'Look at that walk,' Linzi swooned.

'He used to be a model,' Sam chipped in lasciviously. 'Once did an underwear catalogue that I keep under my pillow for lonely nights.'

Linzi licked her lips to buff up her lipstick and slowly rose to her feet again. 'I like him more and more.'

'Gaetano, this is Linzi,' Leon said smoothly. 'She was just demonstrating the flexibility of her knees.'

'Very impressive,' Gaetano murmured.

'I like to keep myself limber,' said Linzi.

Kerry covered her mouth with her hand and hiccuped back a laugh. Sam turned away in disgust.

'Are you a dancer?' Gaetano continued.

'Are you asking?' asked Linzi.

Kerry rolled her eyes.

'If something good comes on then maybe we could . . .'

The heat that flared between them was palpable. Kerry looked at her watch as an excuse to avert her gaze. It was almost ten. 'Aren't we supposed to be meeting Eddy in the pub?' she asked in desperation.

Linzi stared at Kerry as though she didn't understand her. 'Eddy? Oh, yeah. Eddy. You can go if you want but he won't be on his own, so you really needn't worry about standing him up. I'm staying here.' She turned her attention straight back to Gaetano. Linzi wasn't about to leave now. Poor old Eddy was already the flavour of last week. Subject closed.

The ear-splitting music suddenly shrank to a slow, sensuous grind. Linzi snaked her way out into the middle of the room to dance with her hands on Gaetano's slinky hips. Kerry turned back to Leon, who was smiling sadly. Sam and Andrew had left the room altogether while Leon's attention had been focused on introducing the girls to Gaetano.

'Well, I guess I must be staying then,' Kerry told Leon. 'Fancy another drink?'

He shook his head. 'Not for me. I'm driving. But I think I

spotted another can of Tennants Extra over there by the buffet. That is what you're drinking isn't it?'

'Oh, yeah.' Kerry blushed when she remembered the can she had been holding. It rather lacked the sophistication of a real Martini with olive. 'I think I've had enough of this actually,' she said, shaking the dregs. 'It's horrible when it starts to get all flat and warm.'

Leon nodded. 'I can't touch the stuff myself.'

'I thought South Africans were weaned on lager.'

'There's lager and there's lager, Kez.'

Kerry went to put the empty can down and nearly missed the table. Either that stuff was seriously strong or she was getting pathetic in her old age. When she had righted herself, she saw that Leon was looking at his watch again. Obviously pretty bored. Kerry searched the deepest recesses of her brain for something remotely clever to say. Leon gazed over her shoulder to the spot where he had last seen Sam. Pinching herself on the thigh through her pocket in an attempt to restore some semblance of sobriety to her head, Kerry flipped through a mental Rolodex of suitable party subjects to broach with your homosexual boss. She never had this kind of trouble when she was at work.

'You look really pissed off,' she announced suddenly. It wasn't exactly an accomplished opening gambit.

Leon turned back towards her with a weakish smile.

'Do I? I don't feel pissed off,' he said.

'Well, you're doing a good impression of someone who is. Come on, Leon. This is meant to be a party. Smile.' She jigged about on the spot and was vaguely aware that she sounded like the kind of person she often wanted to punch. 'Party! Party!' she added lamely.

'It isn't exactly where we planned to be tonight,' Leon sighed.

'Really? I thought that Lance Sylvester's soirées were the only place to be any night.'

'Right,' said Leon. 'If the alternative is purgatory. You know, it was a year ago tonight that I first met Sam at the "O" Bar. So I guess you could say that today is our anniversary, though he didn't stop sleeping with his last boyfriend until we had been seeing each other for three months.'

'Oh.'

'Yeah. Sam got me a surprise present,' Leon continued. 'He

bought us two tickets on Eurostar to Paris. He's got a friend there who was going to lend us his apartment in Pigalle for the weekend. Sam had it all planned. Dinner on a boat floating down the Seine. Champagne breakfast looking out on the Eiffel Tower. He was really excited about it.'

'I would be too. What went wrong?'

'I couldn't go. I can't risk travelling through customs at the moment.'

'Why not? South Africans don't need a visa to go to France do they?'

'Getting into France wouldn't have been the problem, Kez. The problem would have been getting back in here. I've got two days left on my visa.'

'Two days? You're kidding. Then what?'

'I don't know. I'll think of something.'

'You'll have to get married to a British citizen,' she joked.

'That's the best idea I've heard so far,' Leon sniffed. 'But I can't see the union of Mr and Mr Landesman going down too well with immigration. Can you? Look, let's stop talking about this or I'll go into a decline. This is, after all, a party and you don't go to a party to stand in a corner and moan. Let's go and moan in the kitchen instead. By the way, Kez, what have you done to your hair?'

'Oh,' she put a hand to her tuft. 'I had it cut this afternoon. Does it look really bad?'

'No, it doesn't look bad at all. In fact it really suits you. I didn't know you had cheekbones. And I love that shirt. Green brings out the colour in your eyes.'

'Really?' Kerry felt her throat tightening at the thought of Leon looking at her closely enough to notice anything more about her eyes than that she had the usual two. 'Do you think so?'

'Yeah, they're totally emerald. Look, I think I will have another drink after all. Do you want me to get something for you?'

Kerry shook her head. His flattery had left her barely able to talk. When he disappeared into the kitchen, she sneaked a look at her reflection in the darkened window. Cheekbones? She'd certainly never noticed those either. While she was checking out their existence, Leon returned from the kitchen empty handed.

'Changed my mind. There's nothing drinkable left.'

Kerry still hadn't quite regained her composure. She looked at her shoes and wished she had cleaned them. 'You've had your hair cut too,' she said suddenly.

'Yeah,' said Leon. 'Highlights my receding hairline.'

Soon it was after two in the morning. There was nothing left to drink and the party had degenerated to the stage where people were sleeping over most of the horizontal surfaces. The host himself had passed out in the bath a couple of hours earlier, much to the disgust of his female guests who became too shy to use the loo. Leon glanced at his watch for the millionth time, and scanned the room once more for Sam, who was still nowhere to be seen.

'I think I might head off soon,' he told Kerry. 'Do you want a lift?'

She nodded eagerly. 'If you've got enough room . . .'

'There'll be enough room. Sam seems to have left without me.'

'But what about Linzi and Gaetano?'

Linzi and Gaetano were sitting on the window-sill. They had danced themselves into a near frenzy of lust and now Linzi was sensuously tracing the lines of Gaetano's palm with her fingers. She was probably telling him, 'You're going to wake up next to a beautiful dark-haired girl.' It was an old and over-used trick but still one of the best.

'I'm afraid we'll have to leave them behind. I've only got one spare helmet.'

'Spare helmet?' said Kerry.

'Yeah, I ride a bike. You knew that?'

'I think I remember you saying so but . . . I mean, when you asked me if I wanted a lift, I assumed you must have a car as well. I've never been on the back of a bike, Leon. I wouldn't know what to do.'

'You don't have to do anything. You just have to hang on to me. It's easy.'

Kerry looked at her thin cotton trousers.

'But I'm not wearing leathers. What if I fall off?'

'You won't fall off. I'm not wearing leathers either, am I? I'll take it really slowly, I promise.' Kerry still looked uneasy. 'You don't have to if you really don't want to, though.'

'No, no,' Kerry protested, feeling her heart begin to flutter against the roof of her mouth. 'I'd love to have a go. Got to live dangerously some time. I'll just tell Linzi where I'm going.'

'I don't think she'll miss you.' Leon steered Kerry away from the window where Linzi and Gaetano were now quite seriously entwined. Linzi had given up tracing the lines on his palm and was instead languorously tracing the outline of his left ear with her long, wet tongue. 'You ready?' Leon reached below the table to find the helmets he had stashed there earlier. 'It's Sam's,' he sighed. 'So you might find it a little bit big.'

'How will he get home?' Kerry asked.

'As far as I'm concerned,' said Leon, 'he can walk.'

Leon's fox-eyed Yamaha 750 waited patiently outside Lance's house like a sleek horse seen through an acid haze. Leon put on his helmet, and helped Kerry fasten hers beneath her chin. Then he climbed on and waited for her to clamber up behind him. She felt a little strange about putting her arms around his narrow waist, but when he fired the engine up she had no choice but to cling on so tightly through fear that she probably left fingermarks.

CHAPTER THREE

Leon took the long way home and by the time they had circled Clapham Common about six times Kerry was almost enjoying herself. At one point, she very nearly opened her eyes wide enough to look at the view. But the best part of the journey by far was its end. As Leon turned the bike into Artesia Road, Gaetano and Linzi could be seen stumbling towards number 67, leaning heavily on each other for support. Leon pulled the bike into the kerb with a growl just behind them and helped Kerry climb off to stand, jelly-legged but proud, on the pavement.

'You OK?' he wrapped an arm around her shoulders and tipped her face towards him. 'You look completely white.'

'Nice bike, man,' Gaetano gave the bike a cursory once-over and muttered something about the Triumph Bonneville he had been restoring for the past eight years. Linzi, who knew nothing about wheels except the colours that she liked them in, was duly impressed. Kerry took off the borrowed helmet and tried to shake her hair loose as casually as if she rode a bike to the corner shop on a daily basis.

'That was great, Leon, thanks,' she said. Now that it has stopped, she added to herself.

'You fancy a quick spin?' Leon asked Gaetano.

'I think he might want to come in for a coffee first.' Linzi wanted to get Gaetano in off the street. She could see her charms fading rapidly beside the sleek shiny lines of the Yamaha. Leon declined the coffee and Gaetano reluctantly declined the ride, much to Linzi's joy and Kerry's disappointment. Gaetano shrugged and mentioned "some other time". Leon got back on to the bike and was gone with a roar before Kerry realised that he had finally said goodbye.

'I can't believe I did that,' she murmured.

'Neither can I,' said Linzi. 'You're usually such a chicken.'

Gaetano returned his attentions to the next best thing after a motorbike. Linzi purred. She had won. It appeared that he would be staying for the duration of the night, after all.

Now it was beginning to rain. The three remaining revellers huddled for shelter in the tiny porch of number 67 while Kerry fumbled to find her keys at the bottom of her deep, black PVC bag. Linzi never remembered her keys, whether she was out with one of her housemates, or not. Her subsequent tendency to wake the whole house up in the middle of the night had been the source of many a bitter breakfast argument.

'Hurry up,' Linzi complained as Kerry pulled out a set of keys only to discover that they were the keys to her office when she tried to get them in the door. 'I'm freezing to death out here.'

Gaetano obligingly wrapped his arms around her to keep her warm, then he tucked his freezing fingers beneath the hem of Linzi's borrowed shirt and she shrieked with the shock of his cold touch on her warm flesh. 'Stop it! No! No! No!'

'Sssh!!' Kerry put a finger to her lips and eased open the door. 'I don't think you ought to risk getting any further on to the wrong side of Fiona tonight.'

'Oh, she won't have heard that,' Linzi nearly managed to whisper. 'Not over Tim's snoring. You must have heard him snoring, Kez. Poor you. It's wonder you can sleep at all, having to have the room next to them . . . I tell you what, I'm sure Tim's related to this pig my grandad once had down on the . . .'

'Ssssh.' Kerry put her finger to her lips again. The sound of tinkling laughter from the sitting room suggested that Fiona and Tim were not yet in bed.

'My grandfather used to keep pigs,' Linzi was explaining to Gaetano. 'Big fat pink ones with black spots. Gloucestershire Old Spots, I think they were called. So I know a lot about them.' Gaetano was so entranced with the pig story that he almost tripped over the front step.

Kerry was right. Tim and Fiona weren't in bed. Instead, they were huddled together on the sofa beneath a duvet. When her housemates walked into the room, Fiona giggled and clasped her section of the cover tightly beneath her arms. They were obviously naked beneath the Habitat-covered quilt. Linzi moved to steer Gaetano immediately up the stairs to her room. Kerry averted her eyes and rushed to the kitchen to get one last glass of water before she followed them upstairs herself. It was so embarrassing, Kerry thought, as Fiona and Tim continued to whisper and giggle. Why couldn't they have stayed in Fiona's room instead of flaunting their sex lives all over the house?

But suddenly the sofa lovers were on their feet, with the duvet still wrapped around them, swaying unsteadily from side to side like a giant, drunken sausage roll.

'Ladies and gentlemen,' Tim boomed loudly, as he swung a champagne bottle and prepared to pop the cork. 'Please be upstanding for the bride and groom.'

Linzi and Gaetano stopped halfway up the stairs and peered down over the banister. Kerry stood quietly in the doorway of the kitchen, sipping from her glass.

'What?'

The cork exploded loudly from the champagne bottle and ricocheted against the bare brick wall.

'Please raise your glasses!' Tim continued. They were staggering about in their duvet cocoon. Fiona was giggling, trying hard not to fall out. 'Ladies and gentlemen . . .'

'What on earth have you done? What's going on?' Linzi ran back down the stairs to hear the news.

Fiona raised her glass triumphantly.

'Tim and I are getting engaged.'

Two more bottles of champagne later, Kerry finally dragged on her plaid pyjamas and slipped between the cold covers of her narrow single bed. If she stretched herself into a star shape she could almost touch all four walls of the tiny room at once. It had become a bit of a ritual, just to check that her life hadn't shrunk a little since the morning. It hadn't. Unless her arms were getting shorter too.

What an evening it had turned out to be. The last thing anyone had expected was for Fiona and Tim to get engaged. The odds on were only just shorter than those on Kerry winning the lottery. Things had been more than a little one-sided between the future Mr and Mrs Harper lately. In fact, Kerry couldn't recall

Tim having phoned Artesia Road at all since they'd moved in.
Instead, Fiona was always chasing him around, calling him up,
going over to his place. Oh well. It was nice to see Fiona happy
for once. So happy that she hadn't even protested when Gaetano
fished his gear out of his pocket and skinned up a celebratory
spliff in the strict no-smoking household. In fact, Kerry was
sure that Fiona had almost smiled indulgently when Tim got
completely ratted and asked Gaetano to be his best man.

Kerry sighed. In the next room, she could hear Fiona and
Tim giggling again, then moaning, then groaning in the throes
of mutual ecstasy. It was a wonder that Tim could even get it
up after all the champagne he had drunk. From the other end of
the house, Linzi was giving out a strangely high-pitched scream.
Kerry pulled the duvet up to her neck and tried to cover her ears
with the stretchy white Alice band she used to prevent her fringe
from causing forehead zits in the night. Alone in the box room
again, while all around her the world was making love. That, it
seemed, was the story of her life.

The last time Kerry had slept with a man had been during
her final term at university. That was almost three years ago
now but the episode with Andrew was probably best forgotten
anyway. She had met him in a seminar on osmosis when he
asked if he could borrow a piece of her notepaper. They went
for a coffee after the lecture and said 'goodbye' at four o'clock
the next morning. Kerry thought she was heading for a perfect
romance. She fancied him like mad and they even seemed to
have a lot in common. He was the only man she had ever met
who liked Roxy Music for a start.

It all fell apart when they decided to go to bed after six weeks
of fairly chaste snogging.

Once he had undressed her, Andrew had put a pillow over
her face and tried to carry on fumbling.

'Hey, what are you doing?' Kerry had thrown the pillow off.
Trust her luck to land herself with the Southampton suffocator.
'Are you trying to kill me or what?'

'No,' he told her quite plainly. 'It's just that if I cover your face
up I can pretend that you're Sonia.' Sonia was his ex-girlfriend.
'I'm sorry, Kerry, but it's the only way I can get a hard-on.'

Kerry made her excuses and left.

It had been a long time before she could think about that

particular disaster and laugh, though Linzi and Fiona laughed
about it on a regular basis of course. Kerry hoped she would
never be that stupid again. The next man for her would be
someone really special. Someone without all that emotional
baggage. And someone who was at least reasonably gorgeous.
Leon had the right face for a start.

Leon Landesman, Kerry sighed to herself. If she had to draw a
picture of a perfect man . . . He was six feet tall, not too big, like
the six-foot-five rower called Ryan who had given her a crick in
the neck. He was dark and handsome, not preternaturally pale
like the ginger-haired accountant with no eyebrows that Fiona
was forever trying to persuade her to date. He rode a motorbike,
not an embarrassing push-bike with Kelloggs Frosties stickers
like the bloke she had accidentally picked up by the broccoli
in Safeway. And he was gay. Not camp as a row of tents but
gay as a gay thing none the less.

Kerry screwed up the picture she had been painting in her
mind.

Was it really too much to ask for? A man who was handsome,
witty and straight? Didn't Linzi have any spares? Kerry suddenly
saw herself ten years down the line, alone in a basement flat
with three mangy cats. Perhaps she should have stayed with
Andrew? After a few months she probably would have been
grateful for the pillow-thing herself. Or Ryan? Had he really been
that bad? All that stretching up to kiss him was probably good
for her posture. And what did she have against ginger hair? That
accountant probably wouldn't have any hair at all eventually.

Kerry wondered if she still had the telephone number of the
deputy warehouse manager with the Frosties-stickered bike.
These were desperate times.

'I just don't want to be on my own,' she murmured to whoever
it was that was supposed to listen. 'Please don't let me end up on
my own.'

Number 67 had at last fallen silent. Kerry rolled on to her back
and looked up at the shadow of her round paper lampshade. She
wondered how long it could possibly last; this barren plateau
in her love life, this plateau in the decline of Fiona and Tim.
And Linzi with Gaetano? Sleeping with him already? That girl
was such a tart . . . Oh well. Kerry closed her eyes and began
to count sheep.

But moments later it started again. This time on the other side of Kerry's bare-walled room. Kerry stuffed her head beneath her pillow. Now even the weirdoes next door were having their annual shag.

CHAPTER FOUR

For Kerry, the arrival of Monday morning was almost a relief.

Sunday had been unbearable. Woken at seven by the renewed sexual celebrations of the newly engaged Fiona and Tim. Put off her breakfast by the tantric tongue tangling of Gaetano and Linzi. Unable to concentrate on the Sunday papers because of the creaking bed directly above the dining table. Unable even to go for a walk across the Common without being reminded that she was on her own by the good people of Clapham with their bloody public displays of affection.

She considered calling Leon. He had given her his home number for emergencies. She could ring and claim that she thought she had dropped her credit cards while she was on his bike, then perhaps casually suggest that they meet in town for a cup of tea. A great idea – though in the end she decided against it. But not until she had almost dialled Leon's number so many times that she knew it off by heart.

So once again, Sunday night for Kerry Keble was Marmite on toast in front of the *Antiques Roadshow*. But with the volume on the television turned up so loud, to drown out the clamour of squeaking bed springs above, that the rock guitarist from next door actually popped round to complain.

Yes, Monday morning came as a relief.

The tube ride to work was eventful.

Unsurprisingly, the Northern Line was experiencing delays due to a defective train at Hampstead and Kerry had a fifteen minute wait in Clapham before the journey even began. She positioned herself right at the end of the platform, knowing that the carriages which stopped there would be emptiest and that she might even, if she was very lucky, get herself a seat. She had a new romantic novel to read in her bag and couldn't wait to crack the spine and dive right in. Kerry didn't like to read on the platform because she was worried about nutters who might try to push her on to the lines. She figured that it wasn't a totally irrational fear, since it was something she often felt like doing herself on a Monday morning.

When the train arrived, she could hardly believe her luck. Everyone in the end carriage was crammed into the space by the doors while the seats that lined the walls appeared to be completely empty. The passengers were obviously all waiting to get off. Kerry stepped forward to claim her chair. The train stopped. The passengers piled out. Kerry and the people behind her piled on. They scrambled for the chairs and Kerry was relieved to feel her bum make contact with the soft blue foam. Success. She had made it. She had her coveted seat.

The guard announced that the doors were closing and the train sped into the dark tunnel like a rat into its hole.

It very quickly became apparent why so many people had quit the train at Clapham South.

'What are you bloody well looking at?'

Kerry peered up from the refuge of her paperback and found, to her horror, that the question was being directed at her.

'I said, what are you bloody well staring at, eh?'

Sitting opposite Kerry was an old woman wrapped up in three coats who appeared to have a tea-cosy crammed down on her head. It was literally a knitted tea-cosy. Kerry could see the hole that had been meant for the spout. In the seat beside the old woman, with a tea-cosy of his own through which protruded his fluffy ears, sat a matching dog. The little brown dog had his chin on the back of the seat and was dozing, dribbling in his dog-dreams over the shoulder of the smartly-dressed man to his right.

'I said, what are you bloody well looking at, young lady?' Mrs Tea-cosy asked once more.

'I . . . I . . .' Kerry was gobsmacked. Was she supposed to answer? 'I wasn't looking at you,' she said in a panic. 'I was just reading my book. Really, I was.'

'Yes,' the old woman narrowed her eyes. 'I know all about you and your books . . . You're taking notes about me aren't you? All of you are,' she waggled her finger at the commuters up and down the carriage. 'You all get money off the Government to do it, I know. Money off the Government to take your itty bitty little notes.' The man with the dog dribble on his shoulder was trying to suppress a smile.

'Do you want to see my stitches?' the woman asked menacingly, leaning forward across the aisle that divided her from Kerry and breathing strongly alcoholic air straight into Kerry's face. Kerry's eyes fixed in horror on a stamp-sized flake of something she assumed to be dead skin caught up in the woman's hair. 'You want to see my stitches,' the woman continued. 'I know. You all do.'

Kerry looked frantically to her fellow passengers for support, but they were all looking in different directions. Staring into space. Not about to get involved. It was as if she wasn't there.

'No, no, thank you, I really don't want to see your stitches.' Kerry opened her book again and tried to concentrate on the words which now appeared to swim like fishes before her eyes. The woman continued to rant about her surgical appliances, rocking backwards and forwards so that the cider smell of her breath hit Kerry in foul waves.

'You do, don't you?' Mrs Tea-cosy pulled on the coat-tails of a middle-aged man who was strap-hanging. He tugged the corner of his Burberry raincoat free from her greasy grasp and continued to read his paper as if nothing had happened.

'Excuse me,' he ventured politely, when she tried the trick again.

The old woman's dog raised his head from the neck rest and looked around slowly as if he had seen it all before. 'Don't you start ignoring me,' the woman raised her voice. 'I said, you want to see my stitches, don't you?'

The man made no indication to suggest that he did.

Which obviously made Mrs Tea-cosy even more upset than the fact that the Government was tailing her. Suddenly, she snatched the man's newspaper from his hand and began to hit him with it about the pin-striped knees. He jumped backwards from her vicious aim, at the same time knocking into a startled young woman who had been teetering on high heels behind him. She shrieked as she tumbled and laddered her tights. The man helped her to her feet while Mrs Tea-cosy continued to rain angry blows on his head with the *Daily Telegraph*.

'Ugh! Hay-yelp,' the young girl started screaming and the fat dog too was suddenly galvanised into action. Mrs Tea-cosy didn't relent in her beating. Her dog began to bark at the man as though he were the assailant and Mrs Tea-cosy the assailed. The crowd who were strap-hanging along the aisle parted like the Red Sea and crammed themselves backwards into the spaces by the doors. Kerry pressed herself back into her own seat as far as she could go, eyes wide with terror.

'Get off me.' The man being hit with his own paper obviously couldn't decide whether or not to throw a punch. His arms wavered between positions of defence and attack. 'Get off me, you stupid old woman.'

Both the woman and her dog were on their feet now and the woman was reaching inside her greasy coats. The next thing Kerry knew, the woman had one of her breasts squeezed naked between her red-mittened hands and was waving it at anyone who cared to look and see.

'Look at my stitches,' she cried to the sky.

The other passengers let out a collective gasp.

'Oh, man, that's disgusting,' said a young black guy who up until then had been laughing through his chewing gum.

The train pulled slowly into the station and the doors opened. Once again, the entire contents of the end carriage poured out on to the platform and tried to cram themselves on to the train a little further down.

The crowd moved along with murmurs of amusement and disgust. Kerry shoved her novel back into her bag and followed the complicated signs to the Bakerloo Line. She wasn't amused, or disgusted. She was worried. How long before that mad old woman was her? All alone in the world and showing her tits to plain strangers.

When she got into the office, she recounted the story to Leon. He laughed all the way through. Then Kerry told him about the surprise engagement announcement. He laughed all the way through that too. Especially the bit about having to listen to a variety of happy couples shagging the night away. Kerry laughed with him, but when she stopped she felt oddly hollow again. Was this really her life she was talking about?

Then the phones began to ring.

'Good morning, Verbal Tix . . .'

Verbal Tix was a relatively new company. The big chief, Serena Winterson, had worked at a huge talent agency for many years, until she got sick of the pitiful commission structure and defected to form Verbal Tix with a number of dissatisfied artistes in tow. Now almost a year old, the company had expanded to employ four people. Leon was in charge while Serena had time off to drop yet another baby. Then there were the three bookers; Celestine, Joshua and Kerry, the new recruit. Leon had interviewed her and offered her the job as he walked her out of the office. They had hit it off straightaway. Kerry liked Josh too but Celestine was proving more difficult to get to know.

Kerry had the desk opposite Leon. On her first day it had been totally clean and empty, but one month into her contract, the drawers were overflowing with showreel tapes and sweet-wrappers, and a selection of fluffy little gonks with googly plastic eyes had formed a defence line between her and her new boss. Kerry's blotter was covered in so many scribbled numbers that she could never find the really important one she had just written down. All numbers were meant to be entered into the database on the computer, but that, despite the extensive experience she had listed on her CV, was one area of modern life that Kerry did not feel inclined to embrace. She could, however, work the switchboard, which foxed both Leon and Celestine. So most of Kerry's working day was spent taking calls and logging vital numbers on her blotter and on Post-its, which always got lost on the floor.

'Hello, Verbal Tix.' No rest for the wicked.

'Yes, hello,' said a plummy voice. 'I'd like to book Lance Sylvester to do three advertisements this afternoon.'

'I'll just check his availability for you, sir.' Kerry put her hand over the receiver and mouthed 'Someone wants Lance Sylvester' across the desk to Leon. 'Make out he's quite busy,' Leon mouthed back.

'This afternoon?' Kerry said to the caller. 'I'm afraid that might be a problem. He's quite busy today. How long would you like him for?'

'Quite busy, eh? What a load of bollocks?' The plummy accent slipped. It was Lance himself on the phone.

'Oh, ha ha ha, Lance,' muttered Kerry. 'If you keep calling me up like this you're only stopping the people who might really want to give you a job from getting through.'

'Sorry, Miss Keble,' he whimpered like a schoolboy then laughed his nasty dirty laugh. 'So, did you enjoy yourself at my party, darlin'? Got any scandalous gossip to tell your Uncle Lance?'

'I don't think so.'

'You got a lift home with Leon,' he reminded her conspiratorially. 'With your legs wrapped around him on the back of that bike.'

'I had to hang on somehow . . .'

'Ha ha ha. Anything happen? Eh? Eh?'

'Lance. No. You've got a one-track mind. Besides . . . you know,' she stuttered.

'Stranger things have happened, I say. Ask Celestine.'

'Lance!!! Look, I've got another call coming through. I'll call you back if anything comes in for you. OK?' Kerry put down the phone and started to chew her pencil. 'Stranger things have happened.' Just what did he mean by that?

At lunchtime, Leon asked her to join him for a sandwich at Pret-à-manger. He paid. But Kerry could hardly take the time to enjoy his generosity or his company because she was so desperate to get back to the office and ask Celestine about Lance's latest insinuations. Stranger things have happened? Was Lance suggesting that Celestine and Leon had got it on? Leon linked his arm through Kerry's as they walked back to the office. He was chatting about Sam and Kerry couldn't find an opportunity to probe about anything else. At Verbal Tix, Celestine was on the telephone to an important client. Kerry willed her to put down the phone. A bubble of excitement was rising in her stomach and she knew that she wouldn't be able to do a thing until she knew the whole story. If Kerry had a ghost of a chance with Leon Landesman she wanted to snatch it right away.

Fiona had been at work since the markets opened at seven o'clock in the morning, and the night before she had had just two hours sleep. But for once she didn't feel tired at all as the big hand crept towards eleven. When Maureen the tea lady came round with the trolley, Fiona bought two Crunchie bars and ordered a nice strong coffee. Maureen had raised an eyebrow.

'So you're off your sugar-free flapjacks then?'

'Life's too good to eat birdseed,' Fiona told her. Cellulite didn't matter anymore. Nothing mattered anymore. Somebody loved her. Somebody was about to prove that he loved her. They were going to take Tuesday afternoon off to choose the ring. Fiona picked up the phone to call Tim's office and doodled a heart on her blotter while his phone rang. It rang and rang. Tim had probably already gone out to lunch with a client. Fiona put down the phone and coloured in the little blue heart.

'Doodling hearts now? You look like you're in love,' Maureen observed as she poured out a strong cup of tea for Fiona's neighbour.

'I am. I am. I am,' Fiona sighed. But she was waiting until she had the ring to tell everybody just how much.

'Well, let's hope that love can conquer this,' said Pete, as he handed her a memo from the powers that be. Pete smiled smugly. He had the desk opposite Fiona and had been in unspoken competition with her from day one. 'Mr Hara wants to see you,' he told her with no small degree of satisfaction. In Pete's considered opinion, you only got a message to make an appointment with Mr Hara, head of the whole conglomeration, if you were on the way out.

'Do you want me to call him for you?' Pete asked eagerly. 'Tell him that you're wetting your pants?'

'Thank you, Peter, but no,' replied Fiona. 'I'll just finish this Crunchie and then I shall call him myself.' Nothing was going to spoil her second day as a fiancée. Especially not Peter Harris. She pushed back her chair and put her feet up on the desk, having first speared the memo from Hara on her spike for receipts.

'Good afternoon, Miss Davenport. I'll just let Mr Hara know that you're here.' Hara's secretary broke into a rare smile.

Miss Koto was known to the boys on Fiona's floor as the 'Komodo Dragon'. She was a hard-boiled woman, who had come from Japan with Mr Hara when he was put in charge of the London offices. Koto was in her early forties or maybe younger but she'd led a very hard life. Rumour had it that she was jilted at the altar by a dashing young army officer, who with embarrassment later committed hari-kiri. Naturally, the deserted bride had been devoid of the milk of human kindness ever since. When Ms Komodo Dragon smiled at you, it didn't necessarily mean that you were favoured. More likely, she knew that your head was about to roll and was actually suppressing the desire to laugh at your pathetic disposable face.

'Go straight in, Miss Davenport,' Ms Koto said, waving her towards Hara's office with a pencil that had been sharpened on a Samurai sword.

Fiona took a deep breath and took hold of the handle on the polished wooden door. She had had enough time to start worrying now. The only other time she had been in Hara's office was when she first started at the bank. On that occasion she had been crammed into the room with twenty other graduate recruits. She had been right at the back and had barely heard a word of Hara's quiet pep talk. Instead she had been looking at the management books that lined his office shelves, at least half a dozen of them written by himself. Mr Hara was a frighteningly successful man but when Fiona walked into his office on this occasion, he rose from his chair behind his desk the size of a football pitch and surprised her by strolling across the room to shake her warmly by the hand.

'Miss Davenport,' he said in his lispy Japanese accent. 'How lovely to see you again. Sit down. Sit down.' He motioned her towards the black leather sofa which flanked one side of the room. Fiona sat in one corner of the sofa. Mr Hara sat in the other. Fiona crossed her legs demurely at the ankle. Was this the new human approach to giving an employee the chop?

'Tea?' he asked.

Fiona refused politely. She didn't really want to be holding anything she could spill in her slightly shaky hands. Hara smiled at her and nodded. Fiona nodded back and hoped she hadn't nodded too deeply because she knew the Japanese had some kind of code about that. Hara took a deep breath and began.

'Well, Miss Davenport, you are probably wondering why I have asked you here today.'

Wondering, thought Fiona. Now she was really wetting her pants.

'Though you may not have seen much of me during your time

here with First Orient Bank, rest assured that I have my finger on the pulse of everything that goes on in the London office and, in particular, I monitor the progress of my graduate recruits with very great care indeed . . .'

Fiona nodded.

'Very great care indeed,' he repeated.

Fiona nodded again.

'I suppose you could even say that I have my spies . . .'

Fiona just nodded. She had a sudden flashback to one terrible lunchtime when she had been spotted blubbing in the loos by the Komodo Dragon. Tim had just cancelled their three-year anniversary date in favour of an old boys' rugby dinner at his college in Cambridge. Fiona felt the first prickles of a cold sweat gathering beneath her fringe. Had that one awful moment sealed her fate? Apparently the Dragon was the kind of woman who thought that taking a whole day off to go to your father's funeral was weak.

Hara continued, 'And we've noticed that your progress has been somewhat different from that of the other employees in your year . . .'

Different? She was finished. 'Well, I haven't . . .' Fiona began to prepare her excuses. Hara raised his hand to cut her short.

'In fact, so different, that I have decided to offer you the placement in our New York office because I feel that it is time for you to spread your wings . . .'

'I . . . I.' Fiona was astonished. She couldn't possibly have heard him right. The New York placement? It was the most prestigious trainee placement that the First Orient Bank offered. And Hara was offering it to her? Everyone had assumed that it would go straight to Peter Harris. 'New York?' she squeaked.

'Yes. New York,' said Hara, with a quizzical smile at her disbelief. 'And you should also be thinking about making applications to do an MBA as well. First Orient Bank has close links with Harvard . . .'

Fiona couldn't close her mouth. 'Harvard,' she murmured.

'Yes, Harvard,' repeated Hara. 'The placement begins in two months' time, Miss Davenport. You would be based out there for six months. Of course the bank will provide funds for your resettlement and take care of your British affairs while you are away. Miss Koto will be pleased to help you with all the necessary

documentation.' Mr Hara paused and smiled. He laid a cool, slim
hand on top of Fiona's which were clenched tightly together in
her lap. 'Of course, I am assuming that you want to go . . .'

Fiona nodded. 'Oh, yes. Of course I do,' she lied. The time
to get out of this mess was later. 'But I had better go back to
my desk now,' she muttered, shell-shocked. 'Got to get some
figures finished for this afternoon.'

'Certainly. Conscientiousness is what we like to see.'

Mr Hara rose to show her out of the room. In the reception
area, the Dragon looked up from her typing and smiled. It was
a real smile this time, one that even involved her eyes.

'Well done,' she mouthed.

'Yeah,' said Fiona. 'Yeah. Thanks.'

When Fiona returned to her desk, she was chalk white. The
New York placement. What a disaster! She knew that what the
choice really boiled down to was six months away from Tim or
the end of her career. Pete and his cronies Simon and James
were already waiting by her desk like vultures, eager to hear
the bad news. Seeing Fiona's stony pale face, they assumed that
they had got what they wanted. A head had rolled.

Simon handed her a cup of tea, ready made. Milk and two
sugars. Not her usual drink at all.

'I thought you might need this,' he told her. 'It's nice and
sweet. My mother always said that it's just the thing to drink
when you've had a nasty shock.' His voice was full of unnatural
concern.

'Thanks,' said Fiona. 'I guess I have had a shock.' She sipped
at the tea silently. Simon perched on the edge of Peter's desk.
James leaned forward across her monitor to stare. They watched
her swallowing slowly as if that cup of tea would be the last thing
ever to pass her quivering lips.

'For Christ's sake, what did old man Hara say to you?' Pete
couldn't wait a second more.

'He said,' Fiona whispered into her polystyrene cup. 'He said
that he wants me to go to New York.'

Linzi was almost horizontal on her desk. The only thing moving
was her index finger, which was pressing the mouse to flip over
the cards in yet another game of Solitaire. What time was it? She
looked at her Mickey Mouse watch. It was only two minutes later

than it had been two minutes ago. Still two hours till lunchtime.
Still seven hours till knocking off time. And about ninety-six
hours until the end of the week.

Linzi was shaken out of her reverie by the sound of a pile of
papers dropping heavily on to her desk. Cymbelline, the graduate
trainee, tried to attract Linzi's attention with a discreet cough.

Linzi pretended not to hear.

'Duncan wants this lot typed up straight away,' Cymbelline
told the top of Linzi's head. 'We've got a presentation to the
client at eleven. And, by the way, it would help if you could
use the approved layout first time, this time.'

'Yes, sir,' Linzi saluted Cymbelline's retreating backside. She
was wearing the creative department uniform of tight-fitting
black trousers and high-heeled suede boots. She really shouldn't
have been. Not with those thighs.

Linzi wearily flicked through the papers that Cymbelline had
given her and opened the word processing package on her desk-
top PC. The approved layout indeed, Linzi snorted. Ellington,
Froggett and Splinter had a special system for their presentations
and every letter, proposal and invoice had to be typed in precisely
the same way. Linzi had caused a complete débâcle in her first
week by using Times New Roman instead of the approved
Century Schoolbook to type a memo to the TV department
head. Big deal? It seemed it was. Linzi complained that nobody
had told her anal retention was a company policy. Was she
supposed to guess?

Bing! The word processing package announced that it was
ready to play with the cheerful little beep that made Linzi want
to push the computer on to the floor with her boot. Every single
time. She entered her password. 'TITS.' Apparently it had been
chosen by the girl who worked there before. Well, thought Linzi,
she must have been a 'right larf'.

God, so this was the heady world of advertising? The creative
department of Elton John, Frog-spit and Sphincter. Six lads
from 'oop North' and a couple of Sloaney just-out-of-schoolgirls
gathered daily around a glass-topped table to put toilet jokes into
the copy for everything from bank accounts to 'boil-in-the-bag'
chicken. Caroline, the boss at Linzi's temping agency – Advertising Angels – had promised that this would be a stimulating job.
Linzi had had more fun sticking her fingers into electric sockets.

She read the yellow Post-it note that was stuck to the top page of the pile to be typed.

'Darling Linzi, approved lay-out, please. And when you've finished this you can come and sit on my face.'

Oh, ha ha ha. A Post-it with extra wit from Duncan the wag. Duncan the wank. The creative department head with the perm straight out of eighties *Brookside*. Linzi took the Post-it note and stuck it into her diary to keep as evidence for the day when she would sue his saggy-trousered arse. If this wasn't sexual harassment then she didn't know what was and the Post-it note was more tangible than the leery winks and the 'accidental' bottom pinch he had given her as she tried to put more paper into the photocopier. Linzi certainly hadn't bothered to wear a skirt to the office after her first unhappy day in this job.

The computer had been standing unused while she sorted through the papers. After three minutes the screen-saver kicked in. 'GET YER TITS OUT!!!' scrolled across the screen in slow motion. Somebody must have changed the saver while Linzi was in the loo. She clicked her mouse angrily to get rid of it. Did they do this to Cymbelline? she wondered. Probably not. In the one lunchtime that Linzi had joined her workmates for a drink, Cymbelline had downed three pints and thrown two of them straight back up again. Cymbelline was one of the lads. Though with red lipstick, of course.

Linzi began to type the first page out. Fourteen point, bold font for all headings. Twelve point, not-bold font for text. She was about halfway down the page and heading for her top speed of forty words a minute when she felt a hand on her shoulder and stumbled on the space bar. Bugger. It was him.

'You've spelt that wrong . . .' he said.

Linzi tried to find the spelling mistake in the words that flickered before her. Nothing was obviously wrong.

Duncan elaborated. 'Penis only has one "n".'

'I'll go back and spell-check it when I've finished,' Linzi said without looking up.

'Ooooh, what's wrong with you today? Get out of the wrong man's bed, did you?'

Linzi took a deep breath. 'I didn't find your Post-it note to me tremendously funny, Duncan,' she said through tight lips.

Duncan rested his belly against the back of her chair. Linzi closed her eyes and gritted her teeth against the mental picture of the tuft of hair that was habitually pushed out between the bottom buttons of his too-tight shirt by copious rolls of excess fat.

'Writing that kind of thing could count as sexual harassment, you know,' she elaborated.

'Woo-oh! Big words! Sex-u-al ha-rass-ment,' he mimicked her voice. 'Oh, get a sense of humour, Linzi. You know that I wouldn't touch you with a bargepole anyway. You're far too skinny for me.' He leaned forward and squeezed her hard around the waist. 'Look, I can get my hands right around you.' Linzi turned on him with a snarl. 'Ooooh!!' Duncan backed off with his hands in the air, shielding his face and crying 'No. Please. Help me!!! The woman's gone mad!!' He appealed to his audience for approval. Cymbelline obliged with a sycophantic laugh.

'It's not funny,' Linzi hissed.

'Everyone else in the office thinks that it is,' Duncan replied in justification.

Linzi bashed at the keyboard blindly until Duncan leaned heavily against her backrest and the sudden jolt made her skip a key. 'I can't type while you're looking over my shoulder,' she told him flatly.

'Looks like you can't type anyway,' Duncan replied. 'How much do we pay you? Seven pounds an hour? Too much for someone who doesn't even know how to bloody well spell. I'll have to ask that fat cow at Advertising Angels to send us a proper girl next time . . .'

'I can spell.' Linzi ploughed on with the typing. 'Customer profile (fourteen point, bold) . . . We must remember that the typical consumer for Butcher's new Soup-in-a-Mug is likely to be a young single mum with only a small weekly budget for food. It is likely that she will not be terribly well educated . . . (twelve point, not bold)' Ellington, Bigot and Splinter.

'When you've finished that, my petal,' Duncan rested his chin on her shoulder. She could feel his hot stinky breath against her ear. 'If you think you'll ever finish it – I need you to send a courier up to Sarah's house with this.' He propped an 'E, F and S' embossed envelope between Linzi's keyboard and monitor. 'Call her and tell her when to expect it. I need ten woolly jumpers for tonight. Patrick Farnham is having a leaving do after work at the Dog and Duck . . . You can come if you like.' He stood up and turned towards his office. 'Though I don't suppose you ever "come" do you, Miss Iron Knickers.' He slipped back behind the glass partition that separated his creative greatness from the proles before Linzi had time to respond. Cymbelline stifled a snigger.

Linzi paused in her typing and stared at the envelope. Then she looked up and glared across the open-plan office straight at Cymbelline. Cymbelline quickly ducked her glossy-haired head behind the cover of her monitor to escape the evil eye.

'Woolly jumpers' was the code for coke and Duncan wanted ten grams of coke at sixty pounds a gram, which meant that the envelope sitting in front of Linzi contained six hundred pounds in cash. In fifty pound notes probably, since Duncan would never carry anything less. It was disgusting, sticking that amount of money up your nose. Linzi briefly considered picking up the envelope and walking straight out with it. But that was too easy. Instead she picked up the dirty white telephone and dutifully dialled first the courier company and then the dealer. To the courier, she gave the reference of the client to whom Duncan would make that morning's presentation so that the trip would be written off against their fee. To Sarah, the dealer, she gave an estimated time of arrival for the 'wool' of a quarter to midday and Sarah promised to have finished her 'knitting' by twelve.

According to Cymbelline, Sarah the dealer had a new top-of-the-range BMW and sent her five-year-old son to a private school so her 'jumpers' must have been the most popular outfits in town. Sarah was always polite on the phone, friendly but businesslike. Linzi tried to imagine how she must look. A mother and a coke-dealer? What kind of a woman would step into such a nasty little world with a tiny child in tow? The kind of single mother who couldn't afford 'Soup-in-a-Mug' on her Income Support perhaps?

When the deal had been sorted out, Linzi dialled Gaetano at his shop, thinking that the sound of his voice might cheer her up. He wasn't there and Linzi didn't leave a message with his assistant. Then she called Caroline at Advertising Angels and begged her to find her a different job.

'Heaven's above, Linzi,' Caroline sighed. 'That's a three-month placement you have there. You've got job security. I thought that you wanted security for a while. You've only been in the job for a week and a half. Give it another chance. It's three months' work, my darling.'

'Exactly,' said Linzi. She just knew she wouldn't last that long. She wondered for a moment whether she should tell her temp controller that Duncan thought she was a 'fat, old cow'. No. Pointless. Caroline would probably put that down to 'jolly japes' before spending the afternoon blubbing in the loo. It wouldn't actually spur her into action.

'Please,' Linzi begged.' Just keep an eye out for something that might suit me a little better, would you, Caroline? I'll do almost anything and you know that I'm reliable. I just don't feel quite right here.'

Cymbelline paused before Linzi's desk en route to the coffee machine.

'Personal phone calls?' she asked, not-at-all-quietly.

'Yeah. It's the Pope actually. I'm confessing my murderous thoughts. Do you want a word?' Linzi covered the mouthpiece and held out the phone.

Cymbelline waddled on by with a tut.

'Stick with it, darling,' Caroline told Linzi when they resumed the conversation. 'Even the most extrovert people among us can sometimes find that we take a little longer than we expect to settle in. Oh, whoops. I've got another call coming through. Speak to you later, sweetheart. Mwah! Mwah! Cheery-bye.'

'Cheery-bloody-bye.'

Cymbelline returned from the kitchen with a trayful of drinks. One for every member of the team – with the exception of Linzi, of course. When she leaned over to put down the coffee she had poured out for Duncan, he hooked a finger into the V-neck of her shirt to get a better look at her cleavage. Cymbelline emerged from his little glassed-in office blushing like an overblown rose.

'Don't get many of those to the pound!' Duncan called after her.

'Obviously don't get many brain cells to the pound in this place either,' Linzi sighed. 'Where's my coffee, Cymbelline?'

'In the machine,' Cymbelline replied.

Linzi finished the pile of typing just before the deadline and all in the approved layout. Duncan took it from her with a grunt, and went to his meeting without reading it. Linzi wished that she could have been there when they got to the section in which she had added her own special opinion that Soup-in-a-Mug was 'reconstituted cack'. Ten minutes later, the cocaine arrived. Same ingredients as Soup-in-a-Mug, but slightly more expensive. Linzi signed the courier's delivery slip and took the coke straight into Duncan's office without opening the padded envelope. He had instructed her to leave it in the bottom drawer of his desk. She opened the drawer and stuck the jiffy bag full of powder beneath his collection of football and girlie mags and the neatly folded issue of *Guardian 2* in which Duncan was hailed as one of advertising's 'brave new yobs'. 'Breaking new ground' according to the interview. Duncan spent more time breaking wind. Linzi closed the drawer with a smile at the thought. Next, she went back to her desk and picked up her bag.

'Where are you going?' Cymbelline asked.

'I'm going to lunch,' said Linzi.

'But who's going to cover the phones?'

'You can, Simper-leen.'

Leaving Cymbelline looking like a goldfish which had suddenly found itself on the dry side of the fishtank, Linzi headed straight for the lift. Cymbelline was probably calling Advertising Angels to complain about her even as she reached the ground floor. So what, thought Linzi. She had no intention of going back to Ellington, Froggett and Splinter. Never ever ever again.

When she got to the phone box on the corner of Soho Square, Linzi dialled the police and quietly tipped them off about the quantity of coke in Duncan's bottom drawer.

CHAPTER FIVE

Getting home from work early meant that Linzi had plenty of time to get ready for that evening's date with Gaetano and since the house was empty, because Kerry and Fiona were still out treading their hamster wheels, Linzi was doubly pleased that she could use Fiona's expensive body oil stuff in the bath without having to ask.

Linzi soaked for almost an hour, topping the water up with extra hot until her fingers got so crinkly that she began to worry that they might not plump back out again in time for her date. She slapped on some of Kerry's best Clarins' moisturiser, just in case, and then made sure that she rinsed the bath clean of all evidence of body oil theft. Last time, Fiona had cottoned on that someone was using her Clinique when she slipped on the slick it had left behind while having a shower. She had almost pulled the shower rail off the wall in an attempt to stop herself falling. It wasn't funny. At least that's what she said.

Linzi raked through her underwear drawer to find a set of lingerie that if it didn't match exactly at least matched in colour. The choice wasn't inspiring. Black or chewing-gum grey. She plumped for the black and reminded herself that she was going to have to do some washing one of these days. Luckily, she had been saving a once-worn Wonderbra for special occasions. So, foundation work done, she set off on a tour of her housemates' wardrobes to find something suitable to sling over the top.

Fiona's wardrobe first. Linzi opened the polished walnut doors wide and stood back. This could be the wardrobe of someone who did night shifts in a dry-cleaner's shop for a hobby. Every shirt, skirt and running-vest hung from its very own padded coat-hanger, and every loaded coat-hanger was covered with a plastic dry-cleaning bag to fend off the dust. The order was absolutely rigid. Like a rainbow, the clothes ranged from red on the left to blue on the right. Black and white basics had their own section at each of the spectrum's ends. This strict organisation made it very difficult to steal from Fiona's wardrobe. She could see at twenty paces whether something had been tampered with and would be waiting by the front door to snatch her best shirt off your back before you could take off your coat and make your excuses.

Besides, thought Linzi, it would be a bit of a risk borrowing something from Fiona that night. Linzi was going to watch Gaetano's band playing in a North London pub she had never heard of but which was apparently quite a prestige venue on the rock circuit these days. DKNY is hardly the kind of thing you want to wear to a heavy metal gig, so Linzi closed the walnut doors of Fiona's wardrobe once more and tried to make sure she hadn't left any incriminating fingerprints on the bright brassy handles.

Kerry's wardrobe was a different matter altogether. For a start, she couldn't fit a proper wardrobe into her tiny room. So, most of Kerry's stuff had migrated out on to the landing and to help solve her storage problems she had bought one of those canvas portable wardrobes on a tent-pole frame which was bulging at the sides like an old man's best dress-shirt. Linzi sometimes felt guilty that Kerry had got such a bum deal when it came to bedrooms but Kerry rarely complained and had once even claimed that she liked it. Looking in through the slightly open door now, Linzi could almost see why. Kerry's room was like a little nest, practically all bed. Cosy. But not really enough room to entertain a visitor.

Linzi unzipped the floppy fabric door of the portable wardrobe. Three crumpled T-shirts sprang out straight on to the floor as if they had just been waiting for a chance to escape. This wardrobe was chaos. Linzi wasn't even sure that there were actually any coat-hangers in there at all. She pulled out a couple of pairs of jeans in an attempt to make some working space for her search and quickly concluded that this collection was the result of at least five years' panic buying. A pair of flared green jersey-knit palazzo pants? Purleese? Linzi had never seen those before. And that orange tube skirt? A real throwback from the eighties (which was probably the last time Kerry had been able to fit into it, she thought unkindly). Linzi draped the offending items over the banister and continued to hunt for something vaguely wearable beneath the frumpy frills and furbelows. No wonder Kerry was always wearing those black jeans of hers.

Linzi spotted a corner of promising red fabric and tugged it out to find that it grew into a skirt of that special proportion, the one that can make even Kate Moss look as though she has fat knees. Linzi held it against her body and snorted. She was surprised to see that it came from somewhere as trendy as Miss Selfridge. Then she piled everything that lay across the banister back into the canvas coffin and zipped it up again, at least as far as the zip would go before it got caught on something inside and jammed.

Linzi retired to her room with the red skirt and a belt she had pinched from Fiona. She rolled the skirt up at the waistband and fastened it in place with the belt. With her own black jumper over the top the ensemble looked almost stylish. Fiona had a lipstick that might even match the skirt. Linzi helped herself to a couple of generous smearings and made sure she was gone before anyone got home to complain.

As she struggled up the road with three carrier bags full of shopping, Kerry caught a brief glimpse of Linzi as she dashed out of the house. She looked wonderful as always. She had such a stylish way with clothes. And, of course, thought Kerry sadly, the figure to carry it off. That red skirt she had been wearing was particularly cool, though. It reminded Kerry of the Miss Selfridge number she had consigned to the back of her wardrobe after just one disastrous airing at a twenty-first birthday bash when she had a snog with a boy who turned out to be her cousin. After supper, Kerry mused, perhaps I'll dig that old thing out and give it another try.

She was glad that for once nobody was in when she got home. It meant that she could soak in the bath for as long as she liked and perhaps even borrow some of Fiona's bath oil stuff.

Fiona had been waiting at the bar of the Pitcher and Piano for almost three-quarters of an hour. When she arrived, the place had been almost empty, but now, with all the offices in the vicinity chucking out their inmates, it was packed with people trying to drink away that Monday feeling. If one more person jostled her at the bar, Fiona thought angrily, she would throw her drink straight over him to save him the bother of spilling it.

Finally, Tim appeared. His head was easily visible above the sea of little people beneath him. As he moved across the room, the crowds parted before him as if they recognised something infinitely superior to themselves in his bearing. Fiona's stony face cracked into a smile as soon as she saw him. She was engaged to that six-foot-four god of a man. Not bad work at all for a girl from Bristol.

'Sorry I'm late,' he told her as he kissed the top of her head.

'It's OK,' she grinned and lied. 'I've only been waiting five minutes.'

'Good job I didn't come on time in that case,' Tim replied without a hint of a smile.

Tim commandeered Fiona's space at the bar and ordered them both a fresh drink. As the barman fiddled about with his taps and tried to find a couple of clean glasses, Fiona just gazed at the back of Tim's neck. At the way his hair curled down on to his collar. At the little raised mole she had wanted to kiss so many times but resisted because she felt that it might be embarrassing for him if she drew attention to it. As he leaned on the bar, Tim's pinstriped suit jacket was stretched tightly across his broad shoulders. This is the man I'm going to marry, Fiona murmured to herself. Tim turned around and caught her silently moving her mouth.

'Sorry, Fi. Didn't catch a word of that. Too noisy. God, it's packed in this place tonight. Why do we keep coming here, eh? Oh look, Wooders and Minky are over there by the door. Hey, Wooders!!!' He waved hello. 'We'll go over and have a chat with him in a minute.'

Fiona nodded compliantly. Tim's best pal from college, Wooders, was her biggest rival for his affections.

The barman put a pint and a half of Guinness down in front of Tim, then presented him with his change and a receipt in a small white dish. Tim scooped up all the little coins and shoved them straight into his back pocket. 'I hate it when they give you your change like that,' he told Fiona. 'What do they expect? A bloody tip?'

Once again, he had forgotten that Fiona hated Guinness. Tim put the half-pint in her hand and began to stride off in the direction of Wooders. The crowd parted before him and closed straight up again behind him, so that Fiona reached Wooders and Minky almost three minutes later than Tim had.

For one of the premier rock venues in London, the Forget-Me-Not and Firkin had a dire record with regard to its provision for ladies' conveniences. Linzi stood with her feet on either side of an unidentified puddle and leaned over the cracked sink full of murky water and fag-ends to reapply her lipstick in a horribly smeary mirror. Gaetano's band had just finished their set. It had been met with what seemed like approval from the audience, though it may just as well have been a collective fit brought on by the erratic strobe lighting. Now Monster Munch were packing up their equipment and loading it into the van so that the Professor, as their bassist was called, could drive it home before coming back to the pub again sans wheels to get slaughtered with impunity.

Gaetano was already waiting outside the ladies' when Linzi emerged repainted. He wrapped his arms around her and pressed a kiss to her newly coloured lips. The sweat from his face wiped off half her foundation.

'What did you think?' he asked excitedly. 'Those last two songs went down well, I reckon. The Professor said that the guy from Malibou Records didn't turn up until then so it doesn't matter if the set was a bit crap.'

'I thought it was all brilliant,' Linzi smiled. She stroked his earlobe lovingly and fiddled with the little silver ring that was stuck right through it. 'Almost as brilliant as your solo performance on Saturday night.'

'Foxy lady!!' Gaetano murmured.

He kissed her again, this time simultaneously bringing his thigh between her legs so that she could wriggle up and down against it. Linzi rubbed against him like a cat. She couldn't wait to get him home. She had been longing for this moment since she had reluctantly let him out of her bed to go to work that morning.

'What are we going to do now?' she whispered hotly into the hollow where his shoulder met his neck.

Gaetano took his leg away from her crotch and fished a fag out of the top pocket of his leather waistcoat. He didn't offer one to Linzi. 'Well, we're going to wait here until the Professor gets back from dropping the van off at his old man's garage. Then we're going to have a few jars and just see what develops. We'll probably hang around here while Mutant Phlegm are on. They're pretty good. Our biggest rivals.'

'Oh.' Linzi was more than a little disappointed. Their first real date and she was already taking second place to a bunch of men who could BO for Great Britain. 'I was thinking that we could perhaps go and get something to eat later on. Just the two of us?'

Gaetano smiled at her as if she had just told him a joke. 'I'm not hungry.' He kissed her on the forehead.

'But I am,' Linzi protested.

'Do you want me to get you some crisps from the bar?'

'No, don't bother.'

The Professor reappeared all too quickly. He had changed out of his Terrorvision T-shirt into something equally unsavoury without sleeves. He had combed his hair too and pulled it back into a frizzy ponytail with a brown elastic band. Linzi didn't like to think of the potential for split ends when he tried to pull it back out. The Professor got the first round in and the band retired to a table which, according to a little beer-stained card sign, was specially reserved for 'artistes'. The man from Malibou Records had told Socks, the band's guitarist, that he enjoyed the show, apparently. However, he didn't have time to stay for a chat and a drink, which was a pity.

'Yeah, and I really liked that bit in "The Virgin is Bleeding" when Socks cut the crap and went for the reverb,' the Professor was telling the boys. 'The crowd went berserk, man!! We are nearly there, man. I tell you, nearly there. This time next year, we'll be wearing our own T-shirts.'

Linzi wondered where he had borrowed the one he was sporting tonight.

'You'll have to stand at the back for the publicity shots though, Professor,' Gaetano told him. ''Cos we don't want to scare any children.' The rest of the band laughed. The Professor looked as though he had heard that one before and hoped he wouldn't have to hear it again. Linzi's heart went out momentarily to the teddy-bear of a man.

'Yeah, Merlin had better go at the front,' Socks thought aloud. ''Cos he's like the singer and all, isn't he?'

Only just, thought Linzi.

'But Gaetano's the most handsome,' she suggested sycophantically.

Bingo! Gaetano turned to Linzi and gave her an affectionate squeeze on the knee. Then his hand moved up Linzi's leg and beneath the edge of her borrowed skirt. 'Can we go back to your place, please?' she whispered desperately. Gaetano looked uncomfortable.

'No, it's best if we go back to yours tonight. But I've got to finish this pint yet.'

Kerry stretched the lead on her CD player as far as it would go and then turned the volume up full blast so that she could hear it clearly while she was taking a bath. She had used some of Fiona's bath oil and topped that up with her own bubbles so that now the bathtub looked like the kind of tub you see on fashion shoots where the model is just sticking her pink-painted toenails out of the foam and staring at the camera with a look of terrible coyness.

Kerry had put on her Roxy Music Live CD. She could only risk doing that when Linzi the Trend Controller was out. This was going to a great bath. Kerry had bought a microwaveable vegetarian curry with rice from Safeway and the minute that was ready she would take it upstairs and jump right in. Bryan Ferry, Biryani and a bathful of bubbles. What girl in her right mind needed a man?

Though she wouldn't have said 'no' if the man on offer was someone like Leon.

That evening, the tube had been out of service at Leicester Square due to 'customer action', which meant that someone must have thrown themselves on to the line, as they always seemed to do so selfishly during the rush-hour. When Kerry re-emerged to make a beeline for Oxford Circus instead, Leon had been passing by on his way to the car park. He had offered her a lift home on the back of the Yamaha. Kerry couldn't accept because she was wearing a pencil skirt, but Leon had been concerned and that was enough to make her subsequent tube journey home almost bearable. She had hardly even flinched when a pixie-faced infant picked his nose and wiped the sticky findings on her jacket as the train pulled into Victoria. Leon had offered her a lift home. God was in his heaven.

The steam from the bath had frosted up the mirror. Kerry drew a heart around her face and started to wipe away the condensation from its middle. When the mirror was clear again, she noticed the white head of a spot nestling treacherously between her eyebrows. It must have been there all afternoon. All the time she was sitting right opposite Leon. She huffed on the mirror in disgust to frost it up again.

Wooders was giving Tim the low-down on the old boys' match he had missed that Saturday. Apparently, someone they knew from college had broken his nose. And bled all over his cream Ralph Lauren jumper, the poor lad's girlfriend, Minky, added to Fiona as an aside. The match hadn't gone as well as the boys hoped and that in no small part, said Wooders, was due to Tim's absence. What was his excuse, eh? Fiona's attention drifted from the best way to get stubborn blood stains out of lambswool as she waited for her moment to step into the spotlight.

'Where were you when we needed you?' Wooders jabbed Tim hard in the side.

Fiona stepped closer to Tim and wound her arm through his, ready to make the tableau of a perfect couple when Tim announced their big news.

'I had to go into the office and finalise some details on this project I've been doing,' Tim said. 'It's a pretty big deal actually, and if I get it right it'll be mega-bucks for my bonus. You know how it is.'

'Yeah, right. That accounts for your day. But what excuse do you have for missing the post-match training, you woman?' Wooders continued.

'I was just too tired after work, man,' said Tim. 'I'll make up for it next week though. Twelve pints at the Iron Horse. I betcha.'

'Twelve pints? You'll be on your knees, mate. Fifty quid says you don't make it to eleven.' Tim and Wooders shook on the arrangement. Then Fiona opened and closed her mouth like a goldfish while Wooders and Tim did a bit of friendly punching-each-other-in-the-guts to reaffirm their allegiance. Too tired to go out on Saturday night? What was Tim on about? Why hadn't he told Wooders that he had been too busy getting engaged to play rugby?

'Are you OK, Fiona?' Minky asked, recognising a face she pulled quite often herself when her boyfriend was pretending that she was part of the furniture.

'Yes. Fine,' Fiona lied but she desperately followed the rest of the conversation between the boys, waiting for the crucial turn to what had really happened that weekend. It didn't come. The boys sank another two pints and Wooders made his excuses. Minky followed Wooders to the door. Tim made some comment to the effect that Wooders was jumping straight into a sick man's bed, then he finished his pint and put the empty glass down on the lid of a shiny grand piano.

'You ready, Fi?'

She had finished her half-pint hours ago.

'Yes. I suppose.'

Fiona shrugged on her coat and tried to follow in Tim's wake to the door.

Linzi stared at the clock above the bar, willing the barman to call time. The gig had been dissected right down to the opening chords of their cover of The Stones' 'Gimme Shelter'. The Professor had drunk himself to sleep. Socks was still holding forth on the advantages of Fender over Gibson or something like that. Gaetano's hand had occupied the same position between Linzi's legs for the past half-hour. She had almost forgotten that it was there apart from the occasional flickering movement of his fingers which was meant to pass for affection.

The barman rang his brass bell to call last orders. Socks said he had to 'shake hands with the governor'. The Professor started to snore.

'Why's he called Socks?' Linzi asked when the man in question had disappeared into the gents.

'Don't know,' said Gaetano. 'He's been called that for as long as I can remember. Might be something to do with him wearing odd socks to school one time.'

'That's original. And Merlin?'

'Because he's magic on the mike.'

'Yes,' observed Linzi. 'He certainly knows how to make himself disappear when it's his round. And why is the Professor called the Professor?'

'Because he's clever. He's the only one of us that got any "O"-levels. He went to university to do a degree in pharmacy and all that. The idea was that when he finished he'd be able to make his own acid and sell it to us cheap but now he just spends his days in Boots in Kentish Town telling grannies how to insert their suppositories.'

Linzi snorted.

'That must be nice. And how about you, Gaetano? How come you haven't got a nickname like the others?'

'Because I'm too cool to have a stupid tag. Believe me, Linz, if we get noticed I'm going to ditch those idiots straight off. The Professor's only in the band as it is because he's got access to his dad's Transit van. He can't play bass to save his life.'

'Oh. That's harsh. I thought he was quite good. Very enthusiastic.'

'Too enthusiastic, if you ask me. That's why he always comes in too early on the chorus of "The Virgin is Bleeding".'

'Practice makes perfect.'

'He's the exception that proves that rule.'

'Enough bitching,' Linzi put a finger to his lips tenderly. 'I think he's waking up.' The Professor stirred slightly in his sleep. 'Anyway, can't we go soon? Only it's pretty late now and I've got to get up early in the morning.'

'What for? I thought you chucked your job in today.'

'Yeah. And tomorrow I've got to start looking for a new one, haven't I?' She leaned towards him and kissed him gently on his long black eyelashes. 'Besides, we've still got a bit of getting to know each other to do.'

Gaetano squeezed her upper thigh. 'I'll just tell Socks we're going.'

But Socks had already got one last pint in.

'We'll just finish this,' said Gaetano. 'And then I promise you, we're gone.'

The live concert version of 'In Every Dream Home a Heartache' was Kerry's favourite song of all time. It was right at the end of the album. Kerry would get out of the tub when it finished. She wasn't feeling too great as it was. The combination of the curry and the hot bath had brought her out in a ferocious sweat and she was feeling rather drained.

So drained that she had to pull the plug out of the bath and lie there until all the water had disappeared before she could even think about moving again. She wondered what time it was. The phone hadn't rung all evening. Linzi and Fiona were probably out with their respective men. Kerry didn't want to think about how long it had been since she last went out with a man after dark.

That afternoon, she had cornered Celestine in the loos in an attempt to find out exactly what Lance meant by 'stranger things have happened'. Celestine just kissed her teeth and said that Lance Sylvester was a no-good stirrer but upon the application of a little more pressure she had buckled.

'I expect he means the Christmas Party,' she said at last.

'Was it a good one?' Kerry asked.

'It was a complete disaster,' Celestine replied. 'We were all in this really posh restaurant, right? Josh couldn't come because he had flu so we had a space in the reservation and we let Lance come along to make up the numbers since he's practically a permanent fixture here as it is. Anyway, Serena's husband got so drunk he could barely see and then accused her of having an affair with Leon.'

'But that's ridiculous. Leon's gay, isn't he?'

'Supposedly,' said Celestine. 'But sometimes he acts like he's not sure.'

'Staying at my place tonight?' Fiona asked as she and Tim waited for a train going their way to arrive at the tube station. Tim cleared his throat and gobbed a big ball of phlegm on to the live line.

'No thanks, I think I'll go back to mine. I need to change my shirt.'

'I've got one of your shirts at my place,' Fiona persisted hopefully. 'You left it last week. I've washed it and ironed it.'

'Which one is it?'

'White with blue stripes.'

'I feel like wearing the pink one. I'll give you a call at work tomorrow.'

'At work? But we've both got the day off, haven't we? You said we were going to go shopping and buy the ring tomorrow.'

'Oh yeah. I did. Sorry, Fi. I forgot to tell you. I've got to work tomorrow. On this project. Nobody's going to be getting any time off for the foreseeable. We'll go into town on Saturday, OK?'

'OK.'

What choice did she have? The train arrived and Tim guided her safely inside a carriage. When they reached Stockwell station, he got off there and left her alone on the train to complete her journey. Fiona waved goodbye until her journey took her on into the tunnel. Tim had only looked back once.

Fiona had to dig her fingernails into the palms of her hands to stop herself from crying. She had decided that Tim had not mentioned their engagement in the pub because he was waiting until he had bought the ring, but that thought was of little comfort to her now that she was on her own. Tim was as distant as he had been for the past couple of months again. In fact, though she couldn't bear to admit it, his sudden proposal had been as much of a surprise to her as it had been to her flatmates. When he said that he had something to ask her that Saturday night, it could just as easily have been whether she wanted to call their relationship off.

Perhaps it was his work. Fiona knew how easy it was to let a bad day in the office spill over into after-hours. She was the closest person to him and as such she was bound to get most of the fall-out. Yes, that was what it was. He did love her really. It was his work.

But the protective bubble of their engagement had already burst. She hadn't even had time to bring herself to tell Tim about New York. A treacherous little tear sneaked its way on to Fiona's cheek. The girl sitting opposite looked at her curiously and drew her boyfriend's attention to the damsel in distress. She whispered something in her boyfriend's ear and smiled smugly, safe in the knowledge that she was loved without needing symbols to prove it. Fiona dug her nails harder into her hands. She mustn't cry. She mustn't cry. She didn't want to look like some kind of idiot in front of all these people. But her lungs were ready to explode with a sob. The train couldn't reach Clapham South quickly enough.

*   *   *

While Kerry was lying like a flat fish at the dry bottom of the bath, the doorbell rang. She leapt to her feet and, suddenly taken by an attack of dizziness, reached straight for the shower curtain for support, ripping the plastic coated fabric from two of its plastic hooks. Bugger, that was half their deposit gone, again. She struggled into her dressing gown to confront her midnight visitors.

Gaetano and Linzi tumbled on to the floor of the sitting room in a kissing heap. Kerry fled back up the stairs to be out of their way.

'Wow,' said Gaetano as he watched Kerry's flight from his vantage point on the carpet. 'Is it my imagination or are Kerry's legs bright purple?'

'Who gives a shit about Kerry's legs?' Linzi silenced him with a kiss. 'Come upstairs and fuck me, you stallion.'

Gaetano followed her dutifully into the bedroom. Since she had hold of his collar, it was clear that he wouldn't be going anywhere else that night. She had her hand down his trousers almost before she closed the door behind them. His penis was as limp as three-day-old lettuce.

'Oh no, Gaetano. I just knew you were drinking too much!'

Fiona waited at the top of the road until Gaetano and Linzi were safely inside number 67. She gave them two more minutes to get to Linzi's bedroom, then she let herself into the house and washed down two Nytol with a quarter-bottle of white wine someone had left unfinished in the fridge.

CHAPTER SIX

Tuesday always seems to go more slowly than Monday. It must be something to do with the fact that you've already been over all the previous weekend's gossip and yet the next weekend is still far enough away to make it seem slightly premature to be thinking about your next lie-in. In short, it's a bit unreasonable to expect any Tuesday to be a real blinder.

'Good day everybody?' Kerry asked as she walked through the door and threw her fake-fur-collared coat across the back of a chair.

Stupid question. Linzi was already installed on the sofa with the duvet tucked around her and a jar of Nutella balanced between her knees, which she was attacking with a tablespoon. Fiona was getting in a couple more minutes on the exercise bike while she waited for her jacket potato to be cooked in the microwave. They were both focused on the television and didn't even seem to notice Kerry coming in.

'I take it that's a "no", then.'

'Huh?'

'I just asked whether everybody had had a nice day at work . . . Oh, never mind. It doesn't matter. You obviously didn't.'

'I didn't go to work today. I quit my job,' Linzi announced suddenly.

'You did what?' Fiona stopped pedalling and stared. 'You didn't tell me.'

'I quit my job yesterday. I couldn't stand it any longer.'

'But you had only been there for a week and a half. What do you mean, you quit?'

'I mean I packed up my desk and walked out into the free

spring air. It was the worst job I have ever ever had to do, Fi. Can you believe that my boss got me to send a courier out to fetch his cocaine and then told me not to think about getting a habit myself because with my lack of skills and experience I'd never be able to earn enough to support one?'

'Nice guy,' said Kerry.

'He was a piece of shit.'

'But the rent is due at the end of the week, Linzi. How are you going to pay? None of us can stand our jobs, but do we quit a week before the rent is due?' Fiona was on a rant again and the louder her voice grew, the faster she pedalled.

'I thought you loved your job, Fi,' Kerry tried to change the focus. 'Counting all that money every day.'

'I do not "count money" every day.' Fiona was offended. 'I work on new international business projects and as a matter of fact I've just been offered a six-month placement in New York.'

'New York? Wow.' Linzi popped up from beneath the duvet like a tortoise at the sniff of a lettuce leaf. 'Wow! That's brilliant. When are you going? We'll be able to come and visit.'

'No you won't. Firstly because you never have any money and secondly because I'm not going to go,' Fiona told her flatly. 'I don't want to.'

'Why not?' Linzi was disbelieving. 'I would cut off my legs for a job in the States.'

'Then you can cut your legs off and have it. I don't want to leave London.'

'You don't want to leave Tim,' Kerry said perceptively.

'We've just got engaged,' Fiona protested. 'If I go away now everything will be ruined.'

'Why? Six months is nothing when you've promised your-selves to each other for a lifetime. It's the Big Apple, Fiona,' said Linzi. 'Just think of the shopping. Macys, Saks, Bloomingdales and all those other ones.'

'Christ. That's about all you ever think about isn't it? Shopping? I'd have to leave everything behind. My friends, my family, just about my whole bloody life. Macys just doesn't mean that much to me, funnily enough.'

'Well, your family live just two hundred miles away now and you only ever see them when Tim's got something better to do at the weekend,' Linzi reminded her. 'New York is only six hours away, Fi. Stop being so wet and go for it.'

'I am not being wet.' Fiona stopped pedalling. 'Just tell me what's wet about not wanting to go through the palaver of uprooting myself and going to a foreign country where they just happen to have the highest murder rate in the world? I don't think that's wet. I think that's pretty sensible.'

'And you could get knocked over by a bus on Balham High Road tomorrow . . . It's the chance of a lifetime so why not live a little . . .'

'What, you mean like you, Ms Career Girl? I don't see you getting on your bicycle and cycling to Heathrow.'

'If I could find the opportunity, I would take it. One day, when you and Tim have finished redecorating all the bedrooms of your semi-detached, you're going to turn around, take a good look at his beer gut and wish that you had done it.'

Fiona opened her mouth but didn't appear able to say anything sharp in return. Kerry hovered halfway across the room, as if she knew that Linzi had thrown a grenade and was waiting for it to explode. But Fiona still didn't say anything. Instead, she jumped off the bike with an exhalation of exasperation, picked up her handbag and sprinted up the stairs. From downstairs, the two girls heard a strangled sob amplified by the acoustics of the bathroom.

'What did you have to say that for?' Kerry asked. 'You know she's sensitive about Tim's gut.'

'He isn't.'

'Do you think she's all right?'

'No.'

'I'll go up and talk to her.'

'About what, Kerry? She doesn't seem to have anything in her life except Tim these days. I remember when we used to talk about going off and working in a place like New York. All three of us together. I remember a time when Fiona was going to be the next prime minister and you were going to be the next Sigourney Weaver. If Fiona doesn't take that placement in the States then she really is the Stepford wife I think she's turning into. Six months in New York! I would kill for a chance like that. And knowing that bank of hers, she'll have some huge relocation package built in. She should try working in some of the places I've had to work in since I've been temping. You would think that it was still the Middle Ages if you met some of the men in the advertising industry.'

'Oh, yeah,' Kerry suddenly remembered that Linzi had quit. 'What happened to you?'

'I had to report my boss to the police for dealing in Class A drugs.'

'Fair enough. So you're not going to go back?'

'Put it this way, I don't think he'll have signed my time sheet.'

About an hour later, Fiona crept sheepishly back down the stairs and squeezed herself into the corner of the sofa that wasn't occupied by Linzi and the duvet. She was clutching a dusty bottle of red wine.

'I've been saving this since Christmas,' she said. 'It's a peace offering. Do you want some?'

'Go on then,' said Linzi. Kerry brought three glasses from the kitchen and sat cross-legged on the rug since the floor was infinitely preferable to the chairs.

Fiona cleared her throat. 'Listen, I know you both think I'm stupid for not wanting to go to New York, but I assure you that it's not as simple as not wanting to leave Tim behind. I mean, I'd have to leave you guys behind as well . . .' Kerry smiled at the sneaky flattery. Linzi punched her on the arm. 'And I really am frightened about the murder rate . . .'

'Most people are murdered by someone they know,' Kerry chipped in cheerfully.

'Great. Thanks. So now you're saying that I wouldn't be able to make any new friends either in case one of them turned out to be the nutter who has it in for me.'

'That nutter could be Tim,' Kerry continued. 'Has he asked you about taking out life insurance yet?'

'I know,' Fiona laughed. 'You're right. It is a pathetic excuse. But it's strange, isn't it? I never thought that opportunity could be such a double-edged sword. I don't want to go to New York, but I know that if I don't take the placement, First Orient probably won't bother to renew my contract at the end of the year.'

'Are you so unsure that Tim would wait for you?' Kerry

suggested reasonably. 'You just got engaged, after all. That proves that he's committed.'

'You didn't just decide to tie the knot because you're up the duff?' Linzi asked flatly.

'No, Linzi,' Fiona reeled in indignation. 'I am not up the duff. Look, if you two stop hassling me, I promise I'll think about it for a bit longer. I haven't even mentioned the placement to Tim yet. He'll probably insist that I go anyway, so that he can have a final fling.' Her mouth smiled but her eyes stayed decidedly unhappy as she raised her glass. 'Not bad stuff this, is it? Happy Tuesday everyone.' The others returned the toast. 'Linzi,' Fiona began again. 'Just out of interest, what are you going to do about this month's rent?'

Linzi would call both her parents, of course, and apply pressure to each by implying that the other would provide for their only child if he or she did not. Linzi's parents had been divorced for almost fifteen years now but the war still went on. In her wildest dreams, she thought that it was perhaps because they still harboured some deep feeling for each other and were longing to get back together.

When the issue of money was resolved, the girls got on to far more important matters. Fiona's mother had recently reported that one of the girls' old classmates had dropped her third sprog in as many years. Guessing who the father might be took up the best part of an hour. Then the demolition of yet another packet of Boasters sparked a great diet debate.

'I've got a brilliant idea,' Fiona said suddenly. 'Instead of just talking about how we're going to get fit the whole time, let's set ourselves a goal and really, really go for it. One of the guys at work was telling me about a half-marathon that he's going to run. It's still a couple of months away so we've got plenty of time to get fit. It's only thirteen miles and you don't even have to run the whole way. What do you think?'

Kerry looked worried.

Linzi didn't even bother to look up to see if Fiona was joking, but remained flat on her back on the floor with her half-full wine glass balanced on her curvy belly.

'Linzi, what do you think?' Fiona persisted.

'I think the whole idea is perverse.'

It was the kind of answer Fiona had expected.

'I'll sign us up,' she continued regardless. 'It's twenty-five pounds each to run but you get that back if you raise enough sponsorship money. It's for some cancer charity, I think.'

'Twenty-five pounds, Fi? I don't know . . .' Kerry began. 'I'm expecting a bit of credit card damage this month. And it'll be painful.'

'Your credit card bill or the marathon?' asked Linzi.

'Both,' Kerry wailed.

'Rubbish. It'll be brilliant fun and besides, you both need to get into shape . . .'

Fiona divided the very last of the Bordeaux between their three glasses.

'Get into shape? But I like the shape I'm in,' Linzi protested. 'What do I want to change it for?'

Fiona sighed as if they were just pretending not to know why. 'Because you are both going to be my bridesmaids, aren't you?' she asked them impatiently.

'Your bridesmaids?'

'I'm getting married, remember? Linzi, you'll do it, won't you?'

'OK,' said Linzi disinterestedly. 'As long as you swear we won't have to wear peach.'

'I swear it. I was thinking along the lines of jade anyway. And you, Kez? You're on for it, aren't you?'

Kerry shrugged. 'I suppose so. Always the bridesmaid, me.' She drained her glass sadly. Fiona's wedding would make Kerry's third bridesmaid job in two years. She wondered how many more times she could get away with it before she would never be able to be the bride. 'OK,' Fiona raised another toast. 'We'll start training tomorrow night.'

'Actually,' said Linzi. 'I can't. I've got a date.'

'Not Gaetano again?' asked Kerry. 'How was last night?'

'Brilliant,' Linzi replied. 'He's fantastic. I'm so glad you made me go to that crappy party with you, Kez. Turned out to be the best move of my life. I borrowed your red skirt by the way. Hope you don't mind.'

'No,' Kerry lied. 'Of course I don't.' At least her wardrobe was having a love life.

CHAPTER SEVEN

K erry picked up the TV supplement and grazed through the listings of the last few programmes for that night. Nothing doing. It was Saturday night, after all. Most normal people were out enjoying themselves in clubs and pubs and bars. Kerry, however, was having to miss a party because she had tried to jazz her hair up with some 'wash-in, wash-out' hair-dye and now she had "Passionate Pecan" tiger stripes all the way down her face and her back. Fiona had warned her not to use the stuff in the shower but it was odd that while it washed happily out of Kerry's hair, which was now back to its usual pale mouse-brown again, any skin that the stuff had touched remained bright red. Kerry's grandmother would have told her that it was God's way of saying 'Stay brown'.

Kerry stuffed the last of the Choc-Chip and Hazelnut Boasters into her mouth in two bites and took her empty mug out to the kitchen. The credits of the film she had been watching played slowly across the screen. When she had rinsed out the mug and left it soaking – since Fiona could throw a convincing epileptic fit over tea stains on the crockery – Kerry switched the television off and headed up the stairs. There was really nothing left to do but go to bed.

The doorbell rang while she was in the bathroom, right in the middle of cleaning her teeth. She spat the toothpaste out into the sink with a curse. It was bound to be Linzi. Why couldn't that girl ever remember to take her house-key? The doorbell rang again. Occasionally, if you left her outside for long enough, Linzi would find her key in the bottom of her bag and let herself in but tonight she obviously couldn't be bothered, or she was genuinely locked out. Kerry wiped her mouth dry on a slightly damp towel.

'Hang on. Hang on,' she muttered. 'You're just bloody lucky that some of us have nothing to do on a Saturday night.'

Kerry opened the door abruptly, causing the late-night caller to jump back a couple of steps. She stared at her visitor for a couple of seconds before she realised that this wasn't someone she particularly wanted to catch her in her Alice band and tartan PJs.

'Leon?'

'Yeah, it's me,' he nodded sheepishly. 'Look, I'm sorry to come round so late, Kerry, but I didn't know what else to do. I had a row with Sam this afternoon and he kicked me out of the flat. When I went back to make it up to him I found he'd had the locks changed. I've got nowhere to sleep tonight. Any chance I could borrow your floor?'

Kerry was already back inside the house and halfway up the stairs to collect her dressing gown.

'Yeah,' she called. 'Of course you can. Come on in. Can you put the kettle on?'

Leon slunk into the house and closed the door quietly behind him. Kerry could hear him going into the kitchen. She rubbed her eyes to make sure that she wasn't asleep, then, reassured yet rather worried by the fact that she wasn't, she made a surreptitious dash for the bathroom, whipped off the Alice band and checked the extent of the Pecan streaks. Wasn't it just Sod's Law that the hair-dye disaster had happened today of all days? Her cheeks were still faintly orange and her hair was a mess. She dragged a comb through her fringe and then wrapped a red bandanna around it. No, that looked ridiculous. It even accentuated the pale tangerine pallor of her skin. She ripped the bandanna back off again. Should she stick some foundation on perhaps? She heard Leon cough nervously in the silence downstairs. Bugger, bugger, bugger. He would have to take her as she was. At least she had managed to half-clean her teeth.

She floated back downstairs with her dressing gown wrapped tightly over the tartans. Leon was sitting on the very edge of the sofa, still wearing his coat.

'Do you want me to take that for you?' she asked him.

'No,' he said. 'I've been out in the freezing cold all bloody day. I need to get some circulation back in my body before my arms drop off.'

'You poor old thing. I'll make the tea.'

'So, what did you row about this time?' Kerry asked as she unscrewed the tea caddie. She heard Leon sigh painfully in the other room.

'Its a disaster,' he called back. 'Do you remember that Andrew guy who was at Lance's party?'

'The one with hair like shredded wheat?'

'Yeah, that's the one. Well, looks like your friend Linzi was right after all. Even after Sam found out that Andrew couldn't get him a record deal, he still went ahead and slept with him. When I tackled him about it this afternoon, Sam told me that he actually thinks he might be in love with the man. He thinks we've outgrown each other lately and says he needs space to mull things over.'

'And he's kicked you out on to the street while he does it?' Kerry emerged from the kitchen with two steaming mugs. Tea with milk and two sugars for Leon, which was how he had it at work. 'That's a bit of a liberty. I thought it was your flat anyway?'

'Well, it's rented but my name is on the agreement.'

'Oh.'

'The locksmith obviously didn't bother to ask.' Leon slipped his padded jacket off his shoulders. Beneath it, he was wearing only a tight sleeveless vest. The top of his left arm was black and blue. Kerry decided not to mention it.

'So, since it is your flat, why don't you just go to the police and get them to demand that he lets you back in?'

'I don't want to get them involved,' Leon sighed. 'Not that they'd do anything about it anyway. A couple of queens scratching each other's eyes out? They've got better things to think about. Besides, what if they ask to see some identification, Kez? I've already overstayed my visa by a week. I didn't want to get anyone else involved. Especially you. I'm sorry, Kez. It's really late. I should have called first.'

'I don't mind,' she said brightly. 'I was just going to have my Horlicks anyway. You're more than welcome to stay and on Monday morning we can talk about that pay-rise you owe me.'

Leon managed a laugh. Then he recoiled suddenly, clutching at his chest.

'What's up?' asked Kerry.

'Just wind, I think. I stopped for a curry on the way over.'

She wondered if he was bruised across the ribs too.

'Listen, Leon, do you think Sam is serious about Andrew or might it just be that he's hedging his bets for when you have to go back home?'

'To be honest, I've been trying not to think about it. I suppose it might be that.'

'Then why don't you suggest that he goes back with you?'

'To South Africa?'

'Yes. I had a friend from school who fell in love with a Kiwi. When his visa expired she went back to New Zealand with him. They got married and now they live in Auckland and Bristol on alternate years.'

'It's a bit different, Kez. Even if Sam does come back with me, it would just be extending the problem. We could never get married, could we? He would have to come home eventually. Besides, he wouldn't come to South Africa in the first place. He's already said as much. I mean, it's hardly the kind of country where two gay guys can hold hands in the street. Sam loves it here. He's trying to break into the music scene. He thinks South Africa doesn't have one. No, the only solution is for me to stay here and the only way I can do that is by getting a British passport.'

'How are you going to do that?'

'I'm not sure yet. Something will hit me. Look, Kez,' Leon said suddenly. 'Would it be OK with you if I went straight to bed now? I don't think I can keep my eyes open for very much longer.'

'Oh, sure . . . Don't you want to finish your tea first?'

He put the full mug down on the coffee table. 'No. I just want to go to sleep.'

'OK.' Kerry hadn't even thought that far ahead. A brief mental picture of her tiny room with its single bed flashed into her mind. He couldn't stay in there. And she had no spare linen for the sofa. She got to her feet and fiddled with the waist-tie of her dressing gown.

'What's up?' asked Leon.

'I'm just thinking where I can put you. I haven't got any bed-stuff for the sofa.'

'I'll share your bed,' Leon said casually.

Kerry's mouth must have dropped open.

'If you don't mind.'

'No, it's not that . . . It's just that . . .' Kerry began to stutter.

'I'll keep my clothes on,' Leon promised.

Kerry giggled. If only he knew how little she would mind his taking them off. Suddenly she was struck with inspiration. 'OK,' she said. 'I'm fine about it if you are.'

'Kerry, I've shared a single bed with a bird-eating tarantula before now. To share a bed with you would be sheer luxury.'

Kerry remembered the words of Celestine in the ladies' loo. 'He acts like he's not sure.' Was she about to get a love life? Breathing quickly, she led Leon upstairs to Fiona's bedroom, passing it off as her own.

'Nice room,' he said, appraising the twee miniature Monet prints that Kerry thought rather naff.

'Thanks.'

She sat down on the edge of the bed, her chest heaving expectantly as she waited for him to untie her dressing gown like the foil wrapper around an exotic chocolate. It didn't happen. Instead Leon slipped straight beneath the clean white duvet, without taking off his vest or his jeans first, and fell asleep almost instantly, leaving Kerry gazing up at the flower-patterned lampshade which hung from the ceiling, still wearing her dressing gown and her pyjamas.

When she was sure that he wouldn't wake up if she moved, she rolled over on to her elbow and looked down on to his face. There was always the morning, she figured. He had said that he was tired.

Kerry snuggled down beside him again and sighed with pleasure as he draped a heavy arm across her body. Who would have thought that she would end this disastrous Saturday with Leon in her bed? Well, in Fiona's bed. Kerry prayed that Fiona and Tim wouldn't have a row that night.

CHAPTER EIGHT

Fiona knew that something was up when she saw that her bedroom door was not exactly the same distance ajar as she had left it the night before. She hoped that Linzi hadn't been raking through her wardrobe again. She was tired of having to argue with her about who had the right to wear her own brand-new trousers first. All she wanted to do now was get beneath the warm duvet and catch up on the sleep she had missed while squished into a single bed at Tim's. She pushed open the door and slung her overnight bag down by the dresser.

'Oh, Christ,' she muttered.

It seemed that she wasn't going to be jumping straight under her duvet after all. Her bedclothes were piled up over two distinct body-sized humps. She recognised Kerry's light brown hair spilling out over the pillow. God only knew who the other hump was. Without saying a word, Fiona crept out of her room again and opted instead for a nice cup of tea and the sofa.

Fiona didn't say anything about the matter until Leon had left the house to pick up the Sunday papers. When she did speak, the first thing she said was 'I thought he was gay.'

Kerry flushed. She sat next to Fiona on the sofa and hugged her knees beneath her dressing gown. 'So did I. I guess he must be "bi" instead.'

Fiona's eyes widened like saucers. '"Bi"? So, tell me more, Kez. What happened?'

'He turned up shortly after you left for Tim's,' Kerry lied. 'I couldn't believe it. We had a couple of drinks and then he asked if he could stay the night. I couldn't ask him to sleep with me in my single bed, could I? So I had to pretend that your room is mine. I'm sorry, Fi. I was desperate.'

'That's OK,' Fiona said graciously. 'It's a bit risky though, isn't it? I mean, sleeping with your boss has to be a fast one-way route to disaster.'

'Oh, we don't have a conventional boss/employee sort of relationship anyway,' Kerry assured her, wishing that they had done something to be worried about. 'Verbal Tix isn't like that.' She picked up the teacup which Fiona had just placed on the floor and put it to her mouth to take a sip.

'Hey,' Fiona protested. 'You had my bed last night and I let you off about that, but you can make your own bloody cup of tea!!'

'Sorry,' Kerry put the cup down again double-quick. 'Anyway, Fi,' she remembered her manners. 'How was your Saturday night? You look done in.'

'Yeah. I could have done with going straight to bed when I got home,' Fiona replied pointedly. 'Last night wasn't too bad though. Tim had some kind of drinking contest with his mate Wooders at the Iron Horse. He drank eight pints of Stella and then he was sick all over the table so the landlord asked us to leave. Needless to say, I took the opportunity to get Tim home straight away. The contest had started at six and was over by seven so by nine o'clock he had been through his hangover and was almost sober again . . . I told him about the New York placement then,' she added, almost as an after-thought.

'You did? What did he say?'

'He helped me to write this.' Fiona unfolded a scrappy piece of paper from the pocket of her jeans. 'I'm going to type it up before I send it, of course.'

'What is it?' Kerry scanned the first few lines. 'Oh, Fi. I don't believe it. You're not going to go, are you?'

Fiona shook her head. She was twisting something on her finger. The new engagement ring. 'No, I'm not going to go. Tim and I have been thinking about having a June wedding. No point in messing around with a six-year engagement, is there?'

'No, I suppose there isn't.' Kerry folded the letter back up and gestured that she wanted to see Fiona's ring. Fiona stretched her left hand out delicately and tipped her fingers from side to side so that the brilliant solitaire diamond glittered blue and yellow in the light. It was almost as big as a peanut.

'It's beautiful.'

'Thanks. It's a little bit loose,' Fiona told her. 'So I'm going to have it adjusted to fit. But it is lovely, isn't it? Tim insisted that we buy it from the shop where his grandfather bought a ring for his Gran. He said that it's actually family tradition for engagement rings to be handed down from generation to generation, but his mother threw hers into the gutter when she and Tim's father got divorced. They never did find it.'

Kerry smiled. 'It's fabulous, Fiona. And I hope you'll have better luck than Tim's mum. OK.' She slapped her hands down on her thighs and pushed herself up from the sofa. 'If you're not going to let me drink your tea, I suppose that I had better go and put some clothes on. Leon will be back any minute.'

'Then it's hardly worth getting dressed again, is it?' Fiona observed.

'I'm not like Linzi,' Kerry laughed as she tackled the stairs two at a time. 'Some of us like to get out of bed at least once every twenty-four hours.'

From Linzi's bedroom came some mutterings in Italian and a high-pitched squeal. Gaetano had stayed off the juice especially that weekend. Now Linzi didn't expect to see sunlight again until Gaetano went to work on Monday morning.

Leon returned to number 67 and let himself into the house with Kerry's key.

'Nice man in that shop at the top of your road,' he told Fiona.

Fiona smiled. The man in the paper shop was a screaming queen.

'I'm sorry to be getting in your way like this,' Leon continued. 'I'm just going to see if Kerry wants to go for lunch and then I'll be gone.' Kerry had reappeared, resplendent in her best Sunday dress, and was already putting on her coat.

'We can go to the pizza place on the other side of the Common,' she told Leon excitedly. 'I think it's half-price on a Sunday.' She ushered him back out into the street, winking at her housemate as she did so. Fiona retreated to her bedroom with relief.

Leon Landesman was no bisexual. What had Kerry been on about?

CHAPTER NINE

The telephone rang. And it was Sunday night, so it was bound to be one of their mothers. Kerry let the phone ring until the answerphone kicked in and waited until she heard the unmistakable voice that belonged to her very own mum.

'Oh, I hate these stupid answering machine thingies,' Mrs Keble began after the bleep. 'I never know what to say when they come on . . .'

'Makes a change,' said Kerry as she picked up the receiver and cut the answerphone short.

'Oh, so you are there, Kerry. I let the phone ring seven times,' she said accusingly.

'I was upstairs, Mum. I was drying my hair. I couldn't hear it ringing,' Kerry lied.

'Have you been using that conditioner your sister sent you?'

Kerry studied a split end which she held tightly between her fingers. 'When I remember.'

'Kerry, you must try to remember. You want to look your best for the wedding, don't you?'

'Oh, yes,' said Kerry sarcastically. 'The wedding. Is that still going ahead?'

'Of course it is. It's going ahead next weekend! Why do you have to sound so bored by it the whole time, Kerry? You really upset Michelle when she called you last Thursday. She said you kept changing the subject each time she tried to ask you when you'd be able to come back for your final dress-fitting. The wedding is less than seven days away now and the sleeves aren't even sewn on your dress yet. Auntie Angela needs to check you haven't grown since last year.'

'Grown?' That was a nice euphemism for putting on weight. 'Tell Angela to model my dress on that old toilet-roll holder of yours. That's what she usually does, isn't it?'

'Kerry!!'

Angela had made the bridesmaids' dresses for the wedding of Kerry's elder sister Miranda to her dream plumber Steve. The dresses for Michelle's wedding were being cut from the same pattern, but using a different colour fabric. Turquoise this time, instead of overblown English Rose pink.

'You've got to come home for a fitting, Kerry,' her mother persisted. 'And Michelle also needs to know if you have decided yet how you want to have your hair done. She's booked you an appointment at Smart Cuts for eight thirty . . .'

'The night before?'

'No, on the morning of the day, of course.'

'But the wedding's not happening until three in the afternoon.'

'I know. But there's the bride to do and then you three bridesmaids and me. Pat needs plenty of time in case anything goes wrong.'

'What can she do with my hair anyway?' Kerry moaned. She was the only one of the three Keble sisters to have inherited her father's unruly mousy mop.

'That's why Michelle sent you the conditioner. You're supposed to be getting it under control.'

'I could have it fluffed up like candyfloss to complement the meringue dress, I suppose,' Kerry mused.

'Kerry, I can see there's no point talking to you about this today. Honestly, you haven't changed a bit since you were a little girl. It's your sister Michelle's big day and all you can think about is self, self, self.'

Kerry didn't bother to argue. But Michelle's Big Day? That was pushing it. Kerry would lay bets that this wasn't going to be Michelle's one and only wedding. After all, Richard was the third guy she'd been engaged to since her sixteenth birthday four years before.

'Anyway, I saw Mrs Davenport in town the other day and she told me that her Fiona has just got engaged to that lovely boyfriend of hers. You didn't mention that when I called last week. Her mother says that they announced it two weeks ago.'

'They announced it last week actually and I'm very sorry I didn't get on the phone to you straight away. Maybe I've just got wedding-itis.'

'Oh, Kerry-love, don't talk silly,' her mother's tone softened. 'It will be your turn one day very soon and then you'll see what all the fuss is about. Talking of which, have you decided who you'll be bringing as your escort yet? I've got to give the stationers the table plans for the reception this week so that they can do the calligraphy. Your "other half" is the only gap I've got left on the top table . . .'

'Oh, mother,' Kerry sighed. 'You know I haven't got an "other half". Can't you just close the gap up?'

'Absolutely not. It would ruin my seating plan. You could always ask Nicholas Faddy. He's such a nice, polite boy and you know that he still holds a torch for you, even after all these years of rejection.' Nicholas Faddy had had a crush on Kerry since junior school, which meant that he spat at her regularly until puberty hit and then started writing her poems.

'It's a bit short notice, Mum. And besides, I haven't spoken to him in two years.'

'Then he'll be delighted to hear from you, Kerry.'

'OK. OK. I'll call him in a minute and I'll let you know what he says tomorrow. All right?'

'Good, that's settled then, except for the final fitting.'

'Couldn't I just take my measurements here and call you with those as well?'

'No, Kerry, you cannot. You've got to be here on Friday morning. Apart from anything else I need to know what you think of my outfit in case I have to take it back to the shop. I went to Berketex again and I was going to have a blue version of the suit I wore for Miranda's do but then Richard's mother turned up and announced that she'd gone for the blue herself. And she did that after we discussed outfits and agreed that blue is most definitely more my colour than hers.'

'That's shocking, Mum,' said Kerry as she began a thorough examination of her fingernails.

'Well, if she wants to look washed out in the photographs . . .'

Almost the instant Kerry put the phone down, it began to ring again. Suspecting that it was her mother calling once more to ask her whether she wanted roses and gypsophila in her hair or just the gypsophila, Kerry almost let it ring. But then she decided that it was probably best to get any more wedding agony over with straight away.

'Yes,' she said rather aggressively.

'Oh, I'm sorry, Kerry,' said Leon. 'Have I called at a bad time?'

'No, no. You haven't.' All sweetness and light again.

'I was just calling to say thank you for last night. For letting me stay and for listening to my ramblings all through lunch. You're a real star, Kerry. I hope you managed to get some sleep with me snoring next to you.'

Kerry felt a flush creep across her body.

'I slept like a log,' she squeaked, despite having spent half the night praying that he would try to keep her awake some other way.

'Good. Anyway, I'm staying with a friend in Willesden tonight so I thought that I should also call to ask if you could try to be in work a little earlier than usual tomorrow, to open up the office for the others, since I haven't the faintest idea how long it will take me to get in.'

'No problem,' Kerry replied. 'I'll be there.'

'I'm sorry to ask all these favours of you, Kerry. I really owe you one. If there's ever anything I can do in return. Except give you a pay-rise, that is,' he pre-empted the usual joke.

'Well, actually,' Kerry smiled. 'There might be something. What are you going to be doing next Saturday?'

As she put down the phone a second time, Kerry felt a malign presence looming behind her. Fiona tapped her smartly on the shoulder. She was dressed from head to toe in royal-blue Lycra, a professional looking pair of trainers on her feet.

'Come on, Kerry,' she said brightly. 'We've got to start training for the race.'

Kerry protested. It was the Sabbath.

But Fiona was insistent. 'If you want to be able to finish this race at all you're going to have to start training now. I'm going to run around the Common. You're going to come with me.'

'What about Linzi?' Kerry moaned. 'How come she's excused?'

Fiona said nothing but looked skywards. The creak of a bed rocking on floorboards again.

'She seems to think she's getting enough exercise already.'

CHAPTER TEN

Caroline Murray of Advertising Angels took off her glasses, closed her eyes and pinched the bridge of her nose in a very weary fashion indeed. Linzi Adams had swallowed her pride and squeezed herself into the hard chair that was jammed into the tiny space between Caroline's desk and that of the other temp controller. She smiled broadly, Caroline just shook her head.

'Well, Linzi Adams, I must say that this is a very pleasant surprise. And what can I do for you today?'

'Got any work for me?'

'You just jettisoned a three-month placement at Ellington, Froggett and Splinter,' Caroline hissed.

'I had to. It didn't suit me. Did they make much of a fuss?'

'No,' Caroline sighed. 'As a matter of fact, they asked if you would go back but I couldn't get hold of you in time because your telephone was engaged all day. I had to put someone else in. Seems like they had a bit of a débâcle at E, F and S after you walked out. Now, this is between you and me, Linzi,' Caroline leaned forward so that her ample bosom displaced her papers to the outer edges of the desk, 'but I know someone who works in another department at the agency who tells me that the dear chap you were working for was found with half a pound of heroin in his desk. Half a pound!! Of heroin!! I never would have thought it of him. Would you? Now, it looks as though he's going to be dismissed. In fact, he will probably end up doing time. So naturally, with him gone, the creative department was in utter disarray and they needed a temp more than ever.'

She leaned back again to gauge the effect upon Linzi of this shocking piece of gossip.

Linzi affected a look of surprise to stifle a blossoming smile.

'But anyway, you've missed that job altogether now. The new girl I've put in there loves it. And they've asked her to stay for the full term.'

'That's a shame,' said Linzi. 'For me, I mean,' she added quickly. 'Not her.'

Caroline put her glasses back on and began to flick through her files. 'Now, Linzi. We are still supposed to be looking for a full-time position for you, aren't we?' Linzi nodded. 'And I've got an updated version of your curriculum vitae here.' Caroline opened Linzi's cardboard folder and looked at the CV with tightly-pursed lips. 'Ah, yes. You're the one with a degree in psychology. Two-one. Not much call for that in the field of advertising these days.'

'So you keep telling me.'

Caroline leaned forward again and pushed her glasses up into her fringe. 'Oh, Linzi dear, what are we going to do with you?' she said with a sigh of concern. 'I think it's time that you and your Auntie Caroline had a wee chattette about your qualifications and training.'

'We've been through this before, Caroline. I've done all the training courses you offer. Freelance, Lotus Works and Ami-Pro,' Linzi counted them off on her fingers. 'I can use just about any computer package now.'

'Exactly,' said Caroline.

'Huh?'

'Bit of a clever clogs, aren't we?' Linzi screwed her eyebrows together. Clever clogs? Caroline reached right across the desk to take her hand and rubbed it comfortingly. 'Oh, darling. You mustn't take that as an insult. Mustn't, mustn't, mustn't. But in today's harsh *employmental* climate, being good at everything quite often doesn't work to your advantage. After all, nobody wants to employ someone who might be after their own job within a fortnight.' Caroline squeezed Linzi's fingers. 'And this is the problem that we have with you ... It's not just your psychology degree, Linzi. You've got diplomas in shiatsu and aromatherapy too. When I send your CV to a client who's looking for an office junior, they're going to take one look at this lovely long list of qualifications and put you straight to the bottom of the pile.'

Linzi was agog.

'Well, why don't you put me in for an office "slightly more senior" job?'

Caroline looked unamused. 'We all have to start at the bottom, Linzi.'

'Oh.'

'What I want to suggest to you, sweetheart,' Caroline continued, 'is that we adopt a new strategy. Let's reinvent Linzi Adams and make her the most sought-after girl in town.' She squeezed Linzi's fingers so hard that Linzi expected to see blood spurt out of the ends. 'OK?'

'What do you mean? Reinvent me?' Linzi was suspicious.

'Well,' Caroline picked a fat red marker out of her desk tidy and popped off its lid. 'We might as well start here.' She drew a thick red line through the section of Linzi's CV that read 'qualifications'.

'You've crossed out my degree!'

'That's right. And all these awards,' the pen hovered over some of Linzi's proudest achievements. 'Just a little bit scary. And we hardly need to tell them about your voluntary work, do we? You raised the money to buy a water-pipe for Africa? Not really all that relevant to any of our clients.' She scored away at Linzi's CV like a hairdresser asked for a crop after a week of doing only shoulder-length bobs. When she had finished, she handed the piece of paper back to Linzi. The only things recognisable beneath all that red ink were her name and her date of birth. 'And we need to change your work experience. To make it show that you can handle responsibility but at the same time not too much. Ever worked in a pub, my dear?'

'No,' said Linzi quietly.

'Waitress in a restaurant, perhaps?'

'No.'

'Oh dear. Well, I'm sure you'll think of something.'

Linzi was in shock. It would take a few moments before she could summon up the energy to be angry again. She stared at her decimated curriculum vitae. Caroline wanted her to leave out her degree. Three years of hard work. Three years of sweaty swotting wiped out in a stroke of red biro so that some fat ad exec would think about letting her make his tea.

Caroline put the red marker back in the green plastic pot and crossed her arms on the table again.

'Now. What you'll need to do is go through to the training room and type your new improved curriculum vitae up on one of the machines. Make me a couple of copies and then I can put you in for these jobs that I have here.' She fanned out a selection of postcards as if they were exotic trips on *Blind Date*, then picked out one to read. 'I have a feeling that you will like the sound of this one, Linzi. It's for a secretary in a marketing company. Nine thousand pounds a year and a free lunch twice a week. Doesn't that sound nice? Yes? The word processors are through there.' Caroline pointed to the way out. She was already looking for the file of the next poor girl, who was standing shyly at the office door, about to lose her PhD in the cause of Advertising Angels.

'OK, Linzi sweetheart. Bye-ze-bye. Off to the typing room with you. Leave it with Stephanie when you're finished.'

Linzi rose from her chair and walked towards the training room like a zombie. Of course! What a fool she had been to think that hard work and qualifications would get her anywhere in this game. She sat down in front of the machine that ran the Ami-Pro tests and opened up a new word-processing file. She began to type her CV out again automatically, keeping nothing of the old Linzi but the barest details of her identity. Out with the A-level results. Tone down those GCSEs. She printed out a copy and read it through. The humiliation was absolute.

'Never hide your light under a bushel,' her grandmother always used to say. She was a senile old bat for the most part, but for once, Linzi thought, perhaps she had been right. Linzi's light hadn't just been hidden, it had been unplugged. And all so Caroline could stuff her in some crappy job and pocket the fat commission. Linzi scrolled through her CV until she got to the section labelled 'work experience'. Was she going to make up some job in a pub? No way. She could do better than that.

A smile spread across Linzi's face as she typed out the details of her extensive experience as a lap-dancer, listed 'frottage' under her interests, and delivered the amended manuscript to the vacuous Ms Ash on the front desk who scanned the document officiously without batting an eyelid. As far as 'Advertising Angels' were concerned, thought Linzi, they could go straight to hell.

But a tour of central London's remaining major recruitment agencies failed to turn up much in the way of a job that Friday morning. Linzi was OK until they got to the typing tests, but as soon as they saw her measly max of forty words a minute it was 'don't call us time' again. After all, as the woman at the Brook Street Bureau said, 'just what is a psychology degree without shorthand?' Perhaps Caroline had been right.

Linzi mooched down Oxford Street, window-shopping as she went. There was a fantastic Romeo Gigli sweater in the window of Selfridges, but she had to get down to the Mr Byrite store near Tottenham Court Road before she could find something that was actually within her price range. Pretty soon, all that sticking her nose on windows had made her desperate for a drink. If she could afford one, she snorted. She really needed to make some money.

She had mooched as far as Soho. Gaetano had once told her that his family owned a cafe on Dean Street. His mother and uncles worked there most days (his father had done so too, until his operation) and some of his younger cousins took over at the weekends. Linzi turned down Dean Street and felt a funny warm sensation spreading through her limbs as she neared the cafe with its tattered brown sunshade overhanging the dirty street. It was exactly as Gaetano had described it. It had to be the one. Gaetano told her that he had cleared coffee cups and wiped tables in his school holidays. The thought of him two feet smaller and without his itchy stubble made Linzi feel weak at the knees.

She gazed up at the canopy with its faded words, 'Carlotta's Café', and wondered how many times Gaetano had unfurled that sunshade. She touched the part of the frame that she could reach, excited to be touching a part of her lover's past.

'Carlotta's Café,' she murmured again and stepped inside.

Behind the shining counter, two men made sandwiches, cutting and buttering with the speed and precision of machines. A small woman, almost as wide as she was tall, was pouring out cappuccino into polystyrene cups for two builders in dust-covered jeans. Only the very top curls of her hair-do bobbed above the coffee machine. She was talking quickly, with a thick Italian accent. She was the kind of proprietress who remembered the names of everyone who came into her shop.

'*Alora*, Dennis, that'll be three pounds and fifty pee to you today. How are your kids? All right? And your wife, she is OK too?' Dennis nodded and handed over the cash. 'OK, darlin' I see you tomorrow again. *Ciao*, Dennis, bye-bye.'

This must be Gaetano's mother. Now that Linzi could see her around the corner of machine she noted with delight that this woman had her lover's deep brown eyes. The man in front of Linzi asked for tea to take-away.

'No sugar for you, innit?' She gave her customer a radiant smile. Linzi couldn't wait to talk to her. She looked so warm. So different from Linzi's own perfect professional mother and her friends. Gaetano's mother was the sort of woman who would only kiss you on both cheeks in the street if she actually meant it. 'OK.' She fixed the plastic lid firmly on to the polystyrene cup. 'Careful you don't spill it, eh. I see you tomorrow, my love.'

'Who's next, please? *Ciao*, bella.' It was Linzi's turn to be served. 'And what can I do for you today, young lady?'

'A cup of tea, please. To drink in.'

'You want sugar? No. OK. You go sit over there and I bring it over to you in a minute.'

The coffee machine let out a huge plume of steam. Gaetano's mother shouted to the kitchen. A boy came out. He was a few years younger than Gaetano, but the look was already there. He pouted as he filled the hissing cauldron. His lips were the same as Gaetano's. He mumbled, 'It's OK now,' in the same displaced Italian-in-London drawl.

Gaetano's mother bustled out from behind her counter. She had to come down a step to enter the seating area of the café and Linzi was surprised to see just how short she really was. She put the cup and saucer down in front of Linzi without slopping a drop and simultaneously whipped a cloth out of her apron pocket.

'Those builders are too messy boys,' she complained as she whisked away the spilled sugar and salt from the wood-effect vinyl covered table. 'I don't know what their mothers teach them at home, eh? No manners.' She turned to walk back to her post behind the coffee machine. A queue of gasping Soho workers was winding almost as far as the door.

'I think I know your son,' Linzi said, suddenly placing a hand on the woman's arm to stop her from racing away. The woman turned back towards Linzi with a smile.

'Which one? Is it my Luigi or my Gaetano?'

'Gaetano.'

The woman rolled her eyes heavenwards. 'Oh, Gaetano! That boy to me! He is just like his father . . . a devil. You know him from your school? Yes?'

'No, not from school,' Linzi laughed. 'In fact I only met him a couple of weeks ago. I suppose you could say I'm his girlfriend though.'

'His girlfriend?' the woman's lip quivered almost imperceptibly.

'Yes. My name's Linzi. I expect he's probably mentioned me to you.'

'Oh, no.' The woman leaned back with her hands on her hips. 'He has not a mentioned you to me. Not by your name. Was it a your place that he stayed last Sunday night when he was supposed to be having his dinner at home with his family?'

Linzi giggled shamefully. 'Oh, whoops, sorry about that. I guess he must have forgotten.'

'So it was your place.' The woman's eyes narrowed and she leaned forward to hiss in Linzi's ear. 'You English girls don't care anything about the family do you? Does your poor mother know that her daughter in London is a whore?'

'I'm sorry.' Linzi wasn't quite sure she had heard correctly. Likewise the members of the coffee queue who all turned their heads to see what was going on.

'I said you are a whore, young girl. Sleeping with my son. Sleeping with any man before you are married to him. You English girls are all the same. You don't have any morality. You think that a man will respect you after you have let him do everything he likes on the first night that you meet? Ptoo-ey!'

Gaetano's mother spat straight on to the table that she had only just wiped clean.

'Get out of my café, bitch. I don't need any custom from a woman like you. And you stay away from my Gaetano!!'

Linzi gathered up her bag and left without bothering to question. She ran towards Leicester Square and couldn't stop her cheeks from blushing furious red until she was on the tube and almost at Charing Cross. Her ears were stinging with embarrassment. She had been called a whore in front of all those people, and worse than that she had been called a whore by the mother of the man that she thought she might be falling in love with.

CHAPTER ELEVEN

That Friday Fiona's parents were in town on one of their flying visits. They had tickets to see a show that evening and would be staying with friends overnight, but between one and three they had time to see their darling daughter. When she broke for lunch at work, they were already waiting for her downstairs in the glittering marble lobby of First Orient. Her mother kissed her lightly on both cheeks then wiped away the little lipstick mark that she had made with her handkerchief. Fiona's father smiled his slightly silly smile.

'Your father has booked us in at The Chop House,' Mrs Davenport began excitedly as she bundled Fiona into a waiting taxi. 'So I do hope you're not going through one of your funny vegetarian phases, dear, because apparently the menu is all rather meaty. Such a shame Tim couldn't join us. What's his excuse this time?

'He's got to work straight through lunch, Mother. His team are on the verge of completing a very important project.'

'What's all that about?' asked Fiona's father gruffly.

'I'm not sure, Dad. He never really tells me much.'

'Been at that firm for almost two years now, hasn't he?' Mr Davenport mused. 'Time he was moving on if you ask me. Time he spread his wings. Got to bump up the take-home a bit now that the pair of you are going to take the plunge.'

'Oh, yes, darling,' Mrs Davenport trilled. 'I almost forgot. You must let me see the ring. Oh wonderful, you did go for the solitaire in the end. How lovely. Just so classy, aren't they? Looks a little bit big though, Fi. You should get it adjusted before you go and lose it. I know what you're like about losing things. Look, Hugo. Tim's bought the ring.'

'Yes, I know he's bought the ring, dear, but has he set the date? That's what I need to hear.'

'Hugo, you haven't even looked at the ring,' Mary Davenport reprimanded. 'Don't pester the poor girl about the date today. We've got plenty of time to sort that out. But has he, dear?' Mary asked her daughter conspiratorially. 'Have you decided when the big day might be?'

'Oh, I don't know, Mum,' Fiona was a little embarrassed. 'Tim's been a bit too busy to discuss that kind of thing in any detail.'

'A summer wedding would be nice though. June? Or July? No hurry.'

The taxi had pulled up outside the restaurant. The family Davenport bundled out of the car and into the lobby. They were shown straight to their table by a young Australian girl who presented the menus with a flourish. She announced the specials with idiosyncratic intonation.

'Get everywhere these colonials,' said Hugo, when the waitress had left them to choose at their leisure. 'All over London now. That chap in the garage was a Kiwi, wasn't he, Mary?'

'I think they do a lot of travelling, Dad.'

'Do too much flitting around, these young people. Though there's not much at home for them except sheep, I suppose. Right, I'm ready to order. Where's that bloody girl gone now?'

'Hugo,' Mary tutted. 'We're not ready yet. Keep your voice down.' After the army and a few years on the trading floor, Hugo Davenport found such on instruction very hard to obey.

'How's Angus, Mum?' Fiona asked.

'Oh, Angus sends his love. Obviously he couldn't come up to town today because he's slap bang in the middle of his finals. I think he's a little bit worried, the poor lamb.'

'Nothing to be worried about,' Hugo boomed. 'He knows he'll pass them with flying colours. If his sister can do it . . .'

Mary shot Hugo a look that changed the direction of the conversation immediately.

'He's had quite a few job offers from the management consultancy firms he's applied to. He thinks that he might go for the one at Atherton Bros. They offer the most holiday time apparently,' Mary smiled. 'I think that's swung it.'

'Lazy little bugger that he is,' said Hugo.

'Well, I must say I can't blame him,' defended Mary. 'He'll have to work terribly hard as it is, Hugo.'

'It's no kind of attitude to have if he wants to get on,' Hugo continued. 'A man's got to take his career seriously. None of this fannying about for five years before going off to have a baby.'

'Your father's secretary has just gone on maternity leave,' Mary added by way of an explanation.

'Oh.'

'But how about you, dear? How's your little job at First Tokyo?'

'First Orient, Mum. My little job's fine.'

'I expect you can't wait to get home every day to make your wedding arrangements now. Have Kerry and Linzi said whether they want to be bridesmaids?' Fiona nodded. 'You'll have to be careful with the colour you choose for their dresses. Linzi will be easy. She's got such wonderful skin and striking dark hair. But Kerry? She might be more difficult to match. Perhaps you could get her some of that wash-in, wash-out hair-dye stuff for the day?'

The waitress had reappeared, armed with an electronic device to take down their orders which looked like something out of *Star Trek* and, by the trouble she was having in getting it to work, was probably technologically of the same era. In the end, she admitted that she would have to resort to old-fashioned memory.

'Not entirely sure she took all of that in,' Hugo muttered as the girl headed off in the direction of the kitchen. 'That's well-cooked for my steak!' he boomed after her. All eyes turned to see who was making such a fuss. Fiona pretended to be fascinated by the shape of the pepper pot.

After lunch, Mary and Fiona left Hugo alone in the dining room while they went to powder their noses. It was Davenport girl-speak for going somewhere to discuss things unmentionable in front of the men, such as gynaecology and career aspirations. Fiona caught her mother's eye in the mirror as they both reapplied their lipstick in exactly the same way. First step, a careful line around the cupid's bow, then both lips together and press hard to distribute the lipstick evenly over the rest of the mouth. Fiona was struck not for the first time by how much she looked like her mother these days. It wasn't just genetic. Fiona could barely pass a mirror without remembering her mother's early warning that she had to keep herself looking nice at all times, for the men. First to get one and then, when you'd got one, to make sure he didn't stray. It was a full-time occupation.

'Are you excited, dear?' Mary asked again. 'About becoming Mrs Timothy Harper?'

Fiona nodded. 'I suppose I am.'

'Oh, it'll be wonderful, sweetheart. He's such a catch. A real Prince Charming.'

'Yes, Mum, so you say.'

'Such lovely blond hair and so very tall,' Mary mused. 'And he's doing well in his career. You know I'm very pleased, Fiona. I couldn't have asked for a better son-in-law. Beats any of the royal family hands down.'

'Mum,' Fiona interrupted before her mother could start reminiscing about the time she had danced with the Prince of Wales. 'Mum, what do you really think about me getting married at twenty-four? Are you sure I'm not too young? I know you married Dad when you were nineteen, but have you ever thought that you might have missed out on something?'

'Missed out on something? Like what, darling?' Mrs Davenport looked very curious indeed.

'Like seeing the world, Mum. Travelling a bit. Perhaps even working overseas?'

'Working overseas? Heavens.'

'Yes. You could have gone to India and taught English there like Auntie Jane did when she finished her degree. What if I did something like that?'

Mrs Davenport screwed the lid back on to her lipstick and dropped it into her bag. 'Well, Fiona, I suppose I must admit that there are times when I think that your father is a belligerent old bugger, but if I had waltzed off to India at the drop of a hat instead of marrying him, I might have ended up with no belligerent old bugger at all to keep me in my dotage. Like your Auntie Jane.' Pleased with her answer, she linked her arm through her daughter's and led her back out to the table where Hugo was subjecting the bill to some extreme scrutiny.

'Think they've over-charged us for the mineral water,' he told his wife.

It was exactly like something Tim would have said.

When her parents had been safely dispatched on a tour of the best shops in Knightsbridge, Fiona returned to her desk and took a slightly dog-eared envelope out of her handbag. It was the letter to Hara, telling him that she couldn't take up his offer of the New York placement for 'reasons of a personal nature'. She dropped the letter into the sack of the spotty boy who collected and delivered the internal post. There was to be no turning back now. Or was it no going forward?

CHAPTER TWELVE

K erry had been waiting three long Underground minutes for the train to arrive. Just how long is an Underground minute, she wondered, since her reasonably accurate watch had counted at least six to London Underground's three. While she was pondering this, the intercom suddenly crackled ominously into life.

'Ladies and gentlemen. I would like to apologise for the delay to your service this morning. This is due to passenger action at Kentish Town. Your next train should arrive in approximately three minutes. I said, your next train should arrive in approximately three minutes. London Underground apologises for the delay.'

The commuters up and down the platform murmured their disappointment. Kerry sighed and moved back to lean against the tunnel wall. She and Leon would be leaving for her sister's wedding straight after work that evening so she was carrying a case full of clothes for the weekend, not to mention the bumper bottle of conditioner that Michelle had sent Kerry to deal with her frizzies. When she left the house the suitcase had seemed light enough, but now the cheap fake leather-covered handle was cutting into her fingers and she longed to put it down. She didn't like to because she had once seen a woman have her bag snatched after doing the same. Though who would want to steal her case, Kerry reasoned with herself. The lads who hung around Balham tube station asking people the time until they found a Rolex to pinch had offered to upgrade her Casio digital to a Timex.

It still hadn't quite sunk in that Leon had actually agreed

to come to the wedding at all. He had been in a surprisingly good mood all week. On Monday afternoon he had gone back to his flat with the reinforcement of a big friend and demanded that Sam let him in. Sam, apparently, had been quite reasonable for a histrionic nutcase. He agreed that Leon should probably be allowed to get over the split in his own flat and had taken his own stuff to his mother's house. Leon had his suspicions that Sam had in fact gone straight over to Andrew's, but he wasn't going to dwell on it. No, he said, much to Kerry's joy, he was going to enjoy this weekend with his favourite colleague instead. He had never been to an English wedding before and he was really looking forward to it.

The electronic noticeboard flashed up 'CORRECTION' and the passengers looked towards the renewed message with the stoical patience of cattle. 'Edgware via the Bank'. Damn, thought Kerry, she needed Charing Cross. The next Charing Cross train wasn't even shown.

But then, suddenly, in the manner that occasionally makes you think that travelling by tube really isn't that bad after all, the commuters of Clapham South were granted a special visitation from the gods of the underworld and the next tube arrived. It was two whole Underground minutes early. And just to ice the cake for Kerry, this surprise train was going to be travelling via Charing Cross.

'Praise the Lord.'

Kerry was stepping forward to board the train when the shouting started. As she put one foot on the train she was suddenly knocked off her feet by a flying commuter, causing her to land chin first on the hard wooden-slatted floor

'What the f . . .' She scrambled to her feet and turned to glare at the man who had knocked her over. But, even as she did so, he was falling on his face too. He hadn't meant to push into her. But he was being pushed.

Behind him, stood a small man with a broom handle at the end of which was attached a battered boxing glove.

'Get on the train! Get on the train!' the man was shouting manically as he pushed the commuters into carriages with his home-made super-shover. 'Get on the train. Quick, quick. Get on before the doors close.' He punched a girl in the back with his boxing glove. Another commuter flew involuntarily into the carriage, pleading 'But I want Bank, not Charing Cross.'

The train was delayed for three London Underground minutes while the police came to fetch the man with the poker. By the time they had restrained him, the intercom was announcing that there would be a delay again, due to passenger action at Clapham South. Of course, the train now standing at the platform would be diverted via the Bank. Kerry decided it was time to ask Leon if he was serious about teaching her to ride a motorbike.

Leon had hired a car for the occasion of driving back to Bristol, since he sensed that Kerry wasn't too happy about tackling the M4 on the back of his Yamaha. They left the office at three o'clock, in a fairly vain attempt to avoid the mass Friday-night exodus from London. Celestine had been a little bit grumpy about being left to hold the fort, since Josh had done a sicky, but Leon promised her that she could take Monday morning off in lieu. When it was time to go, Leon picked up Kerry's bag. His knees buckled a little under its unexpected weight.

'What on earth have you got in here?' he complained.

'Nothing much. Girls' things, you know. Extra knickers. Hairspray and stuff.'

'Hardly travelling light, are you?' he laughed.

'Well, I need everything I've brought,' she replied.

The traffic crawled out towards the M40 and, through the centre of London, they were frequently overtaken by pedestrians. Fortunately, Leon had the foresight to bring some tapes to keep them amused. He asked Kerry to make the choice and pointed to a Tesco carrier bag bursting with cassettes which he had stowed behind her seat. Kerry fished out 'Boys and Girls' straight away.

'Brilliant! Can I put this on?' she asked eagerly.

'Sure.'

'I didn't know you were into Bryan Ferry?'

'Neither did I, but you went on about him so much, I thought I'd give him a second chance. It's a bit schmaltzy, Kez. Don't think I'll listen to your musical opinion in the future.'

Kerry pushed the tape into the cassette deck joyfully anyway. At least he had listened to her once.

'It grows on you,' she assured him as the opening chords began to issue weakly from the speakers in the back.

'So does ringworm,' said Leon. 'I'll play you some proper music later. Now tell me, before I have to ask your mother, who is it that's getting married again?'

'It's my younger sister, Michelle,' Kerry told him for at least the third time that day. 'I've got two sisters. Miranda's older and she's already married to a guy called Steve. They thought they ought to do it before they christened their second child. That was last year and I was bridesmaid then, too.'

'Fun?'

'A nightmare. You have to wear a stupid dress all day and everyone keeps telling you that it'll be your turn next. Except that it wasn't to be, because Michelle beat me to it.'

'Who's she marrying?'

'Richard. He's OK. They've been going out for a couple of years. Before that she was engaged to Jason, but he wouldn't set a date for a wedding so she chucked him.'

'Sounds harsh.'

'I think it was for the best. He worked as a fishmonger and it wasn't much fun having him around the house on a hot day. Not to mention the fact that he used to beat her up.'

'That's bad news.'

'Yeah, I told her that the first time she came home with a black eye. But Michelle and some of her friends . . . they've got this strange attitude. They think that if someone's jealous or violent it's only because he feels so strongly for you. They stand around in the ladies' saying things like: 'Ooh, he's lovely. He only beats her up at weekends.' Richard's not like that, thank God. But I sometimes get the feeling that Michelle rushed into their relationship because being with Jason made her feel like she couldn't cope on her own.'

'Could she?'

'Of course she could. She's a really bright girl.'

'Like you.'

Kerry blushed.

'How old is she? Your little sister.'

'She's twenty-one.'

'That's young.'

'Listen, in my family they think you're on the shelf once you hit twenty-four. That's why I had to drag you along to be my "other half" today.'

Leon snorted with laughter. 'I take it you haven't told them much about me, then?'

'Leon, I don't tell my parents much about myself.'

'Aren't you close?'

'Oh, we're close enough. It's just that they worry so much. Every time I go home it's: Are you saving up for that mortgage? Have you sorted out your pension plan? Have you got a boyfriend? I know that they just want me to be settled down so that they don't have to worry about me any more. But the thing is they don't have to worry anyway. I mean, I'm doing all right.' Leon nodded. He was convinced.

'But when I spend any length of time at home I end up thinking that they're telling me how it really is. Maybe I should have a mortgage by now. Maybe I should have a pension. Maybe I should have a man. I see those down-and-outs that sit near our office and start thinking that it could be me if I don't get things right before it's too late. Lost and lonely. With no one to talk to but a whippet with mange.'

'I think we all think like that sometimes.' Leon turned the car on to the motorway. 'But it doesn't happen to most of us even though most of us fuck things up once or twice in our lives. Hey, I'm really looking forward to this wedding. Aren't you?' He deftly changed the subject. 'I can't wait to meet your mum.'

Two and a half hours later, they hit the driveway of the Keble family home in Bristol. It was teeming with strangely clean and well-polished cars. Even Kerry's father had decorated his old white Mondeo with a pink ribbon that came down across the bonnet in a Victory V. The windows of the house were already decked with rosettes and flowers in readiness for the morning. There was no mistaking that something was going on.

Mrs Keble was standing on the front step before Leon had time to finish parking. Her hair was in curlers, covered over by her one and only Hermès headscarf, a twenty-first birthday present from a glamorous maiden aunt. The faces of Kerry's cousins and her nieces crowded at the windows now, displacing the decorations as they fought to catch a glimpse of Kerry and her legendary new beau.

'Hello, Kerry Love.' Mrs Keble kissed her last spare daughter so hard on both cheeks that Kerry felt her Mum's pink lipstick being pressed into her pores. 'Did you have a lovely drive, dear, all the way from London?'

All the way from London? London was less than three hours away, but it was the furthest any Keble girl had ever gone. Or any Keble at all for that matter, not since Uncle Tony went North in dubious circumstances.

'And this must be Leon?' Mrs Keble was talking through an orchard of plums. 'It's very nice to meet you at last. We've heard so much about you from our Kez.'

'Mum!'

Leon raised an eyebrow to Kerry while Mrs Keble gave him the lip stamp treatment as well.

'Come on in, you two young lovers. Miranda, get the kettle on. Your little sister's home. Michelle's having a facial with that mobile beauty salon girl,' Mrs Keble said in a stage-whisper as they passed the dining room. 'So you had better not go in there. Don't want to catch her with a green face.'

'Hi, Kerry!' Michelle the bride-to-be called out from beneath her cucumber face pack. 'I'll be out in a minute when me pores are done. Hi, Kerry's new man!!!'

Kerry's new man? Leon was struggling to keep anything like a straight face.

'Earl Grey or Tetley?' Mrs Keble asked another prospective son-in-law. 'Then we'll sit down and you can tell us all what's happening in *Neighbours* back home.'

'Mum,' Kerry sighed. 'Leon's from South Africa.'

Michelle had decided to spend her last night as the penultimate Miss Keble at the Keble family home. It was a bit of a joke, since she had been living with her fiancé Richard for the past eighteen months, but Michelle was superstitious like that.

It was a full house. Leon had to share the sitting-room floor with cousins Malcolm and Derek and for the first time in about fifteen years, Kerry found herself sharing a bed with her sister. They went up to bed at ten o'clock on the strict instructions of their mother who was concerned that Kerry's under-eyebags would never go down, despite having kept her under a pair of cucumber slices for an hour that afternoon. Kerry lay to the left of the bed. Michelle lay to the right with her arms on the outside of the covers so that the duvet dipped and divided them down the middle. They said 'good night' and closed their eyes. Each

waited for the breathing of the other to slow into the familiar
pattern of sleep.

'Are you asleep yet, Kez?'

'No.'

'I'm not keeping you awake, am I?'

'No.'

'Are you excited about tomorrow?'

'Nn . . . yes.'

'I'm not . . .'

There was silence for a moment.

'What do you mean, you're not excited about tomorrow? It's
your wedding.'

'I'm terrified, Kez.'

'Oh. That's to be expected, Chelle,' Kerry tried to sound
comforting. 'It's your big day isn't it? The spotlight will be on
you. Don't worry though. While you're up at the altar pledging
your troth most of the congregation will be concentrating on my
arse in that meringue of an outfit.'

'Don't you like your dress?'

'Put it this way, I don't know if I'll be wearing it out next
weekend.'

'I hate my dress, Kez.'

'What do you mean? You're the bride.'

'I mean, I hate it. I'm going to look like a bloody cotton-wool
ball when I go down the aisle.'

'But you chose it . . .'

'I didn't, Kez. Richard's bloody mother chose it. She insisted on
coming with me when I went to Pronuptia. I wanted something
a bit more, you know, a bit more modern. No sleeves. Quite
straight. A sheath dress or something like that. But she kept on
making me try on these dreadful puffball things instead. Kept
on about how lovely I looked and how it was as if I was the
daughter she never had. She said that mine was going to be the
perfect wedding that she had always dreamed of arranging.'

'Oh.'

'I didn't know what to do. I tried on this dress that I really
liked and she just sort of screwed her face up like she'd smelled
something horrible. She said it wasn't decent, having your arms
on show like that when you're getting married in the house
of God.'

'And so you bought the puffball?'

'No. I didn't. She bought the puffball. She said she had been saving up to buy a wedding dress for her future daughter since she got pregnant with Richard in 1969. She was devastated when she found out that she couldn't have any more children after him and so she kept on saving for her future daughter-in-law's wedding dress instead.'

'And did she choose the bridesmaids' dresses as well?' Kerry was horrified.

'No, Mum suggested those. She thought it would be cheaper to use Miranda's old patterns and we got the material from that fabric shop in town after all the stock had been ruined in a flood. That's why it's a slightly different colour on the bodice. I'm sorry, Kez. I know it's not exactly your style.'

'It's just a dress,' Kerry told her. 'And by this time tomorrow night it'll be wrapped up with its mothballs again. You've got to think of your dress as one of those little things sent to try you, Chelle. I guarantee that by the time you and Richard are having rugrats you'll be saving up to humiliate your own first daughter-in-law.'

Michelle made a funny snorting noise in the dark. Kerry wasn't sure whether it was the beginning of a laugh or a sob.

'Oh, Kez.' It was a sob. 'It's not just the dress. That's just the tip of the iceberg. Since her husband died, Richard's all she's got and she keeps on interfering. She's already come round our house and had him put a dado all the way down our hall. I hate those things. And she's coming to the hairdressers' with us tomorrow morning. She's going to make me have all my hair cut off to show that I'm a married woman, like those Russian brides, I know it. It's the beginning of the end for me, Kez. I'm never going to be able to be myself again. You don't know how lucky you are. You're living in London. You've got an exciting job. You're going out with an incredible-looking man. You wouldn't believe how much I envy you!'

Kerry smiled in the dark.

'Michelle, things are never quite as they seem. You wouldn't believe how much I envy you.'

'How can you envy me?' Michelle sighed. 'I spend all week filing boring car insurance claims and all weekend traipsing round garden centres and DIY shops in search of the perfect trellis. I didn't want to work in insurance. I wanted to be a dancer on a cruise ship. Or a nanny in America. Even a gaucho in Argentina once when we did about them in Geography. I wanted to see something of the world. OK, so we're going on honeymoon to Majorca but Richard has said that'll be our last holiday for five years because we've got to start saving for when we have children. I'm twenty-one years old and I haven't even seen the Niagara Falls.'

'Linzi says they're not as big as you think they're going to be anyway.'

'That's not the point. The point is, she's seen them and I haven't.'

'But Michelle. It's not all bad. I mean, you've got security with Richard. You've got your own house. You've got a car. You've even got a washing machine. You've got a start in life. It's three years since I got my degree and all I have in the world amounts to a double duvet and a broken sandwich toaster.'

'Life's not about having things, Kerry. It's about doing things. It's taken me signing away a week's wages every month on a washing machine and tumble dryer to realise that. Our house could burn down tomorrow, but Linzi's memories of how small Niagara Falls seemed will be with her for ever.'

'But even if your house did burn down, you'd be able to replace it from your insurance,' Kerry reasoned, as she totally missed the point. 'You have got insurance, haven't you?'

'Of course we've got bloody insurance, Kerry. I am marrying Mr Anus after all.'

'Mr Anus? That's no way to talk about your future husband.'

'I believe you dubbed him that after he insisted that we get a doggy bag at Pizzaland.'

'Oh, yeah. I think I did. But I like Richard, Michelle. I really do. I think you'll be good for each other.'

Michelle sighed and rolled over on to her side.

'I wish I was so sure. Hang on to your independence, Kerry, or you could spend the rest of your life wandering round B & Q in your spare time like me and Miranda do. I don't want to go through with this bloody wedding. I've been trapped into it by our folks and his mum. You are the only one of the three of us sisters that can escape all this shit now.'

*   *   *

But at three o'clock the next day, the prize puffball and her attendant meringues strode proudly down the aisle.

When they reached the altar, Kerry stepped forward to take Michelle's bouquet. Michelle met her eyes with a smile. All the misgivings of the night before seemed to have melted away in a dream of forever love. Michelle turned her gaze to Richard, who was so nervous that he looked as though he was trying to hold in a fart when he smiled. Richard was a kind and gentle guy, thought Kerry. Michelle was going to be all right with him.

Kerry ushered the younger bridesmaids into their seats by the aisle. They were level with her mother, who was sitting next to Leon. Mrs Keble sniffed discreetly as the vicar began his spiel about the sight of God. Leon fished in his pocket and brought out a clean, ironed handkerchief, which he lent her to dab at her eyes. He was the perfect escort, smiling, smarming, singing out loudly for all the hymns.

While the bride and groom signed the register, the choir sang 'Wonderwall' and the organist tried to keep up. The vicar had originally said that only hymns could be played in his church, but Richard's mother had slipped him a couple of hundred quid for the vestry fund and the musical policy had been mysteriously changed. Unfortunately, that money covered the painful rendition of 'Lady in Red' as the bridal party proceeded out of the church as well.

But it was a beautiful wedding and Mrs Keble was staggering with emotion as she walked proudly back up the aisle on Leon's arm. Either that or the cooking sherry.

CHAPTER THIRTEEN

The wedding reception was being held in the banqueting hall of a local hotel, Hawthorne House. As children, Kerry and her sisters had often played in the ruins of Hawthorne House as it then was. It had been decimated by a fire in the twenties which was supposedly started by the cook's eldest son when he found out that his father was in fact lord of the manor. In the mid-eighties property boom, the red-brick shell had been bought and restored to its former glory by the Post House Group, and where once there had been grass poking up through singed flagstones, there was now that familiar carpet – dark blue pile with an attractive golden monogram. Michelle had always said that she intended to live in Hawthorne House when she grew up. A night in the honeymoon suite was almost a wish fulfilled, Kerry guessed.

There were three wedding parties at Hawthorne House that day. When the Keble party arrived, they were ushered straight out on to the rolling lawn for their complimentary glass of feeble Bucks Fizz. It wasn't the most glorious of days and Kerry was starting to wish that she had a little more puff in her sleeves to keep her warm. The official photographer had a set-to with the manager because the party which had arrived shortly before the Kebles were taking too long with their photographs and hogging all the best scenic spots.

By five o'clock, Kerry felt grinned out. Her sister and her new husband finally got to have their photocall on the precarious swing by the ornamental lake and the Keble party were called inside for the wedding breakfast. Breakfast? Ha ha. Kerry's stomach had been on the verge of rumbling throughout the service. She had only been able to have one piece of toast that morning because Angela had cut the dress just a little on the small side. Mrs Keble reminded Kerry that it was her own fault, since she hadn't managed to attend a single dress-fitting since the very first one almost eighteen months before.

As chief bridesmaid, Kerry sat to the right of the best man. Leon had been placed three spaces down, between Michelle's new grandmother-in-law and Kerry's Great Auntie Jean. He was still smiling and nodding while Jean probably told him about her problem waterworks. While the waiters were pouring out the first of many glasses of champagne, Leon turned and caught Kerry's eye. He winked at her and raised his glass. She felt herself blush and got some bubbles up her nose.

'That your boyfriend, is it?' Derry the best man asked as he broke a bread roll into a pile of clumsy crumbs. 'Bit flash, in't he? Saw his car outside. Still, I 'spect they're all like that up in the big city, mind.'

'It's not his car,' Kerry explained. 'He just hired it for the weekend. He usually rides a Yamaha 750.'

Derry's eyes widened. 'Bloody hell. I knew he was a flash bugger. That's one of the fastest bikes you can have on the road.'

Kerry knew it too.

'How come you didn't ride up on that then?'

'I wouldn't have been able to fit my suitcase on the back of it.'

'What? I wouldn't let no bloody woman's bag stop me from riding a Yamaha 750,' Derry commented through a mouthful of bread. 'I'd have told you to take the bloody train and I'd meet you here.'

'I guess that's why Carina broke off the engagement,' Kerry replied acidly.

'She was unfaithful to me.' Derry was hurt. 'And after I painted her name on the side of my Escort and all.'

The wedding breakfast segued almost without event into the speeches. One of the younger bridesmaids threw up in the loos and Kerry was dispatched to deal with it. When she returned, feeling a little queasy from the experience herself, her father stood up to give his speech as 'father of the bride' and ended his little monologue of Michelle's most embarrassing childhood memories with 'Two down, one to go'. He even publicly offered Leon a fiver to take Kerry off his hands. Derry said he would do the job for just three pounds.

From the Hawthorne House Hotel, they proceeded to the 'wedding disco' at the Lions' Rugby Club. The lobby to this draughty hall was still caked with mud brought in by that afternoon's rugby practice but the hall itself had been really tarted up for the occasion. All the plastic tables had had their cigarette burn scars covered with pink paper tablecloths. At the centre of each cloth was a pink and white floral arrangement to which was attached a helium-filled balloon. A fair arch of balloons graced the buffet table. But when Michelle walked into the room she burst into angry tears.

'I told her to match the balloons to the bridesmaids' dresses,' she wailed.

'They had a special offer on the pink,' comforted her new husband.

Michelle and Richard missed the first dance while she reapplied her tear-stained face in the toilets.

The guests who hadn't been quite important enough to warrant an invitation to the wedding reception proper drifted into the rugby club between seven and eight. They brought with them a terrifying posse of small children who drank too much fizzy orange and started to run around as though somebody had taken part of their brain circuitry out. Leon and Kerry were sitting at a table with Great Auntie Jean.

'There'll be tears before bedtime for that lot,' she remarked. And sure enough, even as she spoke a three-year-old lad in a blue velvet waistcoat collided head-on with a little girl in pink jeans. The adults recoiled from the sickening crack.

'See? What did I tell you?' said Great Auntie Jean. She was the kind of person you wouldn't want to sit next to on an aeroplane.

Pretty soon, Mrs Keble rolled up to their table. She was still wearing her hat, which had been firmly pinned to her head that morning though it was beginning to slip to one side. 'Oh my goodness,' she said in a stage whisper. 'If Richard's cousin Cheryl doesn't take control of her children, I swear I don't know what I'm going to do. I'll give them bloody cracking their heads together. That little kiddy ripped a cloth off the buffet table just now and ran off with a bowl full of crisps. How are you doing, Jean?' she softened her voice a little. 'Has our Kerry's Leon been looking after you? He's a lovely boy, isn't he? From Down Under, you know. Did you recognise his accent?'

Leon smiled obligingly as she ruffled the top of his hair drunkenly. Kerry just prayed that her mother wouldn't pinch his cheeks.

'Isn't he nicely dressed?' She talked about him openly in his presence. 'Not like our Miranda's Steven. I ask you, Jean. His own sister-in-law's wedding and he turns up without a tie. I had to borrow one off some old chap who was in the churchyard putting flowers on his wife's grave. Amazing, isn't it, how obliging people are when they know you've got a wedding on?'

'You should have said, Mrs Keble,' Leon piped up. 'I was carrying a spare tie myself just in case I spilled something down this one.'

'Oh, Leon,' she plopped down in the chair beside him and placed a hot hand on his knee. 'This man is such an angel. I tell you, Jean, I was just about to burst into tears as our Chelle came down the aisle looking so beautiful, when Leon pulled out a handkerchief. And not just a paper one. It was cotton and pressed. I suppose you must have noticed, Leon, how our Kerry just shoves toilet paper up her sleeve. Honestly, I don't know where I went wrong with my girls.'

'I don't think you went wrong at all, Mrs Keble,' Leon smiled. Kerry tried to hide her reddening face on the pretence of getting an irritating bit of gypsophila out of her fringe. Leon's besotted boyfriend impression was completely spot on.

'Thank you, Leon. You're such a comfort to an old woman.'

'Not an old woman, Mrs K.'

'Oh, you cheeky monkey.' Then she did pinch his cheeks. 'Right, come on, our Kerry. You're Michelle's chief bridesmaid so you're supposed to be helping me and your father to entertain her guests. Go and see if you can't control Cheryl's little menace will you? Since it doesn't look as though she intends to take him in hand herself.'

Kerry rose from her chair dutifully. 'Mum, you do know that Leon and I have got to drive back to London tonight, don't you?' Leon stalled her with a wave of his hand.

'Not until your lovely mother and I have had a dance.'

By the time Leon had done the rounds of all the ladies of a certain age, it was out of the question that they would be driving back to London that night. Kerry's mother insisted that they stay over until the next day and Leon, to Kerry's surprise, raised not one word of protest. When it came to bedtime, Mrs Keble took Kerry aside and said that, since Michelle had gone on her honeymoon to Majorca and this was the nineties and all, she had no objection if Leon wanted to take up Michelle's side of the bed in her absence. Kerry protested feebly on the grounds of decency, since that was what she thought she was supposed to do, but Leon seemed only too happy with the arrangement.

'I couldn't spend another night with your cousins,' he told her when they finally got behind closed doors. 'They spent the whole time having farting competitions in their sleeping bags. Honestly, I felt inadequate.' He crawled into the saggy double bed beside her. The springs had been knackered for as long as Kerry could remember. 'I think we're going to get a bit of roll-together in this,' Leon commented. 'Hey, is that you in that picture?'

He pointed at a photograph of the three sisters in primary school uniform which stood in a dusty frame on a shelf.

'Yeah, that's me in the middle. Stopping the other two from kicking the living daylights out of each other. They used to fight all the time.'

'I can't believe that. You've got such a lovely family, Kerry,' Leon whispered. 'But then, someone as nice as you had to be brought up by nice parents, I suppose.'

'Like my mother says,' replied Kerry dryly, 'she doesn't know where she went wrong.'

'They're all so friendly. They really welcomed me into the fold.'

'I'm sure they're just like any other family, really.' Kerry was feeling strangely embarrassed by the flattery.

'Not mine,' Leon sighed. 'Do you know that this June it will be three years since I last saw my mother? And my father? I can't even remember how long that's been. I've got an older sister, but I haven't seen her either. She sided with Mum when we fell out and refused to return any of my calls. I was quite surprised about that.'

'What did you fall out about?'

'What d'you think? Me coming out of the closet, of course. Me doing "unnatural things" with some sailor I met in Cape Town. Mum just tried to deny it at first. Then, when I told her that I was actually going to move in with him, that was it. She cried for three days and then cut me off without another word.'

'Shit, that's rough. But why do you think your mum was so upset? I mean, I think that my parents would stand by me whatever I did.'

'Believe me, I thought the same. I suppose Mum might have been embarrassed. We lived in a very small town. And I think she was worried about not having any grandchildren too. My sister never had a boyfriend in all the time I can remember. She's destined to die an old maid. I suppose Mum thought I was the only hope for the continuation of the Landesman family line.'

'I'm lucky I've got two sisters to do all that for me. Miranda had Hayley before she left school. But did you ever have any girlfriends?' Kerry asked casually.

'Yeah, I had a few. In high school I went out with this girl called Janine for almost five years. It started when we were twelve. Mum thought that she was going to be the one. After we split up I would come home every other night to find Janine and my mother sitting at the kitchen table plotting how they could get us back together. I felt bad about that. I mean, I don't dislike girls even now. And I would love to have children one day.'

Kerry could almost hear the beating of her heart.

'It's just that I'm attracted to the whole person,' Leon mused. 'I think gender is pretty irrelevant if everything else is there. You know, if you've got total empathy with someone.'

Kerry nodded in the dark.

'Unfortunately, since I hit eighteen I've tended to find that total empathy only with the boys,' Leon added with a faint laugh.

'But it's not impossible that you might turn straight again,' Kerry whispered hopefully. 'I mean, if you found a girl you had total empathy with?'

'Turn straight? Well I suppose you should never say never,' Leon laughed. 'If I found the right girl.'

'Leon, what are you going to do about your visa?' Kerry asked when he had fallen silent again.

'I was trying not to think about that.'

'You're always trying not to think about it. You're going to have to sort it out soon. I mean, I'm sure it'll show up that you're still working illegally when the company gets audited.'

'I don't think the tax office is connected to immigration.'

'Look, it's better to sort it out now than be caught a year down the line. If they have to deport you you'll never be allowed back into the country. Ever. We might never see you again.'

'I'm not ready to go home yet.'

'You might not have to. You could say that you were planning to get married to someone British and that you need a bit more time to make sure you're making the right decision.'

'Married to who, Kez? Are you offering?'

'Are you asking?'

Leon snorted. 'That's a pretty ridiculous offer but thanks all the same. Look, I'll see you in the morning, Kez. I'm knackered now.' He put out the bedside lamp.

'I don't want you to have to go,' Kerry whispered in the dark.

'What?' Leon murmured in his half sleep. He lay his arm across Kerry's waist and began to snore in her ear.

It wasn't until late that Sunday evening that Leon finally pulled the hire car up outside Kerry's door. He undid her seatbelt buckle for her and sat back to wait for her to let herself out. The engine was still running.

'Thanks for coming to Bristol with me,' Kerry said shyly. She wanted desperately to invite him in for a last cup of tea, but she had had his undivided attention for almost a whole weekend now. He probably had other things to do.

'My pleasure. You know that I really enjoyed it anyway. It was something different and your Great Auntie Jean was a real scream.'

'She thought you were lovely too,' Kerry told him. 'She asked me when the big day is going to be after you caught the bouquet.'

Leon blushed. 'Yeah. I don't think I was supposed to have done that. It's a "girls only" thing, isn't it?'

'My cousin Jenny was a bit disappointed, I have to say.'

Leon looked at the bridal bouquet which was wilting fast on

the back seat of his car. He reached over and fetched it. 'Here. I don't think I've got much use for this.' He handed the roses to Kerry. 'You could dry them out to preserve them. Hang them upside down until the petals go crispy. There's something else you should do to them to make them last forever but I can never remember what it is.'

His fingers brushed lightly against Kerry's as he passed her the bouquet.

'I'll try that,' she murmured.

The engine was still running. Leon straightened himself up in his seat again. It was a sign that he was ready to go. Kerry pushed down on the handle of her door and put one foot out on to the pavement. 'Thanks again,' she told him. 'You really made my weekend.' Then she leaned over the gear stick and planted a soft kiss just to the side of his mouth. She was sure that his lips puckered to meet hers. Taking her heart in her mouth, she kissed him again.

'I'll see you tomorrow morning,' he told her. 'Nine o'clock sharp.'

'OK.' She clambered out of the car.

Kerry stood on the pavement with her bags around her feet and waved until the tail-lights of his hired car had turned the corner and were gone. She looked at the bouquet in her hand. One of the heavier roses had already dropped out of the soggy oasis base and lay like a dead butterfly in the oily puddle at the side of the road.

CHAPTER FOURTEEN

'Kerry, I need to have an urgent word with you.' Fiona didn't even wait until Kerry had taken her coat off. 'You just won't believe what Linzi has done now.'

Kerry racked her brains for the answer. 'Let me guess,' she began. 'She turned the heating on outside designated hours? Left pesto in the sink for three days?'

Fiona's upper lip twitched angrily. 'No, it's far worse than that.'

'Worse? Don't tell me. She left a tap running for the whole weekend?'

'Ha ha ha.' Fiona wasn't in the mood for a joke. 'No. You're not even close. She's moved Gaetano in.'

'Moved Gaetano in?'

'She's moved Gaetano in.'

Fiona pointed to the four pairs of men's shoes that had joined their boots beneath the hat-stand to illustrate her point. 'He turned up on Friday night with a car full of bags and boxes. He says that his mother has thrown him out of her house. Can you believe that she objects to him going out with a girl who isn't Italian? Anyway, Linzi let him straight in to stay without even asking whether it would be OK with you and me. She said that he was going to go and see his mother on Saturday morning to try to sort things out. But it's Sunday night now, Kerry. And Gaetano is still here. In fact, I don't think he's been out of the house at all since he arrived.'

Kerry surveyed the room, looking for further signs that a cuckoo had indeed been making itself at home in their nest. An ashtray overflowing with the dog-ends of roll-ups balanced precariously on one arm of the grey Draylon sofa. A dented, empty lager can lay on the floor beside it.

'And he smokes in the house.' Fiona followed Kerry around as she walked from lounge to kitchen and kettle to fridge, whispering all the time like a latter-day Iago. 'And he has about as much clue as Linzi about the ethics of taking your turn with the washing-up. We talked about this before we even moved in, Kerry. We decided that boyfriends staying overnight is OK, but no one is allowed to actually move someone in on a permanent basis.'

'Not that I could move anyone into my room if I wanted to,' Kerry muttered.

'OK, so I know it's a bit small, Kez. But we'll swap rooms in a couple of months, I promise. It's just that . . .'

'I know. I don't have a proper boyfriend. And you and Linzi do. You see, if Linzi had the small room, Gaetano wouldn't be here.'

'Ha ha ha. But the fact remains, he is here. And what are we going to do about it?'

'I'm not going to do anything. It's only been two days and I'm sure it's just temporary,' Kerry sighed. 'Linzi will have fallen out with him by the end of the week if he even stays that long.'

'Do you really think so?'

'Of course. You know what Linzi's like with men. Gaetano will be old news by next Saturday.'

Linzi's bedroom was above the kitchen. With the sound of the kettle boiling, Kerry and Fiona had almost missed the rising squeak and creak, but now the kettle had stopped its furious bubbling, they found their attention being drawn to the ceiling. To the sound of a badly made bed rocking frantically on creaking floor boards. Kerry and Fiona groaned simultaneously.

'Do you still think he'll be out before the end of the week?' Fiona asked.

'We've got to tell her to get that bed fixed,' said Kerry.

'I swear she's never been in love for this long before,' Fiona whined. 'I'm sure she thinks that he's the one for her.'

They resolved to tackle the question the next morning at breakfast. But breakfast came and went without event. Linzi had called in sick for that week's temp job and returned to her warm bed and lover before the subject of unwanted guests could be properly broached. Fiona and Kerry walked together to the tube.

'If he's going to be staying for more than a week, we'll have to work out his share of the rent and the bills,' Fiona began. Kerry just shrugged. 'Oh, how selfish of me. I almost forgot to ask,' Fiona continued. 'How was your little sister's wedding?'

'Romantic,' Kerry admitted.

'Lovely! Tell me all about it from the start. What were the dresses like?'

Kerry couldn't wait to get to work.

Fiona was feeling particularly intolerant of Linzi's misdemeanours because she hadn't seen Tim all weekend. The Old Boys' rugby team was having its annual reunion do and as an ex-captain of the college side, Tim was, of course, obliged to go. Fiona didn't expect him to come back before all the drinking games were done but she was a little disappointed that he hadn't even phoned to say 'hi' by Sunday night. On getting into the office, the very first thing she did was check her voicemail to see if he had called. No new messages since Friday afternoon. She picked up her handset and dialled Tim's desk at BFO Schwartz, the merchant bank.

'Tim,' she said automatically when the phone was picked up at the other end.

'No, Tim's not at his desk. This is Ryan.'

'It's Fiona, Ryan.'

'Oh, hi, Fi. How's tricks?'

'Well as can be expected on a Monday morning, thanks.'

Ryan had the desk opposite Tim. They got on very well. Apparently they had a mutual friend who had been at Ryan's prep school and in Tim's tutorial set at Cambridge or some such spurious connection like that. Once or twice, Tim, Fiona, Ryan and Ryan's girl of the moment had been on a double date. He was thickset and handsome with curly blond hair. In fact, not unlike Tim but without the cauliflower ears. Ryan might have been just Fiona's type if she wasn't already engaged to his workmate. 'Where is he, then?' Fiona asked impatiently. 'Throwing his guts up in the loo, I suppose.'

'He's not coming in today,' Ryan replied.

'Oh really. Did he call in sick?'

'No, he booked a day's holiday at the beginning of last week.'

'He didn't tell me.'

Ryan spluttered. Fiona sensed that he knew he had put his foot in it, right up to the ankle. 'Oh, no. You must be right, Fi,' Ryan back-pedalled. 'He must have called in sick before I got in this morning. I was getting him mixed up with one of the other boys. Yes. That's it. Tim's sick. Rugby this weekend, wasn't it? I expect he's throwing up right now.'

'Thanks, Ryan. I sincerely hope he is.' Fiona put the phone down and blinked back the prickle of tears gathering behind her eyes in disbelief. She prayed that Ryan had been wrong. She couldn't believe that Tim would have taken a day's holiday when they were meant to be saving up all their leave for a nice long honeymoon. She dialled his home number. He wasn't there. Perhaps he was still in Cambridge. Fiona couldn't concentrate on her screen and managed to accidentally delete all the hard work she had done on Friday afternoon.

Tim called her shortly after lunchtime. He claimed that he had dawdled back from Cambridge with Wooders that morning, having called work at the crack of dawn to tell them that he was sick with food poisoning. He arranged to meet Fiona after work at a bar near her office. He hadn't proposed the meeting readily and Fiona put down the phone with a strong sense that he would rather have stayed at home and nursed his head. But she didn't give him the opportunity to cancel and at half past five she made a dash for the loo to put her face straight, adding an extra coat of mascara. Linzi had once said that she could tell by the thickness of Fiona's mascara whether she thought she was just about to be dumped. Fiona sniffed back the thought. But it was true. She only bothered to accentuate her good points when she wanted to warn Tim to be grateful for what he had. This make-up truly was her war-paint. A knot tightened slowly in her stomach which didn't let her loose until Tim walked into the bar and hugged her hello. Then he ordered a couple of Diet Cokes. A sure sign that he had made a new week's resolution never to drink again. Ever.

'Did you have a good weekend?' Fiona asked automatically.

'Oh, it was a great match,' Tim began. 'And, as ever, I was the man of it. We showed those young pups a thing or two about rugby, I can tell you. They were absolutely pony and crap, Fi.

No wonder the college has slipped right down in the league. Apparently they've got this strict new entrance system which means that the undergraduate applicants are chosen purely on academic merit these days. How can they expect to get a decent rugby team together with a policy like that? Bloody ridiculous if you ask me.'

Fiona wasn't in the mood for an education policy debate. Instead, she went straight for the jugular.

'I called you at the office this morning and Ryan said that you had booked today off.'

'No,' said Tim patiently. 'I called in sick.'

'He said that you had booked the day off,' Fiona repeated as she angrily stirred the ice and lemon around in her Diet Coke with a straw. 'Taken a day's holiday.'

'OK. I did. But so what?' Tim couldn't be bothered to try to hold out under questioning while his head still thumped like a Kiwi warrior's dance hall floor. 'I booked a day off. Big deal.'

'So, when we were supposed to be buying the engagement ring you told me that you couldn't get any time off because of this terribly important project you've been working on. And after that, we decided that it would be a good idea to save up all our leave for an extra long honeymoon anyway. Then you go and blow a whole day on messing around with that bloody idiot Wooders.'

'Calm down, Fi. It was time off in lieu, I swear. Besides I'm sure that I mentioned it to you last week.'

'You did not.'

'Sheesh!!' Tim blew his floppy blond fringe out of his eyes. 'It won't happen again, Herr Führer. I promise.'

'Have you even told him yet, Tim?'

'Told who what?' Tim leaned back in his seat and spoke into his glass, misting it up as he did so.

'Have you even told your best friend that you just got engaged to me?'

Tim put his glass down noisily. 'Of course I have.'

'I don't believe you,' Fiona countered. 'When did you tell him?'

'I told him on Friday. When we were driving down to Cambridge. I told him in the car.'

'And what did he say?'

'He said that he was very pleased for us both and that he wishes us a very long and happy marriage.'

'Rubbish. He wouldn't have said that. Wooders would have said that you were out of your mind, Tim. He hates me. I'm the last girl on earth he would want you to marry.'

'One, he doesn't hate you, Fiona, and two, perhaps there is just a vague possibility that he really is pleased for us.'

'Ha ha ha, Tim.' Fiona wasn't convinced. 'Look, I've told Mr Hara that I'm not going to New York because we're getting married this summer and now I want you to set a date. I want you to tell all your friends that we're engaged and then set a date on which we will be married come hell or high water. It doesn't mean anything, this bloody ring, if we're not allowed to tell anybody about it.' She took the ring off and held it threateningly between her thumb and forefinger right in front of his face.

Tim's forehead was wrinkled with panic. 'Fi, I'll tell everybody at the next rugby practice, I promise.'

'And we'll set the date?'

'Of course,' he gulped. 'When for?'

'June, like we discussed when we were deciding whether or not I should go to New York,' Fiona announced. 'June the fifteenth to be more exact. It's a Saturday and it'll be my parents' silver wedding anniversary on the same day.'

'Christ, Fi. June the fifteenth? It's a bit short notice. Can't we . . .'

'Set the date or call this wedding off altogether, Tim Harper. There's your choice.'

Fiona didn't hang around to hear him choose but flew off in the direction of the ladies' as if the hounds of hell were on her tail. She waited three minutes, hyperventilating over a toilet bowl and trying not to cry. Why had she given him an ultimatum, she asked herself in despair. Tim was the type of idiot who would call her bluff on principal. She reapplied her mascara, poking herself in the eye as she did so and instantly making it look as though she had been crying even though she had just barely managed not to. When she finally re-emerged, with the blood thudding in her head as though she had just finished a five mile run, Tim had been joined at their secluded corner table by Wooders. Fiona wondered whether she should walk straight out again. She couldn't believe that Tim had told Wooders where they would be on their quiet evening out after spending the whole weekend in his company. Tim muttered something quietly to which Wooders responded by spitting out a mouthful of beer and slapping Tim heartily across the back.

'Good God, Tim!' Wooders shouted so that the attention of every customer in the bar was drawn to their corner table. 'You're out of your tiny little mind!!!'

Fiona stalked hurriedly across the room and stood before the table with her clenched fists resting on her hips.

'What's going on?' she snapped.

Tim smiled sheepishly. Wooders continued to snort with laughter.

'I was just telling Wooders that we're getting married in June.'

CHAPTER FIFTEEN

The phone rang. Linzi was pretending to be out, but Gaetano answered the call and forgot that he was meant to say that Linzi wasn't in. It was Caroline, from Advertising Angels. She proudly announced that she had arranged an interview for Linzi at a very smart advertising agency in the West End. The position was for a personal secretary to one of the directors and they were offering ten grand to start and a twenty-five pound Next voucher after five years' continuous service without sick leave.

'So, you see,' said Caroline triumphantly, 'I know you weren't very happy about it at first, but my idea about toning down your CV worked after all. You've got an interview, darling. Don't you think your Auntie Caroline always knows exactly what she is doing?'

'Yeah, thanks.'

But Linzi was puzzled. Hadn't they seen the bit about frottage?

'I have had to put a couple of other girls forward for the job of course,' Caroline continued, 'but I don't mind telling you that I think you have by far and away the best chance of success. I've pencilled you in for three thirty. You'll be interviewed by Mr Gerrard himself. He's a lovely man. I'm sure you won't find him scary at all. But you will remember to take your nose ring out won't you, darling? I'm not sure how old Mr Gerrard is, since we've only spoken on the phone, but my guess is that he is in his middle years and I think we both know that body piercing generally does not go down too well with men of a certain age. Have I made myself clear, sweetheart?' Linzi grunted an affirmative.

'Good. Right, you'll need the address. Do you have a pen? You do. OK. Here it is. I think you'll find that Tottenham Court Road is the nearest tube. Better make sure you're there a couple of minutes early in case of emergencies. Don't want to have to nip out for a tinkle halfway through the interview, do we?' Linzi rolled her eyes. 'OK, darling. Wishing you the very best of British. Don't forget to call me the minute you get out to tell me how you've done. Mwah-mwah. Bye-ze-bye.'

'Bye-ze-bloody-bye.'

Caroline had already hung up.

'Got an interview?' Gaetano asked.

'Yeah,' Linzi told him. 'Don't think I'm going to go through with it though.'

'Why not?'

'Because it will be crap, G. Because every single job interview that stupid woman sends me to is crap. She doesn't need to send out girls. She should just send out loo-rolls. I'm not going to go.'

'I think you should,' said Gaetano without looking up from his paper.

'Oh, yeah. And why's that?'

'Because you need a job, that's why.'

'Why do I need a job? I get my allowance and my dole. I think I can cover the rent until my housing benefit comes through.'

'You said yourself that your father has threatened to cut off your allowance if you don't get yourself some work before the end of the month. You don't have to do it forever, Linz, just show willing for a while.'

'You're supposed to be on my side.'

'I am on your side. Look, Linz, falling out with your family isn't much fun, you know.' He was going misty eyed over a full-colour illustration of a plate of pasta smothered in rich tomato sauce. 'Just make out like you're trying for a little while and your father will be off your back again before you know it.'

'You're worse than the people at the dole office.'

'And it'll give you something to do while I'm at the shop this afternoon.' Gaetano put down his paper and pulled Linzi towards him for a hug. 'Besides, just think of all the presents you'll be able to buy for me with your first big wage-packet.' He nuzzled into her ear.

'And when are you going to buy something for me?'

'When I'm rich, *cara mia*. When the band has its first number one album, I'll buy you a diamond-studded speed-boat and take you around the world.'

'I get sea-sick,' said Linzi flatly, as she freed herself from his arms.

Linzi decided to borrow Kerry's navy-blue suit to wear to the interview. Fiona's black DKNY number would have been more stylish and a far better fit, but Fiona had already read the riot act to Linzi that week over Gaetano's extended residence and at that moment, to wear her clothes without permission just didn't seem like such a great idea. Linzi did, however, borrow a pair of Fiona's smartest Pied-à-terre shoes. Fiona's shoes were easier to get away with because she had yet to work out an infallible footwear filing system.

The Soho offices of CPIDG Ltd (named, very creatively, thought Linzi sarcastically, after the directors' initials) were rather fantastic. The receptionists looked as though they were supermodels dressed by Armani and sat behind a burred oak desk that was as big as a small boat. As she waited on the edge of a buff leather sofa, Linzi began to wish she had taken the risk and come DKNY after all.

'Miss Adams,' said the receptionist who moonlighted as Naomi Campbell's body double. 'Mr Gerrard will see you now. Take the lift to the third floor and someone will meet you there.'

At the third floor, Linzi was met by a vision of a boy in black leather jeans. He took her to the anteroom of Gerrard's office and asked her whether she wanted tea or coffee. When she asked for coffee, he offered cappuccino or espresso. She went for espresso for fear of getting a milk moustache. The leather-vision told her that they had proper coffee machines on every floor of the CPIDG headquarters.

As she waited for her summons, Linzi watched the beautiful people of CPIDG drift by. It seemed that everyone was smiling. A man in his forties bent down to pick up a bundle of papers a young girl had dropped on the floor without even pausing to think of the opportunity to get a quick flash of her knickers. By the time Mr Gerrard poked his heard around the door, Linzi had almost forgotten how pissed off she had been on the way there and decided that she wanted a job in this place, even if it was just making the tea.

She got out her best interview technique and shook him warmly by the hand.

'Sit down,' he implored her, as he pulled out a chair. 'Linzi, isn't it? George Gerrard's my name, but you can just call me George.'

He resumed his position on the other side of the desk, and looked down at a piece of paper in an Advertising Angels folder. It was her creative CV. He quickly refreshed his memory of it and smiled broadly.

'Ah, yes,' he said. 'Frottage. Perhaps you should start by telling me some more about that.'

Linzi had to admit that she'd only seen pictures.

George Gerrard was nothing like the man Linzi had expected to meet that afternoon. He was not, as Caroline had suspected, in 'his middle years'. Rather he was only just the wrong side of thirty and his body was resisting all temptation to spread. He was dressed in a beautifully cut suit, possibly Paul Smith, and a white shirt with a Nehru collar that circled a tanned and well-muscled neck. As he spoke to Linzi about her CV, he rolled up his sleeves to reveal a Breitling diving watch on one brown wrist. Linzi wondered idly how deep he could go.

'Well,' said George, when Linzi had admitted that the three GCSEs on her CV were in fact supplemented by four A-levels and a degree, 'I think that's about all the questions I have for you, Linzi.' She made a move as if she was about to stand up and shake his hand goodbye. 'No, hang on, I've got one more.' He leaned back and tapped his silver pen against his pearl-white bottom teeth while he decided whether or not he should risk asking it. 'Do you fancy coming for a drink?'

'A drink?' Linzi exclaimed, as if it were the hardest question she had ever been asked. 'With you?'

'Yes. With me. Why not? It's a beautiful day and I fancy having a quick half before I head home. I think you should come with me. We need to build up some kind of a rapport if we're going to be working together.'

'Working together?'

George was already slipping on his jacket. 'Come on.' He opened the door to his office so that she could pass on through

before him. He let his temporary secretary know that he would
be out for the rest of the day and then guided Linzi into the lift.
She wasn't sure quite what to say. Had he just offered her the
job? It seemed as though he had. Her heart was beginning to
do little skips of delight. After everything he had told her about
the company and her prospects should she join them, she found
that she couldn't wait to accept it. And he would be such a great
guy to work for, far better than that chauvinist moron at E, F
& S. George Gerrard seemed really keen that his PA should
have the opportunity to get on within the company rather than
moulder behind a monitor. Even the ice-maiden receptionists
waved goodbye cheerily as George and Linzi stepped out into
the street. He was obviously well liked by the other employees.
She had a job. Gaetano would be thrilled. And maybe even
Fiona would get off her back for a bit. She was so excited that
she found it difficult to cross the road and stepped out in front
of a moped.

'Hey, careful,' George yanked her back on to the pavement.
'My car's over there,' he pointed towards the multi-storey car
park.

'We're going in the car? I thought we would be going for a
drink around here.'

'You're not in a hurry, are you?' She shook her head. 'Then I
thought we'd get out of town. Who wants to sit outside a central
London pub on a day like today? Breathing in all that crap in
the air.' He pulled an exaggerated face of distaste. 'No, I know
a great place down by the river. It's got a beautiful garden and
more importantly, it's also got real ale.'

He opened the passenger door of a navy-blue BMW 325i. It
had a soft top, which he rolled down. 'Don't get to use this often
enough in England,' he commented. 'And these days I hardly
ever get the time to drive down to my place in the South of
France.'

'The South of France?'

'Yes. Near Cannes. Do you know the area?'

'Vaguely,' Linzi lied.

'Thought I might take my lap-top and my new PA down
there for a bit. Got to take advantage of the communications
revolution.'

'Absolutely.' Linzi settled back into the deep leather passenger seat and ran her fingers ponderously over the polished wooden dash. She really couldn't believe her luck. What a great day. What a great guy.

They drove to the pub by the river and sat at a picnic table right on the bank until the sun began to creep down the sky. Midges danced in the air, suddenly buoyed up, then dropping down in the thermals. Each time he went to fetch them a drink, George came back to sit a little closer to Linzi. Now they were side by side, just an inch or so between them. George was flipping a beer-mat between his fingers.

'So, do you think you could work with me?' he asked her.

'Oh, yes,' said Linzi. 'I think we'd get on very well indeed.'

'Good. Do you want another drink? They've just called last orders.'

'No. I think I really ought to be getting back home. Will you be OK to drive? You've had a few . . .'

George laughed. 'Do I look drunk? I'll be fine. I'll drive you back to town, no problem. Where abouts is it that you live, again?'

'Clapham South. Well, it's Balham really. Just doesn't sound quite so good.'

'Ah yes. I know it. Do you live on your own?'

'No, I share with a couple of friends. Fiona and Kez.' She didn't bother to mention Gaetano, but George still looked a little disappointed.

'Will they be at home tonight?'

'I don't know. I think so.'

'Shame.' George swilled the last dregs of his pint around in his glass and then swigged it back. 'A real shame,' he repeated. Linzi felt a strange creature with pins for feet jogging up her back and subconsciously scanned his left hand for signs of ownership. There were no signs. 'Come on,' he said, getting to his feet suddenly and grabbing her hand. 'Let's get you back to Clapham South before curfew.'

This time, he put the hood of the car up. It was very different to be sitting next to him in the dark. As he pulled out of the pub gates into the narrow country lane and changed gear, Linzi felt his knuckles brush lightly against her leg. Suddenly, the rough material of her borrowed skirt seemed very, very thin indeed.

When he placed his hand fully on her thigh, Linzi felt as though she were on fire.

'George!' she said, her voice rising in surprise. 'What are you doing?'

'You've got beautiful legs, Linzi,' he told her flatly.

'I don't think you should be . . .'

'Don't think I should be what?' He moved his hand slowly towards her crotch, bunching up the skirt beneath his hand. His fingers rested right at the top of her thigh. Linzi's body responded with a fully blown hot flush. 'Do you really mind?' he asked.

'Well, I . . . No.' Her reply was almost a sigh.

'Will your housemates be at home?' he asked again.

'Probably,' Linzi squeaked. His fingers brushed against the cotton of her knickers.

'Damn. I can't really stay then.'

A lump rose in Linzi's throat. He wanted to stay at her place? Well, he could have stayed, but Gaetano was probably already warming up his side of the bed. 'No,' she told him, covering his hand with hers and pressing it hard against her pubic bone. 'I guess you can't.'

George took his hand from between her legs to take a narrow corner. Linzi found to her surprise that her body already ached in the absence of his touch. George was scanning the side of the road, looking for a place to pull in and park. He found a spot by a five-bar gate and by the time he had turned off the headlights, his tongue was in Linzi's mouth.

'Oh, yes,' Linzi murmured as he struggled into the passenger side of the car on top of her and tipped her soft leather seat back as far as it would go. She could already feel that he had a hard-on beneath his beautifully cut trousers. His kiss was so rough. So different from Gaetano's. It took the breath right out of her body and bruised her lips until she felt they might be bleeding. He had his hand up her skirt again now and had pulled her knickers to one side. Linzi groaned with delight and arched her body upwards against his.

With his free hand, George tugged down the zip of his flies and worked his wood-hard penis free. Linzi slid her hands in between their bodies and touched it. Then George pushed her skirt up until it was around her waist and tried to force her legs apart.

'No way,' Linzi protested. 'Not without a condom.'

'Damn,' George swore. 'I haven't got one.'

Linzi pushed his body away. George crossed the gear-stick barrier again and slumped panting in the driver's seat.

'Aren't you on the pill or anything?'

'That's hardly the point, is it?'

'I suppose you're right, but God, Linzi, I really want to fuck you right now.'

'You do?' Linzi felt strangely flattered by his desperation.

'There could be other opportunities,' she said coquettishly, stroking his wilting penis gently as if to make up for his disappointment.

She leaned across the transmission tunnel and guided his dick into her mouth. George sighed as though he was relieved. Then he put a hand on the back of her head and pushed her down further so that his stiffening shaft went deeper into her throat.

'Yes, yes,' he murmured. 'Suck me harder. Yes, baby, do it like that.'

'Well, give me some space to breathe,' Linzi spluttered.

She elbowed her way upright and took a huge breath.

'You OK?' he asked impatiently, his hand already on the back of her head.

'Sorry,' said Linzi insincerely. 'It's just that you're so very big.'

He pushed her down again and since there was nothing else for her to do in that position, she sucked him as far into her mouth as she could without gagging. George's breathing grew deeper and deeper. She prayed that he wasn't going to be the kind who liked to think about football teams and prolong the occasion. Luckily, it was mere seconds before George began to moan more urgently. She felt the bottom of his penis twitch and knew he was about to come.

'Whoah!!' Linzi turned her head away as the white arrow shot from the jerking head. It made a graceful, glittering arc in the air before landing with a splatter on the polished dashboard.

George didn't even bother to tell her whether it had been good. Instead he got a handkerchief out of his pocket and feverishly began to wipe the dashboard clean.

CHAPTER SIXTEEN

'And what time did you get in?' Fiona asked the next morning. 'Old lover-boy was going up the wall. I thought he was going to walk out on you. He didn't though, worse luck.'

'I went for a job interview,' Linzi told her smugly.

'What? Until two o'clock in the morning?'

'Yes, until two o'clock in the morning. My future boss asked me to go for a drink with him afterwards, that's all.'

'Oh, sounds very friendly I bet Gaetano really loved that.' Fiona bit into her toast with a wink and slid out of the kitchen as Gaetano walked in. He didn't even kiss Linzi hello.

'I'm going to work now,' he announced curtly.

'OK, G. I'll see you later on. Yeah?' Linzi stretched up on tiptoe to plant a kiss on his cheek but Gaetano turned his face away 'Charming,' she muttered once he had left. 'It was him who told me that I needed to get myself a job.'

'Yeah,' said Fiona, removing her margarine tub from Linzi's grasp. 'You do. What time is it now?'

'Seven thirty.'

'Cool. I've got a late start today so I think I might try to find out what all the fuss over this *Big Breakfast* programme is about.' Fiona ambled towards the television. Linzi flew out of the kitchen to stand in front of it.

'Don't!'

'What?'

'Don't watch the *Big Breakfast*. It's rubbish, Fi. Honestly. It'll spoil your morning and if I start watching television now, I'll never get anything done today.'

'Linzi. What are you talking about?' Fiona tried to get past

her. Linzi employed her best netball marking tactics to keep
Fiona back. 'And why is there a tea-towel over the screen?'
Fiona, who had always been placed in goal attack, zipped past
Linzi easily and whipped the cloth away.

'Shit,' Linzi gave up her defence. 'I'm sorry, Fi. I was going to
get it fixed later today. I will get it fixed. I promise. I swear. I
think it's only the buttons that are a bit bashed in anyway.'

'What?'

Fiona gazed in disturbingly quiet annoyance at the control
panel of her television. It had indeed been caved in, as had the
little speaker below it.

'I'll have it good as new by this afternoon. No, better than
that. I'll get you a completely new television,' Linzi burbled.
'I mean, this set must be getting on for ten years old by now.
It's ancient. I'll get you something state of the art. Absolutely
brand-new. Flat screen. Surround sound?'

'With what, Linzi?' Fiona asked coldly. 'With what? You've
got no money to replace this. Besides, it's not that the television's
worth all that much, what's really upsetting is the fact that this
damage is hardly accidental. Someone appears to have kicked it
in. Did you do it?'

'Fi . . . I . . .'

'Gaetano did it, didn't he?' Fiona narrowed her eyes.

'Well, yes,' Linzi squirmed. 'But it was my fault really. He just
got a bit wound up while he was waiting for me to come home
from the interview and we had a bit of a row and . . .'

'He thought it would be a good idea to kick my television in to
show you just how much he missed you? That's great. But what
confuses me is how on earth he managed to miss the screen with
his big feet?'

'Fiona, I've told you that I'll pay for the damage. I can't do
anything more.'

'No. You won't. Gaetano broke it, so he should replace it and
when he's replaced my television he should get out of this house
before I get mad and kick him in. He's a bloody thug.'

'He's got nowhere else to go,' Linzi pleaded.

'I don't care. Why can't he get a bedsit like anyone else in his
position? Tim would never impose on us like this. When he first
came up to London he lived in a horrible little place in Hackney
and had to share a single loo with sixteen other residents.

Gaetano just lazes about here, using all the hot water, eating all the food and never washing up and as if that wasn't enough, it now appears he feels free to rearrange the furnishings.'

'So, Tim's a saint and Gaetano isn't.'

'No. I didn't say that. Tim acts like a grown man, there's the difference. Oh, this is just bloody typical. I've got a late start at work and now all I want to do is go in and get behind my desk as quickly as possible. You've got to get rid of him, Linzi. I don't care how you do it.'

Fiona left her toast unfinished and flounced back up the stairs to fetch her briefcase. She walked out of the house without bidding Linzi goodbye. Instead she hissed 'Sort it out' as she closed the door.

The shouting had woken Kerry up. When she managed to struggle out of bed, she found Linzi in the kitchen, sitting on the work-surface next to the sink with a knife in the toaster.

'What are you doing?' Kerry shrieked. 'You'll electrocute yourself.'

'That's what I'm trying to do,' said Linzi dryly, though she was actually just salvaging a wonky piece of toast that had got itself stuck on the filaments and was starting to burn. 'Honestly, Kez, I don't think I can do anything right these days. I went for a job interview last night and because I came back late, Gaetano kicked the television in a rage and spent the night sleeping with his back to me. Then this morning, I have to face rage number two from Fiona because Gaetano has ruined her telly. She's told me that I've got to kick him out but he's got nowhere else to go. I don't know what to do. I'm just stuck in the middle. What do you think, Kez?'

In reality, Kerry thought that the house was way too small for the four of them and was getting a little bit tired of finding her toothbrush already wet when she went to use it. But she didn't say so. She could see that Linzi was nearly on the verge of tears and had a very strong aversion to being responsible for pushing someone over that verge. 'I don't mind,' Kerry reassured her. 'I understand that he can't go home yet and I hope that one day someone will do me as big a favour as you've been doing for him. Just keep him off the furniture, eh? And get him to bung Fiona fifty quid for the damage. Anyway, I'm sure she'll forget all about this morning once she's talked wedding guest lists with the wonderful Tim.' The girls swapped comedy grimaces.

'Yeah. Guess we'll have to be measured up for the bridesmaid dresses soon.'

'I'd rather be measured for my coffin.'

Kerry had restored a smile to Linzi's face, but the way that week had been going, it was no surprise that it ended in a screaming match. Kerry was still lying in bed when the countdown started, enjoying the Saturday morning pleasure of knowing that you could hit the snooze button on your alarm clock for just about as long as you liked if you felt so inclined. The morning noises had begun. Somebody had got up and had themselves a shower, and from the deep hacking smoker's cough, Kerry guessed it was Gaetano. A few minutes after that, the front door opened and slammed shut behind him. The house was silent for a short while again, unless you counted the screaming of next-door's two young children which could have penetrated six-feet-thick stone walls.

Eventually, yet another high-pitched rendition of 'Mummy, I didn't do it,' rising to a full-lunged keening scream, drove Kerry from her little bedroom and downstairs to the kitchen. En route, she picked up the post. A red envelope addressed in her mother's neatest hand and a postcard from her honeymooning sister in Majorca which she must have sent the moment she touched down at the airport to make sure that it arrived on time. 'Wish you were here,' the postcard said. A strange note to write from your honeymoon suite.

. As Kerry waited for the kettle to spring into life, Fiona padded down the stairs behind her. She too must have heard Gaetano go out, because she was wearing her stripy nightie and fluffy Garfield slippers. She hadn't come downstairs in such a state of undress since the day their unwanted lodger first moved himself in.

'Making coffee?' she asked sleepily.

'Yeah,' said Kerry. 'There's not much milk though.'

'That's OK. I'll have it black. No sugar.'

'I thought you'd given coffee up?'

'I've taken it back on.' A recent report had shown that caffeine helps your body burn more calories in a resting state.

'He's used all the hot water again, you know.' Fiona usually gave the day five minutes before she started a diatribe about Gaetano. 'Selfish beast. I can't bear having a bath when it's tepid.'

'I've put the immersion heater on already,' said Kerry.

'Costs us a bloody fortune,' Fiona muttered. 'When Tim stays he only uses the cold tap.'

'Yes, well. Tim's obviously a nutter.'

Kerry poured out their extra-strong shots of instant life and shoved the last crust of a mouldy brown loaf into the toaster. 'We need some more bread,' she observed.

'It's Linzi's turn to buy but I'm not eating bread any more anyway,' Fiona replied. 'I think I may have an allergy to yeast and that's what makes me get so bloated the whole time.' She patted her washboard-flat stomach, then moved yawning to the sink and started to feel her way along the window-sill, lifting up the sorry-looking shrivelled plants in their pots without really seeing them.

'What are you looking for?' Kerry asked.

'My engagement ring,' Fiona replied through a yawn. 'I forgot to put it back on after I did the washing-up last night.' Her hand continued to creep along the sill like a blind man's. 'That's funny,' she said. 'It's not where I usually leave it.' She took the cup of coffee that Kerry offered while she knitted her brows together in deep thought. 'Perhaps I left it in the bathroom? No. I wouldn't have.' She took a sip from the scalding coffee and then put the cup down on the draining board. She leaned over the sink, careful not to let the ribbons around the neckline of her nightie drag in the cold dirty water of the night before, and scanned the sill more thoroughly. Nope. The ring definitely wasn't there.

'Maybe it dropped into the sink while you were washing up?' Kerry said helpfully, as she scraped a burnt layer off her toast and into the bin. The last slice was too precious to waste.

'I sincerely hope not.' Fiona rubbed nervously at the place where the ring had once been. Then, rolling up a sleeve and closing her eyes, she stuck a hand into the full sink with no small measure of distaste and felt around in the cold, food slime at the bottom. She spiked her finger on a forgotten fork and recoiled, wincing. 'This sink is just too disgusting,' she muttered. 'We've got to rewrite that cleaning rota.'

Kerry watched Fiona trawling through the sludge with the kind of squeamish joy you get when watching a gory horror film. Disappointed, Fiona pulled her hand out of the mire and rinsed it thoroughly clean beneath the hot tap.

'Nope. It's not in there,' she sighed.

'Perhaps you should have pulled the plug out.'

'Then it would have gone straight down the sink, stupid.'

'Oh, yeah. But hang on. You say that you washed up when you got home from work last night and, knowing the way you are about sinks, you would definitely have pulled the plug out when you finished. Right?' Fiona nodded. 'Which means that this water here is left over from Linzi's after-dinner attempt at household hygiene. Perhaps the ring went down the sink before Linzi even started to wash up.'

'Well done, Sherlock,' Fiona rolled her eyes. 'That's really good news.'

'Don't worry. If it has gone down the sink, it'll probably be stuck in the U-bend. That's what it's for. To catch stuff. When I was little, my mum lost one of her favourite earrings down the sink. Dad unscrewed the pipe and it was just sitting there in the U-bend. It had a little bit of sludge on it, but otherwise it was OK.'

Fiona had already opened the cupboard beneath the sink and was looking in despair at the twisty white pipe beneath.

'That's where it'll be,' Kerry pointed at the relevant curves.

'I just don't believe this,' Fiona moaned. 'It took me an age to persuade Tim to buy it, and now, less than two weeks later, I've managed to lose the damn thing.'

'Don't panic. We'll find it in there and Tim need be none the wiser.' Kerry was rather excited at the prospect of being proven right and once again asserting her position as the 'practical one' in the house.

'Are you sure we should be doing this?'

Kerry put a dirty pan beneath the U-bend to catch anything that might be lurking in the pipe. 'Trust me,' she said, 'I've never done this before in my life.'

But the U-bend provided no answers, just a horribly sulphuric smell adding fuel to the girls' theory that the previous tenant had dissolved his estranged wife in acid. An extensive search of the flowerpots on the window-sill proved equally inconclusive. As did the bathroom theory. And likewise a foray around all the possible flat surfaces in the sitting room. Fiona's composure was slipping. She collapsed on to the sofa, still in her Garfield slippers, and took her head in her hands.

'What could I have done with it, Kez? We've looked everywhere. I can't think of anywhere else it could be.'

They went through the possibility that she could have lost it somewhere outside the house. But it wasn't possible. After doing the washing-up, Fiona hadn't moved from her seat in front of the patched-up television until it was time to go to bed. There had been nothing to go out for. Tim was in Cambridge. On an old boys' rugby training weekend, again.

'The last time I saw it,' Fiona said painfully once more, 'was when I put it down on the window-sill before I did the washing-up. I wouldn't have let it fall into the sink. I know I wouldn't. I'm always so careful. It's got a thousand-odd pounds worth of diamonds stuck into it.'

Kerry didn't think this was the right time to mention that Fergie had managed to mislay half of the Crown Jewels at some American airport.

'Tim is going to kill me.'

'That'll save me having to buy a wedding present.'

Fiona wasn't amused.

'Kerry,' she whined, 'stop mucking about and help me out. As far as I can see, the only other possible answer is that I did leave it on the window-sill but that someone else had taken it by the time I got up this morning.'

'Don't be ridiculous. Nobody's been in here except the people that live here and why would any of us want to steal your engagement ring?'

At that moment, Linzi sloped into the sitting room wearing her boyfriend's best Motley Crue T-shirt. 'Hi guys. Has anyone seen Gaetano this morning? Nope? He must have already gone out. Can't believe the bastard didn't kiss me goodbye again.'

Fiona gave Kerry a very knowing look.

By the time Gaetano came back from the market with a new leather jacket draped over his arm, his guilt had practically been sealed. When he let himself into the house, with the extra key that Linzi had cut for him, against Fiona's express request,

he found the girls lined up along the sofa like a police interview panel. Fiona sat in the middle, still wearing her Garfield
slippers.

'I cannot believe that you actually think . . .' Linzi lamented.

When Gaetano walked into the room the girls fell suddenly
silent.

'Morning ladies. Looking lovely as usual. Do you want to see
what I just picked up at the market? It was a real bargain.'

He opened the plain white plastic carrier bag to show the girls
his new leather coat.

Fiona burst into tears and fled up the stairs.

'Jesus,' said Gaetano. 'What's the matter with her?'

'Nothing,' Kerry and Linzi said in unison as they followed
swiftly after her. Gaetano was left alone in the middle of the
sitting room with the leather jacket hanging half out of its bag.

'Are you going to ask him or do I have to?' Fiona hassled Linzi
upstairs in her bedroom.

'No way, Fiona. I am not going to ask my boyfriend if he has
stolen your engagement ring. It is a waste of time. He wouldn't
have done that to you. I can't believe that it even crossed your
mind that he would.'

'Well, I must admit that it didn't cross my mind that Gaetano
would be the type to cave in my television set until he actually
did it. What other explanation do you have for my ring's
disappearance?' Fiona countered. 'Last night it was on the
window-sill in the kitchen. This morning my ring is gone and
Gaetano has a new leather jacket.'

'Oh, come on. If he had stolen your ring do you think he
would be stupid enough to go out, sell the ring, buy himself
a new wardrobe with the proceeds, then come back here and
show it to you the very same morning? You've gone mad, Fiona.
Are you sure you've checked everywhere in the house?'

'I have looked everywhere,' Fiona was finding it difficult to
keep her voice down. 'My engagement ring is not in the house.
It is probably sitting in some East End pawn shop right now
and you're so blinded by lust for that stupid Italian that you're
refusing to see the truth.'

'The truth? For God's sake, Fi. Whose kind of truth is that?'

Kerry, who had been sitting on the edge of Fiona's bed trying to keep out of it, suddenly looked towards the door and widened her eyes in a desperate gesture to get them to shut up. The door creaked open. Gaetano stood in the doorway, the new leather jacket still grasped in his hand.

'What's going on?' he asked. 'What are you all whispering about? It's something to do with me, isn't it?'

'Yes. No,' the girls chorused at once. Fiona rose slowly from her seat at the dressing table, rubbing the spot where her ring had once been like some tragic Shakespearean heroine. 'Gaetano,' she cleared her throat, 'have you seen my engagement ring?'

He shook his head.

'Are you sure? Only, last night I put it on the window-sill in the kitchen while I washed up and this morning, when I went to find it, the ring wasn't there.'

Gaetano shrugged.

'We've searched everywhere in the house . . . Have you taken it?'

'Fiona!!!' They could practically see the smoke pouring out of Linzi's nose.

'What do you mean, have I taken it?' Gaetano asked quietly.

'I mean, have you moved my engagement ring? Did you see it on the sill and put it somewhere else for safe-keeping perhaps?'

Linzi shook her head in despair. She didn't dare look at Gaetano but she knew only too well the furious expression which would at that moment be forming in his eyes.

'What you're really asking is whether I have stolen it, right?' Gaetano stared straight at her. Fiona nodded automatically and stared back, her chin jutting out proudly. 'And the answer to your question is no. Of course I haven't taken it. I've got no need to go stealing things like your poxy little ring, Fiona.'

'It is not a poxy little ring,' Fiona said indignantly. 'It is worth more than two thousand pounds.'

'And I can win two thousand pounds on a single night at the greyhound track. I've got no need to steal anything of yours, you bitch,' he hissed. 'Unlike you, I've got my pride.'

But Gaetano moved himself and his pride out of number 67 that very night. Had she been able to, Linzi would have followed him. But, since he was going back to his family home and she already knew exactly what Gaetano's mother thought of her, it didn't seem like such a good idea. However, she arranged to meet him at the pub as soon as he had dumped his stuff. In view of the mood he had been in since she stayed out all night at a 'job interview', Linzi didn't want to leave him alone to brood for too long. Fiona decided to go to Tim's house for the evening. Kerry was just relieved to have them both out of the house. Despite the fact that in the confusion caused by the missing ring they had both completely forgotten that it was her birthday.

Kerry opened the red envelope from her mother. Inside was a floral card printed with 'Happy Birthday Darling Daughter' in gold and signed by Mum, Dad and The Dog. As she opened it, a twenty pound note fluttered to the floor. For a moment she considered blowing it on two bottles of vodka and drinking herself into Monday. What a miserable way to turn twenty-five that would be.

But then the phone rang. She picked it up on the second ring.

'Hey, what are you doing in on a Saturday night, Cinderella?'

Her heart did a little back-flip of joy.

'And it's your birthday isn't it?'

'Leon?'

'That's me. How come you're not out partying, Birthday Girl?'

'Oh, I don't know. There was a bit of a disaster here today. Fiona has lost her engagement ring and she's blaming its disappearance on Linzi's boyfriend. You know him. Gaetano.'

'Mmmm. Of course I know him. Have to say I wouldn't be surprised . . .'

'Whatever. Anyway, they were too busy arguing with each other to remember what day it was.'

'And they forgot your birthday? Those people you live with are unbelievable, Kerry. They're supposed to be your friends,' Leon sighed. 'But listen, my darling, all is not lost. I just called to say Happy Birthday. Didn't expect you to be in really but Jeremy and I are going to Heaven tonight. Do you want to come along?'

'Heaven? Sure. What's that?'

'It's a club. You'll love it. We're on the guest list. I think Jeremy used to sleep with the guy that's doing the lights so we won't have to pay to get in.'

'But I'm not on the guest list, am I?'

'You will be by tonight, Cinderella. Look, I can't yack on, because I'm using Jeremy's phone. Can you believe I got cut off? I gave Sam the money to pay the bill last month but he obviously put it towards the joint bank account of Dolce & Gabbana instead. I'll meet you outside the club at ten o'clock. Its near Charing Cross. You know that alley that goes down to Embankment? Wear something funky, birthday girl. Wear that green shirt of yours. I'll see you at ten.'

'Yeah. See you then.'

Kerry put down the phone. It was already eight o'clock. Two hours hardly seemed anywhere near long enough to get ready for an evening with Leon.

CHAPTER SEVENTEEN

Two hours wasn't anywhere near long enough to get ready for an evening with Leon.

When Kerry got off the tube at Charing Cross, she was half an hour late. She scanned the queue for Heaven nervously, praying that Leon wouldn't have gone inside without her. It took a couple of minutes before she caught sight of him with great relief. He was standing near the front of the queue, wearing a pair of white jeans and a tight black vest beneath his silver puffa jacket. His companion, who must be Jeremy, was a tall shaven-headed man in tartan trousers and a tight white T-shirt. Smooth-finished was obviously Leon's type.

Leon seemed very pleased to see Kerry. He kissed her on both cheeks and pulled her into the queue beside him. A thin-faced man standing behind them tutted at her intrusion and she was sure she heard him mutter 'fag hag'.

'Take no notice of that bloody queen,' Leon whispered. 'He's been driving us nuts for the last half-hour. Keeps telling his mate the story of how he once met Boy George at some rave. But darling, I said, haven't we all?' The thin-faced man fumed quietly.

The queue shuffled forward three or four steps before the bouncer fastened the red rope gate behind the lucky few once more.

'I can't believe this queue,' Leon's friend complained. 'How long have we been here? Twenty-four bloody hours?' He picked up Leon's wrist and pushed up his sleeve to look at his watch. 'Oooh, that's a nice piece, Leon. But what happened to your Tag?'

'Sam borrowed it . . .'

Jeremy raised an eyebrow.

'And then he put it in the wash.'

'I thought that they were meant to be waterproof.'

'Yeah, they are. I don't think they're designed to take Persil Colour though.'

'How come we're waiting in the queue?' Kerry asked suddenly. 'I thought that we were going to be on the guest list.'

'Darling,' said Jeremy. 'This is the queue for the guest list. I certainly had no idea that Marvin knew so many people and to be frank with you, I'm gutted. I'm also Jeremy, by the way.'

'I guessed you might be. I'm Kerry.' She extended her hand and retracted it somewhat awkwardly when Jeremy looked at her overly polite gesture with surprise.

'You're the birthday girl, aren't you?' he continued. 'Leon tells me that all your nasty friends have forgotten you today.' She blushed bright crimson. Had he introduced her as 'Kerry-no-mates'? 'But we're going to make sure that you have a wonderful time tonight, aren't we, Leon?'

Leon nodded. 'We certainly are.'

'If we ever actually make it inside, that is,' Jeremy added with a sniff. 'Who would have thought that this little shit-hole would become quite so popular with our set?'

The queue moved forward again. Leon and Jeremy slipped beyond the barrier. The bouncer stopped Kerry with a rough hand against her chest before she could follow.

'Wait there,' he said gruffly.

'But she's with us,' insisted Leon. 'Her name's on the list.'

Genghis couldn't have cared less. 'Are you a lesbian?' he asked her bluntly. Kerry felt her mouth fall open. She hadn't expected this. Was she supposed to be? It suddenly struck her that she hadn't seen a single other girl in the queue.

'I'm with them. I'm on the guest list actually,' Kerry squeaked.

'I didn't ask if you're on the list, I asked if you are a lesbian.'

'Oooh, don't be so personal . . .'

The bouncer was suddenly joined by a seven-foot-tall version of a young, black Danny La Rue. 'Come on through here, dear,' the transvestite smiled and lifted the red rope from her path. He fingered Kerry's furry fake ocelot collar enviously as she passed through. 'I do like your coat. Where's it from? Can I try it on?' he asked, already plucking the coat from Kerry's shoulders. It was a small price to pay to get past Genghis Khan.

But putting the said coat away was only slightly more straight-forward than getting through the door. The queues for the cloakroom wound almost right around the dance floor and when Kerry finally did get to the front, the boy in charge of hanging up the coats didn't seem to want to know. Seeing three boys in sailor suits push in front of her, Leon finally came to her rescue and handed Kerry's coat over himself. The cloakroom attendant handed Leon a ticket with a wink.

'This place is weird. It's like I'm invisible because I'm a girl,' Kerry said in disbelief as they waited again at the bar.

'I can see you and you look divine.' Leon gave her a hug. 'I'll admit it must seem a little strange here but you'll soon settle in. It's a great place to people-watch.' He jerked his head towards a blond twenty-something Adonis who was standing on the shiny bar and grinding his pelvis against an aluminium pole erected expressly for the purpose. The blond was wearing nothing but a black leather G-string and some painful kind of harness made from heavy silver chain. Leon sighed. 'No wonder they call it Heaven.'

Kerry looked up at the taut brown buttocks gyrating inches away from her head. 'Yeah. I see what you mean,' she replied. But she felt a pang of jealousy that Leon could be interested in something she most definitely was not and would never be. Whatever happened to the 'whole person thing' Leon had talked about at Michelle's wedding? Leon handed her a beer and a bottle of Evian.

'Is this for you?' she asked, looking at the Evian.

'No,' he said. 'But I've got one for me as well.'

'I didn't really want any water.'

'You will in a minute. Come on. I said we'd see Jeremy over there as soon as we got served.'

They pushed their way through the crowd towards a tiny tunnel between the bar and the cloakrooms that was lit with fluorescent purple light and papered with pictures of variously naked and strangely-clad male torsos. As they moved forward, people stepped aside to let Leon pass, but they moved only grudgingly for Kerry. It was as if she didn't know the magic word. She bumped into the greased up biceps of someone twice her size but when he turned around to say 'Sorry' it sounded as though he had just taken a suck from a balloon filled with helium.

Jeremy was already in the tunnel, deeply involved in conversation with a man who looked almost as out of place as Kerry did in his pale blue jeans and neatly tucked-in chambray shirt amongst all that glitter. The man disappeared into the crowd again before Kerry and Leon reached them. Jeremy was grinning. He gave Leon the thumbs-up sign. 'Got three,' he mouthed.

'How much was it?' Leon asked.

'Fifteen each.'

'Not bad, I suppose. I'll pay for Kerry's.'

'Pay for my what?'

'For your birthday present, of course,' Leon smiled.

'Oh Leon, you didn't have to get me anything.'

'Well, just have it now before I change my mind and keep it for myself. Reach for my hand like you're going to hold it. Don't look at what I've given you until you're in the loos and behind a locked door. I know you, Kerry Keble, you're indiscreet. You'll get us thrown in jail.'

'Hey? What do you mean? What is it?' Kerry asked excitedly.

'Its an "E",' said Jeremy in a stage whisper. 'Ecstasy. You must have done one before?'

'No, I haven't actually,' Kerry told him prissily.

'Oh, then this should be a real laugh. You'll have a great time tonight, my dear.' Jeremy put his hand up to his mouth and, though he didn't seem to have put anything into it, he swallowed, then gave a little shimmy of delight. 'It'll make you feel sublime.'

'I don't know if I really want to do this,' Kerry started to tell them.

'Don't be such a chicken, Kerry,' Leon told her. 'You'll be OK. Everybody does it here. It's the only way I can stand this stupid music. You won't have visions or anything like that. It'll just make you feel really mellow and like you want to dance all night. I promise you, you'll have a great time.' He pressed the small white tablet into Kerry's hand. 'You can just take half of it if you want.'

'No way,' Jeremy butted in. 'That's when people start to have

bad trips. You've got to take the whole thing at once.' Kerry
looked from one to the other in confusion. She knew plenty of
people who had taken ecstasy but had never thought that she
would be one of them. Now she had been handed a tablet by
her boss. The school drug-talk pictures of pushers and broken
down heroin addicts sitting in the gutter seemed a thousand
miles away from this glittery reality.

'Do you take this stuff often?' she asked Leon.

'Often enough. I took one at your sister's wedding to help me
get through the reception.'

'Leon!! You didn't!' Kerry's jaw dropped to her chest.

'I'm afraid I had to. How else do you think I managed to dance
with your Auntie Jean for so long? I could have used some acid
as well that night to be honest with you.' Leon's face cracked
into that familiar friendly smile. Kerry couldn't believe that he
had taken ecstasy at her sister's wedding. She hadn't noticed him
behaving particularly oddly then.

'Look,' Jeremy continued his lecture. 'It's no worse than
drinking alcohol, right? And you won't feel half so out-of-control
as you do when you're pissed. Just remember to keep drinking
water so that you don't dehydrate and you'll be fine. Oh, damn
it. Leon, I forgot to get some chewing gum again.'

'Good job one of us is on the ball.' Leon fished a packet of
Spearmint Wrigley's out of his pocket and handed a bendy stick
to his friend.

'Leon, you're a true life saver. I tell you, there's nothing worse
than waking up the morning after a fabulous night out with a
mouth ulcer the size of a saucer. You'll need some of this stuff
too, Kerry. It's in case you start to grind your teeth.'

'Grind my teeth?' Kerry stood between them, still holding the
tablet tightly in one fist and now the stick of chewing gum in
the other. 'That sounds terrible. Is there anything else should I
know about this stuff?'

'Nothing. Just get on with it, Kerry,' Leon insisted. 'The night
is slipping away.'

'I'll go and take it in the loo,' she told them. 'Swallowing tablets
always makes me gag.'

'OK. Be quick.'

She left them in the tunnel and headed for the ladies.

Once safely inside a cubicle, Kerry opened her fist. The tablet

Leon had given her was as small as a contraceptive pill, a pill she had been taking every day for the last three years though she hadn't had the faintest whiff of a shag in all that time. What was the difference, she asked herself, between taking a prescribed tablet that fucked up her ovaries every day of the month and taking one illegal tablet, once only, that at the very worst would make her dance all night? She stared at the little white circle which was stamped with a tiny dove. Ecstasy had been used in some bona fide medical cases, hadn't it? That meant that it must be safe in moderation and surely one tablet was moderate. But then again, Miss Sensible butted in, what if it had been cut with something terrible? Something like those horse tranquillisers that made you instantly paralysed from the neck down. She'd heard about that. And the thought of being unable to stop herself from grinding her teeth wasn't particularly appealing either.

She could just flush it down the loo and pretend to have taken it. Kerry could dance about like a loon with the best of them.

But how long could she seriously hope to pretend to be deliriously happy for?

And how long would they actually expect her to pretend to be deliriously happy for?

Kerry unscrewed the lid of her water bottle.

'It'll be OK,' she told herself. She put the tablet on the tip of her tongue. 'I'm here with Jeremy and Leon. Loads of people are taking E. I bet Linzi does it every weekend. Everything will be OK.' She swallowed the tablet, feeling it sliding slowly all the way down the back of her throat as if it were the size of a frozen pea. Then she drank half the bottle of Evian straight off to prime her kidneys for the dehydration, just in case. She'd gone and done it now.

When she came out of the cubicle, Kerry looked at herself carefully in the mirror, paying particular attention to the size of her pupils. She looked exactly the same as she had done a few minutes before. Exactly the same. Nothing had happened yet. She sneaked a glance at the other girls waiting patiently in the queue. No one seemed to be regarding her any differently than before. She wondered how long she had before the insignificantly tiny tablet started to take effect.

When she found Leon and Jeremy again they were jigging

from foot to foot on the spot, like two greyhounds in the
trap at the start of a race, raring to go. They smiled widely.
Leon mouthed 'You've been ages. You OK?' The music seemed
louder already, though that might have been simply because
they had turned the volume up. Leon led the way out on to
the dance floor. Kerry unwrapped her chewing gum and started
chewing. She took another swig of water. It seemed really easy
to dance.

'It's like putting on the "red shoes", isn't it?' Jeremy commented. 'You know, the "red shoes" in that film that made the
girl dance until she died from exhaustion?'

Kerry nodded. It had been one of her favourite films as
a child.

'It's going to be a good night tonight. I can tell. I can smell it. I
can feel it in the air. Who-ooh!!!' Jeremy stripped off his T-shirt
and started to samba his way deeper into the crowd. 'Watch out
sailors, dancing queen coming through.'

'I'll stay right next to you,' Leon promised as Jeremy disappeared. 'Are you still feeling all right?'

Kerry smiled and nodded. 'I think so.' He had touched her
arm and the place where his fingers had brushed her skin was
still vibrating at that touch. She was getting into the music in
a way she had never imagined possible before. The bass notes
seemed to be coming from somewhere inside her. She chewed
her gum harder and grinned.

'Yeah, yeah. I think I'm OK.'

CHAPTER EIGHTEEN

When Linzi arrived at the pub where she had promised to meet Gaetano for a drink, he was already there, sitting at a table by the jukebox, with two unfamiliar girls. When she joined them, Gaetano didn't bother to introduce her or make any attempt to bring her into the conversation. Linzi nursed a pint of lager silently until the girls decided they should leave to make sure that they got into the club they wanted to go to. As they were leaving, the taller and more attractive of the two leaned across the table and kissed Gaetano very firmly and unashamedly on the lips. Her long blonde hair fell across his smug face like a curtain.

Linzi fumed.

'Thanks for introducing me to your friends.'

Gaetano shrugged and took a swig from his pint.

'Who were they?'

'Fans of the band.'

'Yes? Well, she certainly seemed to be a very big fan of yours.' Linzi sneered at the retreating back of the taller girl, whose short black skirt was clinging for dear life to the flesh of her thighs just below her buttocks.

'You're not getting jealous, are you?' Gaetano asked, as he tried to suppress a proud grin.

'I think I'd have every right to be if I was.'

'You are getting jealous.'

'I am not. But I am supposed to be your girlfriend, Gaetano. You could show me just a little more concern.'

'Oh, really,' Gaetano sneered. 'So, if you're my girlfriend, why didn't you show me some concern and stand up for me this afternoon when your stupid friend accused me of stealing her engagement ring?'

'I did stand up for you.'

Gaetano snorted into his drink.

'Well, what was I supposed to do, G?' Linzi protested. 'Other than say that you didn't do it? Call for forensic tests? You hardly handled the situation very well yourself. You know that Fiona has had it in for you since the day you ruined her television.'

'And whose fault was that?'

'What are you suggesting? That it was my fault?'

'If you hadn't stayed out all night putting yourself about to get some stupid little job, I wouldn't have been so angry when you finally got home.'

'I wasn't putting it about.' Linzi felt her cheeks flushing red. 'I was having a friendly drink with my future boss. He offered me the job and then he asked me to have a drink with him to help us to get to know each other. What was I supposed to do? You can hardly refuse your new boss's first request, can you?'

'You could have gone for one drink and been home long before you were,' Gaetano hissed.

'We got talking. We were getting along really well.'

'You don't talk to your secretary all night without wanting something more from her than her typing speed. Did you give in to his second request as well?'

'Gaetano, we've been through this a dozen times. I thought that we'd sorted it out. Nothing happened between me and that man.'

'I don't know if I can trust you any more.'

'Trust me? What about you? How can I trust you?' Linzi tried to change the angle. 'I walk in here tonight to find you sitting with another girl who kissed you like she knew you very well indeed when she got up to leave.' Gaetano shrugged. 'Perhaps we should go back to your place now so that I can kick your television to pieces in a blind rage. Or perhaps your mother's television. After all, there wouldn't be much love lost there.'

'Leave my mother out of this,' Gaetano said quietly.

'Why? She hasn't kept her nose out of my business so far,' Linzi snarled.

'You know what, Linzi? I'm beginning to think that what my mother says about you might be true. You English girls really don't have a sense of decency. You've got no modesty. Shouting at me and making a show of yourself in a public place. When it comes down to it, none of you are any good to a man. You deserted me today on the word of your mad friend, instead of standing by me when she accused me of common theft.'

Linzi was open-mouthed. 'Gaetano! How dare you say that? You know that I believe you . . .'

'I'm not so sure.' Gaetano drained his pint and got to his feet. 'I'm going now. I said I would meet the Professor in the Dog. You can go back to your stupid friends if you want.' He stalked towards the door. Linzi gathered up her coat and skipped after him.

'Wait, G. You can't just walk out like that after saying all those things to me.'

'Just try and stop me.'

Gaetano crossed the road outside the pub and headed for the Dog and Duck. As they reached the other pavement, Linzi managed to get just close enough to him to grasp the sleeve of his leather jacket.

'Get off me,' he spat.

'Gaetano. Come on. This isn't fair. Why won't you listen to me for a minute? Why is it always you that's right?'

'Get off me,' he hissed in warning.

'No, I won't get off you. I want to sort this out now. I'm sick of your black moods. I've had to put up with Fiona getting at me the whole time and now you're having a go as well. I was doing you a favour, letting you stay at my place. You spoiled it. You were the one who didn't make an effort to fit in. You wrecked the television. Honestly, I don't think I've met anyone so childish in the whole of my life.'

Linzi's head was flying backwards before she felt the back of his hand make contact with her cheek. When she regained her balance, her face was stinging as though it had been branded with a red-hot iron. She clasped a cool hand to her burning skin. Gaetano was frozen to the spot in front of her. His hand hovered in mid-air.

'Oh, my God. You hit me?' Linzi said the words as though she couldn't quite believe they were true. 'You hit me. You fucking bastard. You hit me.'

Gaetano just stared.

Linzi brought her fingers down across her lip. 'I'm not bleeding am I?' She took her fingers away from her face to look at them. They were clean but the pain in her head had grown so bad and so quickly that she though she might black out at any moment. 'God, I can't believe you just did that,' she murmured. 'I don't think I ever want to see you again.'

But Gaetano had taken hold of her arms now. His face was creased into a terrified frown. 'God, Linzi. I'm sorry. I didn't mean to do that to you. You forced me to. Are you OK? I'm sorry. I'm really sorry. You made me do it. Say that you believe me.'

Linzi's jaw hung slack. She had never been hit before in her life. Not even as a child. Her parents were far too liberal. Whenever she read about such things happening in *Cosmo* she would close the magazine with a snort, unable to see why those stupid battered women hadn't run away at the first slap. Why they just stood there and waited to become a human punchbag. Now she was just standing there too.

'You hit me,' she whimpered again.

Gaetano was crying now. The fat tears ran down his cheeks and into his open mouth which was still wailing lame excuses. 'I didn't mean to do it. I was too drunk to stop myself,' he wailed. 'I didn't want to hurt you, Linzi. I swear I didn't. You made me do it, Linzi. You made me . . . I was angry because I love you.'

'I really, really love you. I really, really love you.' An hour and a half after taking her first E, this single thought was beating through Kerry Keble's head in time with the music. 'I really, really love you.' She gazed straight at Leon. He was dancing with his arms above his head. His eyes were closed. His mouth curled upwards at the corners in a beatific smile. 'I really, really love you.' Kerry felt the same smile stretch across her face until her head was almost split in two by a grin. She wanted to tell Leon what she was thinking. That she really, really loved him. It seemed so important that he should know right now. She reached out and took hold of one of his hands. He carried on dancing as he leaned in close to hear what she had to say. Both still dancing. Never missing a beat.

'I really, really love you, Leon,' she told him.

'Hey, yeah,' he cracked his chewing gum. 'I really love you too, Kerry.'

He kissed her, right on the mouth, then he raised his hands high in the air and turned in a little circle. Jeremy moved back towards him until they were almost bumping hips. They pulled Kerry in between them and danced like a skin sandwich for a bit. As they were dancing like that, Leon kissed Kerry on the top of her head. Kerry in turn planted a wet kiss on Jeremy's bare chest just above his left nipple. It made him squeal.

CHAPTER NINETEEN

Tim was cooking. A rare occurrence. Fiona assumed that he was donning the apron to cheer her up after the most terrible day of her life. She had called him in Cambridge and hearing how distressed she was about the disappearance of her ring, he had actually excused himself from another night of drinking away the benefit of the rugby match he had played that afternoon. If he hadn't, Fiona told him, she didn't know what she might have done in her grief.

Now Tim was chopping an onion silently while Fiona sat at the kitchen table and nursed a glass of chilled rosé.

'I can't believe it,' she began again. 'I was always so very careful with that ring. I took it off every single time I washed up to protect it from the suds and made sure that I put it on again afterwards. I can't think how I could have forgotten. Maybe it slipped my mind when the telephone rang as I was drying up. It was a call from Mum. She wanted to know if it would be all right to invite some of the neighbours to the wedding. I said, yes. That's OK with you, isn't it?'

Tim shrugged.

'Anyway, we searched absolutely everywhere. Got the cushions out of the sofa, everything. Checked beneath the sink. The only possible explanation is that the ring isn't in the house at all. You should have seen Gaetano's face, Tim. He looked so embarrassed when I confronted him.'

'I would be embarrassed too if someone accused me of theft,' Tim reasoned as he tipped the onions into a saucepan.

'Only if you had something to hide.'

'How can you be sure it was him, Fi?'

'Because if he was innocent, Tim, he wouldn't have left the house in such a hurry, would he? He would have stood his ground. And that's another dodgy thing. I mean, Linzi kept on and on about how Gaetano couldn't possibly go home because of the row he had had with his mother and then, as soon as it suits him, the supposed dragon welcomes him back into the nest with open arms. He is as guilty as sin. I don't know how Linzi can live with herself.'

Tim was raking through the drawer for the tin-opener. It wasn't where he had left it. In fact, whenever the tin-opener went missing it usually turned up somewhere really bizarre. Like on the shelf in the bathroom. He had a suspicion that it was something to do with his housemate, another guy who worked at BFO Schwartz. He was a little older than Tim, a bit higher up the company and often stayed away on business. When he was around, Tim tried to avoid him.

'You need to be able to trust your housemates,' Fiona continued. 'If you had done to Linzi what Gaetano's done to me, I know exactly whose side of the argument I would have come down on.' She turned the wine bottle around and studied its label. Tim didn't comment. Probably, like Fiona, he knew that in such a situation she would have been at his side in a shot.

'Is it covered by the insurance?'

Tim sighed. They had been through this on the phone that afternoon and five or six times since then. 'Yes, it is on the insurance. Are you trying to catch me out on this or something?'

'No. But are you really sure, Tim? Doesn't your credit card just cover things for a few days after you've bought them?'

'The ring is covered, Fiona. You don't think I would have spent that much money without taking out some kind of insurance, do you? I mean, you could chuck me next week and hurl the ring into the gutter just like my Mum did. Then where would I be?'

'You're not insured in case we split up, are you?' Fiona was horrified.

'No, of course not,' Tim smiled. 'You can't get insured for that kind of thing.'

'I sincerely hope you haven't looked into the possibility.'

Tim snorted. There was the germ of a great business idea there.

'How long do you think it will take for a claim to go through?'

Fiona continued. 'It's strange, but I feel naked without it already. Sometimes, when I'm not thinking about it, it almost feels as if the ring is still there. I was just getting used to it. But we don't actually have to wait for the money to come through before we get a new one, do we? If you use your credit card again we could get one on Monday and you won't have to pay for it until the end of next month. We could meet up at lunchtime. Now that we know what we're looking for it shouldn't take us half as long as the first trip to the shops did.'

Fiona's voice was momentarily drowned out by the frantic sizzling of the onions as the oil heated up and began to cook them transparent.

'Monday lunchtime?' Fiona repeated hopefully. 'What do you think, Timbo?'

Tim shifted his weight from one foot to the other and continued to stir the onions around in the pan. He didn't turn to look at her as he began, 'I don't know, Fi. My credit card's nearly right up to the limit as it is. I might have some kind of emergency this month and if I've filled up my card, I'll be stuffed. You can wait a while, can't you?'

Fiona rubbed at the naked base of her middle finger.

'You mean until next month?'

'Or the month after?' Tim said hopefully. 'That would be better for me.'

'But Tim,' Fiona whined. 'We'll be right into preparations for the wedding by then! I can't go through my whole engagement without having a ring to wear!'

'Fetch a couple of plates out of the cupboard, could you?' Tim commanded.

'We could get it on my card and you could pay me back. Or you could get your credit limit extended. You've had a pay rise. It shouldn't be a problem.'

Tim took the cold plates from her hands and put them under the grill to warm up as he cooked.

'How about that?' she asked hopefully.

'Let's talk about it later,' Tim replied. 'I'm burning the onions.'

'You want onions on this?'

Linzi sat on the hard plastic bench beneath the unforgiving UV light in an all-night café. Gaetano was at the counter. Getting their hot dogs. The man behind the counter seemed to be taking ages with the unnaturally orange sausages. Gaetano didn't want to be away from Linzi for too long. In case she decided to give him the slip.

Linzi was playing with the salt cellar. Pouring out a few thousand grains of salt at a time and forming them into a pattern. She made a heart, then smashed it into nothing with her finger. Gaetano sat down opposite her and placed her hot dog where the heart had been seconds before.

'Say something to me,' he pleaded. 'You haven't said anything to me since outside the pub.'

Linzi picked a long, stringy piece of burnt onion from the top of her hot dog and folded it into her mouth. What was she doing here? She wanted to go to the bathroom and look at her cheek. Check out the damage. It was still stinging like crazy. She picked up the ketchup, squeezing the unyielding plastic bottle momentarily distracted her from the pain.

'Oh, come on, Linz. You know I'm sorry. I've said it a thousand times. What more do you want me to do? You know that I'm not normally like that. I'd never have hit you if you hadn't got me so fired up. I was jealous about that guy who took you for a drink. You're the most beautiful girl I've ever met, Linz. I don't want to lose you to some flash bastard, that's all. I'll never meet anyone better than you if you go. You're beautiful even when you're crying . . .'

Linzi looked up from her hot dog, which she had no intention of eating, and met Gaetano's eyes for the first time since it had happened. His gaze penetrated hers desperately, begging for forgiveness.

'If we weren't in the middle of a café, I would go down on my knees for you right now,' Gaetano insisted. 'I swear I would.' Linzi looked unimpressed. 'Ah, what the hell. I will.' Gaetano slid from his seat until he was on his knees on the dirty floor beside her. He buried his head in her lap. Two beery middle-aged men in Arsenal shirts told him not to do it. Not to propose.

'Linzi,' Gaetano continued in a low whisper that she had to bend over to hear. 'I need you. I know that we've only known each other for a short time, but if you call things off now, I don't know what I'll do without you. You're part of my life now. I've been making all my plans around you. I can't carry on if you're not there.'

'Gaetano,' Linzi murmured. 'You can get up on your seat again. Everyone's watching you, you're ruining your trousers and I think that I've just about got the message.'

'Are you still going to go?' He scrambled back into his seat. His eyes were wet with tears.

Linzi reached across the sticky table and took his hand. 'No,' she told him. 'I'll give it one more chance.'

Gaetano lifted her hand to his mouth and kissed it extravagantly. 'You won't regret it, Linzi. We're going to be perfect together. I promise you.'

The men at the counter shook their heads sadly.

'All downhill from now on, mate,' the fatter guy said wisely.

When he had eaten both their hot dogs, Gaetano drew a couple of hundred pounds out of a cashpoint and insisted that they make it up immediately in a rather bland Covent Garden hotel. Later, when he had fallen asleep, Linzi listened to the white noise of the air-conditioning and wondered whether she had done the right thing. She looked at Gaetano's face. Relaxed, relieved, reformed. She decided that she had.

After all, even her mother's King Charles Spaniel had been allowed three bites before it was put down.

CHAPTER TWENTY

J eremy had been right. It had been a great evening, possibly one of the greatest nights in a club Kerry could ever
remember, but she was still pretty glad when Leon announced
that he'd had enough and wanted to go home, saving Kerry
the embarrassment of being the first to flake out. There was
no queue at the cloakroom window now and the attendant
even managed a smile as he handed Kerry their coats. In fact
everybody seemed to be smiling. Leon collected a couple of flyers
from Kerry's transvestite heroine on the way out.

'Coming again next week?' Leon asked Kerry as he helped
her to slip on her coat, for which the transvestite had offered
fifty pounds in cash.

'Maybe,' Kerry replied.

'So you had a good time?'

'I did.'

'You feel OK?'

'OK? Leon, I feel like I've been plugged straight into the
mains.' The music was still pumping in her head even though
they were outside now. It felt as though her brain was shimmy-
ing against her skull.

'That's good,' Leon told her. 'But take it easy now, yeah? For
a moment earlier on I was pretty worried about you.'

'I was just a bit scared, that's all. I didn't know how I was
going to react, did I? I don't normally "do drugs".'

'Do drugs?' Leon laughed. 'You make it sound like we spent
the evening shooting up heroin. Where's Jeremy gone now?'
Jeremy was lingering by the cloakroom, extracting a phone
number and a quick tongue wrestle from a man twice his

width and half his height. Kerry winced. It didn't look terribly romantic. Just rough.

'Jeez. That man has such bad taste,' Leon commented.

Short Fat Baldy disappeared back into the crowd and Jeremy came skipping out into the street after Leon and Kerry, wearing a gormless, pleased expression on his face which Kerry had no doubt had often lived on hers. Especially lately.

'Strike three,' Jeremy said exultantly. 'Three telephone numbers in one night. Am I the hottest thing in this place or what? And how did you two fare, my dear little children?'

'You know I'm not in the mood for casual affairs any more,' Leon reminded him.

'Which means that he couldn't even manage to pull a muscle,' Jeremy translated. 'And how about you, Birthday Girl?'

'I was hardly in the market,' Kerry laughed.

'What on earth do you mean, Kerry-darling? There was a girl in the bar upstairs who was the absolute spit of kd Lang.'

'Jeremy,' said Leon. 'I don't think kd Lang is exactly Kerry's type.'

They wandered up the narrow road that led to The Strand. Leon and Kerry linked arms. Jeremy walked along in front of them, weaving from one side of the pavement to the other, doing the occasional pirouette, feeling, he claimed, 'as light as a feather'. The sky was clear after a cloudy day and though you couldn't see many of the stars because of the dreadful ambient light central London gives off, Kerry had a feeling that there were a lot of them up there. They were all twinkling down at her, wishing her a 'Happy Birthday'. And it was.

'Where to now, folks?' Jeremy asked, when they had reached The Strand and stood at the edge of the pavement as though they stood on the bank of the Thames. 'Anybody ready for a bit of rough Trade?'

Trade was the place where everyone who was anyone went after Heaven. It didn't start until most other clubs had finished and it went on way past dawn.

'I don't think so,' said Leon. 'I'm not sure we'll be able to get Kerry in for a start. They've been having a crack down on girls lately. Besides, I could use some sleep tonight.'

'So I'm on my own,' Jeremy pouted.

'I guess you are.'

'Then cheerio, *mes chers*.' He kissed them farewell on both
cheeks and disappeared in the direction of the nearest black
cab, sharing a fare with a couple of guys who were wearing
matching blue feather boas. In the meantime, Kerry's legs had
given in and she was sitting on the edge of the pavement. Leon
crouched down and lifted her up by the armpits.

'Can't stop there,' he told her. 'We've just got to make it across
Trafalgar Square to the Nightbus. Then you can fall asleep if
you like.'

'But I need to sit down now, Leon. Please,' Kerry pleaded. 'I
don't think I've ever danced so much in my life. My legs are
broken. I swear they are.'

She swayed dangerously. Leon himself was too tired to hold
her up for very long.

'OK,' he conceded as his knees buckled beneath her weight.
'Plan B. We'll get as far as the fountains. Then you can splash
your face to wake yourself up a bit and we'll catch a cab home
instead.'

'No, no more water!!!' she wailed.

'Just for your face,' said Leon. 'You don't have to drink it.'

'Are you coming back to my house with me?' Kerry asked
pathetically.

'I think I better had, don't you? I don't suppose you can even
remember the right address.'

'I can. It's 67, Archeesia, I mean, Artesia Road.'

'Right.'

The traffic lights changed and they limped across The Strand
to Trafalgar Square. All around, people were gathering at the
Nightbus-stops but the square itself was almost empty. Leon
walked Kerry as far as the nearest fountain and helped her
clamber on to the marble wall that surrounded it. She trailed
a hand in the cold, black water and tried ineffectively to splash
her face once or twice, getting more of it down her neck than
on her cheeks. Then she shut her eyes and leaned back so far
on the narrow wall that Leon thought she was going to fall in.
Thinking that it was probably a good idea to get her away from
anything potentially fatal for a while, Leon led her instead to the
foot of Nelson's Column and the great bronze lions that guarded
it. There, he popped her on to the wall, then quickly climbed up
beside her and took her icy hands in his to warm them.

'Where's your circulation gone, Kerry? You're scaring me now,' he said. 'Are you sure you're feeling OK?'

'I'm just really tired,' Kerry whined. 'And I feel a bit sick from drinking all that water. I just want to go home.'

'We will in a minute, I promise.' He rubbed her hands briskly between his palms until they began to tingle and Kerry pulled them away. Then she leaned back into him and tried to tuck herself inside his coat to keep warm. Leon pulled one arm out of its sleeve to make it easier for her.

'Can we go home now?'

'Not while you still look like you might be sick. No taxi driver is going to pick us up until you've had a bit of air and come round. The quicker you look sensible, the quicker we can go.'

'I'm always sensible. My mother says so.'

'Yes, I'm sure she does. But your mother also keeps saying that I'm an Australian.'

He tried to do the puffa jacket up around Kerry's back but had little success. Instead he pulled her closer into his arms. 'Warmer now?'

'Mmm. Cuddle me,' she murmured. 'People will think that we're in love.'

Leon gave a grunt of amusement. 'I suppose it is kind of romantic this, isn't it?' he mused. 'Sitting in Trafalgar Square in the middle of the night.'

'Mm-hmm,' Kerry agreed.

'Sometimes,' Leon continued, 'when you're living in London you can start to forget just how beautiful the city really is. I mean, look at the National Gallery now. And that church over there. Look at all these lovely buildings around us. London is as beautiful as Paris ever knew how to be tonight. Except that I never did get to see Paris, did I?'

He looked up at the sky a little sadly.

'And it's a full moon, Kez. Means that the lunatics are out.'

'You've made me into a lunatic,' she mumbled. She tried to look up at the moon with him but contented herself instead with burying her nose further into the shoulder of his puffa jacket. Leon smoothed her hair away from her forehead and smiled.

'You know what, Kez? You're one of the best people I've met since I've been living in this country. You're so sweet and caring. You really would do anything for anybody, wouldn't you?' Kerry nodded into the quilted shoulder. 'I mean, you're about the only person round here who really cares about what's going to happen to me if I can't renew my visa. Sam's deserted me. Even Jeremy will soon find himself a new best friend, whatever he says to the contrary.'

Kerry nodded again. 'I don't want you to go back to South Africa,' she mumbled.

'Join the club,' Leon sighed. He tipped her face towards his so that he could look into her eyes. 'Kerry,' he bit his lip. 'You know what you were saying the other week after your sister's wedding? About what you'd do to help me out? Did you really mean that?'

Kerry nodded. Then added, 'What did I say again?'

'You said that you would marry me if that's what I had to do to stay in the UK.'

'What? I said that? I didn't?'

Kerry suddenly came back to life as if one of Nelson's lions had blown smelling salts straight into her face. She pulled away from Leon to stare at him and swayed backwards dangerously.

'You said that you would marry me so that I could get a visa. Remember?'

'Leon!! Of course I do. But I thought you weren't interested in doing that. You said it was a stupid idea.'

'I've changed my mind.'

'Are you serious? Why?'

'I don't know what else I can do, Kez. I've checked every possible avenue and I think it's the only one left open. Would you really do that for me? Would you get married to me so that I could stay here in England?'

'Oh God, Leon. I'd love to. Yes, of course I would! Yes, yes!!!'

'It's not a proper proposal,' Leon reminded her tactfully but Kerry threw her arms first around Leon's neck and then jumped up to hurl her arms around the nearest all-seeing lion. 'Yes, of course I'll marry you. I can't wait. Oh, Leon. You and me. It's going to be such a laugh.'

'Kerry,' Leon looked concerned. 'Hang on a minute. You know what this means, don't you? You know that we're going to have to live together until immigration are off our backs and if we get caught out you'll be in just as much shit as me. You could even end up in jail for helping an illegal immigrant stay in the country.'

'Leon, of course I know all that. But we're not going to get caught out, are we? It's going to be brilliant. A match made in heaven.' Leon raised an eyebrow. 'I can't believe you asked me. My mum is going to be ecstatic. She already has you ear-marked for a son-in-law.' Kerry hugged him again and kissed him all over the face. Leon held her at arm's length for a moment. 'When are we going to do it?' she asked.

'Well, I suppose we've got to do it as quickly as we can. My visa gets more out of date every day.'

'We've got to have a party after the ceremony.'

'I . . . er . . .'

'Leon, we've got to have a party. It's got to be convincing, hasn't it? Oh, this is so incredible. And do you remember how it was you who caught the bouquet at my sister's wedding? That was an omen, Leon. An omen.' Kerry got to her feet and climbed astride the lion as though it were a horse. She punched the air with a fist.

'You're going to be able to stay here for ever,' she laughed. 'And I'm going to be married. Before Fiona! I can't believe it. She'll be sick with envy. This is the craziest birthday I have ever had. I'm afraid I'll have to have an engagement ring, Mr Landesman,' she reminded Leon gravely.

'Of course,' he said. 'I'll sort it out. But I want you to think about this seriously, Kez. Really, really seriously before you make up your mind.' She nodded, but he wasn't sure that she'd heard what he'd said.

'Shall we go and get that cab now?' he asked.

Kerry didn't look as though she was about to puke anymore.

'Yes. I feel perfect now. Completely perfect.'

Leon slipped down from the wall and braced himself to catch Kerry when she jumped. As she landed, she wrapped her arms around his neck and hung on tight.

'I had a great time tonight,' Kerry told him sincerely. 'I would have had a crappy birthday if it wasn't for you and Jeremy. Especially you. Thanks, Leon.'

'My pleasure entirely.'

'I can't wait to tell the girls about the wedding.'

Leon put a finger to her lips. 'No, Kerry. Not yet. I don't think we should tell anyone what we're going to do until everything is arranged.'

Kerry frowned. 'Really?'

'Really, Kez. You've got to promise me that you won't.'

'OK. I promise, fiancé of mine.'

Leon took his finger away from her lips and kissed them instead.

CHAPTER TWENTY-ONE

The sound of the postman woke Linzi up at half past ten. She stumbled grumpily downstairs. He was delivering something that Fiona had ordered from a catalogue (probably books about how to live with phantom cellulite), a bank statement for Kerry and a letter in an embossed cream envelope for herself. Linzi recognised the emblem of CPIDG excitedly. It had to be the letter confirming her appointment as assistant to George Gerrard. She bounded up the stairs two at a time to her bedroom where Gaetano was still sleeping, having crept in without Fiona's knowledge the night before. Linzi ripped the envelope open as she leapt on to the warm bed beside him.

'It's a letter about that job,' she told him.

Gaetano opened his sleep puffy eyes just the merest crack.

'I don't know why I feel so nervous,' Linzi said as she unfolded the crisp cream letter inside. 'I mean he near as hell said that the job was mine and we got on so well. It's bound to be a letter of acceptance.' She scanned the first few lines and her face suddenly clouded over. 'My God. I don't believe it. The bastard. How could he? He's bloody well gone and given the job to someone else. But he promised it to me. He promised it to me.'

Gaetano was not quite awake. 'Did you get it then?'

She scrunched the letter into a screwed up little ball and hurled it in the direction of the open door. 'No, I bloody well did not,' she bawled. 'After all that bullshit he gave me at the pub it's gone to someone whose "qualifications more accurately fitted the job description". I don't understand it. He told me that I didn't need any specific qualifications. He told me that I was perfect for the job. What a fucking, bloody bastard!!'

'Hey, calm down, *cara mia*.' He pulled her back down under the duvet. Gaetano wasn't ready to get up.

At a quarter to one, Gaetano managed to drag himself out of the pit. Linzi was downstairs, eating toast disconsolately as she flicked through the previous day's *Evening Standard* and checked out the depressing columns full of secretarial jobs, nearly all requiring shorthand despite the none-too-recent invention of the Dictaphone.

'Look at this,' she complained bitterly. 'They want a graduate with fluent French to do the nine-to-five for eight grand a year. They'll be bloody lucky.'

'It's more than the dole,' Gaetano commented.

'Only just. Shit. Shit. Shit.' Linzi dropped her toast butter-side down on the carpet. She had forgotten to sign on. Again. 'Do you think they'll let me sign on this afternoon instead?'

Gaetano shook his head. 'No way, man, that's your money gone for at least a fortnight.'

'Why didn't you remind me I had to go in this morning?'

'You didn't tell me to remind you.' He picked up the piece of toast that Linzi had dropped on the floor and fitted it into his mouth in two bites, carpet fluff and all.

'I can't go on like this any more.' Linzi was in a foul mood. 'How is anyone supposed to live on thirty-seven pounds a week anyway? We can't even get any Marmite for the toast! If my father could only see how he is forcing me to live . . .' Gaetano slung a comforting arm around her shoulder. 'I mean, your mother threw you out of the family home for having sex before marriage and she still sent you an allowance even though you've got a full-time job and she wasn't talking to you.'

Gaetano shrugged. 'Well, I guess family is just more important to the Italians.' He looked at his watch. 'Shit, I said I would cover for Louis at the café this afternoon because I don't have to go into the shop until tomorrow.' He shrugged on his jacket. 'I'll see you tonight, at the Duke of York. I'm meeting the Professor at seven to get set up for the gig. *Ciao bella!*' He blew her a kiss.

She hated it when he said that. He reminded her of his mother.

With Gaetano gone, Linzi uncrumpled the letter from CPIDG and read it through one more time. Qualifications? That was a laugh. It was more likely that she lost the job because she had let that chauvinist bastard come all over his precious dashboard. Well, if George Gerrard thought he had heard the last of Linzi Adams he was very much mistaken. She rang the switchboard of CPIDG and, to her surprise, the receptionist put her straight through to the director.

'George, this is Linzi Adams. You may remember me from last week? I *came* for an interview with you.'

'Linzi,' he knocked her off her stride by being disarmingly charming from the start. 'Of course I remember you. How are you, my dear?'

'Not too great this morning as a matter of fact. I just received a letter on your headed notepaper. I thought you said that I was going to get the job.'

George Gerrard cleared his throat. 'Did I say that, Linzi? I think there seems to have been some kind of misunderstanding.'

'Oh, really. And which bit of the sentence, "You've got the job" did I misunderstand?'

'Linzi. In the first place I did not formally offer you the job, and in the second place I think that under the circumstances it would have been most inappropriate for me to do so.'

'What? Inappropriate? Why?'

'Well, I think that we may perhaps have overstepped the mark when it comes to interviewer/interviewee relationships.'

'We overstepped the mark? I think it was more the case that you pushed me over it. Look, Gerrard, I could make a very serious complaint about this you know.'

'And it would be your word against mine. A company director and a failed job applicant. Who do you think they'd believe?'

'You really are scum,' she hissed.

'Linzi, there really is no need for things to get nasty. It must have been obvious to you that I was very much attracted to you and I realised during the course of our evening together that an attraction that strong could put an unnecessary strain on the working environment.'

'Oh right. So you would have given me the job if I hadn't been so good at giving blow-jobs?'

'Linzi, calm down. I'll make it up to you. I promise.'

'Oh, you'll give me the opportunity to retrial will you? Perhaps if I swallow this time instead of making you come all over the dashboard things will be different.'

'Linzi! I can't give you the job here but I promise I'll make it up to you.'

'How?'

'Sit by the phone. I'll get someone to call you back within half an hour.'

'Really . . . and . . .'

George had already hung up.

The phone did ring again exactly thirty-one minutes later. But it wasn't George Gerrard. It was Caroline from Advertising Angels.

'Linzi, darling!!'

'Oh, it's you. You'll have to be quick, I'm waiting for a call.'

'Now, now, Linzi. I'd be grateful if you could sound a little happier to hear from your favourite Auntie Caroline. Especially when she's the bearer of such good news for you.'

'You are? Go on. Thrill me.'

'Linzi, you really do have something of an enthusiasm problem this morning, don't you?'

'So would you if you'd just been turned down for yet another poxy job.'

'CPIDG?'

'Yes.'

'I know, my dear. But it's not the end of the world, is it now? In fact, I've just had that lovely Mr Gerrard himself on the telephone. He says that he found it terribly hard to choose between you and the girl who eventually got the job but in the end she just tipped you on shorthand and typing speeds.'

'Right,' Linzi snorted. He hadn't given her a typing test.

'However, Mr Gerrard was so impressed with you that he has been ringing round his friends in a desperate attempt to place you elsewhere. He'll have me out of a job one of these days. Ha ha ha! Anyway, he's done it. He's placed you. He has a lovely friend at Manatee Records who is simply gasping for an assistant. Mr Gerrard has recommended you most highly and you'll start on Monday morning. If you want to, that is. He's gagging to meet you.'

'I'll bet he is,' Linzi sneered. 'How much?'

'Oh, negotiable,' Caroline breezed. 'I'll call you just as soon as I know. You do want the job don't you, Linzi? It is the music business we're talking about here. Very exciting. You can even wear smart casual clothes to work.'

'Smart casual clothes? You should have said,' Linzi sighed sarcastically. 'Caroline, I'll see how it goes.'

'Good, good. And you know where the Manatee office is? Right near Hyde Park!! Wonderful for lunchtime in the summer. You see, I knew we'd find a place for you if we just kept trying. George Gerrard was terribly impressed, you know. I wonder what you did to make him take such a shine to you?'

'Yes,' muttered Linzi. 'I wonder.'

When Linzi arrived at the Duke of York that evening, the only other person in the bar was the Professor. He raised his half-pint glass in greeting and gestured her towards him. He was wearing his dirty blue jeans and a faded Little Angels T-shirt with a big rip under one of the arms for ventilation.

'They're not here yet,' he said, stating the obvious. 'They said they'd be here half an hour ago. I had to set up all the gear on my own. But it looks as though it's not going to matter whether they turn up at all anyway. The place is totally empty and we won't get paid if the bar doesn't do well enough.'

'Don't be such a pessimist, Professor. It's only half past seven,' Linzi consoled him. 'People will start pouring through the door in an hour or so, I promise you. Most of them are still getting home from work.'

'I hope you're right. You know, I could have been working tonight,' the Professor said flatly. 'Could have earned sixty-odd quid doing a bit of locum work in the East End.'

'Locum work. Really? I thought only doctors did that?'

'And chemists,' the Professor explained. 'You know how there has to be a late-night chemist in the area? Well, if the shopkeeper doesn't want to do it himself, he can get another chemist in to do it for him. Usually someone who's just qualified and hasn't got a shop of his own, like me. It's all right sometimes. Depends on the area you end up in. You don't want to be doing somewhere near King's Cross after dark.'

'I can imagine,' Linzi nodded. 'Too many drug addicts trying to supplement their prescriptions, I suppose?'

'Yeah,' the Professor drained the last of his drink. 'They come in after methadone and jellies.'

'Jellies?'

'Temazepam. Sleeping tablets. You can melt them down and inject them. It's all right, actually. They leave most of the really interesting stuff though.'

He ordered another pint for himself and one for Linzi.

'But I don't know how much longer I can stand being a chemist, you know,' he told her now that buying her a drink had bought him the right to moan. 'I didn't think that it would take us this long to get a record deal for Monster Munch. I mean, we had loads of interest last month and we sent off all those demo tapes but we haven't heard a thing back from anyone. The majors are only interested in something that's going to be a banker with the first single. The only way we're ever going to get a record out is if we do it ourselves and try to get our own airplay.'

'You mean take it round the clubs?'

'Yeah. I've got plenty of contacts. The only problem is that it'll cost us a couple of grand to get a single cut. I don't have that sort of money to spare and Gaetano certainly doesn't. He spends everything he owns on grass and clothes.'

Linzi smiled ironically. Gaetano had pleaded poverty that very weekend.

'Two grand isn't so much. There has to be some way to get that kind of money, Professor. If you're serious about it. Couldn't you go to a bank? You could pretend to be setting up a label and get a small business loan?'

'Get real, Linzi. A chemist, a clothes shop manager and two out-of-work sparks getting together enough money to put out a record? They'd laugh us out of the bank.'

'And I thought I was cynical,' Linzi commented.

'Anyone who isn't cynical, is stupid,' the Professor told her seriously. 'I'm rapidly coming to the conclusion that crime is the only business that pays these days.'

'Well, you just carry on being cynical, Professor,' Linzi smiled. 'But by this time next week things could be very different for us all.'

'How come?'

'I've got myself a job.'

'Oh, well that's great for you,' the Professor said without enthusiasm. 'Where?'

'At Manatee Records.'

'Manatee Records? You're kidding.'

'I'm not. I'm starting on Monday morning. I'll give myself a couple of days to get to know a few people, then I can take the Monster Munch tape into work and force the people who matter to listen to it.'

'That's really good of you, Linz. It'd be a real help.'

'I'll stand right over them until they sign you.'

'That'd be fantastic.'

At that moment the door to the bar swung open. Gaetano and Socks walked in carrying two battered guitar cases and the mike stand.

'Shit,' Gaetano muttered as he noted that the bar was very, very empty. 'What happened to the audience?'

'Never mind about the audience,' Linzi piped up. 'I just got a job at Manatee Records.'

'That's great, man,' said Socks, dropping his guitar case and punching her on the arm. 'Our own industry insider. Linzi, you're brilliant!'

Gaetano picked Linzi up and swung her around.

'You're a star, Linz. I knew you could do it.'

For a moment it didn't matter that even their singer had failed to turn up to the gig.

CHAPTER TWENTY-TWO

Kerry's plan to bring peace to number 67 by cooking a house meal had been scuppered. As she filled the refrigerator with the goodies she had just picked up from Safeway she noticed a note stuck to the door. Fiona had scrawled, 'Gone to Tim's'. Beneath that Linzi had written 'Gone to the pub'. Both of them knew that Kerry had intended to cook that night and had gone out regardless. Kerry tore the note down with a huff. She was desperate to tell them about the impending wedding (in strictest confidence, of course). The news was burning such a hole in her brain that she thought she might start stopping people in the street and telling them soon. And to make matters worse, neither Linzi nor Fiona had remembered her birthday either. So much for her two best friends in the world.

Kerry's foul mood was compounded by the fact that Sam had dropped by the Verbal Tix office that day. He was looking for Leon, who was out with the newly-returned Serena seeing the bank manager with regard to Verbal Tix's ever-expanding overdraft. Sam had decided to wait for his return and made himself at home on the corner of Kerry's desk. He told her that he intended to get Leon back. That he'd realised what a terrible mistake he had made by running off with Andrew. Sam was sure that the minute Leon saw how sorry he was, their relationship would be back on again immediately. And deep down, Kerry knew that Sam wouldn't even have to pretend to be sorry to reinstate himself in Leon's heart.

Sam said he had tried to call Leon a hundred times but it seemed that he had decided to unplug his phone. Kerry raised an eyebrow.

'Is he missing me?' Sam asked. 'I don't suppose he is. He's been out two Saturdays in a row. Kerry, has he told you whether he's started dating anybody else?'

Kerry shrugged. 'He doesn't really tell me much about that kind of thing but I think that he is interested in someone.'

'Oh, God, no.' Sam bit his lip. 'Tell me it's not that awful Jeremy.'

'No, it's definitely not Jeremy.'

'Who is it then?'

Kerry bit her lip and tried not to look smug as she announced, 'I think it might be a girl.'

'No!!! Not again!!!' Sam left the office straightaway in tears, begging Kerry to let Leon know that he had been there. Not again? Kerry basked in Sam's parting words. Not *again*.

Leon returned just moments later, having left Serena to browse through Mothercare. He must have passed Sam unknowingly in the street. Leon looked hassled. 'You'd think that we'd asked him for the money to set up a gay brothel. Anybody called?' he asked.

'No,' Kerry lied. She concentrated on her screen so that Leon wouldn't be able to look into her eyes. Thank goodness Celestine had decided to go home with a migraine. Josh hadn't made it in at all that day. 'Not a peep from anyone.'

Later that afternoon, Leon called British Telecom and tried to get his telephone line reinstated. Not until he had paid his bill in full and with interest, he was told. Sam had run up a bill of four hundred pounds calling an ex-boyfriend in Canada.

'It's so annoying,' Leon complained. 'Anybody could be trying to get hold of me.'

'Including immigration. Besides, if they couldn't get hold of you at home they would ring you at work, surely,' Kerry reasoned.

'Sam wouldn't. In case Serena picks the phone up. They hate each other's guts. He thinks that she messed him about on some soundtrack deal.'

Kerry remembered what Celestine had said about the alleged affair, combined with Sam's parting words and wondered if that was the real reason. If it was, then there was definitely hope for her.

'I miss him like crazy, Kez,' Leon continued. 'We were together for a very long time.'

'If he was all that bothered about you he would have come round by now, wouldn't he? Serena or no Serena.'

'Yes,' sighed Leon. 'I suppose you're right. You know what, without Sam I wonder if it's worth my while staying here in England at all. I'd be putting you in such an awkward position for nothing . . .'

'Not nothing, Leon. You'd be able to stay with your friends,' Kerry reminded him, desperate for a scrap hinting at affection. It was the first time he had mentioned the wedding since the weekend and he sounded as though he was unsure about going through with it already.

Leon smiled wistfully and murmured, 'Yeah, my friends. There's always them.'

At home in the empty kitchen, Kerry stabbed a potato named Sam right through its potatoey heart.

Fiona knocked on the door of Tim's flat with a peculiarly nervous sensation in her stomach. She hadn't called him first to let him know that she was coming round. She heard his moccasined footsteps padding down the hallway towards her. He opened the door and met her with a look of rather worried surprise.

'Fi? Hi. I thought you were staying in tonight.'

'I know, I was going to but Linzi decided that she was going to stay in as well and so the atmosphere was pretty tense.' She was still standing on the doorstep. 'Well, are you going to let me in or do I have to stand out here in the cold all night?'

'Oh, of course. Sorry.' Tim stood aside and Fiona wandered straight towards the sitting room taking off her coat as she went. She began to tell Tim the story of her day but she stopped abruptly when she walked into the sitting room and discovered that Tim was not alone. Minky Bingham was perching on the edge of the navy-blue Ikea special sofa, nursing a half-full glass of red wine.

'You know Fiona, don't you, Minky?'

Minky smiled shyly. 'Yes, I think we've met before.' She put her glass down on the scratched-up coffee table and straightened her little skirt so that it barely covered her knees.

'You're Adam's girlfriend, aren't you?' Fiona asked pointedly.

'Well, I was.' Minky shuffled her court shoes on the rattan rug. 'I'm afraid we split up last weekend.'

'Oh, I'm sorry to hear that.'

'Thanks. But I think it was for the best. No point prolonging the agony, is there?' She sneaked a look at Tim, who was avoiding Minky's eyes as he brought Fiona a drink.

Fiona installed herself in the armchair opposite Minky and made no further attempt to prolong the conversation. Minky took two more sips from her glass.

'Listen Tim,' she said suddenly. 'Thanks awfully for the wine but I really ought to be going now. Got an early start in the morning. I'm doing a presentation for some tanning shop clients. I work in PR,' she explained for the benefit of Fiona. 'Beauty PR.' She gave her long blonde hair a gratuitous flick and started to stand up. 'I'll see you soon, no doubt. Down at the Pitcher and Piano probably. Seems to be where everyone ends up after work these days.'

Fiona smiled tightly.

Tim helped Minky to put on her jacket and escorted her to the door. He was gone a long while. Fiona strained to hear their too-quiet whispers, desperately fighting the urge to take a peek out of the window and find out what was going on. When Tim came back into the sitting room and took the chair opposite her, Fiona was suddenly aware that he hadn't even kissed her hello.

'I didn't know that you knew Minky all that well, Tim?' Fiona began.

'She lives quite near here.'

'I seem to remember her saying to me that she lived in Fulham which isn't all that near Stockwell, if my geography's not too bad.'

'She was on her way to see a friend in Clapham,' Tim explained. 'She just popped in to say "hi" en route. That's all.'

'Right, Tim,' Fiona sneered. 'And you weren't expecting her at all which is why you've got a fucking great chocolate gâteau defrosting on the kitchen table. Not even you could be planning to eat all that on your own.'

'Christ, Fiona. Are you sure you don't work for MI5?' Tim muttered as he lit a cigarette from a packet of Marlboro Lights which Minky had left on the arm of the sofa.

'I thought you'd given smoking up.'

'I had. But I've just started again.'

'So, had you invited Minky to stay for dinner or not?' Fiona persisted.

Tim took a long, thoughtful drag on the cigarette before addressing Fiona in an uncommonly quiet tone of voice.

'Look, there's something you need to know, Fi, and that is that you do not have the right to barge in here and tell me what I should be doing every moment of my life and who I should be doing it with.'

'What?'

'If I want to have Minky over for dinner then I will.'

'Then you had invited her over for dinner?'

'I had, yes. Big deal. Call the police if you like.'

'Why didn't you tell me?'

'As I mentioned just a moment ago, I didn't think that I had to tell you everything.'

'Instead, you just let me barge in here unknowing, making me look totally stupid in front of her. She must have been embarrassed too. There was absolutely no need for her to leave so suddenly unless the pair of you were up to something.'

'Fiona,' Tim groaned. 'I think you made her feel pretty uncomfortable.'

'I did not make her feel uncomfortable. Look, Tim, I don't want to get into an argument about this. I just want to know why we can't share these little things with each other. After all, we are supposed to be engaged. Engaged to be married.'

'Yeah,' said Tim cagily. 'And that's another thing we need to talk about.' He took another deep drag on the Marlboro Light and stood up to look out through the window.

'What do you mean?' Fiona panicked. 'Another thing we need to talk about?'

'I mean,' Tim began without turning back to face her. 'I mean, I feel like you've twisted my arm over this whole June wedding thing, Fi. I made a bit of a hasty decision under pressure and now, with the ring having been lost and all, I think perhaps we should take a couple of steps back to the way we were before.'

'What? You mean put the wedding date off again? We can't, Tim.' Fiona began to count off the reasons on her fingers. 'I've already talked to my parents about it . . . Mum's looking

into the possibility of using the same church, where she and
Dad . . .'

'No, stop there. Please. What I mean to say is, let's take a step
back to the way things were before we were engaged. It wouldn't
be so very different.'

Fionas lower lip began to tremble violently. 'What are you
saying, Tim?'

'It just might make me feel a bit happier if we dropped the
whole engagement thing for a while. I don't think I'm old
enough for all this commitment yet. We're both at vital stages
in our careers and I think we should be devoting more time to
that right now.'

'Careers, Tim? But you just told me to turn down a six
months placement in New York so that we could get married
this summer,' Fiona shrieked. 'That was my career. Hara went
insane when I told him . . . I'm finished as far as First Orient's
concerned.'

'I didn't tell you to turn the placement down, Fi,' Tim replied
calmly. 'You made that decision yourself. I just helped you to
write the letter.'

'I thought you didn't want me to go.'

'I don't know. Maybe I didn't. Maybe I did. I really didn't want
to influence your decision either way.'

'How can you say all this now? Now that I've thrown away
the New York placement, which means that in all probability
I've also thrown away my whole career, and I've told my family
and all my friends that we're getting married in June. If you call
the wedding off now, Tim, I will die of embarrassment.'

'Embarrassment isn't fatal, Fi.'

'Tim, if you go ahead with this crazy plan of yours, you know
you will ruin my life.'

'If we go ahead with this wedding, I think you know as well
as I do that it will ruin both our lives. Look, I really am sorry that
I let things get this complicated before I realised what a mistake
we were making.' He looked steadily at a spot on the floor. 'But
I can't carry on like this in the hope that things might get better.
I thought it might make a difference but marriage won't change
anything between us if we shouldn't be together. I'm sorry, Fi.
I really am.'

'Believe me, Tim,' Fiona hissed as she rose unsteadily to her feet and tugged on her coat. 'You don't know what sorry is. But you will.'

'Fi, sit back down. You don't have to go right now.'

Fiona headed for the door. 'Call me when you've come to your senses.'

She stormed out into the night and walked all the way from Stockwell to Clapham Common, crying with every painful step. Tim watched her go from the front door she had left open and prayed that she wouldn't do anything stupid. But he didn't follow her to make sure.

CHAPTER TWENTY-THREE

There was no way that Fiona was going to be able to go into work the day after Tim told her it was all over. She lay in bed, awake but unmoving from five in the morning until one in the afternoon. When she finally managed to drag herself downstairs she called her office and told them that she had twenty-four hour flu. Her supervisor sympathised, there was a lot of it going around.

She couldn't eat anything. It was difficult even to get a cup of tea past her dried out lips. When she could bring herself to look in a mirror, she could barely see her eyes, so puffed up were her eyelids with all that crying.

She sat by the phone for half an hour while her fingers hovered over Tim's number. Maybe he had calmed down a little now and was already regretting the terrible mistake he had made. He wouldn't call her from work to tell her that, of course, because they would need to have the kind of conversation that you didn't really want your workmates to listen in on. They had split up once before and he had called her the second he got home from work the next day to make things better.

Besides, it was natural that he should be nervous about the step they were taking together, wasn't it? They had promised each other the rest of their lives. Those boneheads in the rugby team had probably been giving him some stick about being under her thumb. God, how Fiona hated the rugby boys. All men together until they needed someone to cook them dinner or iron their shirts. And anyway, Tim wasn't under her thumb. She let him have plenty of freedom. She didn't mind him having Minky Bingham round for dinner, it was simply the

fact that he felt he had to keep it a secret from her which was
a problem.

And she had her own life outside him, she reminded herself.
There was the half-marathon for a start. She could do with
devoting a little more time to preparing for that. Yes, when Tim
called that evening, as he inevitably would, Fiona wouldn't try
to prolong the argument, she would get straight in there with the
solutions. They could cut down on seeing each other to just once
or twice during the working week so that they weren't so tired
and irritable when they got together. She would train for her
marathon and when that had finished she would start training
for another one. Or perhaps she could do some voluntary work.
She could help out at the dog's home or something. Yes, that
was the key. Separate interests. She should go out with her
friends more often, too. Kerry was usually at a loose end on a
Saturday night.

By the time she had told herself all this, Fiona was almost
convinced that the previous night's argument with Tim was the
best thing that could have happened. She took a shower and
lay down on her bed for half an hour with an ice-mask over
her eyes to bring down the swelling. Then she listened to some
happy music and flicked through an old copy of *Brides*.

Outside, the sun was shining. It seemed like the perfect
moment for the new Fiona to start her regime. She forced down
a bowl of Weetabix while she laced up her trainers. Yeah, she just
needed to become a little more independent, that was all. Tim
didn't really want to call the wedding off, he just wanted to make
sure that Fiona knew the status quo before they took the plunge.

She bounced out on to the sunny pavement and touched her
toes a couple of times.

He would be so proud of her if she finished this race in
good time.

When Fiona reached the other side of the Common, she
stopped sprinting and swung forward to put her head between
her knees and catch her breath. Her chest ached as if it were
about to burst. She put it down to the combination of having run
and having cried so much the night before. Maybe she should
take it easy on the way back? Right now, she needed a drink
and a sit down. She went into Burger King and ordered a huge
Diet Coke.

'Hey, Fiona.'

She turned around to see who was calling her name and immediately wished that she hadn't. Sitting by the cloakrooms, flanked by two of his dodgy-looking long-haired friends, was Gaetano. And he was all smiles.

'How come you're not at work today? Surely you're not doing a sicky?' he asked loudly.

'Sort of,' replied Fiona. She changed her order from eat-in to take-away. The counter assistant looked pained.

'I'll have to key it in again,' he whined.

'Don't bother,' Fiona told him. 'Just give me a straw and a bag.'

'Come and sit here with us.' Gaetano was still talking to her. Fiona was just waiting for the subject of the ring to be brought up and for things to turn nasty. 'Fiona lives with Linzi,' Gaetano was explaining to his friends. As if he hadn't already told them all about her – the wicked witch of Artesia Road. 'Move up so she can sit down, Professor. Be a gentleman.' The tall dirty-looking blond with his baseball cap on backwards obliged. Fiona stopped by their table in passing but didn't sit down.

'Thanks, but I really can't stop today. I'm right in the middle of writing up a project for work and I ought to get back to it. I'll see you around.' She managed a sweet smile for Gaetano's companions before heading for the door in double-quick time. She heard a commotion behind her. Gaetano was putting on his jacket.

'Hang on, Fiona,' he called after her. 'I'll walk back that way with you.'

She pretended not to hear and as soon as she had cleared the door she started to run. Seconds later she was flat on the floor face-down in the icy spilled contents of her drink. 'Oh God,' she murmured.

She just wanted to close her eyes and disappear. Everything hurt. Everything. Especially her chin.

'Bloody hell, Fiona,' Gaetano had caught her up. He was panting. Even jogging the few steps between Burger King and the prostrate Fiona was too much for him. 'Are you all right?'

'I don't know,' she groaned as she tried to lift her face from the paving slabs. 'I think I've got concussion.'

'You just took one hell of a fall.' Gaetano helped her until she was in a sitting position on the kerb with her feet in the gutter. A small crowd had already gathered around them. Fiona put a finger to her stinging lip. It was bleeding.

'Oh God, no. Why did this have to happen today?' she fought back the urge to cry.

'Let me have a look.' Gaetano gently turned her face towards his. 'You've cut your lip pretty badly. Perhaps we should get you to casualty.' An elderly woman with a shopping trolley and a small dog nodded.

'He's right, you know,' she told Fiona. 'You might be concussed.'

'No, really. I'm all right. I really am.' Fiona pushed the concerned hands away. 'I'll be fine. I just need to have a sit down for a minute. Got to get my breath back.'

'Well, while you're down there,' said Gaetano, 'perhaps you ought to do up your shoelace.'

'Thanks, smart-arse.' As she reached down to tie her treacherous lace, her elbow complained like crazy. When she turned it towards her for a better look at the damage she saw that the white sleeve of her sweatshirt was stuck to her skin with bright red blood. 'Oh, shit,' she muttered. 'I've ruined my top.'

'We've got loads like that in the shop,' Gaetano comforted her. 'I'll get you another one cheap. Come on. Up you get.' He tucked his hands beneath her armpits and lifted her to her feet.

'Are you going to take her to the accident unit?' the old woman asked.

'No, she doesn't live far from here. I'll take her straight home.'

'You want to be more careful,' the woman told the limping Fiona as Gaetano escorted her across to a low wall. 'All the silly exercising young girls do these days and then they wonder why none of them can have babies. Running themselves into trouble, they are.'

'You're right,' Fiona replied. 'I promise I'll never jog again.'

Satisfied that the young girl had learned her lesson, the old woman and her dog waddled off in the direction of the bank, leaving Fiona sitting on the wall feeling very much like Humpty Dumpty must have done after the plunge.

'Ready to go?' Gaetano asked.

Fiona put her hand to her forehead. 'No, I'm not. Can't you just leave me here to die?'

He couldn't. Gaetano offered Fiona his arm.

'Honestly, I'll be fine in a minute. Just go back to Burger King with your friends, will you?'

He wasn't about to give up.

'If you try to get back home on your own, you might collapse in the middle of the Common. Who'll help you then? Come on, Fiona. Let me walk you back. I promise I won't try to steal any of your jewellery.'

Fiona narrowed her eyes at him.

'Did you find the ring?' he asked casually.

'No. I didn't.'

'It'll turn up when you least expect it. These things always do.'

Fiona glared but Gaetano tucked his hands under her armpits anyway and physically set her on the path home. Realising that she was not going to get away from him now, Fiona shook herself free of his hands so that she could at least limp alone. She walked as purposefully as her bruises would allow, looking straight ahead, answering questions only. She was not going to make conversation. Gaetano's innocence had been protested but not proven.

'So, they let you work from home now?' Gaetano asked jovially. Fiona nodded. 'Must be nice. Means you don't have to get on the tube in the morning.' Fiona nodded. 'Linzi's got herself a job at last.' Fiona nodded. 'Hope she can stick at it for a while. Might help my band to get a record deal. Christ, Fiona. Are you just going to nod at me all the way home?'

Fiona turned to Gaetano. Her face was horribly creased, as though she was trying to hold something from the *X Files* back behind her cheeks.

'Look, I didn't steal your fucking engagement ring, all right, if that's what you're thinking?' Gaetano was suddenly defensive. 'I don't want all this frosty stuff. I just wanted to do you a favour.'

'Oh, God!' Fiona sobbed suddenly. 'I'm sorry. It's not you. Really it's not. I'm just having a bad day and I want to be on my own. Just leave me here, will you? Leave me alone.'

She collapsed on to a moss-covered bench and covered her eyes with balled-up fists. Gaetano crouched beside her and tried to pull her hands away. 'Shit, Fiona. Are you sure you don't want me to take you to casualty? Are you in serious pain?'

'Yes, I am,' she wailed. 'But there isn't a doctor in the world who can make me feel better!! Go away from me. Go away.' She swatted at him with her hands.

But Gaetano didn't go away. Instead he sat down beside her and shrugged his shoulders.

'Why do these things always happen to me? Why doesn't he love me any more? All I ever did was try to make him happy.'

'You talking about Tim?' Gaetano ventured perceptively.

'Of course I'm talking about Tim,' Fiona snapped. 'Nobody else has ever loved me, have they? But now he's gone and got himself another woman. And I've already made out our wedding invitation list.'

'It's not the end of the world, Fiona.' It seemed like the right thing to say.

'It is the bloody end of the world. I've been jilted by my fiancé, Gaetano. Don't you understand? My mother is going to go insane.' Gaetano nodded this time. He knew about mothers. 'I've told everybody that I'm getting married. I've even turned down a job in New York because of it. They're all going to laugh at me. I'll be the biggest joke in London. They probably already think I've made the whole engagement thing up because I haven't got a ring. I can't go on without him. I can't go back to work. I can't even face my friends. He's ruined my life. Absolutely ruined it and all for some tart with a name like a hamster.'

'What's she called?' Gaetano couldn't resist finding out exactly what a hamster's name was like.

'She's called Minky,' Fiona sneered. Gaetano thought it was a better name for a rabbit. 'Minky Bingham. Minky Binky Bloody Bingham. And she's the fastest bike outside the Tour de France.'

'You got her phone number?'

Fiona shot him a look.

'I'm sorry, Fiona. It was meant to be a joke.'

'Ha ha ha. Well, it wasn't a very funny one. You see, you've started making a joke out of my misery already. Pretty soon everybody will be sniggering about me behind my back. Bob Monkhouse will probably dedicate a whole show to "Fiona Davenport, jilted of Balham". This kind of thing is supposed to happen to Kerry, not me.'

'Hey, come on, let's keep going.' Fiona was beginning to rant and Gaetano was getting twitchy. 'Look, you're even attracting a crowd.' A group of pigeons was strutting past purposefully. Gaetano fished a Burger King napkin out of his jacket pocket and gave it to Fiona for her nose. 'Come on.'

'Do you think he still loves me?' Fiona asked later as they staggered on past the bandstand. 'What's going on in his mind?'

'I can't tell you what's going on in Tim's mind,' said Gaetano, wishing they'd never started this conversation. 'Most men don't even know what's going on in their own.'

CHAPTER TWENTY-FOUR

B ack at Artesia Road, Fiona locked herself in the bathroom while she changed out of her jogging gear and surveyed the damage caused by her fall. She dabbed antiseptic lotion on the worst of the grazes, bringing tears flooding back to her eyes. Despite their pleasant enough conversation as he helped her to cross the Common, she was not especially happy to be alone in the house with Gaetano. Something about him put her on edge. It was nothing to do with the missing ring even. She had felt it the second time they ever met. And it was worse now that she had blurted out the story of last night's row to him. She hoped that if she took long enough in the bathroom, Gaetano would be gone by the time she emerged again. Then she heard music strike up from the direction of Linzi's room. He was making himself at home.

Fiona steeled herself. She paid rent on this house. If she was uncomfortable in his presence then she was perfectly entitled to ask him to leave. She knocked on the door to Linzi's room, feeling only slightly more composed now that she was wearing trousers which covered her sticky knees. When Gaetano didn't answer – the volume was too loud – she went straight ahead and pushed open the door.

'Ahem.'

Gaetano swivelled around with the look of a cornered rat. He was using the cover of Linzi's prized signed Boney M album as a flat surface upon which he could roll up his joint. When he remembered that there was no one but Fiona in the house, he visibly relaxed again.

'We're a non-smoking household, actually,' Fiona told him stiffly.

'I know,' Gaetano shrugged. 'I was just making this one for the walk home.' He licked the length of a Rizla to make it sticky and continued to construct the T-shaped skin regardless. 'You feeling any better?'

'Yes, thanks. Did you find what you wanted? The CDs Linzi borrowed?'

'Dunno. I haven't really looked yet.'

'Look, Gaetano,' Fiona began. 'I'm afraid you'll have to turn the music down while you're searching. I can't begin to work with that noise going on.'

Gaetano fished in his pocket and brought out a little plastic bag with what looked like a very shrivelled dandelion head inside. He opened the bag and sniffed its contents, a wide smile spreading over his mouth as he did so. 'Wow. The wonder of skunk. You should smell this.' Fiona recoiled. 'No? But it's really great. I could get high just sniffing it.' Then Gaetano took a cigarette out of his packet and broke off the filter. He applied a freshly licked thumb to the seam of the cigarette body and the paper rolled apart obligingly to reveal a naked sausage of tobacco beneath.

Fiona stepped across his cross-legged body with some difficulty and turned the stereo down herself.

'Hey,' Gaetano looked disappointed. 'What's the matter with you? I would have turned it down myself in a minute.'

'But I need to start working now. I'm sorry.'

'You're strange, Fiona. One minute we're walking along having a conversation like we might even actually like each other and the next minute you're biting my head off again. No wonder Tim's pissed off with the idea of marrying you. You need to chill out more.'

'Chill out?' Fiona sneered. 'You mean like you? You mean get stoned and lie on my back all day laughing at the pretty woodchip patterns on the ceiling? Is that "chilling out"?'

Chuckling to himself at the mere thought, Gaetano began to crumble the skunk on to his delicately-arranged Rizlas, taking great care not to let any stalk or seeds contaminate the mix. 'Yeah. Something like that.'

'Well, for your information, some of us don't have time to "chill out",' she spat the words with extra contempt. 'Some of us have work to do.'

Gaetano twisted the end of the fat spliff so that it looked like a skinny miniature icing bag. Then he looked around to find something from which he could make the roach. The spare flap of his Rizla packet had gone that way days ago. Instead, he plucked a greetings card off Linzi's cluttered pinboard and ripped a little rectangle out of the back.

'Don't you think she might have been saving that?'

'She won't mind. It's just an old card. Unlike you, Linzi doesn't think with her anus.'

'You're the only anus round here.'

Gaetano snorted and turned his attention back to the very delicate job of inserting the roach into the open end of the spliff. At first, it seemed that he had made it just a little too big. The roach was removed to be more tightly rolled. He tried it again and Bingo! Gaetano held the completed spliff between his thumb and forefinger and admired it as if he had just blown the thing in molten glass. 'Perfect,' he murmured. 'You still here?' Fiona stood in the doorway with her hands on hips.

'It is my house.'

Gaetano brought out his personalised Zippo.

'You can't light that thing up in here. This house in a no-smoking zone.'

'I'm in Linzi's room, she doesn't care if I smoke.'

'Linzi isn't here.'

Gaetano flipped the Zippo up into the air and caught the flint as it came back down. A flame sprang up obediently and he applied it to the end of the spliff so that the twisted paper burned away. Then he put the smouldering joint between his teeth and held the flame to it again until the tobacco caught and it began to burn properly. Fiona stared as he dragged on it deeply and then exhaled a plume of thick grey smoke.

'You want some?' He held it out to her.

'No. Thank you. I don't.'

'It'll make you feel less uptight. Honestly, Fi, the world's a better place with skunk.'

'I don't think you know how silly you sound, Gaetano.'

'I don't think you know how silly you look standing there with your hands on your hips like you're forty years old. Try something different for once.' He held the joint towards her. 'Act your age, not your bust size.' That was just thirty-two.

'Gaetano, why do you have to make this difficult for me?'

Fiona tried to reason. 'I let you into the house to look for your CDs, now all I want to do is get on with my project in peace. In silence.'

'Hang on a minute,' he replied. 'I thought I was the one doing you a favour. I made sure you got home safely, didn't I? Now I need a rest from that walk. You haven't even so much as offered me a cup of tea in gratitude. I'll keep the music down.'

'You won't. You never did.'

'OK, have one toke on my pipe of peace and then I'll go away. You know it's breaking Linzi's heart that you and I don't get on so well.'

'It breaks my heart that you and she do get on so well.'

Gaetano took another drag on his spliff then held it towards her.

'I've never smoked before.'

'Sure you have. Everybody has.'

But Fiona really hadn't ever smoked before. Not even a single B & H with the girls behind the caretaker's shed at school for fear of an embarrassing expulsion. Now she took the spliff from Gaetano and held it gingerly between her thumb and forefinger.

'I should throw this straight out the window,' she said, waving it in the direction of the closed curtains.

Gaetano looked worried. 'Please don't. That would be such a waste. Just have one drag. Go on. Be a devil.'

'Tim doesn't like me to smoke.'

'Tim, Tim, Tim,' Gaetano mimicked. 'Then if I were you, I would smoke forty a day. Men like a wayward girl.'

'Do they really?' she asked a little desperately.

Gaetano nodded. 'Yeah. That's what I like about Linzi.'

'I don't think that Tim would be terribly impressed . . .'

'You'd be very surprised. A little bit of subversion might be exactly what he is looking for. You're getting old before your time, Fi. If you ask me, this row you guys had about the wedding was about his last-ditch attempt to have a bit of fun before settling down. If he thinks he can have fun with you, then Bingo! Wedding's back on.'

'Do you really think so?'

'Listen. My father ditched my mother two weeks before their wedding. She went out on the town with her sisters that night and sent him wild with jealousy by dancing with another man. He was on his knees the very next day. Begging for forgiveness. And my elder brother, born eight and a half months later, is the only blond in the family.' Gaetano laughed.

'Tim won't be made jealous if I have a smoke.'

'No, but Tim is expecting you to mope around, Fiona. If he calls up tonight and you're caned, you'll sound happy. He'll be round like a shot to find out why.'

'Really?'

'Try it.'

'Oh, this is ridiculous.' But Fiona put the damp end of the spliff to her lips anyway and closed them tightly around it. The grey smoke continued to whirl out from the end like a ghostly dancer. She hadn't yet inhaled.

'I don't even know how to do this,' she said, taking it back out of her mouth again.

'What you've got to do,' Gaetano explained. 'Is take it really gently. Really slowly. If you rush you'll only end up coughing.' He placed a hand on her shoulder, like a doctor showing his patient how to inject insulin for the first time. 'Just inhale a little bit and hold the smoke in your mouth.'

Fiona obliged. Her cheeks blew up like a cornered puffer-fish. Gaetano's mouth slid into a smile. 'Now, when you're ready, breathe in naturally and take the smoke down into your lungs. Just breathe as if you were on a hillside, taking in fresh air.'

Fiona raised her eyebrows frantically and shook her head. Fresh air? It was like sucking on an exhaust pipe. Her cheeks were still stretched out to twice their normal size.

'You can do it, Fi. Just breathe in naturally. The smoke will be really cool by now. It won't hurt. Breathe naturally.' he demonstrated the flow of air with his hands. 'I sound like an ante-natal class, don't I?' He took the spliff from Fiona's hand and inhaled once more himself. 'Like that.' He forced the smoke out again between clenched teeth.

Fiona was going slightly pink. She had yet to breathe at all. Finally she could hold the air in her mouth no longer and exhaled like Old Faithful, sending the smoke straight back out into the room. None of it had touched her lungs.

'I can't do it, Gaetano,' she panted. 'I've never smoked. It's just not me. I'll only end up having a choking fit. And I've got to get on with my work.'

Gaetano drew on the spliff again and passed it back to her patiently. He was on a mission now, and if it was the last thing he ever did, he was going to get Fiona stoned. It should be a laugh in more ways than one. He took her by the elbow and guided her hand back up to her lips. 'One more time,' he told her. 'Remember the attraction of subversion.'

She turned her head away from the approaching roach like her mother's terrier when it refused to take antibiotics.

'I can't smoke it. I really can't. Isn't there anything else we could do? You can make it into cakes can't you? I've heard that lots of times. I think I've got some flour and stuff downstairs.'

Gaetano shook his head. 'You're thinking along the right lines, Fi, but you can't do that with this stuff. It's grass, isn't it? If you try to heat it, grass just burns. You need the resin to make cakes.' He nudged her elbow upwards. 'Try one more time. It'll be really worth it. I've never had such a good feeling as the one I got the very first time.'

Fiona licked her lips nervously. 'OK. One more time and then I'll give up.' She slipped the roach between her lips once more and sucked some smoke into her dry mouth. 'I must breathe naturally, I must breathe naturally,' she chanted to herself. Holding the smoke in her mouth for a moment longer, she breathed in through the nose to fill out her chest. She felt the smoke and air rush on down, flooding the tiny chambers of her lungs, and her eyes widened with surprise. She breathed out again and saw a faint plume of smoke escape via her nose.

'Yeah, that's right.' Gaetano gave her a one man round of applause. 'What did I tell you? I knew you could do it, Fi. Welcome to your misspent youth.'

'God, I feel weird. I'm going all light-headed.'

'Not yet you aren't. It's just the shock of christening your lungs. Have another go now, while you've got the hang of it.' He tipped her elbow upwards and the spliff went back into her mouth. Fiona followed the steps she had learned before. Into the mouth, cool the smoke down, air through the nose, and down into the lungs. She couldn't help smiling as she completed the steps without coughing her guts up on to the floor. She held the spliff away from her and looked at it in admiration almost exactly as Gaetano had done.

'You're right,' she told him. 'This stuff's amazing.'

Gaetano laughed. 'I told you so.' She passed him the spliff and he gave it the same doe-eyed look of love. 'But it's such a bad habit. Once you start, you can't think why you never did it before.'

'I didn't because I was scared.'

'We've established that,' said Gaetano. 'You're scared of a lot of things, Fi. But you're not so scared now, are you?' He inhaled deeply and exhaled two perfect little smoke rings that floated off across the bedroom like lost halos.

CHAPTER TWENTY-FIVE

Linzi must have really tried George Gerrard's patience. He had indeed found her another job, but what kind of job was this? Linzi had been more than a little pissed off when she arrived at Manatee Records to discover that her 'truly covetable position' was in fact in the company's dingy basement post room. Hardly the best place to begin her Monster Munch promotion campaign. That morning she had franked three and a half thousand postcards to announce the imminent release of a new single by the heavy metal combo Dyer Ria. To alleviate the boredom she had readdressed the card bound for the PR department at Radio One with her home address and scribbled 'Dear Kez and Fi, Wish you were here . . . instead of me.'

At lunchtime, the pink-haired girl to whom Linzi was meant to be reporting, came down to the post room and looked at the pile of cards left to be franked with a critical eye.

'How's it going?' she asked through her chewing gum.

'I'm surviving,' Linzi lied.

The pink-haired girl bit her lip, unconvinced. 'We've got to get a whole load of cards out for Tineka Bovary's new album this afternoon. I'd better call for someone else to come in and help you.'

'I'll manage,' said Linzi valiantly. The only thing worse than being holed-up in this dingy basement would be being holed-up in the dingy basement with someone else.

'I don't think so,' said the pink-haired girl. 'I'll call the agency.'

Three-quarters of an hour later, Linzi was joined by Freya from Sydney, who was willing to do just about anything to get the money together for her European tour.

'Hiya.' She was unnecessarily cheerful. 'I was sent here to help you by Advertising Angels.'

'No good looking so happy to be here,' Linzi informed her. 'We've got to get through all this lot before they'll let us go home.' She waved her arm in the direction of ten brown-cardboard boxes, each one of which was filled with a thousand postcards. 'Do you know how to use a franking machine?' Freya nodded quickly. 'Good. Then you can get going on these. I need a fag.'

Freya got to it. She didn't know that Linzi wasn't her boss. Two boxes of postcards later, Linzi let her in on the secret. Two cigarettes later than that, they were fast on the way to becoming firm friends. Freya told her how excited she was to be in the UK. And everyone had been so kind. Particularly Caroline at AA.

'But what I don't understand is,' Linzi began to tell her, 'why all you Australians want to come to England in the first place. I mean you've got everything out there. Sunshine, sandy beaches. The latest series of *Neighbours*. And you decide to give all that up and come to London instead. And it's a dump. I mean, where do you live when you're over here? Earl's Court, I suppose.'

'Actually, I'm sharing with some friends in Hackney.'

'Hackney?' Linzi gasped. 'You couldn't pay me to live there. It's so dirty and rough.'

'Oh, we've got a really lovely place there though. Three bedrooms and a sitting room.'

'How many of you are living there?'

'Just eight at the moment.'

Linzi's jaw dropped. 'Eight?'

'Six flatmates and two dossers. I'm just dossing because I only came over from Bangkok last week, so I've got the mattress on the landing. But Finola is going back to New Zealand next month so I'll be able to move into her room then and share with Sandy.'

'Share a room? Doesn't that drive you up the wall? I'm sharing with just two girls in a three-bedroomed house and most days it seems like the place isn't big enough for the three of us. How on earth do you all manage to get in the bathroom before you go to work?'

'Oh, we've got a rota for that,' Freya said cheerfully. 'It starts at six a.m. Unfortunately the dossers get the worst bathroom spots so I'm in at ten past six.'

'Ten past six?' Linzi wasn't sure she had ever seen that particular time of day unless she had forgotten to go to bed the night before. 'Ten past six?' she asked again as if Freya had got her figures wrong. 'That's mad. Why on earth do you want to put up with that?'

'It's worth it,' said Freya dreamily as she slit open another box of postcards. 'It's the only way I can afford to stay in London while I save up to do a tour of Europe. I really want to see the whole of the world before I die.'

Linzi fed the first of a million postcards into the franking machine. She hadn't seen that much of the world herself. Just France on half a dozen family holidays before the family split up. A few Greek islands. Amsterdam on the obligatory student smoking weekend. And a month travelling in the States after finals. On the front of the postcard she was franking, the popstar to be promoted was standing in the foamy surf that crashed against the white beach of an unspecified Caribbean island. Yeah. It would be nice to travel. See the world. If only she had the money.

'If you'd like to go Down Under sometime,' Freya told her happily, 'you could always use my place in Sydney as a base. My flatmates are really cool about houseguests.'

'Then you'd better give me your address today,' said Linzi. 'Because I don't think I'm going to come back here tomorrow.'

Freya duly scribbled down her address on the back of a Tineka Bovary postcard and Linzi responded in kind. Linzi folded her postcard and stuck it into the back pocket of her jeans, wondering if she'd ever get to use it. Not unless the DSS started to hand out international travel grants, she thought dryly.

'Are you really not going to come back tomorrow?' Freya asked.

'I don't think so. I thought that I might be able to meet some influential people, you know, push my boyfriend's band. But I haven't seen daylight since I got here, let alone the A & R department.'

'What kind of music is it?'

'Heavy metal, I suppose,' Linzi said apologetically. She reached into her bag and fished out the Monster Munch tape she had brought with her. 'You can have this if you want it,' she told Freya. 'Do your ear-drums some damage.'

'Thanks. It looks really interesting. But Linzi, don't you think you're giving up just a bit too soon? Won't Caroline be mad?'

'Doubtless, she'll be livid. But you can tell her I said "bye-ze-bye".'

CHAPTER TWENTY-SIX

Fiona was now completely prone at the foot of Linzi's bed. Gaetano was lying on the bed itself, occasionally passing the spliff down to Fiona who would take a deep toke in-between attempting to plait the fringed edge of Linzi's orange bedspread.

'No, I'm sure I'm better off without him. I mean, he would never do anything like we're doing now. I don't think he'd even breathe in if he walked into a room where someone was smoking a spliff. He is so uptight I'm sure he only shits twice a year. It was him that made me like I was, Gaetano. I was a nightmare, I know it.' She passed the spliff back up to Gaetano. 'I gave you and Linzi such a hard time.' Gaetano reached his hand down towards Fiona and she knitted her fingers through his.

'You're not so bad,' Gaetano said soothingly. 'Anyway, like you said, Tim will probably call you when he gets home from work tonight and everything will be back to normal before tomorrow. You know it will.'

'Do you think so?'

'I know what men are like. He would never have asked to marry you in the first place if he didn't have very strong feelings for you. Even though he's now retracted the offer, that doesn't take away from the fact that he made it and that, at that moment in time, he really felt something for you which won't just have vanished into mid-air because of all this trouble.'

Fiona sat up and rested her chin on the edge of the bed. 'What?' Her brain was having trouble keeping up.

'I mean, he probably still loves you, Fi, doesn't he?'

'I really hope you're right.'

Gaetano had been looking at the woodchip on the ceiling but now he turned so that he was facing Fiona. He exhaled carefully, so that the smoke didn't go straight into her eyes. Fiona locked her eyes on his. Linzi had been right about them. Gaetano's eyes were like two big chocolate buttons, slightly melted to a gloss by the sun. Gaetano casually licked his full red lips. Fiona moved imperceptibly closer, so that there was less than an inch between their trembling mouths.

'I'm not so sure that I even care if he loves me or not any more,' Fiona murmured. 'After all, there's plenty more fish in the sea.'

'And I'm a halibut,' replied Gaetano.

Fiona laughed.

Gaetano took hold of the back of her head and pulled her mouth down upon his.

CHAPTER TWENTY-SEVEN

Linzi bumped into Tim on her way back from the tube to Artesia Road. He was fresh from work, still in his suit, and carrying a huge bunch of bright red roses beneath his arm.

'Hello, Tim,' said Linzi. 'You must have done something really bad to turn up with those.'

He looked a little embarrassed as he spun around to see who was addressing him. 'Oh, hi, Linzi.' He waved the bunch of roses at her as if they had suddenly appeared beneath his arm by magic and he had nothing to do with them being there. 'Fi and I had a little bit of a fight last night. I called her at work and they said that she had twenty-four hour flu, so I think I must have upset her pretty badly.'

'Either that or she really has the flu,' said Linzi.

'I don't think she was coming down with anything yesterday.'

'Did you call her at home?'

'If she's in, she didn't pick up the phone.'

'Probably sulking. Or shopping. Retail therapy. Harvey Nicks is marginally cheaper than seeing a psychiatrist.'

'Look, Linzi,' Tim said suddenly. 'I don't mean to put you in an awkward position or anything but what do you think of us? I mean, what do you think of me and Fi? Do you think that we ought to get married or what?'

'Oh, whoah,' Linzi backed off with her hands in the air in a gesture of surrender. 'Don't try to get me involved in some heavy debate about marriage before I've had a drink.'

'But, Linzi, you live with her and you know me well enough. What do you think about us?'

Linzi sighed. 'Fiona is one of my very best friends, Tim. Obviously, I think that the man who marries her has got himself a really good catch. Anyway, you've been together for four years. You should know whether you like her enough to marry her or not by now.'

'Yeah, you're right,' Tim nodded. 'We've been together for ages without too much hassle, haven't we? No reason why it should all change when we get married, eh?'

'Not in theory.'

'Could even get better?'

'Could do. I don't know.'

They had turned into Artesia Road but there were no lights on in number 67. Linzi glanced up at the bedroom windows. No sign of life up there, either. That was odd. Perhaps Fiona really had given up moping about Tim and gone out to meet some friends, though she hadn't exactly kept up with anyone but Linzi and Kerry since meeting the man of her dreams, so which friend would she have gone to see? Linzi really didn't know. 'You're more than welcome to hang on here until she comes back,' Linzi told Tim. 'She'll be really pleased to see you.'

'I hope she will,' Tim said sadly.

Linzi put her key in the chubb lock. It was already open, which was very strange. Fiona never went out without first making sure that the house was fastened up tighter than Fort Knox. Relationship disaster or no relationship disaster. She must be in and asleep. Linzi didn't let Tim know what she was thinking.

'Make yourself a cup of tea. I'm sure you must know where everything is by now. You can put the television on too . . . As long as it's not rugby.'

Tim forced a smile. One of the reasons that he didn't come round to Artesia Road so much any more was the ban Linzi had put on television sport, which was heavily enforced by the other girls. 'Yeah, Tim. You know you're doing the right thing.' Linzi put a hand on his arm as she passed and gave him a little squeeze. 'Besides, Kerry and I have already bought the bridesmaids' dresses.'

Linzi heard the sound of giggling as she turned at the top of the stairs.

'Shit, someone's in!'

The voices were coming from her bedroom. Linzi froze on the

landing, not really sure that she wanted to investigate. Were they being burgled? She almost screamed to Tim to give her backup.

'Ow, what was that?' The burglar had just stubbed his toe.

There was definitely someone in there. 'Tim, come quickly!' Linzi called.

Tim bounded up the stairs, taking them two at a time until he reached the top.

'I think there's someone in my bedroom.'

He had already picked up the poker that stood unused in the fireplace and now raised it up in readiness to bring it down again on someone's head. He put his hand on the doorknob and the world seemed to hold its breath. Linzi crammed her fingers in her mouth as she got ready to stifle a scream.

'Tim! No!'

Fiona appeared in the doorway with her arms raised to cover her head in defence. Gaetano ducked down behind her. The rod slipped out of an astonished Tim's hand and over his back to the floor.

'Tim?'

'Fiona?'

'What are you doing in my room?' Linzi asked.

'What are you doing with him?' asked Tim.

But Tim didn't wait around for an explanation. Instead, he was out of number 67, Artesia Road with the speed of a hurricane, ingloriously stuffing the peace-making roses in the dustbin as he passed.

'Tim, Tim.' Fiona ran out on to the empty street after him. 'Wait for me. Hang on, Tim. Let me explain.' But he had sprinted off around the corner and she couldn't follow him that far in her bare feet.

When Fiona gave up the chase and came back inside, Linzi was sitting halfway down the stairs. Gaetano hovered a few steps behind her, subtly buttoning up his shirt.

Linzi stared at her dishevelled housemate and her sheepish-looking boyfriend. 'OK. Is someone going to tell me just what is going on?'

'I got Fiona stoned, that's all,' began Gaetano. 'We bumped into each other at Burger King and I asked if I could come over and pick up some of the CDs that I left here. I was rolling a joint for the walk back and Fiona asked if she could have some.'

'Fiona wanted a smoke?' Linzi asked incredulously.

'Yeah,' Gaetano shrugged. 'I thought it was strange too, but I guess she was feeling a bit down what with the row with Tim and all. But I didn't know she'd never smoked before so she got completely caned after two tokes. She fell asleep on your bed and that's what must have happened to me too. It was skunk, Linz,' he added, pulling out the bag to prove it. 'It must have been pretty strong stuff.'

Fiona repeated the story almost word for word. Between sobs. Then she tried to call Tim, but he either hadn't made it home or wasn't answering his phone. Later that evening, when Linzi finally managed to get past his answerphone on Fiona's behalf, Tim told her in no uncertain terms that he didn't believe their excuses at all.

'But you believe me, don't you?' Fiona pleaded with Linzi when she put down the phone.

Linzi nodded. She did. She had to.

'Look, Fi,' she said softly. 'I think that your best bet is not to call Tim for a while. Give him a chance to cool down. He obviously wanted to make it up with you after last night. Give him a day or so and he'll be straight back on the phone.' But something told her that Tim had no intention of giving Fiona the benefit of the doubt. Fiona had made his big decision for him. She had quite unwittingly let him off the hook.

For his part, Gaetano decided that it might be a good idea for him to risk his mother's wrath and spend the night at Artesia Road with Linzi.

CHAPTER TWENTY-EIGHT

When Kerry got home from work that evening, she thought at first that the house was empty. Fiona had retired to her room to sob. Linzi and Gaetano were reaffirming their commitment to each other in the bedroom. But Fiona crept downstairs again when she realised that Kerry had come back home and Kerry knew the moment she saw Fiona's red-rimmed eyes that something very serious indeed had gone wrong. Her first line of action was to put the kettle on. Then Fiona began to tell the story. She got as far as sobbing that Tim had broken off the engagement before her intermittent sniffing and wailing became so loud that Kerry didn't have a hope in hell of finding out why.

'He'll call tomorrow, I'm sure,' Kerry reassured her absent-mindedly. They had broken up before. Tim would come crawling back as he always did. After all, getting himself a new girlfriend might actually require making some effort. Right now, Kerry had something far more worrying on her mind than the end of Fiona's doomed engagement.

That afternoon, Mrs Keble, Kerry's mother, had called her at Verbal Tix. At the moment she called, Kerry was on the cappuccino run but her mother felt she knew Leon well enough after the wedding to leave a very delicate message for him to pass on.

'She wants to know if you've seen your sister Michelle,' Leon told Kerry as she tried to get the plastic lids off the polystyrene cups without scalding herself to death.

'Of course I haven't seen my sister,' Kerry replied. 'She's on her honeymoon, isn't she? I shouldn't imagine she's even seen daylight since she got to Majorca.'

'Oh dear. You'd better call your mum,' said Leon.

Mrs Keble explained the dilemma in a whisper. It appeared that Michelle was no longer on her honeymoon at all. She had disappeared. When Richard woke up alone in the room that morning he assumed that she had gone for an early swim, but when she didn't come back after an hour, he got up to join her and found that she had left him a note on the kitchenette table. It said quite simply, 'Richard, I can't go on like this.' She had taken all her belongings with her in the smaller of their two new leather suitcases, which had been a generous wedding gift from Auntie Jean.

Richard had searched the whole of the resort and when that course of action drew a blank, he simply had to inform the island police. He didn't see how Michelle could have got too far since he had their tickets home and all the holiday money. However, a routine check of the airport revealed that she had indeed left the island that morning, flying back to Gatwick. She had paid for her ticket with a credit card! Visa! Imagine that! Richard didn't even know that she possessed a credit card and he certainly wouldn't have allowed her to get one because he doesn't agree with that kind of thing.

'She should have landed at Gatwick at one o'clock this afternoon,' Mrs Keble continued. 'It's gone five o'clock now, Kerry. Are you sure that she's not with you?'

'I haven't heard a word, Mum. Honest I haven't.'

'Are you sure, Kerry, because so help me God if you're keeping her hidden from us and her husband, I'll give you such a hiding. And her and all, when I catch up with her. You can tell her that. Worrying us all to death, she is. It's so selfish. I've had Richard's mother round here all day. She can't stop crying. Your father's gone out to the garage to fiddle with his car and he says he won't come back in till everything's sorted out, not even for his tea. If Michelle is with you, Kerry, you just better make sure she knows how selfish she's being. You can't leave your husband on your honeymoon!'

'Mum, if I see her, I'll let her know that she ought to get in touch, but I promise you, she isn't here with me.'

'Oooh, I don't know what I've done to deserve such terrible daughters,' Mrs Keble sighed. 'Your other sister was round here last night saying that she wants to leave her Steve. None of you can stick at anything for long.'

'Mum, I've got to go. I'm at work. Remember?'

'Leon won't mind you talking to me. He's a lovely lad. Now listen, Kerry. Make sure you call me the minute you get home to let me know whether she's been at your place. And don't you ever go causing me trouble like the other two have. Try and stick with something. Hang on to that Leon. There aren't many men like him about these days.'

'You're right, Mum,' Kerry sighed. 'You're right.'

Kerry reported the conversation to Leon.

'Bloody hell,' he snorted. 'She's not going to be too happy when we get a divorce, is she?'

Kerry smiled sadly. They hadn't gone through with the ceremony yet and Leon was eager to plan the end of their marriage already. That afternoon he had told her that he was prepared to pay her two thousand pounds for her involvement in the scam. Kerry refused. She wasn't doing it for the money.

When Fiona had finished a first sniffly draft of the great engagement break-up story, Kerry picked up the phone and dutifully called home to file her report on Michelle. It took her almost half an hour to persuade her mother that she was telling the truth when she said that Michelle hadn't been in touch. As she put the phone down again, even Kerry was beginning to feel a little concerned for her sister's safety. Where could she have gone? As far as the family could tell, Michelle knew no one outside Bristol except Kerry.

It was while Kerry was worrying about this that the doorbell rang and she opened the door to find Michelle herself, brown and bedraggled but still smiling, on the front step.

'My God, you're in trouble,' Kerry told her sister. After an unwarranted ear-bashing from their mother, Kerry was in no mood to return Michelle's joyous hug.

'I know, I know,' Michelle said wearily. 'I just tried to call Mum from the callbox at the top of your road but she's engaged. Probably yacking on to Richard's mum about what they could have done to end up with such terrible children.'

'Actually she was yacking on to me about what she'd done to end up with such terrible children. She's worried sick, Michelle.

We are all worried sick. What on earth happened? Where have you been?'

'My marriage broke up,' Michelle announced dramatically as she dropped her bag in the hallway and threw herself on to the sofa with a sigh. Fiona looked up from her tea and momentarily felt that perhaps hers wasn't the worst life in the world.

'Your marriage broke up? But it's less than a fortnight old for goodness' sake.'

'I know, Kerry, I know,' Michelle sighed. 'But even as we were getting on the plane I realised that we weren't going to last the honeymoon.'

'What? How did you know that?'

'I can't really explain it.'

'You're going to have to try.'

Michelle straightened herself up in her seat and began. 'Well, I think that the main problem was that nothing was different. I mean, just little things like the fact that Richard still insisted on taking the window seat on the plane and putting all his rubbish on my tray while we waited for the stewardess to collect it.'

'Oh, for heaven's sake. If he always did that, where was the problem?' Kerry didn't understand.

'I suddenly realised that I'd married him because I thought that it would make things better. But it hadn't. I thought it might make us more of a partnership but it was obvious that was just a distant dream. I still felt like I was Richard's donkey, not his wife. Make us a cup of tea, will you, Kerry? I'm gasping.'

'I don't know if you deserve one.'

'Oh, give me a break.'

'You hardly gave Richard one, did you?'

'I gave it nearly two years of living in sin and a few days of full-blown marriage, Kerry. How much more of a break can you give a man? I was miserable. Even the sun and sangria didn't help to cheer me up. When we went out for dinner he would always insist on eating something we could have got in any number of places back home and he moaned like mad when the waiter at this one place said they had no HP sauce. I wanted to see the local sights, eat paella and go a bit Spanish. He just wanted to sleep until the bars opened and then watch the football from home on satellite television. We weren't matched, Kez. We never were matched, we never will be and no piece of gold is going to make enough of a difference. In fact sometimes,' she added dramatically, 'it was almost as if that wedding ring was cutting off the bloodflow to the rest of my body.'

'God only knows what Mum is going to say about this.'

'I don't care what other people are going to say any more. Especially Mum. That's how I got myself into this mess in the first place. Caring too much about appearances and not upsetting Mother. Now I've been unfair to myself and to Richard. You know, I opened a separate bank account without telling him six months ago and then I went and got myself a credit card. I've been gearing myself up to leave him for ages. I just didn't realise that that was what I had been doing.'

'So that's how you managed to fly back here without your ticket. That really confused him.'

'Everything I do confuses Richard.'

'But Mum said that your flight would be in at one o'clock. It's nearly nine now. Where on earth have you been all day?'

'I've been at the Australian Embassy,' Michelle announced. 'I've been getting myself a visa and a work permit.'

'Michelle!'

'I'm flying out to Hong Kong tomorrow night. I got a courier flight so it's dead cheap. Then I'm going on to Sydney.'

'You're going to Australia?' Kerry was almost hysterical.

'It's only the other side of the world, Kez. Stop acting like you're our mother.'

'Oh God, Michelle. You had better call Mum right now. She is going to go insane.'

'Exactly. And I can't face that tonight. I've had one hell of a day already. You call her instead, Kez. Please. Tell her that I'm here with you and that I'm safe. Tell her that I'll talk to her tomorrow morning before I fly. But you can also tell her not to bother driving over here to try to make me change my mind because I'm not going to and I don't trust Dad's driving skills in the dark.'

'You've gone nuts, you have. Completely bonkers.'

'Maybe I have. But I feel much better for it.'

'If Mum has another go at me because of you, Michelle . . .'

Kerry flew into the kitchen to grab the phone and break the news. Michelle finally noticed Fiona's red eyes.

'What's up with you, Fi? You look like you've been crying all day.'

'I have. Tim's broken off our engagement,' Fiona sniffed pathetically.

'I guess I should say I'm sorry,' Michelle began. 'But believe me, Fi, you just had a lucky escape.'

CHAPTER TWENTY-NINE

Linzi traced the outline of Gaetano's nipples through the soft black hair on his chest. He had been lying on his back for the past half-hour, just staring up at the ceiling. When Linzi snuggled into his side he made a half-hearted attempt at a hug.

'What's up with you?' she asked finally.

'Nothing. I'm just thinking.'

'How can it be nothing if you're thinking about it?'

'I mean it's nothing that you would find interesting. I'm just thinking about the band, that's all.'

'What about it?'

'You don't want to know.'

'I do now. The sound of your brain ticking over is keeping me awake. Come on, G, spill the beans.'

'It was right, you know,' Gaetano began, 'what The Professor was saying in the pub the other night.'

'About what?'

'About promoting the band. We can't just sit around waiting for someone to sign us up any more. We're going to have to go for it by ourselves. We've got to put a CD out on our own label.' He sighed heavily. 'It's the only way. You remember Mutant Phlegm? They put out an EP last year. Apparently they got back everything they paid for it and generated enough interest to get themselves a deal.'

'Good for them. But where will you get the money from to make the CD in the first place?' Linzi protested. 'The Professor said that it would cost you at least a couple of grand to get the thing pressed and that's before you've even thought about distribution and promotion.'

'Listen to you. A whole day in the music industry and you're spouting all the terms already.'

'Then you'll be pleased to know that it was my last day in the music industry.'

'What do you mean?'

'They put me in the bloody post room. I'm not going back there again.'

'Oh, great. That's one less contact than we had this morning. We've got no chance of getting in via an A & R man now.'

'I'm sorry, G.'

Gaetano sighed. 'It doesn't matter, Linz. I'm sure it wouldn't have made that much of a difference anyway. Monster Munch are just too off the wall. Those A & R men never have enough vision to introduce something really new. We've got to put something out ourselves. We've all got to pull together. The Professor has got some money saved up. Merlin's a bit of a wash-out financially but Socks could sell his car.'

'Socks sell his car? You've got to be joking. He loves that car more than his own mother.'

'His mother's dead.'

'Oh, I'm sorry,' Linzi said reflexively.

'It doesn't matter. They never got on. He bought the car by selling her bungalow. But even he will have to see that when we hit the big time he can buy himself a thousand bloody cars like that rust heap.'

'And what about you, what have you got to sell?'

There was silence for a moment except for the sound of Gaetano breathing in and out. Finally he answered. 'Nothing material, I admit. But I've got my expertise, haven't I?'

'Your expertise?' Linzi repeated slowly and, she hoped, not too incredulously.

'Yeah. I've got an amazing plan. You remember what we were talking about with the Professor the other night?'

'What?' Linzi yawned. 'How Zildjian make the best possible cymbal?'

'No, apart from that. Before then. When we were talking about his job?'

'Surely you're not going to train to be a pharmacist?' Linzi laughed. 'You'll be retiring before you make enough money for the CD.'

'No chance. What use is a degree to anybody these days anyway?'

Linzi rolled away from him with a snort. 'Quite.'

'Look, I wasn't trying to get at you but it's a fact, isn't it? You've got to do something a bit different to get ahead now. Do you want to hear my plan, or not?'

'Go on. Amuse me.'

'It's not about amusement, Linzi. This is serious stuff. If you don't think you can handle anything heavier than licking stamps in the post room of a record company, then it's best you don't get yourself involved.'

'Me get involved? I have no intention of getting involved. Since when have I been a member of Monster Munch?'

'You're my girlfriend, Linzi. You're supposed to be behind me all the way.'

'How many paces is that?'

Gaetano rolled over onto his side, increasing the physical distance between them. Linzi reached out in the dark and put her hand on his silhouetted shoulder. She knew that she was taking out her frustration on him for her shitty day at Manatee and for the incident with Fiona that she had claimed she didn't even believe took place. 'Hey, come on,' she whispered, 'you just touched a raw nerve with your comments about the post room, that's all. Of course I want to hear what your plans are. Of course I want to help you in whatever way I can.'

Gaetano rolled onto his back again. He reached over to the bedside table for his packet of cigarettes and lit one up. His face looked stony with concentration in the brief glow shed by his flaming Zippo and the tip of the cigarette. Linzi stroked the top of his arm, hoping to smooth the hardness away. 'Come on, spit it out,' she murmured. 'What's the big plan?'

'OK. But you've got to tell me that you love me first, yeah? So that even if you decide that you don't want to be a part of this, you won't ever tell anyone what I am about to say.'

'Of course I won't. I love you.' Linzi was aching to hear the story now. He had never been so serious in all the time she had known him. 'Just tell me what you want me to do.'

'Linzi,' Gaetano said slowly. 'We are going to do a robbery.'

'What?' Linzi sat bolt upright in the bed. 'A robbery? We? I think you had better elaborate.'

'OK.' Gaetano elaborated. He had hatched the big plan while listening to the Professor talking about his job. The Professor was always taking on locum work whenever he had a spare evening, trying to supplement his wages and then ploughing the proceeds back into the band. Some of the shops he worked in had been robbed before. People had got away with thousands of pounds' worth of controlled drugs and had never been caught. Not just once but dozens of times. The smaller shops in particular had minimal security systems. They were cheaply installed and easy to disable. Sometimes the Professor would have only one assistant to man the tills while he made up the prescriptions and most of the time that single assistant would be some stupid young girl. There was one shop in particular which would be very easy pickings. He was due to do a night's locum work there later in the week.

'The Professor reckons that he can put the cameras out of action before we arrive,' Gaetano concluded.

Linzi's heart was pounding against the walls of her chest.

'We're going to rob a pharmacy?'

'I can get a car,' Gaetano whispered. 'You can drive it for us. You can drive, can't you?'

'Yes, I can. But you're not really serious about this?' Linzi murmured to his shadow.

'Of course I'm serious about this, Linzi. I don't want to be a loser working in a clothes shop for the rest of my life. I want to be a somebody. I want to get Monster Munch a record deal and this is the way to make the money to do it. Are you going to help me or what?'

'No way am I. What you're asking me to do is illegal and dangerous,' Linzi said flatly.

'Well, I can't deny that it's illegal,' Gaetano began. 'But it won't be dangerous, Linz. No one will get hurt. The Professor will pretend that he doesn't know what's going on and he'll persuade the shop-girl to co-operate. There'll be no violence, no blood and no risk of getting caught because the Professor will have dealt with the cameras and the panic button to the police station.'

'The panic button to the police station? You didn't mention that. Oh my God, Gaetano. You're being ridiculous now.'

'I told you, the Professor will have disabled it. If there even is one. He says that it's easy, just a matter of unscrewing the buzzer. No one will notice. It'll give us extra time.'

'But what's in it for me?' Linzi continued. 'I'm afraid that the glittering future of Monster Munch is a little too abstract a concept for me to want to end up in prison for it.'

'You won't end up in prison, I swear. And you'll get a cut of the money. A quarter if that's what it takes to get you on board. It'll be about a thousand quid. You could do another course.'

Linzi smiled. 'No thanks. My shiatsu days are over.'

'It could be a lot of money.'

'It would have to be a lot of money to make me take that kind of risk,' Linzi snorted.

'C'mon Linzi. There must be something you're dying to do. All you need is that elusive grand and you can go and do it.'

'You said a quarter. How many of us would be involved?'

'Three.'

'Then why wouldn't the money be split three ways?'

'Because three-quarters of the cash has to go towards putting out the single, of course.'

'I think my help would be worth more than a quarter.'

'OK, a third. Will you do it for that?'

'Well,' Linzi mused, remembering that afternoon's conversation with Freya. 'I was thinking that I might try to travel a bit this year. I've hardly seen anything of the world except France and the Greek islands. But I was also thinking more along the conventional lines of working hard and saving up to pay for the trip.'

'Saving up? You're going to have to get better at holding down a job if that's your plan,' Gaetano pointed out.

'Not fair. I could hold down a job easily if someone would give me something exciting to do.'

'Isn't my idea exciting enough for you?'

'I said "exciting", not "terrifying".'

She felt Gaetano move so that his leg was across hers. He nuzzled her ear beneath her hair and whispered. 'If Monster Munch make it big because of this, I'll take you anywhere you want to go, first class.' Linzi laughed out loud. Gaetano put his hand down between her legs and began to gently massage her crotch. 'So you'll be our driver?'

Linzi bit her lip. 'I didn't say yes.'

She felt Gaetano's leg slip off her own again. 'Look, I'll think about it, OK?' she said to salvage his affection. 'But you've got to give me more details first. You know, I can't really believe you're asking me to do this at all. It's like going out with someone in the Mafia.'

'Hey, you. Shut your mouth.' Gaetano put on his best God-father accent. 'Some of my favourite relations are in the Mafia.' Linzi smiled. His mother could certainly have put the frighteners on a wimp like Joe Pesci.

'When would we have to do it?' Linzi asked after a while in a quieter, more serious voice.

'The Professor is going to be working in this shop on Saturday night. It's in North London. A rough area. There'll be hundreds of natural suspects in the housing estates around the shop and if it gets as far as an identity parade, the Professor says he'll pick out the first bloke he sees who looks anything like the A & R man from Malibou.'

'Gaetano, you're nuts.'

'Yeah, but you love me for it.'

CHAPTER THIRTY

W hen Kerry arrived at work the next morning, Leon insisted that she leave again straight away to sort her family obligations out. Mrs Keble had been on the phone the minute the Verbal Tix office opened to tell Leon exactly what was going on and Leon was both sorry for her and anxious not to get on the wrong side of his future mother-in-law (though they had yet to detonate that particular bombshell).

'At least make sure she gets to the right terminal at Heathrow,' Leon instructed Kerry. 'She could be gone for ages. She's your little sister. You've got to keep in touch.'

Kerry wasn't really all that bothered about giving Michelle a good send-off. She was angry that her younger sister seemed able to cause such chaos and still get away with it. When Mrs Keble's first fit of hysterics had passed and she had persuaded Michelle to talk to her in person, she seemed to forgive her youngest daughter everything. In fact, when Michelle handed the phone back to Kerry, Mrs Keble even said 'She always was the bravest of you all. She'll make something of herself Down Under. I know she will.'

What happened to the selfish, irresponsible and often impossible girl who had left her husband weeping in their honeymoon suite?

Kerry and Michelle shared a largely silent taxi-ride to Heathrow.

'Which terminal?' the taxi driver asked. Michelle looked at her ticket blankly.

'I can't see it, Kerry. Which terminal do you think we want?'

Kerry took the ticket from her and scanned it for the relevant information.

'Four,' she announced. 'Terminal Four.'

'Thanks,' Michelle took the ticket back. 'I didn't have a clue what I was looking for. You always were the practical one, Kez.'

'And you were always the exciting one,' Kerry sniffed.

'Yeah, right. Don't exaggerate. Look, Kez. You will come and visit me, won't you? When I've got myself settled in? You'd love it in Australia. I'm sure you would. Nicky Hazel said that she didn't want to come back after her year out there.'

'Nicky Hazel didn't have all that much to come back for.'

'Leon wouldn't miss you for a week or so, would he?'

'No, I suppose he wouldn't. You get yourself settled in and I'll see what I can do. Though I don't suppose I've even earned any leave yet. I've only been at that job for two months and I've already had to take two days off because of you, what with the wedding and making sure you get to the right terminal today.'

'I'm eternally grateful. You know you're my favourite sister, Kez.' Michelle squeezed her hand. 'I always looked up to you. All through school.'

'Yeah, well. In that case, don't do anything I wouldn't do.'

'I'll see you in Australia then.'

'I said perhaps.'

'Look, Kez. Try to be happy for me, won't you? I expected Mum to be the difficult one but I feel like you're the one who is most pissed off with me over this whole thing. You wouldn't have wanted me to rot away in St Paul's with Richard for the rest of my life, would you? I'm going to take control of my own destiny now. You're going to be proud of me. You'll see. Everyone's got to follow their dreams. At the end of the day, you're the only person with your own best interests at heart.'

'I know you're right, Michelle. It's just that it's all so sudden. And I'm worried that you'll be disappointed when you get there.'

'In some ways, I won't care so very much if I am. It would be far worse to live with the question of what might have happened. Nothing ventured, remember, Kez?' Michelle sniffed a little sadly. 'You said that to me when I first met Richard. When I didn't know whether he fancied me or not and he was too shy to ask me out.'

'I remember.'

'Well, I ventured then, didn't I? I asked him out and discovered that he did fancy me after all. I know it's all gone a bit pear-shaped now, but we had some happy times together and I got you to wear a stupid dress at the end of it.'

'Yeah. I won't ever forgive you for that.'

The taxi driver pulled up outside the terminal. Kerry helped Michelle to drag her bright new rucksack into the departures lounge.

'Is this going to be enough for a whole year?'

'You've got to be a portable girl at times like this, Kez. You don't really need that much stuff to survive.'

Kerry shrugged. But it was hard to imagine how Michelle would cope without her hairspray and curling tongs.

Kerry took the tube back from Heathrow to Clapham South. She had kissed her little sister goodbye at the gate which led to the duty free shops. As she passed through the gate, Michelle suddenly remembered that there was something she had to ask Kerry to take home for her. She pressed her wedding and engagement rings into Kerry's hand.

'Give them back to Richard, could you?'

Kerry nodded.

'It's funny, isn't it?' Michelle continued. 'To think of these two things as symbols of commitment when, in reality, they don't mean anything without the right feelings behind them. Why do so many people seem to spend their lives chasing a little piece of gold, eh?'

'Who knows?' Kerry sighed.

'So long, sis.'

One last kiss goodbye.

'I'm off to chase some sun.'

Now, Kerry fished the two rings out of her top pocket as she sat on the tube. The glittering sapphire and cubic zirconia cluster and the plain gold wedding band. She remembered the first time she had seen the engagement ring. It had been Christmas Day, two years earlier. Michelle's smiling face. Richard's shy request for her hand. She remembered how jealous she had been of them then.

Kerry slipped first the engagement ring and then the wedding band on to the fourth finger of her own left hand. Well, not so much slipped, as wedged. Michelle had much more slender fingers. Kerry turned her hand to watch the ring glitter as she had seen Fiona do with her ring so many times when she thought no one was watching. You couldn't really tell that the cubic zirconia weren't real diamonds. The stones were so pretty. And the gold was so smooth.

Kerry's gaze wandered momentarily from the brilliant rings to the tips of her fingers. She noted with disgust her chewed and stumpy nails. She would have to have a manicure before her big day.

CHAPTER THIRTY-ONE

The next Saturday was a big day for all the girls at 67, Artesia Road. After a week of pleading phone calls, Tim had finally given in to Fiona's demands for a summit meeting and had agreed to see her that very evening to talk things through just one more time. Linzi seemed to be unusually on edge and would sigh and snort with irritation every time someone went near the phone. She said that Gaetano was planning a special evening and she was anxious to know the details. The moods of both Linzi and Fiona were still preventing Kerry from announcing her surprise engagement but she was looking forward to a Saturday almost as good as the last. Leon was taking her along to a Gay Pride march.

The party atmosphere began on the tube. Kerry and Leon could feel their hearts speeding up to follow the beat as they sailed down the escalator at Tottenham Court Road surrounded by a sea of Carmen Mirandas all blowing into their new pink plastic whistles. The noise was hellish. Leon looked a little embarrassed. He turned to Kerry, who was standing one step above him and said, 'No wonder we've got a bad name.'

He turned to face the direction of the escalator again. Kerry stared at the back of his head, at the way his hair swirled in two different directions at the crown. She wanted to kiss it. When they reached the bottom of the escalator, the crowd on the platform surged towards an incoming train. Leon grabbed Kerry's hand and helped to pull her on board. Once in the carriage, he didn't let go, but squeezed her hand tightly as they were pushed backwards against the wall by the sheer volume of revellers.

'If we get parted,' he told her, 'get out at Bethnal Green and wait by the exit.'

'OK,' said Kerry. 'I'll see you there.' But there was no way she was letting go of his hand.

Linzi's telephone vigil was rewarded when the Professor finally called at half past five to confirm the address of the shop where he was working that night. There were just two security cameras in Patel's Pharmacy and General Goods Store. One at the front of the shop and one in the pharmacy itself. The Professor was alone as he had hoped, except for the daughter of the chemist who owned the shop. Manjri Patel was dressed in a bright orange and gold sari and hid the fashion magazine she was reading beneath the counter as though it were a girlie mag whenever the doorbell rang and someone walked in.

The Professor made her acquaintance pretty briefly, then installed himself in the pharmacy on the pretence of checking supplies. The layout was the same as that of any chemist's shop he had worked in before. Pills and potions lined up alphabetically along the shelves. Weighing scales. A pill counter that counted the tablets quite accurately if you dropped them through so slowly that you might as well have counted them out yourself. A list of stolen prescription pads to look out for was scribbled on a Post-It note stuck to the computer that printed out the bottle labels. The controlled drugs were kept in a locked cabinet that was further complicated by a code. The Professor fingered the unfamiliar key which now hung from his belt. Each time the bell sounded when the door opened, his heart hammered against the inside of his chest.

While Manjri dished out another packet of Fisherman's Friends, the Professor gazed at the security camera which filmed the pharmacy. He followed the cable down from the camera to the socket where it was plugged in. All too easy to get to. It was basically an ordinary video camera. A proper cowboy job. The Professor kicked the switch off as he walked through to the main body of the shop. He didn't even have to bend down. Manjri wasn't disturbed by the click.

'What a way to have to spend Saturday night, eh, Andrew?' she said when he emerged into the main shop to see if the camera there had been immobilised too. He was too absorbed in his mission to answer her question.

'I said,' she repeated, 'this isn't much of a way to spend Saturday night, is it?'

The Professor looked at her smiling face a little guiltily. He didn't think it terribly wise to tell her that things were only going to get worse.

'There's a really good band on at the Forum tonight, as well. "Radioactive Survivors". Have you heard of them?'

The Professor nodded. In fact, he knew and loved every song they had ever done. Hardly thought they'd be Manjri's kind of band though. 'Yeah,' he said. 'Did some song about bleeding wounds didn't they?'

'That's the one. Though I have to say that "Stigmata" is far from my favourite track off their new album. Bit too gory. Even for me.'

'So, you're into heavy metal?' the Professor asked. He had dreaded having to force himself to make conversation. To act normal. At least she was making it easy for him with the topic she had chosen. 'You don't look like you are.'

'Well, I don't go out in this, do I?' Manjri said, holding the folds of her beautiful sari out like butterfly wings to reveal the battered sixteen-hole Doc Martens she wore beneath. 'I have to go to my friend's house to change first. Our Dad's a bit traditional,' she explained. 'Especially when me or Sangita are working in the shop. He likes his neighbours to think that he's got two perfectly respectable little Hindu daughters. No conversation with the opposite sex before marriage. That kind of thing.'

'Is he really strict?'

'To be honest,' Manjri admitted, 'he's not so bad now that I've left school and I suppose he was only ever trying to look out for us in the wicked Western world.'

'You've got a really strong London accent,' the Professor commented inanely.

'Yeah? Well, I grew up here, didn't I?'

A little old man, with a back so curved that he was almost polo-shaped, came into the shop at that point and asked for some Kaolin and Morphine. The Professor retreated into the pharmacy. This was something that Manjri could deal with alone. When she had bagged up his purchase and counted the old man's money out into the exact amount of coppers and five pence pieces, she poked her head through the door and tried to pick up the conversation.

'So, as I was asking, where do you usually go on a Saturday night?'

She caught him nervously chewing at the skin on the side of a fingernail. 'Eh? Oh, I go to gigs sometimes. Maybe to a club.'

'If you like my kind of music, perhaps we could go somewhere together one night next week,' she added hopefully.

'Yeah,' said the Professor. 'That'd be nice. I'll give you a ring here, shall I?' The doorbell sounded again and Manjri popped back into the shop like the sunshine girl popping out of a weather house. She was nice. Really nice. It was a pity that, after tonight, the Professor knew he would never be able to see her again.

Pride's headlining acts had finished and it seemed as though everyone who was anyone was now crammed inside one of the sweaty dance tents, so that the only dance anyone could do was one which involved jumping up and down on the spot. Kerry was completely exhausted. She felt as though she had lost three stones in weight that afternoon and was in desperate need of a drink. She had been separated from Leon by two huge guys who were both dressed as brides in matching white dresses and veils. Wedding fever was in the air. When she caught a glimpse of Leon again around the edge of one man's puff-sleeved elbow, she was more than a little relieved as he gestured that he too was ready to leave although it was still only nine in the evening.

They fought their way to the exit. Kerry made it first and collapsed against the springy side of the tent. On the grass around the marquee lay beautiful young people in combinations of boy/boy, girl/girl, boy dressed as girl and so on, catching the last of the evening sun. A girl with cropped hair dyed pink and a ring through her eyebrow gave Kerry a beautiful smile. Just as she was returning it, Leon broke free into the open air.

'Oxygen!! At last!!' He leaned against the tent next to Kerry and the guy-ropes strained disturbingly. 'I don't think I have ever felt this hot in my life.' He took hold of the bottom of his T-shirt and pulled it off over his head. Kerry tried not to look at his chest. 'Phew, that's better. You OK?'

'Sure. I'm fine.'

The pink-haired girl raised an eyebrow quizzically in Kerry's direction. When she got no response, she shrugged her shoulders and walked away. Kerry wondered whether she had actually just scored.

'Jeremy is having an After-Pride party later on but I really don't know if I can be bothered to go now,' Leon continued. 'Do you want to?'

'I guess I might,' said Kerry. 'If I'm invited.'

'Of course you're invited. He loves you. Especially now that you're my fiancée.'

'Did you tell him? I thought we weren't supposed to tell anybody yet.' In fact they had barely talked about it between themselves since the afternoon when Leon said that he had no reason to bother staying on now that Sam had gone for good.

'I had to tell Jeremy,' Leon explained. 'He got drunk and rang up blubbing. He said that he wouldn't have a friend in the world when I went back to South Africa. When I said that I wasn't going to go back to South Africa, he wanted to know how I'd wangled it, of course. He wants to be best man. I've told him I'll think about it. Only thing is, he's so bloody camp, it might be a bit of a giveaway that I'm gay too.'

'But we are going ahead with it?'

'Of course we are. Didn't think I'd jilt you at the altar, did you?'

Kerry smiled with relief. 'I was hoping not. I've already chosen my dress.'

'Don't go too over the top.' Leon looked concerned.

'Won't it look a little odd if I don't?'

'I suppose so. Talking of which, I've got something totally over-the-top for you back at my place. Want to make a move?'

'What is it?' Kerry asked excitedly.

'Wait and see. Though I'm sure you've already guessed. You definitely ready to go?'

'Definitely. Apart from this mysterious present, I'm desperate for the loo and the queue over there at the Portaloos is ridiculous.'

Leon shrugged. 'That's because hardly anyone goes into the loos at Pride for a quick slash.' Kerry winced at the thought. Leon slipped his T-shirt back on. 'Feel a bit skinny with all

the beefcakes round here,' he explained. 'Come on. Let's go.'
He started off in the direction of home.

As they walked towards the tube station, Leon linked his arm
through hers. The gardens of the grotty flats which flanked the
park were full of local residents, leaning menacingly against
their garden gates, occasionally pausing in the slow necking of
a warm beer to hurl abuse. A bald-headed man wrestled with
his muscular dog on the lawn. It wasn't the kind of place Kerry
would have wanted to find herself in after dark and alone.

'Bloody perverts,' shouted a woman with a naked and fairly
grubby baby tucked under her arm like a bundle of rags.

'Charming,' laughed Leon. 'I hope her baby grows up gay.'

'You sound like a wicked stepmother,' Kerry observed.

'No,' Leon protested. 'I thought I was your Prince Charming.'

CHAPTER THIRTY-TWO

Linzi was feeling more than a little bit sick as she waited outside the Esso garage in the car Gaetano told her he had borrowed from a mate. It was a white Ford Escort. Common enough for the area. But it had a thick red 'go-faster' stripe down both sides and 'Speedy' written in curly red letters on the bonnet. Linzi wondered if Gaetano had told his friend why he needed to borrow the car. When he got back in on the passenger side with a bar of chocolate in each hand, it was the first thing she asked him.

'Don't be stupid, Linz,' he told her. 'I said I was taking you for a romantic night out, didn't I? When the job's done, we'll dump it and I'll tell Lance that it got nicked from a car park while we were having our meal.'

'Lance?'

'Yeah, Lance Sylvester. The man who brought us together. He'll be glad of the insurance money now that Verbal Tix is going down. OK, worrier?' He kissed Linzi on the end of the nose and pressed a Mars bar into her hand. She put it straight onto the dashboard.

'I don't know how you can eat anything right now,' she said.

'I need my strength.'

They drove erratically to Patel's Pharmacy. Linzi stalled the car at some traffic lights and had to fight back tears when it wouldn't restart first time. They turned into the narrow side street at three minutes before ten. The Professor was expecting them at ten exactly. Gaetano told Linzi to do a U-turn and drive back in the opposite direction for a little while. It wouldn't do for them to get there before the Professor was ready and have to hang about just asking to be recognised.

Gaetano had lost his smile now. He held the specially prepared bobble hat with its ragged cut-out eye-holes tightly, screwing it up like a dishcloth in his sweaty hands. He was wearing a jacket he had bought from a charity shop that afternoon. His jacket, his trousers and even his socks were black. Everything completely black and plain. Not a distinguishing mark on him. Unlike 'Speedy' the car.

Linzi turned back into the right road. Two minutes to go. She felt as though she might be about to get a migraine.

'Are you sure you want to do this, Gaetano? We could turn back now. What if the Professor hasn't been able to turn the cameras off? What if there's a customer in the shop?' Linzi began to babble. 'There has to be a better way to get the money.'

Gaetano looked at her with a frighteningly expressionless face.

'Linzi. Shut up. There'll be no customers to worry about because the shop will be about to close. The alarms will have been disabled and so will the cameras. I've known the Professor since school. He would never let me down. He wouldn't dare.'

Linzi wondered whether the Professor had ever been put in such a difficult position before but she clammed up and dutifully pulled the car to a standstill near the kerb outside the chemist's shop. She kept the engine running, like she'd seen on any number of films. Gaetano pulled the woollen hat down over his face.

'Good luck,' she murmured, though it hardly seemed appropriate.

'Thanks, bella.'

Gaetano leapt out of the car and seconds later he was springing through the open door of Patel's Pharmacy and General Goods Store.

'Come on. Tell me what the present is.'

'Wait until we get back to the flat. God, I bet you are a nightmare at Christmas.'

Leon lived near the City. He had a third floor flat in a modern development with a gym downstairs and even a doorman. 'You'll have to excuse the mess,' he muttered as he struggled with his key in the lock. 'I didn't have time to sort the place out before coming to meet you this morning. And I didn't expect to have anyone back here tonight or I'd have hidden my pants beneath the sofa.'

But the room that he opened the door on to looked immaculate. The walls were painted plain white. Along one stood a huge blue sofa with deep squashy seats dotted with red and green cushions. The opposite wall was flanked with thousands of pounds' worth of matt black stereo equipment. A bright woollen rug formed the centrepiece on a polished wooden floor.

'Wow,' Kerry breathed. 'No wonder you don't want to leave London.' She was slightly embarrassed now that Leon had been anywhere near Artesia Road, with its furniture borrowed from two different but equally tasteless generations. However, the embarrassment was quickly replaced by delight. After all, this palace was where she would have to live after the wedding. 'You've done this place up beautifully.'

Leon was dead-heading some of the sunny orange flowers which stood in a vase on the coffee table. 'It was all Sam really. He studied interior design before he decided to become a singer.'

Suddenly, Kerry wasn't sure she liked that blue sofa so much. Maybe it was a little bit too chic.

'I wasn't even all that keen on renting the place until Sam pointed out the possibilities,' Leon continued. 'It's really light. In the daytime, of course.'

'Where's your loo?' Kerry asked.

'Oh sorry, Kez. I forgot you were busting.' Leon pointed her in the direction of the half-finished bathroom. 'Mind that pile of tiles under the sink. I can never get myself into the right mood to start grouting. Though the landlord's promised us a bundle off the rent if I do.'

Kerry wasn't listening. 'When I come out again, I want my present.'

She carefully negotiated the DIY booby traps and sat herself down on the cold loo seat. The bathroom was being decked out in tiles which were the same blue as the sofa, mixed in with a few slightly lighter ones so that the overall effect would be like a reflection of the sky in the sea. The white bathtub sparkled, as did the sink. Towels the same colour as the lighter tiles hung in a fluffy array from a shining chrome rail. Kerry went to wash her hands and studied her face in the mirrored bathroom cabinet. At some point that day she had caught the sun and had a little white stripe on her nose where her sunglasses had been. That was a pain, but over all, she decided, she just looked a little healthier than usual. She dragged her comb through her hair and scrubbed at her teeth with a finger loaded with toothpaste.

She could hear Leon moving about in the background. There was the sound of a tap being turned on. A kettle being filled. He walked across the bright wooden floor of the sitting room in his squeaky trainers and switched on the wide-screen television. For a moment, Kerry allowed herself to day-dream about their future together. When they were married she would hear these sounds every night.

Kerry looked at the bathroom cabinet again, but this time she wasn't interested in her reflection. She wondered whether the cabinet door would make a noise and give the game away if she tried to open it. Slowly, she tugged at the little silver handle. Only the merest well-made click. She opened the cabinet door wide.

Kerry wasn't sure what she expected to find. More toothpaste. Indigestion tablets. Proplus. A packet of Nurofen. Three bottles of aftershave. Eternity. Obsession. Egoïste. She knew that he wore Eternity. A tube of KY jelly.

'What are you doing in there, Kerry?' he called suddenly. 'Having a bath?'

'Nothing. I'll be out in a minute.' She flushed the loo hurriedly and closed the cupboard while the sound of rushing water would hide the guilty noise. Then she splashed her face with water in an attempt to cool it down. Obsession and Egoïste? Had Sam left them behind, or was he back? Leon hadn't really mentioned him for days but the sudden re-emergence of the wedding question suggested that something had changed Leon's mind.

Leon had installed himself on the sofa. When Kerry came into the room he pointed at a mug of tea he had already put in front of her place. He had sugared it perfectly. She murmured her thanks.

'There's never anything on television on a Saturday night, is there?' he complained. 'I suppose we're all supposed to be out strutting our funky stuff. I hope you wanted tea. I've got some stronger stuff out in the kitchen but I figured that you probably feel as dehydrated and knackered as I do. I'm getting too old for this partying lark. It's time I settled down.'

'You sound like my mum.'

'I'm probably nearly as old as your mum. No, today was fun, but I can't do it every weekend any more. I used to. Sam and I would go to Heaven until that finished and then straight on to Trade. God, we didn't get home until Sunday afternoon sometimes. Though I think that E had more to do with my staying power than youthful stamina then . . .'

'I had a good time,' Kerry told him.

'Good. I'm glad you weren't bored.'

'The bands were really great.'

'Not really. Honestly, they drag the same old queens out year after year. If I have to see Erasure one more time I swear I'll go straight.' Kerry smiled weakly. 'At least we didn't have to sit through Jimmy Somerville. I used to date a guy who looks like him. Talk about love being blind.'

Kerry slipped off her shoes and curled her feet up under her bottom. 'Are we going to go to Jeremy's party later on?'

Leon sighed. 'Not me. I don't think I can move from this seat again tonight. You can go if you want to. I'll give you the address. It's in Hackney. Chris and Ian will be there. You know them. Remember?'

'Oh, yeah.' Chris had advised her to get her hair straightened. Professionally. 'I don't think I'll bother if you're not going to.'

'Sorry. But I think I'll go straight to bed when I've finished this. I'm just an old wuss, Kez. I'll call you a cab if you like.'

Kerry whispered to hide her disappointment. 'Yeah. Thanks. But I want this present you've been talking about first.'

'What? Oh, yeah.' Leon reached beneath the cushion. 'I was just pretending that I'd forgotten.'

Leon passed the small golden cardboard box over to Kerry. She read the carefully matched gift-tag. 'To my dear, dear friend Kerry, All my love, Leon.' Then she pulled gently at one end of the ribbon so that it unfurled. Inside the box was a smaller, velvet-covered jewellery case.

'I thought as much,' she grinned widely as she opened that up.

'Oh, it's nothing.'

'Nothing?' It was as if the light reflected by the ring inside that box was illuminating Kerry's face. She picked it out and held it up for a closer look. 'Nothing? Leon, this is beautiful. It's the most beautiful thing I've ever seen. Put it on me.'

'What?'

'Put it on my hand for me. I want to do this properly.'

'If you insist.' Leon took the ring from Kerry and slid it on to the appropriate finger. She held her face out for a kiss and closed her eyes. He placed a dry peck on her cheek.

'Oh, Leon. This is so incredible,' Kerry murmured. 'The best thing ever.' She was looking at the ring again now, turning her hand so that shards of light struck the wall. 'And it looks so expensive. Fiona will be so jealous.'

'Yes. Well, I thought you could sell it afterwards since you don't want to take any money now. You can buy yourself something useful. Put a deposit on a bike.'

'But I'll never sell it,' Kerry replied indignantly. 'Don't talk like that. This is my engagement ring.'

Leon smiled stiffly. 'Shall I call that cab for you now? I promised I'd go into the office early tomorrow to help Serena with some figures.'

'Oh, I don't remember you planning that.'

'She called last night.' Leon was already dialling for a cab. 'Artesia Road. What's your post-code there, Kez?'

'Hang on,' Kerry took the phone gently from Leon's hand. 'There might not actually be much point in your calling a cab. I'm not sure I've got my house-keys.'

'What?'

'I had a root round my bag while I was in the bathroom.' Kerry picked up her bag and made a show of looking inside it again. 'Bugger. Looks like I was right,' she smiled sheepishly. 'No keys. I'm locked out.'

'Won't your housemates be in?'

'I'm not sure. I was hoping I could stay with you. I know Linzi's gone to a party tonight and Fiona may have gone home to see her parents for the whole weekend. Would it be OK if I stay? I want to make you breakfast as a thankyou for this, anyway.' She waved her newly ringed hand at him.

'Honestly, Kez. You're doing me the favour where that's concerned.' Leon was already searching the back of the sofa for her keys.

'Where else have you been in here?' he asked her.

'Only the bathroom.'

'Well, I don't think I saw them in there. Where did you last see them?'

'I put them in my pocket when I left the house this morning. Perhaps they dropped out at Pride. It could have happened when we were in the dance tent. I was getting knocked about quite a bit, perhaps they fell out then.'

'You'll never find them again if that's the case,' Leon sighed. 'Do you want to use my phone and call home? It's pretty late. Someone might be in by now.'

'Oh, yes. Thanks.' Kerry picked up the phone and began to dial. But while she dialled she held her thumb over the button that cuts the caller off. She pretended to let the phone ring. Once, twice . . . five times. 'Doesn't look like there's anyone in,' she told Leon as she replaced the receiver.

'Why don't you leave a message, then they can call here and let you know when they get back.'

'Oh yeah,' Kerry picked up the phone again. 'But what if they don't get back until really late?'

'I don't mind,' Leon said flatly through a yawn. 'And the cabs run all night.'

Kerry dialled her number and kept her finger over the cut-off button once more. This time, when she figured that five rings had passed, she waited for the duration of an imaginary answerphone message and left a message in return. 'Hi, girls, it's Kerry. I've managed to lose my keys. Can someone call me at Leon's place? Soon as you get in. Thanks. Bye.'

Leon had gone through to the bathroom. She heard him open the mirrored cabinet. 'Nope. Nothing in here,' he called. 'Perhaps we should check with the man downstairs, in case you dropped them on the way up here and someone's handed them in?'

'I'm sure I didn't,' Kerry replied.

'And you haven't been in the kitchen, have you?'

'No, I haven't.' Kerry was disappointed. It was nice that Leon cared enough to help her look for her keys, but now he was getting just a little too keen to find them. Why couldn't he just let her stay with him and promise to have another look for the damn things in the morning?

'Well, you must have dropped them at Pride,' he was saying

now as he delved into the airing cupboard and emerged with
a couple of blankets. He dumped them next to the sofa, then
disappeared into his bedroom and came back with a pillow. 'So
they're lost for ever. You'll be all right out here, won't you?'
he asked rhetorically. 'It's not that cold tonight and the sofa's
really comfortable. I've spent many a night on it myself,' he
added with a little snort. He pressed the pillow into Kerry's
arms. 'Good night, Kez.' He didn't even kiss her on the cheek
before he went back to his wide double bed.

Kerry sat down on the edge of the sofa with the pillow still
clutched in her arms. What was wrong with him? As she lay
back on the cushions and stared up at the ceiling, she could
hear him turning over in the next room, groaning and moaning
a little as he tried to get comfortable in his ocean-wide bed. He
had given her just two sodding itchy blankets. He really didn't
want her there at all. No, she was misinterpreting his tiredness,
that's all. When he was tired at work he was exactly the same.
Monosyllabic, matter of fact, wanting to be left alone. The next
morning over breakfast everything would be all right again. She
would go out and buy croissants. She thought that she had seen
a decent shop on the corner as they turned into Leon's road.

She took one last look at the new ring adorning her left hand.
It must mean that she was allowed to tell the girls and her mother
at last. And the people at work. Lance would be surprised.

Kerry draped the blankets across her fully clothed body. The
heat of the day was just a memory now, disappearing up into the
clear sky. That week, London had been like the Sahara Desert.
Baking in the day and freezing at night. With only her new ring
to keep her warm, Kerry wrapped the blankets around her and
pulled them right up to her chin.

CHAPTER THIRTY-THREE

'Get down on the floor, you fucking Paki!'
The Professor caught the look of horror in Manjri's eyes as she fell to the floor beneath a single blow from Gaetano's fist. Instinctively, he ran out into the body of the shop to see whether she was OK. Gaetano pushed him away from her roughly.

'Keep away from her, fuck-face. Just open the bloody till.'

Jesus! Gaetano was playing the armed robber for all he was worth.

'What? Fuck!!!'

Gaetano elbowed the Professor in the back. He couldn't be sure but it felt as though Gaetano might even be holding a knife against the thin material of the white chemist's coat. He was really going the whole way. 'Open the fucking till!!!' he shouted again. The Professor opened the till hurriedly and laid the contents bare before him.

'Get some bags.'

He pulled a handful of carriers out from a drawer and shoved them helplessly in Gaetano's direction. Gaetano began to load the bags with that day's takings. Notes first. Scrunching them up as he grabbed. Then he tipped up the drawer to empty out the coins while the Professor watched and actually felt afraid.

'How much do you reckon is in here?' Gaetano asked, not forgetting for a moment to sound ferocious.

'I don't know,' the Professor said feebly. 'Maybe three hundred. I'm not sure.'

'Three hundred? Christ. I thought you said there would be more.'

'Yeah. Well, it's been a quiet night, man . . . I . . .'

Gaetano silenced his friend with a stare. Beneath their feet, Manjri was moaning. She had curled into a little ball, almost wrapped herself around the Professor's ankles.

'Andrew,' she groaned.

The Professor shrugged his shoulders.

'Sort her out, will you man? Fuck. This is hardly worth it.' Gaetano slammed the till shut. 'We need some more stuff. What's in the pharmacy?'

The Professor's eyes widened.

'Tell me what's commercial,' Gaetano demanded. 'Tell me what I can sell.'

The Professor looked down towards the poor girl who was climbing her way up his trousers legs. Blood trickled from her nose to her upper lip.

'I . . . I . . .' he stuttered. 'I'm not sure.' Seeing the girl move, Gaetano swung the bag of money, heavy with coins, straight into her face to set her back on the floor again, catching the Professor's legs at the same time so that he almost buckled on top of her. 'Come on, for fuck's sake, man,' Gaetano was heading into the pharmacy, pulling packets off the shelves as he went and shoving them straight into his bags. 'Hurry up.'

'What's this?' he asked, waving a package at the Professor who could not free his ankle from Manjri's grasp.

'It's for cystitis,' the Professor told him. 'You don't want to bother with that.'

'Well, what the fuck do I want to bother with then? I don't bloody know, do I? What's cystitis anyway? Get that fucking girl off your feet and come through here, will you, you fucking idiot? You're the pharmacist. Tell me what to take.'

Manjri was beginning to right herself again. She was on her knees now, slowly dragging herself up by the waistband of the Professor's trousers. He sagged a little under her weight, his hands hanging helplessly by his sides as he wondered whether he should try to help her or help his friend. Gaetano stood in the middle of the pharmacy, knees slightly bent, ready to spring into action. He looked like a snarling IRA hitman on a supermarket trolley dash.

'Tell me what to take,' he snarled.

The Professor licked his lips and tried to speak. Manjri was still groaning. He looked at her face. One side of it was all blood now. Her brown skin shiny red. 'Take . . . take . . .' he stuttered.

'Take what? Take what? For fuck's sake, man. Tell me what to take. We haven't got much time.' Gaetano clutched at the carrier bags full of cash until his knuckles started to go white. He scanned the shelves desperately for a name that he recognised. The Professor still said nothing. He was transfixed with horror as Manjri loosened her bloody grip on his trousers and slipped back on to the floor. She was completely out of it. Unconscious.

'Take what the fuck you like,' the Professor screamed suddenly. 'You've nearly bloody killed her. You promised me no one would get hurt.' The Professor fell to his knees and tried to get a better look at Manjri's bleeding face. He put his fingers to her bloody neck and tried to find a pulse.

'You promised me no one would get hurt. I think she's dying man, for fuck's sake!!! You've fucking killed her.'

Gaetano swept his arm along a shelf and caught as many of the falling packets as he could in an open bag.

'You're a fucking idiot,' he told the Professor as he stormed back into the shop. 'A fucking, bloody idiot.' The Professor looked up only to be cracked hard in the nose by an angry fist. He buckled and landed heavily on his wounded assistant before Gaetano grabbed him by the hair and pulled him almost upright again.

'I'll fucking see you later, you twat.'

Then he hurled the Professor back to the floor and booted him in the side of the head for good measure.

Gaetano burst out into the street where Linzi was still waiting in the Escort, having seen nothing but the dusty dashboard in front of her. She pushed the passenger door open as he ran towards her and leapt into the car. Then she slammed her foot down hard on the accelerator and skidded away from the scene of the crime before Gaetano even had the door closed.

'Drive, drive, drive,' he shouted as he pulled off the mask. 'Don't stop at the fucking lights, you stupid cow . . .'

Linzi had been slowing down for an amber signal but instead she put her foot to the floor and roared on through, eyes shut tight. Behind them, the scream of brakes and horns told her just how close she had been to disaster.

'Oh God, Oh God,' she whimpered. 'Did you do it? Did you do it?'

'Just keep driving, for fuck's sake. Go faster. Everything's OK.'

They drove until they were out of the City, then dumped the car on the forecourt of a deserted factory and legged it to the nearest tube. As they had been driving, Gaetano had transferred the contents of his shopping bags to an anonymous black sports holdall. He dumped the face mask and jacket in some innocent punter's dustbin.

At twenty-five past ten, the black leather bag sat between Gaetano and Linzi on the southbound Victoria Line. They spent an unnatural amount of time not looking at it and not mentioning it to each other.

CHAPTER THIRTY-FOUR

It was no good. Kerry couldn't get to sleep on the sofa. She stood up and folded the blankets carefully, then she walked silently across the immaculate room and hovered outside Leon's bedroom door. She could hear him breathing, even the tiny whistle as the air passed out through his nose. She put her hand on the door handle and gently pressed it down. Please, please, please, she begged as the door opened without a protest of hinges. Please let me be doing the right thing.

He was fast asleep. The sound of the door swishing across the plush carpet didn't disturb him at all. Kerry crept across the room to the foot of his bed. He was sleeping on a futon and where the street light filtered through the flimsy curtains she could see that his bedclothes were purest white. He was sleeping on his back, with his head turned slightly to the left, his thick black hair in stark contrast with the white pillow. His broad brown shoulders were naked against the cotton.

Kerry walked up the side of the bed and stopped to look at his face. She had never experienced such a strong feeling of love for anyone before. All she wanted to do was bend down to kiss his lips and after that the world could just disappear for all it mattered to her. The fingers of his right hand, lying on top of the sheets, twitched a little as he dreamed. Kerry sat down on the edge of the futon and stared. What was he dreaming about? Did he ever dream about her as he slept?

Taking a deep breath, Kerry picked up the edge of the duvet and slid herself beneath it. Leon murmured and rolled a little further towards the other side of the bed but still he didn't wake up.

Kerry lay next to him, facing towards him, watching his profile in the weak orange glow of the street light. 'Leon,' she whispered. 'I think I love you.' He didn't seem to hear her. 'I mean really love you. I'm not just pretending so that you don't have to go.' That said, albeit unheard, she slid down the bed so that her head rested on the pillow and closed her eyes. Satisfied that he wasn't going to be woken by her presence, she allowed herself to drape an arm over his chest.

In the street below Leon's window, a passing drunk staggered into a car and set off its alarm. Leon woke up.

'Ohmigod.' He sat bolt upright and sprang backwards from the figure which lay beside him in the bed. He turned on the bedside light and got a good look at the intruder. 'Kerry! It's you. What do you think you're doing in here?'

Kerry had fallen asleep. Now, at the sound of his voice, she too woke with a start and suddenly realised that she was in deep shit. Leon just stared at her, the duvet pulled around him like an embarrassed child. He was naked beneath it. 'You're meant to be in the other room.'

'I know. I know. I didn't think you'd mind though,' she squeaked. But Kerry was terrified by the tone of his voice. She had never heard him speak like that before and he definitely wasn't amused.

'Come on,' he told her just a little more softly. 'You've got to get out of here.'

'I . . . I . . . I was scared,' Kerry began pathetically. I couldn't get to sleep out there. I thought that I might have a better chance of dropping off in here with you.'

'But you haven't got any clothes on,' Leon exclaimed.

'I don't sleep in my clothes.'

'Kerry. I don't want to sound harsh or anything but you can't sleep in here with me. You've got to go next door.'

'Why can't I?'

'What do you mean, "why can't you?" This is my bed, Kerry, and I want to be in it alone. You can't sleep with me. Especially not naked.'

'You slept in the same bed as me at my house.'

'That was different. There was nowhere else for me to sleep at your house. And I was wearing all my clothes.' Leon got up from the futon now, protectively covering his nakedness with a pillow, and shrugged on his dressing gown. 'I'm sorry, Kerry. One of us has got to sleep next door or you have got to go home. Haven't your housemates called yet?'

'No, they haven't,' she whimpered.

'Jeez.' He ran his fingers through his thick hair irritably. 'Why don't you try them again? Just in case they didn't pick the message up.'

Kerry hid her eyes behind her hands. She could feel the unfamiliar coldness of her new ring against her eyebrow and at the thought of it she felt tears begin to prick the back of her eyes. Her cheeks were burning. Leon was sitting in the chair by his dressing table now, just staring at her in his bed as if she were the most disgusting thing he had ever seen.

'Why don't you want to sleep with me?' The voice which came out of her mouth belonged to a stranger. It was a pathetic, frightening sob. Leon's mouth dropped open in a mixture of horror and sorrow as tears began to force their way out on to Kerry's cheeks. 'I thought you liked me,' she continued. 'I thought we got on really well. And we're going to get married.'

Leon pulled his dressing gown tighter around his body. Kerry dropped her hands from her eyes and started to sob openly. Her shoulders lurched up and down as she cried uncontrollably.

'Oh, my God, Kerry, what is wrong with you?' Leon threw her the box of tissues which had been sitting unused on his dressing table for months.

'I thought we could get things together.'

Leon snorted. 'How, Kerry? How could we get things together? I'm gay. You've known that since you met me. It's not you I'm not interested in, it's women in general. You know that.'

Kerry sniffed loudly. 'But you told me that you'd had girl-friends before.'

'Yes, when I was a teenager. Before I admitted to myself that I am gay. None of the relationships I had before that actually meant anything to me. I'm gay, Kerry, that's the bottom line. Here, blow your nose.' He had got up from the chair and was sitting on the edge of the futon again. He fished a tissue out of the box and handed it to her gently. 'You haven't been feeling like this all along, have you? Tell me you haven't.'

But Kerry nodded solemnly.

'Oh no. Whatever made you think that I would be interested in seeing a girl again?'

'After my sister's wedding, you told me that it wasn't gender that mattered to you. That what you cared about was the person underneath. You told me that you didn't think anyone had ever understood you as well as I do.'

Leon rolled his eyes. 'I do think that, Kez. But the gender thing . . . Well, I was probably only saying that to justify being gay to you, not to make you think that I could swing the other way for true love. Here,' he handed her another tissue. 'Dry your eyes. You'd had better put some clothes on, too.'

Kerry dragged her T-shirt back on.

'And you asked me to marry you,' she continued.

'You know why I did that,' Leon protested.

'Yes, but I thought . . . I thought that maybe if we spent enough time together you might start to feel differently about me . . .'

'This is unbelievable. Look, do you want a cup of tea?' Leon asked quickly. He had to get away. Kerry nodded and sniffed away another tear. 'Do you want sugar in it?' She nodded again. Leon headed off into the kitchen, put the kettle on and leaned on the breakfast bar with his head in his hands.

Kerry fell back on to his pillows and began to cry again immediately. She buried her face in the place where his head had lain. It smelled of the wax that he used on his hair. Now she was embarrassed as well as sad. How could she have been so stupid as to think that he was just being shy when all along every time she had got near him physically, he had so obviously tried to get away. She remembered the nervous kiss in his car after her sister's wedding. He hadn't been trying to make it something more, he had been trying to make it something less. She had been absolutely stupid and now everything was ruined. She had tried to turn a friend into a lover and lost him on the way.

The kettle whistled. She could hear him pouring the water into mugs. He was probably desperate to get rid of her now. Kerry sat up and caught a glimpse of her face in the dressing-table mirror. Her mascara had marked out the tracks of her tears in muddy black lines. She would drink this tea, then call a cab. The key to her house was, after all, still in the bottom of her bag.

She would have to call him tomorrow and apologise in the cold light of day. She could blame it on the ecstasy she had taken at

Pride. She hoped she hadn't been wrong about him being the kind of person who found it easy to forgive mistakes.

Then the front door to the flat opened and suddenly they were no longer alone. Someone crossed the living-room floor in rubber-soled shoes that squeaked across the wood.

'Mmm. I don't recognise this jacket. Have we got visitors?' the intruder asked. 'I hope you didn't pick up some old slapper at Pride, Leon Landesman.'

'No, I did not.' Leon replied seriously. But then Kerry could hear Leon giggling. Someone was tickling him. Someone was kissing the back of his neck. 'It's just Kerry from work,' she heard Leon whispering. 'She's lost her keys and she can't get home. that's all.'

'Oh, buggeration,' said the intruder. 'Where is she?'

'In the bed.'

'In our bed? That's just great. And all I wanted to do was come home and roger you senseless all night. I guess I'm going to have to be on my best behaviour now. Quick, give me a kiss.' This was followed by more giggling.

'No, sweetness. Don't! Can't you wait until tomorrow morning?'

'Wait until tomorrow? But I've been wanting you all day. Do you know how hard it was for me to get through my shift thinking about you enjoying yourself at Pride? I cannot wait a moment longer.'

'But Kerry . . .'

'Jesus Christ. So what if Kerry's here? She knows you're gay, doesn't she?'

'She's a bit upset tonight. I don't want to rub her face in it.'

'Oh, Leon,' the intruder whined. 'I'm not going to have to put up with this on a regular basis until you get your divorce am I?'

'I don't want to upset her. I need her to marry me, don't I?'

'Yes, but it's not like a real marriage, Leon. You don't have to worry about sleeping around. There are no emotions involved here.'

'Just act a bit restrained for half an hour or so, can't you? I'll get rid of her. It's just that I think she might have got the wrong idea. I didn't realise she was so emotionally dependent on me.'

'Jesus, Leon! Sort it out. I don't want to have to share my

home with some pathetic little fag hag! She's already tried to keep us apart before. She didn't tell you that I called by the office that day because she hates me. She's a vicious little cow and if she thinks she's going to have some kind of hold over you just because of some dumb pretend wedding, you're going to have to call it off and find another bride.'

Kerry scrambled out of the bed and pulled on the rest of her clothes.

'Leon, forget the tea, I've found my keys,' she called as she fled through the sitting room. She tried to slip past the kitchen without looking, but she already knew the other man was Sam. He was back.

Gaetano opened the sports bag and shook its contents out on to his bed. They counted the money. Just two hundred and fifty-seven pounds. Not even three hundred as the Professor had said. Between the three of them, it was nothing. They could have done better taking the money they had spent on preparing the whole thing and betting it on a three-legged greyhound at the dogs. Gaetano scanned the boxes he had whipped off the shelves in the pharmacy with a critical eye.

'Are we going to be able to sell these?' Linzi asked.

'Fuck knows,' Gaetano was not at all happy. 'The Professor went completely pathetic on me and wouldn't tell me what to take. I just grabbed whatever I could reach.'

He picked up a packet of capsules and flipped it over to read the label.

'What do you think of this, Linz? You've got a psychology degree. See any names you recognise? Anything good?'

'Not straight off. No, hang on. I recognise this.'

Linzi picked up a slender package printed with turquoise-blue writing. Turning it over, she laughed a little ironically. Gaetano looked up eagerly, hoping to hear he had done well.

'What are they?' he asked.

'Well,' said Linzi, trying not to smile. 'This is the morning after pill, and these,' she added, picking up a tub of one thousand little capsules, 'are what you take for constipation.'

Gaetano didn't see the joke.

'What do you mean?'

'I mean, this is something you take to stop yourself getting pregnant after unprotected sex and these are laxatives. They give you the shits if you can't go.'

'Oh, fuck off, you stupid bitch. Stop messing around. What are they?'

'Whooah, partner. Calm down. That's really what these things are, I'm afraid. How much money did we get again?'

'Practically nothing. Absolutely fucking nothing.'

'Three-way split, remember?'

'You and the Professor didn't do a third of the job,' Gaetano snarled.

'I drove the car.'

'Yeah, but I got the car for you to drive in the first place. You could hardly keep it on the road. You were fucking useless, both of you. I risked my neck for you two and now I find out that the Professor's palmed me off with a pile of fucking laxatives. I'm gonna fucking kill him tomorrow morning.' As he spoke, Gaetano's lips bared clenched teeth. He didn't look as though he was joking.

'He was probably just trying to make it look convincing, G. If he'd been too helpful it might have been obvious that he was in on the whole thing.'

'He nearly bottled out completely. When he comes round here looking for his share of the money I'm going to make him eat all this shit.'

Gaetano picked up the tub of laxatives and hurled them against the wall. The impact made the tub pop open, scattering thousands of tiny brown capsules, which rolled off into the far corners of the room to be found jamming the Hoover from then until eternity. Then Gaetano scrunched up a fistful of the contraceptive boxes and threw them in the same direction.

'You gotta go,' he hissed. 'My parents are opening the café late tonight for all those fucking homos on their march. You gotta go before they get back.'

'OK,' said Linzi, sensing that a swift exit was probably for the best in this instance anyway. 'I'll see you tomorrow morning. It'll seem better by then. Really it will.'

Gaetano didn't even look at her.

She picked a fiver out of the haul for her taxi-ride home.

CHAPTER THIRTY-FIVE

K erry sprinted down the stairs from Leon's flat but by the time she got to the bottom, she could barely see for tears. She wrenched at the door to the block so hard that her arms nearly left their sockets until the doorman pointed out a night door-release button with a faintly amused smile.

Outside, Kerry collapsed onto the pavement, not caring what her knees landed in. She clutched at her head as she tried to catch her breath again. Then it occurred to her that Sam might be watching her from the window and laughing, so she crawled into an alleyway that was lined with overflowing bins but away from critical eyes.

How could it be that in one day she had hit both the highest high and the lowest low of her life, she wondered as she sat upon a vaguely hygienic looking cardboard box. She had no money left in her tattered purse and though she had her tube pass, she couldn't remember the number of the Nightbus home or even how to get to Trafalgar Square to catch it. Alone and cold in the alleyway, Kerry headed in the direction of traffic noise. Maybe she could find a cabby who was prepared to wait for her while she went to a cashpoint. If only she had some transport of her own.

It was then that she saw Leon's bike. Parked at the top of the alleyway where it was light enough to be reasonably safe. She had grown to like that bike, but now, even that inanimate object looked smug. It was as if every cog and valve knew what she had done. She would never be able to sit behind Leon on that bike again. Kerry cleared her throat and spat at it. But then that didn't seen enough.

She delivered a smallish kick to the back wheel. Then the front wheel. Then she punched at the springy leather seat. Then she karate-chopped the number plate with her heel. Then another punch to the soft parts. A swing with her bag. And a kick and a kick and a kick.

Until a two-footed kick that could have won her points in a karate competition knocked the bike off its stand and crashing down on to Kerry where she lay in the gutter, toppled by her own clever move.

The bike's alarm started screaming.

Kerry scrambled out from beneath it and started to run.

CHAPTER THIRTY-SIX

Pretty soon, Kerry's bruised shins were hurting too much to run anymore. It took almost an hour to get back to Artesia Road at a limp. From time to time, Kerry was sure that she heard the warming up warbles of an early dawn chorus as she trudged the empty streets of South London.

Number 67 was perfectly silent. Kerry flicked on the light switch and tried to ascertain who was in by counting the shoes behind the front door. Linzi's favourite Doc Martens were missing. Fiona's rather more delicate ankleboots were there. The answerphone was disappointingly empty of messages and when she dialled 1471 to see if perhaps someone had called but not left a message, the number that the stilted woman gave was not a number that she recognised. Kerry poured herself a glass of water. She felt completely sober now, with that horrible clearheadedness that comes from having sat your hangover out and thought for far too long about something embarrassing. She wished it was earlier. She wished that Fiona was still awake to listen to her tale of woe and sympathise. The only glimmer of consolation was that it was Sunday and Kerry had twenty-four hours of potential sleep before she had to see Leon again at work.

She climbed wearily up the stairs and decided to skip cleaning her teeth. She eased herself beneath her duvet without bothering to undress but soon found that she was desperate for a wee. Kerry padded back across the landing. The bathroom door was blocked.

Kerry pushed the door and felt it give a little, so it obviously wasn't locked from inside. What had probably happened, she decided, was that someone had hung too many towels on the back of the door and one of them had fallen down to jam it. It had happened before. The only thing to do was shove like crazy until it gave way and have a word about the towel crisis tomorrow.

But it wasn't as easy as shifting a towel. When Kerry had given the door seven hard pushes to no avail she had to switch on the landing light and investigate further. A triangle of fabric poked out from beneath the door. It was silky, not towelling. Like Fiona's dressing gown. Kerry got down on her hands and knees to see just what was getting stuck here. She peered through the tiny gap between door and frame.

'Oh, God! No!' There was a body on the floor.

Fiona had been expecting to see Tim that night. As she waited for him to arrive after a week of agonising silence, she had dressed herself in the outfit she knew he liked the best. She had piled her hair up on top of her head and outlined her eyes with mascara, though the finished result was pretty ineffective compared with the shadows that hung beneath her eyes.

She was ready an hour before he was due to arrive. The others had gone out. She sat alone in the sitting room with the television turned up extra loud to block out the sound of people walking past in the street outside. Every time she heard a car door slam, she thought that she might be sick with the pain of seeing him again.

Half an hour after he was supposed to have turned up, she called him.

'You're meant to be here,' she said.

'I know,' he replied. 'I was going to give you a call in a moment. I'm not coming over.'

'Why not?' she asked him.

'I don't think it's such a good idea, that's all. How are you?'

'You called off our engagement, how do you think I am?'

'Look, if you're just going to scream at me, I'm going to put the phone back down straight away. OK?'

'I don't want to argue,' Fiona pleaded. 'I just need to talk to you, Tim. We still need to sort some things out.'

'I don't think there is anything to sort out any more. We

couldn't have gone on as we were, Fiona. You know that as well as I do. I was going up the wall.'

'Then why did you ask me to marry you?'

'I thought it might make things different . . .'

Fiona didn't quite know what to say in reply to that.

'You're seeing Minky now, aren't you?'

She heard Tim sigh. He didn't answer her question.

'You're seeing her aren't you? I knew what was going on even before we split up.' She sobbed tragically. 'When I came round and found her at your flat that day.'

'Look, Fiona. Minky isn't the reason why I called off the engagement.'

'But you are seeing her?'

'She's been round a couple of times, that's all. It's nothing serious.'

'Nothing serious? Then why did you throw what we had away for her?'

'It had nothing to do with Minky.'

'I don't believe that. I think it has everything to do with her. She got dumped by her boyfriend and so she decided that she would split us up and have you instead. You know what she's like. She was sleeping with Wooders less than a month ago. Well, if you want his sloppy seconds, Tim. If you want to go to bed with a slag who'll sleep with her boyfriend's best friends.'

'Fiona. Shut up. You don't know what she's really like at all.'

'I don't know if I want to know. She's there now, isn't she?' Fiona spat. 'Isn't she, Tim? Isn't she?'

Tim put the phone down.

Fiona had stared at the silent receiver for a long, long time.

When Linzi got home, half an hour later than Kerry, she went straight to the kitchen to get herself a drink. And she was hungry too. The anticipation of that night's work had made her feel like throwing up whenever she passed a kitchen, but now that she had regained her composure, she thought she might fry up the whole of a packet of bacon she had bought the week before. Even if it was a little out of date.

She didn't notice the note that Kerry had left on the refrigerator door until she was closing it again. She pulled it off and read it while she waited for the kettle to boil.

'Linz, Fiona's been taken very ill. Gone to Casualty. Please come and meet me there as soon as you get in. Kez.'

Casualty? What had that mad cow Fiona done to herself now? Linzi took her time with her sandwiches. Let the bacon crisp up really nicely. Then it struck her that perhaps it wasn't just for altruistic reasons that she should go along to the hospital. A housemate emergency might be just the kind of alibi she needed at a later date.

CHAPTER THIRTY-SEVEN

Linzi didn't feel quite so pleased with her clever plan when she actually got to the hospital. Kerry sat alone in the waiting room on one of the hideous red plastic chairs – designed to hide the mess, Linzi guessed. Kerry looked awful. Her face was completely white apart from the black rings around her eyes. She didn't notice that Linzi had arrived until she sat down right next to her and put a cold hand over Kerry's tightly clenched fists.

'What happened?'

Kerry looked at Linzi with wet eyes.

'I don't know exactly,' she sniffed. 'I came home from Pride and found her collapsed on the floor of the bathroom. There was an empty bottle of vodka downstairs and she had a packet of sleeping tablets in her hand. I think she might have taken an overdose.'

'Jeez.' Linzi rolled her eyes. 'You're kidding. What a bloody idiot!! I bet it was over Tim. But she told me that she was getting over him. An overdose? That's such a loser's way to do things.'

Kerry's expression silenced Linzi at once. 'There's no point sitting here calling her a loser now. We don't even know if she's going to survive.' She gave out a strange, strangled sob. 'Her face was completely blue, Linz. The ambulancemen had to give her oxygen.'

Linzi's brows tipped towards the middle of her face in an approximation of concern. 'She'll be OK, Kez. She's pretty fit with all that training for the race. Where did they take her?'

Kerry indicated the corridor with her thumb. 'In there. But I think they might have had to take her up to intensive care since.' She wiped her nose across her sleeve and sniffed loudly.

'Have you called her folks yet?'

'I tried, but they're on holiday in Gran Canaria according to the housekeeper. Oh God, Linzi, what are we going to do?'

Kerry buried her face in Linzi's shoulder. Her tears soaked through the thin fabric of Linzi's shirt and on to her skin. Linzi patted her friend's back comfortingly and looked towards the door through which they had taken Fiona. She would be all right, of course. Linzi had never heard of an attempted overdose case dying once they had been found. As a nurse passed by, Linzi feebly called out 'excuse me'. The nurse waved a hand dismissively. She didn't have time to comfort weeping hangers-on that night. 'Why do you think she decided to do it tonight?' Linzi asked.

Kerry tried to rearrange herself comfortably on the hard plastic chair. 'I don't know. When I set off for Pride, she seemed to be happy enough. She told me that Tim had agreed to see her. He was supposed to be coming round to talk about things. Perhaps it didn't work out.'

'You're probably right. I don't think she's got a hope of getting him back.'

'He doesn't believe that she didn't do anything with Gaetano.'

'That's just an excuse, Kez. Tim was waiting for a concrete reason to call the engagement off. Nothing happened between Fi and Gaetano. Tim knows that as well as I do.'

Kerry raised an eyebrow.

'What do you mean by pulling that face?' Linzi had noticed.

'Oh, nothing. Look. There's the doctor that took her through. You try and get his attention.'

But he had already gone. Then, as Linzi looked towards the door in hope of news, it opened slowly and a tall man was brought through in a wheelchair. He held a wad of bandaging to his nose but it was soaked through with blood already. The nurse pushing his wheelchair leaned over to explain that someone would appear to take him to X-ray in a few minutes. He nodded painfully, then put his hand up to the side of his face and winced in agony.

Linzi was sure that she recognised him even through the mask of wadding and blood.

She did.

'Professor!!'

Kerry struggled upright in her seat when she heard Linzi call out. Linzi was already on her feet, dashing across the waiting room to the side of the man in the wheelchair. He reached out and took hold of her hand. Linzi marvelled at the deep purple setting he had gained around his eye.

'Christ!! What on earth happened to you, Prof?' She knew it was to do with the robbery of course. 'What are you doing in a wheelchair?' Gaetano had promised that no one would get hurt.

The Professor tried to take the bandage away from his nose so that he could speak but thought better of it. Instead he kept the bulk of it pressed to his nose and lifted the corner away from his mouth.

'The chemist's shop I was working in got robbed,' he began to explain in a barely audible mumble.

'Oh, God. And they beat you up?'

The Professor nodded slowly. 'And my assistant.'

'Your assistant?'

'Kicked her head in. She's had to go up to a ward, I think.'

Linzi's eyes glittered with panic but as Kerry was standing right behind her now she had to pretend that this was all news to her. 'Was she unconscious?' Linzi asked.

'Yes,' the Professor sniffed. 'Completely out of it. They think that he might have fractured her skull. Ow. Sorry, Linzi, it's really difficult to talk. My mouth's all swollen up. I've got to have an X-ray. Might have cracked my jaw.'

Linzi sank slowly into the red plastic chair nearest to his wheelchair. Kerry wondered momentarily why she seemed so upset by what had happened to this curious guy but she was too interested in finding out the gory details of his injuries to dwell on it for long.

'Have they got any idea who did this?' Kerry probed.

The Professor shook his head. 'The bloke had his face covered with some kind of mask. A balaclava thingy. I couldn't even tell if he was black or white and after he put Manjri out, I was too scared to start noting details. It's like my mind went out of focus.'

'They will find him eventually,' Kerry reassured the poor man. 'Somebody in the area must have seen him leave the shop. Perhaps he had a car. Did you hear anything? Did you recognise the sound of a particular engine? A car description can narrow things right down.'

'Kerry,' Linzi broke in. 'He'll have to put up with a load of questions from the police. Give him a break.'

'I'm sorry,' Kerry told the Professor. 'I didn't mean to pry. Honestly,' she sighed. 'What a night this has been. When I got home tonight I found our housemate Fiona passed out on the bathroom floor. Suspected overdose. We're waiting to see if she's OK.'

'I think I met her once. Wish her my love,' the Professor murmured. At that moment a porter appeared with a clip-board. 'Andrew Montgomery?' he asked.

'That's me,' the Professor said feebly. It suddenly struck Linzi that this was the first time she had ever heard his real name. Andrew. It suited him. A big, gentle name. 'I've gotta go for my X-ray now. Guess I'll see you at the gig on Tuesday, Linzi, if I can make it.'

'Yeah. Tuesday,' Linzi replied distantly.

'Who was that?' Kerry asked as the porter carted the Professor off, keeping up a running commentary on football that Linzi knew would be boring the musician in him rigid.

'Friend of Gaetano's,' Linzi explained. 'Plays in the band. Works in a chemist's shop. Says they're always getting robbed for drugs and that.'

'God, some people are real scum, aren't they?' Kerry spat. 'What kind of guy beats someone up like that? And God only knows what kind of state the girl is in. She's probably going to be scarred for life and not just physically. He must have been an animal.'

Linzi nodded in agreement.

'Friends of Fiona Davenport?' The doctor who had supervised Fiona's care had finally reappeared. Kerry waved her hand to attract his attention. He strolled across, flicking through his notes, smiling a little sadly.

'How is she?' Kerry asked desperately.

'Oh, she'll be OK,' the doctor told them. Kerry felt all the muscles of her body give out a collective sigh. 'She's gone into the recovery room now. We'll keep her in overnight, just in case. Did you manage to talk to her parents?'

'No. They're in Gran Canaria.'

'Bit of a nuisance, that. Still, if you could leave their details with the receptionist we'll try to get hold of them first thing. You may as well go now. She won't be able to see you until tomorrow. Good job you got home when you did.'

The doctor was called away by a nurse to deal with a drunk who had been getting out of hand while she tried to apply a bandage to his nasty glass wound. Linzi began to button up her coat.

'You're not going now?' Kerry asked.

'You heard him. He said that she's all right.' Kerry looked betrayed. 'Look, I've got to go, Kez. I need to catch Gaetano at home before his mother comes back. I left my wallet there. I won't see him until Tuesday otherwise.'

'Will you come back here afterwards?' Kerry asked.

'Yeah, of course. Or I'll see you at home.'

Linzi made a break for the automatic doors, almost having a fatal collision with an incoming RTA victim's trolley as she dashed to the nearest phone.

CHAPTER THIRTY-EIGHT

Linzi punched Gaetano's telephone number into the key pad. He had promised her that nobody would get hurt if they did over the chemist's shop. Now the Professor was sporting a broken jaw and some poor girl was lying unconscious in hospital.

The telephone in the Carlotti household rang and rang and rang. Just as Linzi was about to give up and put the receiver down, Gaetano picked it up.

'I need to talk to you,' she said, her voice shaking.

'It's the middle of the night, for fuck's sake,' said Gaetano. 'I want to go to bed. I'll see you tomorrow.'

'No way, Gaetano,' Linzi insisted. 'I need to talk to you now. I've just walked out of the accident unit. And guess who I saw there?'

'Who?' he asked petulantly. 'I don't know, do I?'

'I saw the Professor. He's got a broken bloody jaw and he says that the girl who was with him is in a fucking coma, Gaetano. I thought you said that nobody was going to get hurt? Just how unhurt is that?'

'Sssh, *cara mia*. We can't talk about this on the phone. I'll talk to you tomorrow morning. I'll come round to your place first thing. Yes?'

'No way. I need to talk to you about this tonight. You realise what you've done. You realise how much more serious this whole thing is now. We're not just talking about robbery any more . . . If she doesn't come round we could be talking about . . .'

'Linzi,' Gaetano cut her short, sensing that she was getting dangerously hysterical. 'I told you, we can't talk about this on the phone. Come over to me quickly. My parents won't be back for another hour. Get a taxi over and don't talk to anyone else about this on your way.'

'As if I could . . .' But he had already put down the phone. Linzi climbed into the next taxi almost before it had disgorged its woeful man with his hand wrapped in a tea-towel, followed by a whey-faced girlfriend who thought he was losing a fatal amount of blood from his pinky.

When she got to his house, Gaetano was already waiting downstairs but he ushered her quickly up to his room. 'If my mother comes home now you will have to climb out the window,' he told her.

'What? Why?'

'Because if she finds you here she will throw me out of the house again, that's why. And I don't want to have to go through all that shit. I've told her that we're not seeing each other any more.'

'You what?'

'It's the way it's got to be, Linzi. I had to. I can't live with you can I?'

'Christ, Gaetano. You're almost thirty years old. You're old enough to rob a chemist's shop with violence but you can't stand up to your own mother?'

'Don't push it, Linzi,' Gaetano warned her. 'You knew that what we were going to do tonight wasn't going to be a tea-party.'

'I know. But I'm really scared now, Gaetano. I don't understand why you had to hit the girl. She's really badly beaten up.'

'The Professor said that she would be soft but she wasn't. She kept trying to get in my way. The Professor couldn't stop her. I had to put her out of it.'

'You hit him as well.'

'It makes it look more convincing, doesn't it? Besides, he's had it coming for a long time.'

'What do you mean by that?'

'I mean he's always acting like he's the only one of all of us that's got any brains. He doesn't like it when someone else comes up with a good idea. That's why he was against my plan for the robbery.'

'Don't you think it might just have been that he didn't want to end up in jail?'

'No one was going to end up in jail. It would have been so simple, so perfect if he had just done everything exactly like we planned. But oh no, he had to get cold feet. He was acting like he wasn't part of it so well that he forgot that he was.'

Suddenly, they heard the sound of a key turning in the front door. High-heeled footsteps on the tiled floor of the hallway. A woman called up the stairs to Gaetano. Linzi instantly recognised the voice.

'Shit, they're back. I'll have to go down,' Gaetano said. 'She's seen my light on from the street. I've got to go and show an interest in how opening the shop tonight went. Since it was my idea to get her out of our way. Another great idea by Gaetano Carlotti. Besides, I need to create an alibi. She thinks I've been in bed sick all evening.'

'Gaetano, you can't go downstairs and leave me here now . . .'

He kissed Linzi on the top of the head. 'Look, the fire escape is right below the window. I'll come and see you at your place first thing in the morning, OK? And don't worry. The girl will be fine and no one will ever know the whole story of what happened tonight except you, me and the Professor. Providing you can both keep your mouths shut.'

With that, Gaetano left the room.

'OK, Mama. Don't come up. I'm coming down now.'

Linzi got up and walked towards the window. It was already half-opened so that she wouldn't have to make a sound forcing it. She looked out at the narrow black metal ladder which descended to the street. This was bloody ridiculous. She hadn't had to avoid someone's parents since she was bunking off school with Kerry. She was reaching one leg out through the window when she saw the corner of the black box peeking out from beneath Gaetano's bed clothes. Linzi pulled her leg back in.

Gaetano must have put the money from the robbery in that box. All the money. Including her share. She flicked back the duvet. The key was in the lock. Laughter and animated chatter floated up the stairs. Gaetano was busy with his folks. Acting as though nothing had happened.

Without bothering to open it first, Linzi silently picked up the safe box and tucked it inside her jacket. Then she climbed out of the window for real this time and let herself down into the quiet street below. Less than three weeks after promising that he would never lay his fist on a female again Gaetano had put one in hospital. There was no way that mother-worshipping jerk was keeping her share of the money for his stupid band now.

CHAPTER THIRTY-NINE

Kerry had fallen asleep in the hospital waiting room. When she woke the next morning, she discovered that somebody had covered her with a blanket and for some reason the tenderness of the gesture made her burst into the tears that she had been fighting to hold back all night.

'You all right, love?' the woman who was cleaning the waiting room asked. 'You been here all night, have you?'

Kerry nodded.

'Who you waiting for? Your boyfriend?'

Kerry shook her head. 'My friend. A girl I live with. Fiona Davenport. She got taken ill suddenly last night. Do you know if she's OK?'

'Not me, love. I don't know anything about the patients. Ask the girl on the desk. She's the one will be able to tell you.'

While Kerry was standing at the desk with the blanket draped around her shoulders, Fiona's doctor walked up behind her. His eyes were sunken deep in his face. He hadn't slept at all that night but he still managed a smile for a concerned friend.

'You still here? Your friend's OK, you know,' he assured Kerry once more. 'But she's asleep now. Go home and get some rest.'

'Are you sure?' Kerry asked.

'Trust me, I'm a doctor.' The girl on reception shared the joke.

'OK. If you're really sure she's safe.'

'I'm sure.'

Kerry wandered out into the early morning car park with the hospital blanket still wrapped around her shoulders. As she passed the phone box, she considered calling Linzi to see if she would come out to meet her in Fiona's car. But then she thought better of it. She needed a walk and some time to think. She needed to be alone.

The sky was grey. The clouds had moved in while she slept. How quickly the weather changes at this time of year, Kerry found herself thinking. Yesterday the sun had been shining with intent to burn, now it couldn't be seen at all. How quickly everything can change, she continued to muse. Her watch told her that it was almost nine. She wondered if Leon was up and about yet. She wondered if she would get home to find a message on the answerphone asking why she had left his apartment so suddenly when Sam arrived.

She had a feeling that she wouldn't. It was completely clear to her now that Leon had wanted nothing more from her than her passport. If she had been a good friend to him, she told herself, she would have helped him out willingly and not asked for anything more than the opportunity for a good party in return. How could she have thought that things could be different? He had even offered her money for her trouble.

As Kerry neared the Underground station, she fished in the top pocket of her jacket for her Travelcard. Feeling the smooth round edge of an unfamiliar object, she pulled it out to remember with disgust that she was still carrying her sister's engagement and wedding rings. Not to mention the tiny emerald cluster which was taking up space on her own finger. Michelle had been right. It was all rubbish, this marriage thing. Even if your fiancé was heterosexual. As relationship sticky-tape, a wedding ring was as useful as the fluffy side of Velcro without the hooks to catch against. Kerry took her ring off and wrapped it in a tissue with the other two then she thanked whoever it was that hung out in the sky that she hadn't ever got around to announcing her fantasy engagement. At least it meant that she wasn't going to have to face the embarrassment of announcing that it was off again. She was, however, going to have to face Leon on Monday morning. If they had been like Tim and Fiona, she could have banished him from her sight for ever. As it was, she could only do a sicky. But that would be too obvious and it would only prolong the agony . . . She could also hand her notice in. But then what?

As Kerry turned into Artesia Road, she tried to comfort herself with the thought that things could only get better. After all, bad things happen in threes and she'd definitely had her three that week. First her sister's marriage going wrong, then the disaster with Leon, then Fiona's overdose.

But when Kerry saw the fire-engine parked outside number 67, she realised that as far as bad things were concerned, one of the above obviously didn't really count.

CHAPTER FORTY

Number 67 Artesia Road had been gutted by a mysterious fire in the small hours of that Sunday morning while Fiona recovered, Kerry dozed in a hospital waiting room and Linzi was God only knows where. The firemen decided that it had been deliberate. On Linzi's bedroom mirror, someone had scrawled 'SLAG' in lipstick as red as blood. And they had lost a lot of things as well: the television, the video, two CD stereos, the remains of which could not be found amongst the charred offering that had become of the sitting room.

The arsonist had robbed them of fingerprints to catch him by, of course, so they had no idea of his identity or motive, but the strangest thing was that Linzi had disappeared. Her room had not just been stripped of electrical goods but of her clothes and most of her toiletries as well. Linzi's mother and father, briefly reunited by the trauma, were trying to obtain funding to make a television programme about sudden disappearances. Unkind people suggested that Linzi's departure was maybe a case of spontaneous combustion.

Fiona came out of hospital the day after the fire. Her parents had flown home from Gran Canaria early and whisked her straight back to Bristol without stopping to pick up what remained of her belongings at Artesia Road. Kerry followed the exodus west a couple of days later. Leon had offered to let her have sick-leave but she told him that she didn't think she was suited to the job any more. Leon didn't push it, which made Kerry sad. Neither did he mention the ring or the motorbike.

Back in Bristol, Mrs Keble seemed to be in her element. Kerry was the second of her little chicks to have flown back to the nest that week. Big sister Miranda had finally ditched Steve the plumber and left him with the house and the kids. Kerry took up residence in her old room and went into a deep sulk. She didn't bother to call back any of the people from school who kept telephoning to find out the truth about the night of disaster on the pretence of being concerned. When Fiona felt well enough, Kerry trawled round to the Davenport residence to visit her on her sick-bed but that was as far as the Keble's once-wandering daughter could be bothered to go. It seemed that anywhere else she went she was dogged by whispers that Linzi had started the fire herself and fled.

Living at home again was like being in a time warp. When Kerry got in one evening from a visit to Fiona, it suddenly struck her that she could be witnessing a tableau from her sixteenth year. Her father had just come home from work. He was sitting at the kitchen table, wearing his shirt and tie to which still clung the oily smell of heavy engineering. Her mother was cooking dinner. Tuesday night: burgers, chips and beans. Miranda was on the telephone arguing with her estranged husband about custody of their children using words of not more than four letters in length. Even Michelle's absence from this family scene was usual. She would have been out snogging in the car park behind the all-night newsagents.

'How was Fiona?' her mother asked.

'Looking better,' Kerry replied.

'Oh, that's good. I spoke to her mother in the post office this afternoon. It's been a terrible time for that family. One minute they're planning a wedding and the next minute their daughter is an invalid. It's like they've got a baby in the house again, her mother said.'

'I don't think it's that bad, Mum.'

Mrs Keble turned the burgers over and smiled patronisingly. 'Your father's got some good news for you, sweetheart. Tell her your good news, Nigel.'

Mr Keble pushed a photocopied piece of paper across the table-cloth to his daughter. 'Bloke at work gave me this today. Says they're looking for secretaries at the place where his wife works. Says if you want it, you're as good as in. What with your exams and all.'

Kerry skipped through the details. The job was for a VDU operator at a big joinery place just down the road. Kerry remembered walking to and from school, seeing the women who worked there hanging out on the fire escape having a quick fag since smoking was strictly prohibited inside because of the sawdust. Kerry hated the noise and the smell of the place. Even walking past it for those few brief moments each day had been enough to make her want to run away into the hills.

'You see, love. All that gallivanting off to London when there's perfectly decent jobs just down the road from your Mum and Dad. You didn't really want to be dealing with that media business. No job security there. Work at Mitchell's, you got a job for life and the chance to get yourself a decent boyfriend. Bunch of hunks at Mitchell's, your sister says. I still can't believe it though,' Mrs Keble's eyes took on a distant look. 'That lovely Leon being one of those "homer-sexuals" . . .'

Kerry felt her eyes begin to glaze over. Miranda came back to the kitchen table in tears. Steve was still refusing to let her see the girls. Mrs Keble slopped beans on to four plates while cursing both her sons-in-law. Kerry's father asked her whether she wanted him to tell his mate that she would have the job? Kerry nodded. Her mother put the hot plates on the table. Kerry took a forkful of the beans and they tasted like sawdust in her mouth.

A week later, Kerry was just about to leave for her first day of work at Mitchell's Joinery when the postman arrived. She opened the front door to him and took the bundle of envelopes straight from his hand. Brown, brown, brown. A pile of serious bills. And a postcard. A postcard of deep blue sea and soft white sand. They didn't know anyone who was away on holiday, did they? Kerry turned the postcard over and read the scribbled message with a quickening heart.

It was from her sister Michelle. Writing to the Bristol-bound Keble family from her new apartment overlooking the Sydney bloody Opera House.

'You're going to be late if you don't get a move on,' Mrs Keble called from the kitchen. 'Don't want to be late on your first flippin' day.'

'Yes, Mum!'

Kerry put the brown envelopes on the table beneath the telephone and stepped out of the house and into the drizzle, still clutching the postcard in her hand. She started in the direction of Mitchell's Joinery, her feet getting faster and faster as she neared the noisy, smelly warehouse, faster and faster as she reached the rusty gate and walked straight on past.

She walked to Fiona's. By the time she reached Fiona's street, Kerry was almost running. She hammered on the front door. Mr Davenport had already left for the office. Mrs Davenport for her class in t'ai chi. Fiona staggered down the stairs, her legs barely in working order after three long weeks in bed.

'You're not going to believe this!!' Kerry thrust the postcard into Fiona's hands. Fiona scanned the scrawled handwriting quickly. As she read her face cracked simultaneously into the widest of wide smiles.

'It's from my sister, to let us know her new address in Australia. But read the bottom bit. Read it. She says that she bumped into Linzi in Cairns.'

'I can see it. Linzi's in Cairns? What on earth is she doing there?'

'Well, I don't know, do I? But I think it's about time we found out.'

They scuttled into the Davenport's bijoux 'telephone room'. A converted cupboard beneath the stairs. Kerry began to dial the number scrawled along the side of the postcard. Frantically. Stumbling over the digits.

'What time will it be over there?' Fiona was concerned. 'You're probably calling her in the middle of the night.'

'Michelle won't mind if we wake her up. I don't know about you, but I think that this is a bit of an emergency.'

The phone was picked up at the other end. The person answering told Kerry, in an accent that was pure Birmingham, that Michelle did indeed live in the flat but that she had gone out to work and he didn't expect her back before midnight.

'Where's she working?' Kerry asked.

'At a bar in town. She only started last week. She got the job through one of her sister's old friends.'

'I am her sister. Which friend?'

'Linzi, I think her name is.'

Kerry made a fist of triumph.

'Thanks . . .'

'Benj.'

'Benj. This is Kerry. Will you tell Michelle that I called? And if you see that bloody Linzi girl on your travels, tell her it's about time she got in touch with her old mates from Artesia Road!'

CHAPTER FORTY-ONE

Three weeks later, Linzi met them at the airport in Sydney. With her newly tanned skin she looked more beautiful than ever, the shadow of London life long since vanished from beneath her eyes. She greeted her former housemates as if they had been apart for a thousand years. She glanced at their new suitcases a little guiltily though. Fiona had lost her Louis Vuitton in the fire.

On the drive back from the airport, she explained in an unbelievable half hour what had happened on the night they last saw her in London. As she told them about the robbery, Kerry remembered the man in the accident unit and was aghast. Linzi told them that Gaetano had made her do it. Fiona found that quite easy to believe. They wanted to know why she hadn't gone to the police. Linzi said that she had been too scared. And rightly so, she had figured, when Michelle told her about the burglary and the fire. Linzi had guessed that Gaetano might be capable of that. Which was why she had to leave so suddenly once she had taken the money from his room. He would have had her head off. Killed her, probably. So Linzi had gone straight to Paris on the first Eurostar of that Sunday morning and from there to Thailand and from Thailand to where they were now.

'How much money did you get from the robbery?' Fiona was desperate to know. It was such a crazy story that she asked about the cash as though she were asking about the proceeds of some company merger.

The shadow of a guilty smile passed across Linzi's lips. 'Not enough,' she admitted. 'But there was other stuff in the box as well. I sold that.'

'Like what?'

Linzi squirmed. 'You promise you won't hit me?' Fiona nod-ded. 'Swear? I am driving after all.'

'Of course. Like what, Linzi? What did you find?'

'Like your engagement ring.'

Kerry clapped her hand to her open mouth in shock. Linzi visibly shrank at the wheel as though she still expected a blow. For a moment there was an extremely uneasy silence in the little hire-car. Fiona broke it. She broke it with the biggest and longest laugh she had ever laughed in her life.

'That ring had two thousand pounds' worth of bloody dia-monds set in it!' she screeched.

'You're kidding!' said Linzi. 'I only got three hundred pounds. But I'll pay you back, I promise.'

'No problem, Linzi.' Fiona had laughed so much that tears were streaming down her cheeks. 'Tim filed an insurance claim after it got lost. When the money came through a couple of weeks ago, he felt so guilty about breaking off the engagement that he sent me the bloody cheque. That helped to pay for our flights here.'

'You didn't cash it?'

'Of course I did. After all he did to me, the very least I deserve is a sun-tan. I'm glad you sold that ring. If you hadn't I would have thrown it straight over there!!'

They were driving past the glittering expanse of Sydney Har-bour. They wound down their windows and leaned out to get a better view of the sparkling blue and white.

That first night together in the Southern Hemisphere was spent at the beach bar and café where Linzi sometimes worked during the day and Michelle did a night shift three times a week. Linzi had already fallen head over heels for a fellow waiter who brought them free beers with such regularity that even she was soon under the table.

When the bar was officially closed and all the punters but the three girls had been pushed out on to the street, Linzi ordered a final round of beers for a last toast. She raised her bottle. 'To my very best friends.' Fiona and Kerry clinked glass upon glass. 'I'm so glad you're both here. I didn't think you'd ever want to see me again.'

'I didn't think we'd ever be able to see you again,' joked Kerry. 'We were terrified that something unspeakable had happened to you.'

'Well, I guess it has,' Linzi sighed. 'I've made myself an exile now. I suppose I'm going to have to stay out here for a while, then keep on travelling until I'm sure that it's safe to come home.'

'I can't believe you're on the run from the police,' Kerry laughed. 'My mum always said you'd end up either on the stage or in prison.'

'Mmmm,' Linzi snorted. 'I think a term in Holloway would beat temping in an advertising agency but I'm not quite ready to find out for sure. Anyway, what's the weather like at home? Having the usual sort of June?'

'Snow and hailstorms?' Kerry nodded. 'Pretty much.'

'You know what day it is today?' Fiona had been very quiet since the hilarity about the ring, but now she piped up again. 'Today is the fifteenth of June. Today is the day I was supposed to get married to Tim.'

Both Linzi and Kerry put their glasses down on the table. It didn't seem appropriate to raise a toast to that.

'Today is the day I would have walked down the aisle and promised myself to that dunderhead for ever. I would have been Mrs Tim Harper. The original Stepford wife.' She leaned on her elbow, looking at the pale amber beer swirling around in the bottom of her glass. Then she raised it, unexpectedly. 'Well, girls, here's to lucky escapes!'

The other girls cheered.

'And here's to not wearing jade!!' said Kerry.

'Did I say jade for the bridesmaids?' Fiona looked horrified. 'I couldn't have done. That would have been terrible with your hair.'

'Anything's terrible with my hair,' sighed Kerry.

'So,' Linzi continued. 'If things had gone according to plan, you would have been starting your married life tomorrow but now you're not. What are you going to do instead, Fi?'

'A week ago I would have said that was a pretty hard question,' Fiona said quietly. 'But I think I've got it sorted out now. I'm going straight to New York.' The other girls smiled. 'Peter, the idiot that they offered the placement to when I turned it down, managed to disgrace himself by getting drunk at a graduate recruitment seminar in Aberdeen. When it came for the moment for him to get up on stage and extol the virtues of First Orient's graduate training scheme, he just dropped his trousers and did a moonie. Hara called me the very next morning and begged me to take the placement up. Didn't seem to be an awful lot of point in refusing this time. It's not as though I'm going to be leaving a great deal behind.'

'You'll have a fantastic time, Fiona,' Linzi assured her. 'But don't forget who your best friends are when you're trekking around Bloomingdales.'

'Sure, I'll bring you back a pretzel.'

'Thanks. It's probably more than I deserve.'

'Your turn now,' Fiona moved the spotlight. All eyes turned towards Kerry, who was peeling the label off her beer bottle with a look of deep concentration upon her face.

'What are you going to do, Kerry Keble? Now that you've come this far.'

'Back to England, I suppose,' Kerry muttered.

'No way. Stay with me,' Linzi suggested.

'I can't, Linz. I've got things to go back for.'

'Such as.'

'My family.'

'But they live in Bristol. Please tell me that you won't end up back there.'

'I've got to get a job sometime soon.'

'You can get a job anywhere. I'll get you one here.'

'I don't know,' Kerry squirmed.

'You're not going back because of a man?' Fiona asked.

'Get real,' said Kerry. 'I'm going to be staying off men for a long while. It's just that . . . I don't know. It's just that I'm not sure that I'm ready for all this.'

'All this what?'

'All this . . . well, for the rest of my life, really. I mean, I'm fresh from my biggest balls-up to date. Falling in love with my homosexual boss. How stupid was that? I've had my heart broken and I've lost my job. I don't think I can handle anything more exciting than a stint at Mitchell's Joinery yet.'

'Well, you blew that one by coming out here,' Fiona observed.

'You're right. I guess I have.'

'Come away with me.'

The girls looked up to see who was addressing them. Michelle had finished her late shift in the kitchen and now stood by their table, drying her hands on a filthy beer-mat. 'You could come on a trip with me, Kez. We could go to the States and to Canada. See the Grand Canyon and Niagara Falls.'

'They're smaller than you think they are,' Linzi said wisely. 'If I were you, I would go to Zimbabwe. Victoria Falls are much bigger.'

'Yeah? Well, we'll still have a great time however big they are. What do you think, Kez?'

Kerry looked sceptical.

'We could go in two weeks.'

'That doesn't really give me enough time to get ready.'

'How long do you need to get ready?' her sister protested. 'What on earth do you need to bring except a toothbrush and a credit card? We'll travel light.' Michelle was sitting on the edge of the wonky table now. She slung a brown arm around her big sister's neck. 'You could use the insurance money from the fire.'

'I might need that money for an emergency.'

'Listen,' Michelle was having none of that. 'What kind of emergency are you going to have in Bristol? A nasty run in your tights?'

'Anything could happen,' Kerry said feebly, knowing even as she said so that it was hardly likely to be true in Bristol.

'Until I married Richard, Kez,' Michelle continued, 'I thought that adventures were for other people. I thought that I wasn't meant to do anything other than live out my days in the place where I was born. I realised that was wrong on the plane to Majorca. I wasn't being held back by lack of money. I wasn't being held back by a baby I'd dropped before leaving school like our Miranda. I wasn't being held back by anything but me. You said that I shouldn't do anything you wouldn't do, Kez. If I'd taken that advice, I would hardly have left Heathrow.'

Kerry blushed.

'You know I'm right.'

Fiona nodded.

'So which is it to be? Logging the planks at Mitchell's Join- ery or a taste of life on the open road? It's the saw mills or

Niagara Falls, Kez. We can sell my wedding ring to help raise more cash.'

'Sounds like a great deal to me,' Linzi chipped in. 'I can give you the number of a man in Bangkok. Come on, Kerry. You've got this far already. Now it's your turn to propose a toast.'

Fiona poured the last of her beer from the bottle. Michelle pinched some of Kerry's. There was silence while they waited for her to take up the challenge. Kerry stared at her own half-empty glass. They were right. They were all right. The only thing holding her back now was fear. She had no man to go back to and no decent job. In a week's time her friends would be all over the place and as for her family, well, in her heart she knew that no matter where she went and how long she went for, there would always be room for her when she got home.

The insurance money would be through before the end of the month.

'Ahem,' Kerry cleared her throat. 'I think I'd like to propose my toast now.'

'What's it to be?' asked Michelle.

'Of course, after way too much hesitation, she said that it had to be to the open road. And as soon as the insurance money came through we booked our tickets out of there and headed for the States. If you'd told me this time last year that I would be spending my first wedding anniversary in Canada with my sister, I wouldn't have believed you, but I don't have any regrets about letting my marriage go now. In fact I can't believe I chose the opportunity to wear a stupid dress for a day over the chance to do this.'

The French girl standing next to Michelle on the *Maid of the Mist* nodded. Then Kerry reappeared, having taken a photo of the Falls from the front of the boat. Her fringe was plastered to her forehead and her clothes were soaked through, despite her regulation blue plastic cape.

'You know what?' she said, pushing back the sweaty plastic hood, and shouting over the roar of the water. 'Linzi was right. They're not really that big.'

Michelle turned to her new friend again. 'Men, marriage and Niagara Falls,' she told her puzzled companion. 'When it comes down to it, very few things are the big deal you think they are.'